LET'S GET PHYSICAL

LET'S GET PHYSICAL

Sherry Ashworth

Hodder & Stoughton

Copyright © 2001 by Sherry Ashworth

First published in Great Britain in 2001
by Hodder and Stoughton
A division of Hodder Headline

The right of Sherry Ashworth to be identified as the Author
of the Work has been asserted by her in accordance with the
Copyright, Designs and Patents Act 1988.

10 9 8 7 6 5 4 3 2 1

A CIP catalogue record for this book
is available from the British Library

ISBN 0 340 75020 0

Typeset by Hewer Text Ltd, Edinburgh
Printed and bound in Great Britain by
Mackays of Chatham plc, Chatham, Kent

Hodder and Stoughton
A division of Hodder Headline
338 Euston Road
London NW1 3BH

For Sara Menguc

Thanks to Julie Leeming and Margaret Curry

Chapter One

'Your name?'

'Cassie Oliver. Cassandra Oliver, actually, named after the ancient Greek prophetess, although I suppose in these politically correct days we should call her a prophet. Perhaps a seer is more accurate. See-er. She could predict forthcoming catastrophes. Singularly inappropriate in my case. I can't honestly say I had a clue—'

'And your address?'

'Thirteen, Sunnybank Brow – one of those cottages near the Three Tuns. Did you know they used to be millworkers' cottages? They were built to a far higher standard than many similar properties in the area because Samuel Ramsbottom, the owner, was a Unitarian and keen on the dignity of labour. A fascinating man. His family still—'

'Age, Cassie?'

'Thirty-nine. Not forty yet, ha, ha! Though my GP said to me, fair, fat and forty – almost to be expected. Fair I'll accept, although it's fading fast. Fat is a little unkind, and forty was pushing it.'

'Do you want to hop on the scales?'

'Oh, all right then. But I know what it's going to be. Thirteen stone three. They weighed me at the hospital. The consultant wasn't too impressed. I told him that in other cultures I would be considered a prize worth having and, anyway, it ran in the family and—'

'Eighty-four kilograms.'

'Oh!' Cassie preferred the sound of her weight in kilograms as it meant nothing to her. She paused for a moment and watched the girl key in her weight on the computer. This office where she was having her fitness assessment reminded her uncomfortably of her GP's surgery. That was why she was so nervous and, consequently, voluble.

'And what do you do for a living, Cassie?'

'Is that important?' She was puzzled.

'Only in that it helps us assess your lifestyle.'

'A sedentary lifestyle, I'm afraid. I guess that's part of the problem. I'm a university lecturer, with a special interest in medieval history. I deal with admissions too. In some ways it's quite a stressful job as the pressure is on us now in a way it never used to be, and as academics we're expected to produce our own original research on top of our teaching load. But on the other hand, I know I'm lucky to have a job with status and which has enabled me to carry on learning.'

Cassie couldn't help but notice that the face of the fitness instructor had assumed that familiar glazed expression she encountered on her students' faces when she was explaining Edward III's economic problems. She stopped herself.

'So, Cassie, you don't get much regular exercise?'

'Well, it depends precisely what you define as exercise. Although I drive to work, I do walk from the university car park to the history building. Once I'm there I move about quite a bit as I have to get from my office to the lecture theatre and canteen, and my office is two flights of stairs up from the main floor. I walk to the library too! I read an article in a newspaper that suggested fidgeting was a form of exercise. And I gesticulate a lot in lectures.' She heard her voice fading away.

'Oh dear, the computer's playing up again. Hold on.' The girl gave all her attention to the computer screen, which had temporarily gone blank.

Cassie looked around her at the posters of fitness equipment, the exercise bike lurking menacingly in the corner, the blood-pressure machine and an unclaimed pair of trainers. There was a rota pinned to a board listing the names of the staff and their hours. Cassie read that. Here was a whole world she knew nothing about. The groves of academia were her stamping ground and she had not stirred from them even briefly. She had never left the world of education since starting school at four.

She'd loved school from the moment she'd set foot in it. She particularly enjoyed her years at an all-girls grammar school, relishing the camaraderie, the institutional feel, and the way that learning was valued. History fascinated her, and she found she had the capacity to turn historical evidence round in her mind like a Rubik's cube, making different shapes and patterns, and writing full, lush essays that delighted her teachers and swept her into Oxford. She joined an all-girls college and felt immediately at home. She had boyfriends because she thought she ought to, then discovered she quite enjoyed male company. She moved to Manchester to take her Ph.D. and ended up staying there.

Cassie recognised her life was circumscribed. It was deliberately so. The past seemed safer than the future in many ways. Its challenges were purely intellectual. She had felt until recently that she had acquired the one thing everybody craved: comfort. She was comfortable: comfortable with who she was, a quirky, sometimes pedantic but good-humoured academic, comfortable with her friends, comfortable in her cottage with its antiques, cat and capacious fridge. Cassie worked hard and food was her fuel, reward and greatest indulgence. Not that she ever thought about it. Instead she thought about her subject, her students, her research, university politics, current events and her friends, first and foremost of whom was Terry.

The trainer interrupted her reverie. 'Ah, that's better. I thought we were going to have to start from the beginning. So, Cassie, what are your objectives?'

'My objectives?' Cassie reoriented herself.

'Your fitness goals.'

'Goals?' She thought for a moment of footballers. 'Fitness goals? Well, you tell me what you think they are.' Cassie remembered she was not leading a tutorial. 'Sorry. It's not so much a matter of fitness, but of weight loss. I've been told I need to lose weight. To be frank with you, it's a bit of a catch-22 situation. The consultant told me that either I must give up fatty food and lose some weight so my gall bladder has a chance to function efficiently, or have my gall bladder removed, in which case I'd need to lose weight so he could operate on me safely.'

Even the word 'operate' chilled her. It was the idea of someone taking a knife and slicing into her body while she lay there, unconscious – unconscious! – like so much meat, an inert white mass, not Cassie Oliver at all. The terrifying impersonality of it was almost unthinkable. It was why she had resolved to take herself properly in hand and join Fit Not Fat, formerly the Sunnybank Health and Fitness Centre.

Still scenes from the last few months haunted her. She could recall vividly the several occasions when her stomach had cramped and tightened and felt like a metal balloon inside her. She put it down to indigestion, and said nothing to anyone until one evening when she and Terry were watching *The Late Show*, having demolished most of the Coronation Chicken salad, and she had ended up writhing in agony in the floor, almost as if someone had punched her. Terry insisted on driving her to Casualty and she had sat there terrified among the drunks and screaming babies until a young, harassed doctor told her it sounded like gallstones.

Gallstones? That did not compute. Cassie had a touching belief that she was immortal and preternaturally healthy, just like her parents and ninety-three-year-old grandmother. She didn't even know what gallstones were except they sounded nasty. Gall, she knew, was the essence of bitterness to the medieval writer and thinker, just as honey was the essence of sweetness. The doctor explained briefly how cholesterol deposits had built up in her gall bladder, and how her gall bladder was trying to expel them to no avail. That was probably the cause of the pain. But only probably. Cassie was given some painkillers and the instruction to see her GP at the earliest opportunity.

Fair, fat and forty, he called her, concurring with the Casualty doctor's diagnosis of gallstones. First, she had to have an ultrasound scan. A few weeks later she was back in the hospital, begowned and benighted, beached on the examination table, having a cold jelly rubbed into her stomach by a rotund Indian radiologist. She chatted to him about the depredations of the British East India Company in the nineteenth century as he peered at her insides.

'Congratulations,' he said. 'You have gallstones.'

Congratulations? She sat up to hear his reassurances that the rest of her was all right, but that gallstones were the sign of a malfunctioning gall bladder, which was better out than in. She was given an appointment to see the consultant. She was Marie Antoinette in the tumbrel, approaching the guillotine. She was sick with panic by the time he entered the consulting room where she was frantically marking essays to re-establish normality. Yet it had turned out not to be so bad after all. She was given a choice. She could – through her own efforts – turn back the clock. If she lost weight and took care of her lifestyle, she could keep her gall bladder. She promised faithfully to do that. It was a reprieve. Her drama had converted to melodrama. All she had to do was lead a healthy life.

'So you want to lose weight?' the girl asked her.

'Yes,' Cassie agreed.

'OK. Obviously you need to pay attention to your diet—'

'I know.' Cassie stopped her in her tracks. 'I discussed that with my GP.' She was uncharacteristically silent. She chilled as she thought of skimmed milk, naked bread, and tart, vinegary salad dressings. Once she had bought and sampled a low-calorie hot drink, which claimed to be chocolate. Its chemical sweetness and artificial flavour appalled her. To think there were women who actually taught themselves to like this! She felt like starting a charity for their benefit. 'Choice', the drink was called, creating the illusion that these women had a choice. She had a choice, and chose never to drink such rubbish again. But now her GP had stated the terms of her choice . . . Come to think of it, the Irish Liqueur Choice hadn't been too bad.

'As long as you realise the importance of diet,' said the girl. 'So what we need to do now is assess your level of fitness.'

'No need,' said Cassie. 'I can tell you that already. Totally unfit.'

'You'd be surprised how many people say that. I'm sure you'll find you're capable of a full exercise programme.'

Cassie hoped she wasn't going to be as fit as all that.

She breathed in deeply, and blew into tubes, and the girl entered more figures on the computer. She breathed in deeply again, and lunged forward along a graded board to measure her flexibility. She was handed a monitor by the girl and instructed to fasten it under her T-shirt so that it picked up her heartbeat.

The act of lifting up her T-shirt made Cassie acutely self-conscious. Whereas the trainer was dressed in a sunflower yellow sweatshirt emblazoned with the words 'Fit Not Fat' and a badge reading 'Jodie', Cassie wore an elderly maroon T-shirt with the seam coming undone on one side. She had found her leggings at the bottom of her wardrobe. They were paisley and stretched uncomfortably over her thighs. She felt she was an absurdity, a fish out of water. Her other self, the respected academic, admired and feared by her students, had ceased to exist. She was just an ungainly lump, compared to the svelte girl who was taking her details. She adjusted the monitor as she was instructed.

'Just hop on to the bike, now,' Jodie said, making it all seem so easy.

Cassie carefully climbed on, and slowly began to pedal. She was surprised to discover it *was* easy. Round spun the pedals, and she thought, I could get used to this. Then Jodie bent down and adjusted the controls. There was more resistance now and Cassie was straining to keep her pace, knew her heart was pumping, felt her chest tightening, but was damned if she was going to give up.

'I can't ride a real bike,' she told Jodie. 'Never have been able to. It's a question of balance. You see, I have poor muscular co-ordination. I can't tell my right from my left, either. Just like the government.' There was no response to her pleasantry. 'Even now, I have to make an L-shape with the thumb and forefinger of my left hand to check I really am turning left when I'm driving. It means taking my hand off the steering-wheel, which I suppose—' Cassie broke off to catch her breath. 'I've never been very sporty. Sport always seemed fairly pointless to me. People either kicking balls or hitting them with sticks or throwing them into nets or over nets – I mean, how exactly has civilisation been furthered by man's ability to throw and catch a ball? Which, now I come to ask it, is an interesting question. You could say—' It was no use. Cassie discovered she could not both talk and pedal.

'You're doing fine,' the girl said.

The words of encouragement surprised and pleased her. She pedalled harder, then immediately regretted it and slowed down. Strange to be pedalling so hard and getting nowhere. Stranger still to be working her body and not her mind. Her mind unfixed itself, floated free and attached itself to the girl called Jodie. She looked no older than Cassie's undergraduate students. It was a droll reversal to be assessed by a student. Cassie found herself getting hot and sweaty. 'How much longer?'

'Just a couple of minutes.'

She pedalled steadily. That it should come to this! She had lived so happily for years and years, stretching her mind but ignoring her body. She'd honestly thought she could carry on like that for ever. Then her gall bladder had mutinied. Cassie knew she was undergoing a process of redefining herself. She had to incorporate the idea that there was something wrong with her – that she was ill. She had recently been in the habit of stopping whatever she was doing and thinking, *I have gallstones*. She consciously prevented herself becoming obsessed with them or boring her friends and colleagues with the details of her condition. Terry had told her that gallstones themselves were fawn-coloured and laced with emerald green, quite beautiful to look at. She'd wondered if that had been his way of letting her know how much he loved her. It *was* romantic, after a fashion, but didn't really cheer her up.

She had gallstones. The knowledge affected her self-image. Parts of her were beginning to wear out because she was no longer entirely young. She was approaching forty – fair, fat and forty. She had never meant to be forty. Her chosen age was somewhere around twenty-eight, grown-up but timeless. She hoped she still thought as if she was twenty-eight. Only her hot, sweaty body pedalling furiously on this stationary bike did not think it was twenty-eight.

'You can cool down now,' Jodie said.

Cassie pedalled more slowly, experiencing a sensation of exquisite relief. There was more tapping at the computer as she surreptitiously wiped her damp forehead with the side of her hand. She watched Jodie enter details on a card, and took pleasure in how remarkably virtuous she felt at having cycled for a full five minutes.

'This is your personal programme,' the girl told her, and invited Cassie to take a look at the card. 'Obviously we're concentrating on aerobic exercise to attack those fat cells. Five minutes warm-up on the rower, fifteen minutes on the treadmill, fifteen on the stepper and twenty or so on the bike. Sound OK to you?'

Not understanding any of this, Cassie thought it sounded perfectly OK. Twenty minutes on a bike wasn't a long time by anyone's reckoning. In fact, she could already feel herself being seduced by the promise of change. Exercise was a novelty to her and, as such, had its attractions. Was it going to be possible to transform herself and become that toned, bronzed woman adorning the poster of gym equipment she saw in front of her? Anything was possible. Feeling fitter already she smiled at Jodie.

'What would you like to do now?' Jodie asked her. 'You could have your first workout, or I could show you how to use the equipment.'

'Just show me how to use the equipment,'

Cassie followed Jodie out of the office towards the gym. The health club was a pleasant place to be, with its clean brick walls, piped music and air of purpose. Cassie passed a studio where a class was taking place. She glimpsed a number of women contorted into odd positions, not seeming to move at all. She thought she might try that class. She passed a glass cabinet of items for sale, sweatbands, towels, T-shirts, heart monitors. Suddenly she became curious about the club, having a premonition that she would be spending a lot of her time here. She began to quiz Jodie. 'Have you worked here long?'

'Nearly a year. That means I was working here before it was taken over by Fit Not Fat.'

'Do you like it here?'

'Oh, yes, loads! I like working with people and keeping fit. Everyone's really nice.'

'And Fit Not Fat, are they good employers?'

'It's too early to say. They're a big company so I suppose it must be better for us in the long run. Actually, they're interviewing for our new manager today. It's exciting!'

9

Together they approached the gym. Cassie's first thought was that it resembled a medieval torture chamber. People had spreadeagled themselves on uncouth contraptions, pounded endlessly on treadmills like demented hamsters, raised and lowered weights, climbed ceaselessly up stairs as in a Piranesi-inspired nightmare. Faces were blank and red with effort. And yet that was only half the truth. Mirrors lined every wall so people could watch themselves exercise. Why would they want to do that? There were TV screens stationed in different positions relaying the news, depicting cricket matches, showing the latest pop videos and Richard Whiteley presiding over *Countdown*. Some pop music she did not recognise played steadily, masking the whirr and buzz of the equipment and the thumping of feet on rubber. The rather large person in the maroon T-shirt and paisley leggings was her, surveying it all. It was impossible to imagine that all this would ever become familiar. Then she remembered the glint in the eye of the consultant at the hospital speaking casually about removing her gall bladder with the insouciance of a latter-day Genghis Khan.

'Show me how it all works,' she said.

Jodie Purcell directed Cassie back to the ladies' changing room. Then she checked her watch. There was just ten minutes to go before lunch. At last! It wasn't so much that she was hungry, but a craving for chocolate had hit her about an hour ago and controlled her with a sado-masochistic glee. A Mars bar? Or a Snickers? No, just a king-size block of Galaxy. Anything so long as it was dark, sweet and mildly narcotic. It was that time of the month.

Then she remembered what was going on at the other end of the building. Poor old Siobhan. She really wanted the job and Jodie thought it was only fair that she should get it. Since Trudy left for Portugal she'd been the acting manager. Garth had applied too. They were saying he wasn't a serious candidate but he thought he ought to apply. And Jodie had seen another woman arrive earlier this morning, someone not much older than her, with her fair hair cut into a neat bob and wide, bright eyes. Jodie took an immediate liking to her, then felt disloyal. There was poor old Siobhan. Except Siobhan wasn't old. It was a pity they couldn't all be the manager. That was why everyone at Sunnybank – no, Fit Not Fat, she must get used to the new name – had been tense for days. Even Jodie herself had been feeling the strain; maybe that was why she couldn't stop thinking about chocolate. Just the thought of something sweet and smooth in her mouth, her tongue curling around the yielding silkiness, the way all her senses concentrated on the experience of the slow release of pleasure, a chocolate orange, maybe, a Galaxy, some Minstrels, or even a trip to Thornton's.

Chapter Two

Jane found it impossible to keep still, impossible to clear her mind and relax, impossible to do anything but pace up and down the reception area, her eyes taking mental snapshots of the features of the club. Semi-circular reception desk with teak wooden panelling, a poster advertising a fun run, two glass-panelled doors leading off, heavy-duty industrial carpet in sun-flower yellow, locker keys hanging on a rack behind the reception desk. Jane sniffed the familiar rubbery trainers smell and heard piped soft rock music. She took deep, calming breaths and was seized by a tremor of terror and delight.

The truth was, she loved interviews. She was fully alive when she was being tested, when she was given the opportunity to show what she could do. And then some. The fact was, the position of manager at Sunnybank's Fit Not Fat would be perfect for her. The permanent manager of the Kearsley Gate branch was shortly returning from her maternity leave and Jane, as acting manager, would be demoted. And Sunnybank was so much nearer her flat. This job was ideal. It *had* to be hers — *anyone* could see that. And it was not fuelled by self-interest, this passionate desire to be manager at Sunnybank. No — she would make damned sure that *everyone* would benefit. She wanted to turn the club round, win the appreciation of the staff, get Sunnybank fit, save lives! And I'm not being over-dramatic by saying that, thought Jane, imagining herself already facing the interview team. The whole purpose of getting fit was to fight off illness, to live a long and healthy life, to feel good about yourself and be *positive*. Running a health and fitness club was a vocation to her—her job had meaning. Yes, Jane had her gospel to preach and consciously loved this sense of being on a mission. A girl, she thought, on a mission, and smiled.

And then she checked her watch. Her interview had been due to start three minutes ago. She was surprised no one had come to welcome her. The receptionist (badge saying 'Kendra', large specs, Kendra, Kendra, Kendra — must remember her name!) had popped out a few moments ago to get someone and left Jane here. Two short dumpy ladies entered the reception area from the car park with sports bags and stood at the reception desk. Hmm, thought Jane. Not good. The desk should never be left unmanned. The ladies threw her a mildly curious glance and for a moment Jane saw herself through their eyes, a young girl (although twenty-four was not *that* young), slight in build (but honed to perfection), flushed, nervous (but excited too).

She tried to work out why Kendra was so long. Perhaps the interviewing team from Head Office was late. Jane knew that the Sunnybank branch of Fit Not Fat had only recently been acquired by the company and she could tell that simply by looking around the place. The furniture was uncharacteristically shabby but the carpet was brand new and glared at her. Time passed slowly, one leisurely second ambling after another. And then everything sprang into action as Kendra returned with Sarah Curtis, the human-resources manager from Head Office, and Jane felt herself living and breathing more intensely and vividly than she could ever remember before.

'Jane!' said Sarah, and Jane responded with an appropriate greeting. 'So sorry I'm late. I was waiting for the fitness-assessment room to be free — it's the only place suitable for interviewing. And then we had to set it up by ourselves. But we're ready for you now.' She ushered Jane through the door to the left of the reception desk and along a corridor lined with posters and glass cases selling sports equipment. Jane passed a rather plump woman in her thirties or forties in a maroon T-shirt and paisley leggings, on her way out, a bemused expression on her face. She glanced into the gym and saw a young girl in sunflower yellow standing dreaming by the filing cabinets in the corner. And here she was, outside the door at the end of the corridor and oh, no! Two other candidates were there, sitting erect on upright chairs.

The competition. Simultaneously Jane smiled at them and tried to read them. One woman, older than her, hard-featured, hair scraped back, stiff grey business suit. One man, good body, nice face, at ease. And Jane was assailed by a welter of conflicting emotions. For if this was the competition she had to beat them. If not, they would beat her. It pained Jane to be beaten. Yet it pained her equally to risk hurting and alienating others by beating them. She could not bear anyone to think badly of her. Rather, *they* should want her to get the job too, so she beamed at them, exuding warmth and enthusiasm.

'Excuse me a moment,' Sarah Curtis said, and disappeared into the office.

Jane was compelled to fill the pregnant silence.

'Hi! I'm Jane Wright. Are you also being interviewed today? For the manager's job?'

'Yes,' said the man, surveying her with interest. 'Garth Taylor, senior fitness instructor.'

His lazy smile had the oddest effect on Jane but she was a mistress at dealing with awkward, inconvenient reactions to people of the opposite sex. The answering smile she gave him dripped professionalism. 'I'm the acting manager at Kearsley Gate Fit Not Fat.'

'I'm Siobhan Murphy, the acting manager *here*,' said the other woman, throwing just the lightest emphasis on her final word.

Jane's stomach dropped like a stone into the depths of her being. It was a put-up job, a fix. This woman was bound to get the job. It was a case of insider dealing. The interviews were going to take place purely to lend authority to the appointment. Adrenaline ebbed back along her veins leaving her limp and defeated. For a moment. And then, in a rush, it came surging triumphantly back. For she would not be beaten. This was a challenge and she was equal to it. As she summoned her resolve the door opened again and Sarah appeared. 'Jane,' she said, 'we'll see you first.'

The panel had arranged the room informally, with a desk pushed against the wall and four chairs in a loose circle. Jane took her seat, both acting and being, she hoped, in control. She sailed through the warm-up questions, discussing the weather, last night's match and her journey to the club with consummate ease. Her eyes flicked to each of the panel in turn, assessing the effect her remarks were making. Afterwards she hardly remembered what they looked like, only how they received her responses, how they smiled at her pleasantries.

'So, Jane, if you could talk us through your career until the present day?'

A deep breath, and she was off, running through her education, her qualifications in Step, Pilates, Boxercise, her employment record, her promotions, her past few months managing Kearsley Gate. She cast herself as a woman who was going places, who was divinely appointed to be the manager of this branch of Fit Not Fat. The trick, she knew, was to believe that she really was this person, this go-ahead, proactive Jane Wright. If she had a talent, it was her ability to create a convincing version of herself for public consumption.

What strengths would she bring to this job, were she appointed? Jane told them. Enthusiasm, first and foremost: the fitness industry was her life. The ability to motivate others, as a manager was primarily a team leader. Drive, determination, proven organisational abilities, she had them all. And then she began to worry that she had sold herself too well and might just have come across as a touch arrogant. That would never do. So in a twinkling of an eye she checked herself and added, 'And I'm willing to learn from my mistakes.' And realised she had back-pedalled too far and, with mounting panic, added further, 'Not that I ever try to make mistakes,' laughed, hated herself for laughing, tried to look serious. Then she recovered her equili-brium. 'I mean,' she said, 'I can be open-minded, but firm. I can listen to others, but know how to make decisions.' A horrible sense assailed her that she was making this up as she went along. There was a moment of complete paralysis as the scene in front of her eyes — three people sitting in a circle as if they were playing a game — froze like a crashed computer screen. And a numbing panic travelled up from her toes, along her legs, and—

'What would you say your weaknesses were?'

Aha! The weaknesses question. Jane had prepared an answer to this one. Yet still there was something terrifying about admitting to weaknesses. It was as if she had been invited to peer into a bottomless chasm. Weaknesses. She coughed politely, paused, to show that she was having to think long and deep about this one. 'Well, I suppose some people might say I work too hard,' and it was true. But working too hard was never really a weakness. It was the necessary adjunct of success. There was something noble in being a workaholic. You could never be too rich, too thin, or work too hard. Everyone knew that.

'And if we did appoint you,' someone said, 'you would be leading a team who might resent you. There are two internal applicants for this position. How would you minimise any bad feeling?'

Jane thought for a moment. She was back on form. 'If members of my team felt they wanted to move on, I'd certainly help them to get good positions elsewhere. But if they chose to stay, I'd delegate – give them new responsibilities to help further their careers. I'd take the time to get to know them, evaluate their skills and show them they were appreciated. It's vital that we work as a team, as team spirit will keep and motivate members — the staff is our greatest asset. Although good marketing will attract clients, they won't stay unless we can offer them that little bit more — in our case, as a small club, the personal touch.'

Jane was aware that she was talking as if she had already got the job, but it was no bad thing. She knew she sounded tremendously positive, which was good. She glanced at the panel. Their faces were pleasantly bland. If only she knew what they were thinking.

They discussed marketing next, publicity, and Jane listened to the history of the club. When Fit Not Fat had bought Sunnybank from Trudy Thompson, the previous owner, it had been making a loss which, given that the club was situated right in the middle of a residential area, was surprising. It ought to be possible to run a highly successful venture here. Then it was discovered only a month after contracts were signed, that Fitness International were planning to open a branch just ten minutes away. So the new manager would be up against stiff competition.

'I thrive on competition,' Jane added. It was true. Sarah smiled. Did she favour her? God, Jane hoped so!

'So we want the new manager installed as quickly as possible. We want to establish Fit Not Fat, Sunnybank, as *the* health club in the area.'

'Absolutely,' agreed Jane.

Then there were the concluding formalities. Sarah said they had no more questions to ask, people rose, hands were shaken and Jane was assured they would reach a decision by the end of the day. And she was free to go. She opened the door, and in a sudden burst of confidence and fellow-feeling said, 'Good luck!' to Garth and Siobhan sitting outside. And it was over.

In a blur Jane left the club, found her car in the car park and drove for the ten minutes it took her to get to her flat, a first-floor one-bedroomed apartment in a modern, nondescript block. It was more of a base than a home. As she unlocked the front door she regretted having arranged to take the afternoon off from Kearsley Gate as the solitude emanating from her flat momentarily depressed her. Just anticlimax, she told herself. That's all.

That sense of anticlimax was also responsible for her light-headedness, she decided. She had tried to eat breakfast, but naturally it had gone straight through her. Now she was beyond hunger, which was a pity, as she needed something to do, like eat lunch, to pass the time until she heard from Sarah Curtis. What else could she do? Tidy up? She glanced around her living room, with its jumble of magazines, documents from work, books on interview preparation, half-open makeup bag, and her heart sank. Another time, maybe. Then she prowled around the kitchen, opened the fridge, saw the remnants of last night's bottle of wine and wondered if she should finish it off. She even went as far as placing her hand around the damp, cool neck of the bottle. It was only twelve fifteen, far too early for a drink. But, on the other hand, she needed some help in coming down after the interview. She tightened her grasp. But then again, she wanted to be sober if Sarah rang. She released the bottle. Only she *deserved* a drink. The bottle gleamed at her. But was this the beginning of alcoholism, drinking alone, and before lunch? Resolutely, Jane closed the fridge. She would indulge tonight, to celebrate or to drown her sorrows. That was what any normal, reasonable person would do.

But am I normal and reasonable? Jane asked herself. Certainly she had put on a good show of it this morning, but now she felt the mask slip. It had all been an act, and the effort of maintaining it had drained her. Now she didn't know what to do with herself or even what she was. What she was, in the eyes of the world, would be announced by Sarah Curtis shortly, either Manager of Sunnybank Fit Not Fat, or (terrible thought!) Not Manager of Sunnybank Fit Not Fat.

Now, in her heightened state of anxiety, poised between two possibilities, Jane thought about herself. She wondered why success was so important to her. Perhaps it was to every female of her generation – in today's world, you had to *be* someone or get trampled underfoot. Yes, that was it. Survival of the fittest. But then, maybe it was just *her* to be ambitious. When she was small she fantasised regularly about being the first girl on the moon, an Olympic athlete winning a gold medal, a rock star with a number-one hit, prime minister, or head of a multinational corporation. The fantasies still seemed perfectly reasonable to her. Without a dream, what was the purpose of life?

And that was the end of Jane's introspection. She knew it was important to keep busy while you were waiting otherwise waiting became torture, and decided that a little extra work on her abs would not go amiss. Physical activity calmed the mind, and sit-ups flattened the stomach. She pulled out her Cybex trainer from the cupboard and lay on the floor doing sit-ups.

One, two, three, four, her ears pinned back for the ring of the telephone, eight, nine, ten, eleven, and then it occurred to her how ridiculous she must look lying on the carpet bobbing up and down for dear life and would have laughed – she certainly smiled to herself – but giggling was a girlie thing to do. If only she *knew* the result of the interview. She could cope then – knowing even bad news was so much preferable to waiting. Twenty-one, twenty-two, twenty-three. She had interviewed well, but had they seen through her? To that other Jane, damned by faint praise in every school report – 'Jane finds this subject a challenge', 'Jane's spelling has improved a little this year', 'Jane must not be disappointed with this result.' Thirty, thirty-one. But Jane *had been* disappointed and couldn't understand why, with all her effort, things weren't coming right for her. Thirty-eight, thirty-nine. She would show them. She would be the best. Forty-four, forty-five. Why was life so difficult? Forty-nine, fifty – and Jane stopped. To her surprise she felt as if she was about to sneeze. She sat up and did sneeze. Perhaps she was allergic to the dust in the carpet. It was giving her a headache too, a prickly pain in her forehead. Or perhaps the excitement had been too much for her. What she needed now was a whisky, or brandy – one of those medicinal alcoholic drinks. A shame there was none in the flat. A malt whisky would relax her throat, which was feeling unusually tight. She swallowed awkwardly and got to her feet.

The possibility that she might be catching a cold crossed her mind. But, no, she believed in mind over matter. She was *not* ill. She was experiencing an inconvenient allergic reaction. Illness was for wimps. Illness was mucky and disgusting and best not thought about. It was why Jane worked in the health industry. An unstoppable sneeze travelled along her nasal cavities and exploded into the silence of the living room. Perhaps it was time she Hoovered after all. She marched resolutely to the hall, seized her vacuum cleaner and clicked it on.

She rather liked the roar it made. Ill? No way was she ill. It was Jane Wright who had won a prize – her only school prize – for not missing one day of school for the whole four years she was at Kingsway Juniors. She had received a trophy at assembly *and* a five-pound book token. Her mother often remarked about her strong constitution, and apart from the chicken pox she had suffered as a baby, and the bout of glandular fever in the sixth form (caught, she imagined, from Michael Crompton who had kissed every girl at that Christmas party), she had never been ill. She had little sympathy with people who were.

She was feeling more positive now, almost like the Jane who had sparkled so eagerly at the interview. As she Hoovered, pushing debris under the settee and armchair, she hummed one of the more cheesy of the recent chart hits and was feeling better by the minute. Then she became aware that the telephone was ringing. Trembling, fumbling, hot and sweaty, she picked up the receiver. 'Hello?'

'Hello? Mrs Wright? This is Alpha Damp-proofing here.

Since our engineers are in your area doing some work we wondered if—'

'Sorry. Not interested.' And under her breath, 'Sod off!'

'What do you think of Siobhan Murphy?'

'She's a distinct possibility. She knows the business like the back of her hand. Only I don't necessarily see it as an advantage that she's been here for such a long time. Could she keep at the appropriate distance from her colleagues? And from her answers to the questions, I reckon she'd want to run the club on the lines of the previous owner. Would she ever make a genuine Fit Not Fat person?'

'I tend to agree with you. To be honest, I found her rather frightening. And it was hard to draw her out. She said very little about herself.'

'Yes, but she knows the club's members well. That must count for something.'

'So does Garth Taylor. How about him? What did you think, Sarah?'

'Impressive in many ways. He certainly came across as knowledgeable about the fitness industry. He's been on a number of courses. And there's something quite attractive about him.'

'To you, maybe. I'm not sure he's experienced enough in management – and there are no business qualifications.'

'We could train him ourselves. I'd be happy to spend some time with him.'

'I'm sure you would. But what about Jane Wright?'

Sarah fanned herself. 'She was very . . . *there*, if you know what I mean.'

'Intense – is that what you're trying to say? I tend to agree, but I find her an interesting prospect. She's young, true, but her references from Kearsley Gate are very complimentary.'

'Kearsley Gate's an easy branch to run. All she had to do was keep it ticking over. I admit Jane gave a good interview – a textbook interview . . . Maybe that was it.'

'There's nothing wrong in being prepared. You've got to concede she hasn't put a foot wrong.'

'A fair comment.' Sarah chewed her lip thoughtfully.

'And, besides, this branch needs someone with a bit of drive, with guts. I reckon she could get this place moving. I liked her development plan. It was forward thinking and innovative.'

'Would the other staff resent her?'

'Bound to, but a good manager would nip that in the bud. There are old wounds festering here, that's pretty obvious. It's exactly why we need new blood.'

'Coffee, anyone?' asked Sarah. 'And is it safe to smoke in here? I'm gasping!'

'Isn't your nicotine patch working?'

'I was allergic. Oh, God, I *hate* having to make decisions!'

Jane had reached the bargaining stage. She had promised the Fates that if she got this job she would tidy her flat properly, cut down her drinking, go to bed early at least five nights a week, not work quite so hard, work harder, go out more and not go out quite so much. She had convinced herself alternately that the job was hers (they would never appoint an internal candidate) and that she didn't have a hope (the acting manager was bound to get it). Her limbs were aching and her forehead was hot. She hated herself for getting in to such a state about a job but couldn't imagine not getting into a state over a job. Yet as each minute ticked slowly by Jane found herself caring less, perversely enjoying the inactivity thrust on her because her future lay in the balance, at someone else's disposal. It was irritating and a wonderful relief all at once.

So when the phone finally rang Jane felt an odd reluctance to answer it. She let it ring once, twice, then got up and lifted the receiver.

'Hello?' (Suspicious, frosty.)

'Is that Jane Wright?'

'Yes.'

'Sarah Curtis here. I'm happy to tell you we want to offer you the position of manager at Sunnybank. Will you accept?'

Yessss! Jane punched the air with delight.

'Well, thank you, Sarah. I'd like to very much.'

'There's lots of work to be done, you know.'

'I do,' said Jane, 'and I'm not afraid of hard work.'

'We know, and that's why we've appointed you. That, and your enthusiasm and the development plan.'

'I won't let you down.'

'We're sure of it.'

As soon as Jane had concluded her conversation with Sarah she went straight to the fridge for the bottle of wine, telling herself that this was the last time she was going to use alcohol as a mood prop because today was the beginning of the rest of her life. She had her first real management position. Today, Sunnybank; tomorrow Fit Not Fat, northern region, then national HQ, and when the company was ready to invest in European sites she would be at the helm. She toasted herself, and laughed at the way her mind had been running on. One step at a time. She thought coolly about Sunnybank, remembered Garth and Siobhan (problem one), the tatty furnishings (problem two), the new branch of Fitness International (problem three) and realised she had her work cut out. For a moment she doubted herself. What if she screwed up? What if the job was beyond her? She was young and not particularly experienced. But no — she would commit her body and soul to the pursuit of success! What one single woman could do to make Sunnybank Fit Not Fat the best club in the North-west, she would do. Jane was serious for a moment as she pledged herself to this. And then she smiled again, and bathed in bliss.

It was time now to let the world know what had happened to her. She thought about ringing her friends, or even Gina and Liz in London, but they would all be at work. She would text them shortly: she didn't want to interrupt them. She remembered her colleagues at Kearsley Gate, and was just about to call them when it occurred to her that really she ought to let her parents know first. She hesitated.

It was possible, it was just possible that this promotion would impress them. Running your own branch was something by anyone's standards. They had been cool when she was applying for the job, purely to help her cope if she didn't get it. Her parents were Stoics, always had been. But now there was a just a chance that they would be seriously impressed. How could they not be? Filling with anticipation, Jane dialled their number. Her mother picked up the phone.

'Hello?'

'It's me, Jane. You'll never guess.'

'Guess what?'

'I got the job. I'm the new manager at Sunnybank!'

'That's nice, dear. I'm glad you rang. Mavis and Gerald have included you on their invitation for their twenty-fifth and I wondered if you could make it.'

'Well, it depends. I don't know—'

'It would be lovely to have you with us. Sunday the four-teenth?'

'I might be at the—'

'Well, let me know if you're coming. And of course I'll pass on your news to your father. But I must rush, Jane. It's my afternoon at the office.'

' 'Bye, Mum.'

' 'Bye, dear.'

Bloody typical, thought Jane. Nothing I do ever pleases her.

She drained her glass of wine. She fought her disappointment valiantly, turning it into grim determination. I'll show her, she thought. One day, and one day soon, she's going to sit up and take notice. She'll have no choice.

Sunnybank, here I come!

Chapter Three

———◦◦◦◦———

Cassie stood in the bathroom contemplating her leggings and the maroon T-shirt hanging over the bath. Should she iron them? Did you iron things you were going to work out in? More to the point, ought she to buy some proper clothes for exercise – from one of those sports shops with eager young acne-bespattered-just-out-of-school sales assistants standing around in posses? Probably not. And who wasn't to say that crinkly maroon T-shirts weren't shortly going to be all the rage at the gym? So she snatched her gear off the hangers and was just about to bundle it into a carrier-bag when the doorbell rang.

She paused and frowned. Who could it be? She wasn't expecting anyone. This was her free Saturday afternoon, in which she had planned her first full workout. Curious, she made her way down the stairs and saw, to her surprise and pleasure, the outline of Terry through the side window. Eagerly she opened the door.

'What are you doing here?'

'Whatever you want me to do,' Terry said, with a mild suggestiveness.

'You could look at the plumbing in the kitchen,' Cassie parried.

'Are you going to let me in?'

Cassie stood aside as he crossed her threshold and thought how different their friendship had become since he had declared an interest in her, so to speak. She had known Terry for some years: he was a friend of a friend of Lynda, and not one of her academic circle. That in itself was a blessed relief. Just to spend time with someone who didn't think in terms of papers, research, student numbers and department in-fighting was sheer bliss. Terry was a freelance journalist, specialising in restaurant reviews. He had taken her as his partner for many a three-course meal, at which Cassie had been morally obliged to eat as much as possible (to be fair to the restaurateur) and had described what she had eaten in sensuous terms to Terry. He had used her description in his lush, sensuous reviews. It was only in the past few months that this same sensuousness had begun to affect their friendship too. They had both been a little surprised by it, Cassie had realised she needed to do some serious thinking, and then the gallstones came along.

'You're not busy, are you?' Terry asked, entering her living room and scanning it for signs of work.

'No. Actually, I was on my way to the gym.'

'The *gym?*'

Cassie glowed with virtue. 'The gym,' she said, relishing the sound of the word in her mouth.

'May I ask why?'

'I thought about what the consultant said and decided to try to avoid the operation. I'm overhauling my lifestyle instead. I've joined Fit Not Fat.'

Terry gave a long, low whistle, and made himself comfortable on Cassie's *chaise-longue*, picked up from a second-hand shop a year or two ago. 'To be honest, I don't see you as the type.'

Cassie bridled. '*What* type?'

'A Lycra princess.' Terry chuckled, crossing one leg over the other and stared at her.

His gaze made her uncomfortable. He had a way of looking

at her that suggested ownership — no, not ownership so much as the sense that he knew her, *really* knew her, which in the biblical sense was almost true, but not quite. His smile also hinted that he knew what would become of her fitness regime — that her membership card would soon find its way down the back of the cupboard to moulder there.

She had to put him right. 'I'm doing this for *health* reasons,' she said, a little sternly. 'Quite frankly, I'm scared of what will happen if I don't.'

'I know,' he said.

Cassie was only a little mollified. She resented anyone detracting from the enthusiasm she had been cultivating for her new regime. She looked critically at Terry. He could do with getting into shape, too. There was just the hint of a bulge above the belt of his trousers, the result of a few too many good dinners. But otherwise she had to admit he was disturbingly attractive for someone who didn't care too much about his appearance. His hair was a little dishevelled, and his favourite navy pullover looked just too comfortable on him, it was true. But his eyes were boyish and mischievous, his face expressive, sensitive without any loss of masculinity — Cassie stopped her thoughts right there. She had promised herself to think rationally about her relationship with Terry and make some conscious choices before she committed herself. Where would it all end? Would she settle down, marry, even have babies? It could happen — these days, forty was the new thirty. The advantage of being nearly forty, surely, was that one went into relationships (at last) with one's eyes open. And, besides, now that she was about to institute some change in her own life, she had to resist the blandishments of Terry, her personal chocolate orange, until she had achieved what she was about to set out to do.

'There's a new venture in Didsbury,' Terry interrupted her train of thought. 'They say it's an experiment in fusion — tikka masala Caesar salad to a background of Pavarotti and Ravi Shankar. Do you fancy it?'

'Sounds appalling.'

'I know. I've reserved a table. I'll pick you up at eight.'

'Yes, but – Look, Terry, I don't think I can. Indian food is terrible – it's cooked in ghee, full of fat, and even Caesar salads come with dressing – and then, if I'm working out this afternoon, it seems rather self-destructive. I'll come and watch you eat, and I might toy with a side salad, but I don't think . . .'

Cassie saw Terry's face fall and she felt guilty. But everything she had said was true. Indian food was hell to digest, and she didn't want to risk upsetting her gall bladder. She sat by him on the *chaise-longue* and took his hand.

'There must be something you can have,' he said. 'Just avoid the obviously fatty food.'

Her problem with Terry was that he always sounded so reasonable. Yet Cassie felt there was more at stake than just a meal. To go out for dinner on the first day of a diet-exercise regime was ridiculous: it would undermine everything.

'Isn't there someone else you could take?'

'I want you,' he said.

'I could meet you in the pub afterwards?'

He grinned at her. 'Just be careful I don't spike your drink with lard!' She laughed. The tension was dissipated.

'So you've joined a gym,' Terry said. 'Strange – I wouldn't have put you down as the masochistic type. But why the gym? Why not take up jogging? Even a small amount of exercise, walking in the park, would make a difference.'

'But would I keep it up? That's the question. It's so easy to find excuses if all you're doing is walking more. One day it's raining, or another day you're rushing around and the car saves time. No, I'm doing this one properly. I'm committing, Terry.'

'But you told me the other day you were shy of commitment.'

'Relationship commitment, not task commitment.'

'I can wait,' he said. 'But will I still fancy the new streamlined Cassie?'

'Streamlined? Give over. I've told you already – read my lips – I'm only doing this for health reasons. I'm not going to change. I don't want to change.'

'Good.'

Cassie leant over to give him a brief kiss on the cheek. She owed him that much. 'But I must go now. I've spent all day dreading this afternoon and I don't want to waste all that anxiety,' she said.

'Just take it easy,' Terry told her.

Take it easy? The whole point of the gym was not to take it easy. Cassie tried to dismiss thoughts of Terry as she strode purposefully along the brick-lined corridors of Fit Not Fat. She would deal with him later. Now she had enough on her plate. She was unaccountably nervous of working, or being seen to work, in the gym and, were it not for the scalpel of Damocles suspended above her gall bladder, she wouldn't be seen dead here.

In fact, to help her acclimatise herself to the gym she had arranged to meet Lynda in the changing room. Lynda was one of the secretaries at work. She and Cassie shared their journey to the university in Cassie's car. Hours spent at a standstill in Manchester's traffic had cemented their friendship, despite their obvious differences. In fact, it was Lynda who had recommended Fit Not Fat to Cassie. She had been a member when it was just the Sunnybank Health and Fitness centre. Her mother was a member too. And her husband.

Crossing her fingers, Cassie hoped Lynda was there now. She pushed open the door of the changing room and then, to her horror, saw women getting changed. They were actually in a state of semi-undress. There was something faintly shocking about seeing complete strangers with only half their clothes on. There were nut-brown breasts, white, dimpled thighs, and even – God forbid! – the odd triangle of pubic hair. The reality of other people's bodies embarrassed her and she looked everywhere but at the other women. At that moment Lynda arrived from round a corner, in a tiny black Lycra top, shiny black cycling shorts and Nike Air trainers. Her mass of dark, curly hair was tied back and she looked every bit the fitness fanatic. Cassie was thoroughly intimidated. She greeted Lynda then shamefacedly got the maroon T-shirt and leggings out of her Sainsbury's carrier-bag.

'I knew you'd turn up,' Lynda said, settling on a nearby bench to watch Cassie change. 'Getting here for the first time is the hardest thing you'll ever do. And your first workout is your toughest workout. From then on it gets easier and easier, believe me. You won't regret this, Cassie. I admire you a lot for what you're doing, and so does my mum, and so does Merton. And there's something else I've been dying to tell you. I was reading in a magazine the other days that it's possible to flush gallstones out of your system if you dose yourself with olive oil. You ought to give it a try. I'll find the article for you. I told Mum to put it on one side. And talking of Mum, did I tell you she hasn't had a dizzy spell for a few days? And that's without the pills. So it might not be her blood pressure after all. I think that's good news, though she said she'd prefer to know once and for all what was causing them. But here I am going on about Mum and haven't asked you how you are. How *are* you?'

The problem with Lynda was that she really wanted to know. She was fascinated by health, her own, her family's, the health of people she knew and even those she didn't. She collected the details of obscure diseases with the enthusiasm of a trainspotter. She was a medical polymath.

'I've been fine, but I've been watching my diet,' Cassie said, as she struggled into her leggings.

'Yes – you should avoid fat at all costs. But it's not easy. And I should know. You'll need all the help you can get. Have you thought of hypnotherapy? You can programme your uncon-scious mind to help you avoid foods and behaviours that are bad for you. My cousin went to a fabulous hypnotherapist who cured her of biting the sides of her fingers. And a friend of hers lost three stone simply by playing these tapes he'd made her. I have his number somewhere. Are you ready yet? Mmm. I'm not sure those leggings do anything for you. But in a few weeks you'll be slim enough to fit into all the trendy gear. We'll go out one lunchtime and spend some of your money.'

Cassie didn't mind Lynda's gentle bullying. She knew Lynda to be warm-hearted, generous and motivated by the desire to ensure that no one she knew was unhappy or, worse, ill. Her religion was officially Judaism but unofficially self-improvement. Together they walked the few yards to the gym's entrance. Cassie took a deep breath.

Once inside, she noticed little of her surroundings. She was enveloped by a fog of self-consciousness occasionally illuminated by a flash of absurdity. In a trice, it seemed, she was on a mat trying out some stretches with Lynda encouraging her, and then on a treadmill with Lynda briskly reminding her how to programme it. Soon the machine was in motion, and she was off.

The art of the treadmill, Cassie soon discovered, was to move your legs at precisely the correct pace to prevent you being carried gently backwards and falling off the end. She clung tightly to the rail in front of her and attempted to do this. Emboldened by success, she let go. She was walking at a comfortable, leisurely pace. Hey! She was actually exercising! The novelty was intoxicating. She looked about for Lynda, who was sitting on a painful-looking contraption, watching one of the TV monitors. Cassie presumed it was doing her good somehow. She broke her concentration briefly to smile and give Cassie a thumbs-up. Cassie smiled back. She was enjoying herself.

Out of the corner of her eye she noticed the door of the gym open and two young women come in, one a trainer in the Fit Not Fat sunflower yellow pullover, and another in a smart pale green suit. The trainer seemed to be showing the gym to the girl in the suit – perhaps she was a prospective client. But the girl in the suit seemed more at home than that and in fact she came over to her.

'Come on!' she said. 'You can go faster than that!' and, to Cassie's horror, she pressed the speed button repeatedly until Cassie was having to scurry awkwardly to catch up, and walk at the pace she adopted when she was late for a lecture.

'That's better!' said the girl. 'That'll get your heart working.'

Cassie was tempted to tell her that her heart was already working and that what she had actually meant to say was that the unaccustomed exercise would get her heart working *faster*, which was an entirely different proposition, but the complexity of the thought splintered in the effort Cassie was having to make just to keep in the same position on the treadmill. She wondered vaguely who the girl was – obviously something to do with the health club. She noticed the instructor speak to her with tight-lipped deference, so she was probably in some kind of authority.

Speculation over, Cassie became aware again of her exercise and discovered that when you think about something else the clock on the treadmill goes faster. OK, she told herself, think of something else. The reasons for the downfall of Richard II? The effect on the English economy of the Black Death? Admission numbers for next year? Such was the mosaic of her life at present. None of it really engaged her, or seemed as real as the fact that she was walking briskly on a never-ending rubber belt going nowhere and, for some incomprehensible reason, this was supposed to be doing her good. Now when she looked at the clock, she discovered that there was only a minute to go, and she kept her eyes fixed on the descending figures and – joy of joy – the treadmill slowed, her walk returned to an amble, and it was over.

Almost out of breath, but not quite, Cassie decided that she had enjoyed herself. In a burst of euphoria she realised she had exercised competently and effectively. Now she eyed the step machines and saw that a lady in her fifties was on one, marching slowly and gracefully. It looked even easier than the treadmill. She walked over to the step machine and frowned as she realised she'd forgotten how to set it up.

'Can I help?' asked a male voice by her side.

She turned to discover a man with film-star looks and a body to die for. Gay, thought Cassie immediately. They always were. She showed him her card and he explained how to programme the machine and helped her position herself on the steps, one foot on each paddle. As the paddles took her weight, Cassie felt herself sink gently to the floor.

'Try a slow march on it,' the man said. 'Like you're going upstairs.'

Cassie pumped the paddles for a few moments, then found herself sinking to the floor again.

'No,' said the man. 'Smaller steps – just to get it moving.'

She tried two or three, but it was hard work as the machine was resistant to her efforts. She sank to the bottom again.

'Watch me,' said the man.

He ascended the machine next to her and began to step. Cassie found herself distracted by his male gorgeousness. Broad backs always turned her on, and the combination of his honed physique with the well-defined bone structure of his face and those baby blue eyes – I like the scenery here, she thought. She tried to step to his rhythm. Impossible. Her legs refused more than two or three steps. She sank to the bottom again.

'Hmm,' said the instructor. Cassie tried to smile at him appealingly. 'You probably don't have the leg strength to do this at present. Just try the machine each time you come until you get the hang of it. For today, just do twenty minutes on the recliner bike instead.'

'OK,' said Cassie, liking the sound of that. The man's name was Garth – it was on a badge pinned to his track-suit top. 'Can you show me how that works too?'

In a few moments she was installed, her legs stuck out in front of her, pedalling steadily. She had to do twenty minutes of this, which seemed an inordinately long time. The thought weakened her legs and she wondered whether she would have the energy and determination to stay here all that time, pedalling, knees going round, feet going round, an unaccustomed tightness in her thighs as they pumped up and down – hard work! It was the pointlessness, the endlessness she found discouraging. She was going nowhere, except, she told herself, as far away from the operating table as she could get. The idea cheered her, and she imagined herself pedalling furiously away from the hospital, gowned surgeons and distraught nurses in hot pursuit, but she was escaping from their surgical-gloved clutches, faster and faster – she was slipping down on the bike and adjusted her seating – pedalling, pedalling . . . She was hot and wiped her forehead with the side of her hand.

Still fifteen minutes to go! Impossible, terrible – whatever could she do to pass the time? She looked up at the TV screen positioned in front of her and tried to concentrate on a pop video of dancing schoolgirls and failed. Her thighs were hurting now and she was uncomfortably hot. A quick glance in the mirror at the side of the gym showed a large, red-faced woman pedalling desperately. Cassie wouldn't own the image. This was torture. Quick – think of something else. A hairy man came in and walked over to the weights. With calm deliberation he selected a pair and lifted them, providing a welcome distraction. She watched him wince with the effort and it made her feel better that someone else was suffering.

It was getting still harder. Her legs were aching and she was slipping again. She righted herself and clutched the handles by her side. She found that by taking more weight on her hands it was easier to pedal. Beads of sweat gathered on her forehead, formed rivulets and threatened to run into her eyes. She wiped her forehead and released a silent volley of obscenities. What am I doing here? she asked herself. Take out my gallstones! I concede defeat. She looked at the clock. Three minutes to go. Just three minutes. I can do it! No, I can't. She looked up at the TV screen again and there was Cher, smiling beatifically down at her, as if she *knew* what Cassie was going through. Saint Cher. *Come on*, she seemed to say, *you can do it! I'm older than you, much older, and look at me! No pain, no gain!*

Cassie smiled back at her, and discovered that smiling helped. Somehow it gave her energy. Thirty seconds, twenty – thank you, Cher! Ten, nine, eight, sevensixfive – gasp – fourthreetwo, one, yess! Cassie's legs slowed and came to a stop. She had done it. Twenty whole minutes on an exercise bike. She was shattered, exquisitely shattered. Sweat was pouring off her. She got off the bike and her legs were wobbling. They only just managed to get her over to the water fountain where she drank cup after cup of ice-cold water.

And as she stood there, something strange happened. She breathed deeply and felt unaccountably light, and happy, and exhilarated, and young again, and tingling, and full of a sense of accomplishment and possibility, all intermingled. She was exhausted, true, but it was *good* exhaustion. It was the closest she had ever come to that sought-after post-orgasm feeling. No – it wasn't the same as that. After sex, she felt as if she had been naughty. Now, she felt good, virtuous, smart, in control. And, besides, sex was all fun. She had to admit she had hated every moment on the bike, but it had made her feel this good. Strange how not enjoying something can produce so much enjoyment. Maybe this was like sado-masochistic sex? But what did it matter? She felt great.

Lynda seemed to have finished whatever she had been doing and came over to her.

'OK?' she said.

'Brilliant,' said Cassie. 'But shattered.'

'Good. It sounds like the endorphins have kicked in. You really should wear a heart monitor to make sure you're working at the right level.'

'How was your workout?' asked Cassie. 'Gruelling?'

'I was only toning today – resistance work is terribly important. It prevents osteoporosis. What are you doing after your shower, Cassie?'

Cassie shrugged. 'Going home. Work. Terry asked me to go and eat with him but I won't – I might join him later for a drink.' She felt just a little sorry for herself and Lynda picked up on it.

'Poor you! And it's Saturday as well. I tell you what. Follow me home in your car and come and spend some time with us. It'll be lovely to have you. You've never met my family properly and I've told them so much about you.'

Cassie agreed. It seemed natural to her that after the novelty of the gym she should be whisked to another new environment. Lynda had told her a great deal about the Cohen family and Cassie felt as if she knew them all intimately, inside and outside. Merton, Lynda's husband, was an optician who suffered terribly with migraine headaches. Marla, her mother, was a widow prone to dizzy spells and hypertension. Lynda had two children, Hannah, enlarged tonsils and suspected asthma, and Josh, who picked up everything that was going, the opportunist thief of childhood illnesses. They all lived happily in a detached house off Captain's Nook.

'That's arranged, then,' Lynda said. 'We'll have a nice, cosy afternoon.'

Driving behind Lynda's convertible Cassie was glad of the distraction this visit afforded. Now that her workout was over she was hungry and regretted turning down Terry's invitation.

One last meal with him would have postponed her new lifestyle only by one day. Sudden change was bad for people, anyway. Better, perhaps, that she should have joined the gym and carried on eating tempting food for a few more days. What was happening to her that she should turn down a free meal? Only it wasn't just the food angle. She hoped Terry didn't think she had rejected him. As much as she didn't think she wanted a full-blown relationship with him, she didn't want to put him off either. It was important to get the balance right. She suspected that this afternoon she'd got it wrong. But the gym had to come first. She had to prioritise it if she was to make a go of learning and living a healthy lifestyle. For she had realised that health was probably the most important thing of all — because what was the point of having money, love, success in your career if you were ill, dying, or even dead? No point at all. Cassie knew it was important to go all out for health. She thought of Lynda's one-woman crusade against illness with a new-found respect.

She knew the exterior of Lynda's house — a modern, sprawling, detached residence with a manicured lawn and neat trees in pots. She had sat outside it on many a morning while Lynda raced around the house giving orders to her mother and searching frantically for her handbag. Now she parked just before the drive and joined Lynda as she ran up to the front door.

'My mother will be thrilled to meet you, Cassie. She's always been so pleased that we go in together with you being one of the lecturers. Ah, here are my keys.' Lynda unlocked the door and immediately Cassie heard a small child crying. Lynda's mother, Marla, appeared with a flushed little girl in her arms. 'Hannah isn't too well,' she said.

Cassie saw Lynda pause to take this in, like an officer informed that the enemy was in sight. 'What's the trouble?' she asked, taking Hannah, feeling her forehead, kissing her soft dark hair.

'She was sick just after you left for the gym. I tried to take her temperature but she wouldn't let me. She wouldn't have a sleep – and she's refused to eat anything, which is just as well in case she's sick again so I don't really know but I think she must be coming down with something.' Lynda's mother was as voluble as her daughter.

'Shall I go home?' Cassie offered.

'No,' said Lynda. 'It won't be anything much – I hope. I'd like you to stick around, just in case. Mum, put the kettle on. Honey, how do you feel?'

'A hurting tummy.'

'You see, Cassie, it might go away of its own accord. Or not. Mummy's home now, petal. Where's Merton?'

'Helping Josh on the computer,' said Marla.

'Men are never there in a crisis,' Lynda muttered. Hannah continued to whimper, playing with her mother's curls. The complicated cogs and wheels of Lynda's domestic life clicked and whirred, and made Cassie feel slightly alienated. Again she offered to go home.

'No, please don't,' Lynda insisted.

So Cassie went into the kitchen to help get some drinks and listened to Marla retell the story of Hannah's indisposition while she cut some slices of carrot cake and put out a plate of biscuits. Marla was easy company – conversation bubbled out of her like a waterfall. She was dressed unostentatiously in a dark skirt and brick-coloured cardigan. Her dumpy figure was appealing, and interestingly at odds with her carefully coiffured hair and made-up face. Cassie took the refreshments out to the front room, and before long they were sitting there together, Hannah on her mother's lap, droopy but content. She was a remarkably pretty child, olive-complexioned with large brown eyes, and thick dark hair swept back into a ponytail. She was dressed exclusively from Gap for Kids. Just now she seemed like a baby again, burrowing into her mother, clinging to her, unable to keep still.

'Are you feeling better, pet? Yes, of course you are, now that Mummy's home.'

'No I'm not,' said Hannah.

Lynda ignored her. 'Cassie had her first workout today,' she announced to her mother.

'Well done!' Marla said.

'Yes, it's part of her lifestyle change. She has gallstones, you see. No, Cassie, put the cake back. There's too much fat in it. I suppose you can have a Rich Tea but you'd be better off with just the coffee.'

Annoyed and taken aback in equal measure, Cassie replaced the slice of cake.

'Gallstones!' said Marla, with delight. 'My sister had her gall bladder removed years ago – before they started with this keyhole surgery. She was off work for weeks. But these days it's so quick – I think they go in through your navel. Do they, Lynda? Now, my cousin Leslie had his gallstones dissolved . . .'

Only recently Cassie would have blanked out such a monologue; now she listened avidly. Once you had an illness, she had discovered, you were greedy for every bit of information relating to it. She supposed it was partly a control mechanism – the more you knew, the less frightening it was. But it wasn't only that: there was always the chance you might hear a story with a happy ending that gave you hope, or some recondite and closely guarded secret cure that only an élite fraternity had ever tried. No, sod it, gallstones really were interesting. She began to question Marla further but was interrupted by Hannah. 'I think I be sick again.'

Lynda was up in an instant and swept the child to the bathroom from where there came some unpromising noises followed by the pulling of the chain. On emerging into the front room Hannah looked paler than ever, and Lynda increasingly concerned, a furrow making itself distinct on her forehead. 'She really isn't well,' she said. 'I hope it's nothing serious.'

Could it be? Cassie wondered. She knew nothing about child illnesses and could offer no reassurance. Surely the chances were that it was only a tummy upset or food poisoning. But if it wasn't? That powerful narrative pull of illness asserted itself. First, a sign that something was wrong. Second, the unbearable suspense while one finds out what it is. Third, the course of the illness. Fourth – the crisis, life and death in suspension. Fifth, the outcome. Faced with the onset of an illness one was filled with primeval dread yet also, perversely, wanted the story to be as sensational as possible. Why else were scholars so fascinated with plagues and epidemics? The Black Death, in fact, was one of Cassie's favourite topics. However, it was unlikely Hannah had bubonic plague and Cassie pulled herself back to the present.

'Get Merton to come down,' Marla was saying.

'Merton! Hannah's been sick again!'

In a few moments Merton appeared, a plumpish, dark-haired man with a shy smile and designer glasses.

'Take a look at her!' Marla demanded.

'Mum, he's an *optician*! What does he know about illness?'

Marla shrugged, and addressed herself to Cassie. 'You'd have thought he'd had some sort of medical training.'

'I'm sure it's just something or nothing,' Merton said.

'Something or nothing!' Lynda reacted as if Merton had insulted her. 'This is your *own child*, Merton!' She nuzzled Hannah protectively. 'Don't worry, chicken. Mummy will look after you.'

'Shall I ring the emergency doctor?' asked Marla.

All was chaos and Cassie could hardly follow the cross-currents of anxiety, resentment and excitement.

'Yes, ring the doctor! Somebody ring the doctor!' Lynda shouted at Merton. Hannah whimpered.

Marla attempted to explain to Cassie. 'She worries a lot

about the children.' There was a note of approval in her voice. 'And with all the talk of meningitis and Hannah not having had her jab yet—'

'Mum, stop it.'

'Shall I come with you to the doctor?'

'No! You just make me worry more, with all your talk of meningitis. Cassie, will you come with me? Hasn't Merton found a doctor yet? There is an emergency surgery, and they're quite good. We've used them once or twice, haven't we, Mum?'

Cassie felt herself being inexorably drawn into this growing crisis. She could sympathise with Lynda. There was no telling what was wrong with the child, partly because Hannah couldn't say precisely how she felt and partly because the most horrendous possibilities could never be ruled out. An upset stomach and fever were the prelude to almost anything.

Merton came in. 'We can take her to the surgery now,' he said.

'Dad!' came a boy's voice from upstairs. 'The computer's crashed again.'

'You stay with Josh,' Lynda commanded. 'Mum, in case we're a long time you'd better stay here too – you know what to do with the chicken. Cassie will come with me. Don't worry, Hannah, you'll soon be better.'

The chaos and panic reminded Cassie of the one time she had attempted to watch *ER*, when hysterical medics had turned an illness into a drama – which was the point, really.

Within a few moments they were installed in Lynda's car, Hannah strapped into the back seat. 'Not that I think there's anything terribly wrong with her,' said Lynda, 'but the point is to be *sure*. I'd never forgive myself if it was anything serious.' Cassie immediately imagined Hannah in a Victorian deathbed scene, matted hair framing a chalk-white face, mother, father, family surrounding her, a forlorn, forgotten teddy bear by her side, a priest reading the last rites – but, no, Hannah was Jewish. 'It could be her tonsils – they're enlarged and prone to infection – and if it is, some antibiotics might be in order, but really it's just to rule out anything else. Hannah, baby, do you have a pain in your neck?'

'Yes, it hurting.'

'Oh, no! Are the lights hurting your eyes?'

'Yes!'

Immediately Lynda turned around and the car swerved dangerously. She righted it in the nick of time. 'Oh, my God, Cassie, did you hear that? Her neck's painful and the light's hurting her eyes! You don't think it's meningitis, do you? Do you have a rash, petal?'

'Yes!'

'This is a nightmare!'

Cassie looked behind her and saw, that if anything, Hannah seemed better. She was agreeing with everything her mother said simply because she wanted to please her. Or perhaps she was a bit of a drama queen too. 'I don't think she understands your questions,' She said. 'She doesn't look that bad.'

'Oh, God, you might be right. I know I'm being silly but you hear such things. And when you love somebody, just the merest possibility that—'

She swerved into the surgery car park and Cassie held on tightly to the glove compartment. In a trice they were out of the car, Hannah in her mother's arms, and they were entering the surgery. The last time Cassie had been here was to discuss the findings of the ultrasound scan with her GP. It occurred to her now that she hadn't eaten since lunchtime, and she felt grateful to young Hannah for having made this possible.

The three took seats at the far end of the surgery. Hannah wriggled off her mother's lap to investigate some battered toys that lay in a heap in one corner.

'It's so good of you to come,' Lynda said to Cassie.

'No sweat,' Cassie said. 'I'm sure there's nothing to worry about.'

'I know, but you do worry, don't you?'

You do, thought Cassie, looking around the waiting room. New-age flute music insinuated itself over the loudspeakers and a TV screen silently played a loop of health advice. No one was watching it. The music was an irritant, Cassie thought, belying the fact that no one was ever relaxed in a doctor's waiting room. Funny, too, how etiquette prevented you speaking to another patient, and if you did, you *never* asked them what was wrong, although that was the thing you most wanted to know. At the doctor's, everyone was at their most human and vulnerable, yet everyone avoided eye contact. A young woman in designer jeans was immersed in a magazine and the old chap in a bobble hat stared vacuously at the wall. It was as if they had begun that slow slide into the terrifying process that turned a person into a patient and robbed them of their individuality.

Cassie remembered how appalled she had been when, at the hospital, she had had to put on a white gown before her scan. She was told to place her own clothes – those symbols of Cassieness – in a hospital bag, and don the garb of anonymity, presumably so that the radiologists were not troubled and distracted by the fact she was a fellow human being. Or was it that in any institution the system triumphed eventually over the needs of the individual? Was the NHS, in fact, like the medieval church? And if it was, did that mean that the summoners, the pardoners and corrupt priests were like—

'Cassie? Did you hear me?'

'Sorry. I was miles away. What was that?'

'Do you think she's looking better?'

Cassie glanced over to where Hannah was having a stand-off with a small boy over a grubby shape-sorter. 'I do,' Cassie said. At which point Hannah set up a demented wail and Lynda rushed over to rescue her.

'Hannah Cohen!' came the receptionist's voice. 'Surgery number two, please.'

'Shall I wait outside?' Cassie offered.

'No,' said Lynda. 'If it's bad news, I'll need you.'

Cassie followed Lynda into the surgery and took a seat as far away as possible from the doctor. Lynda clutched Hannah to her, but Hannah wriggled off her mother's lap and, retreated to Cassie's knee. Lynda explained her symptoms.

'I'm sure it's nothing serious,' the doctor said, 'but I'll just give her a quick examination. Hannah?'

Cassie felt a hot little hand grip hers.

'Come on, Hannah. The doctor won't hurt you,' Lynda cajoled.

'I want to make you better,' he said.

Hannah remained motionless. Cassie had every sympathy with her. She didn't trust doctors either. They gave you bad news, they cut you up, they knew things you didn't. She was on Hannah's side.

'Come to Mummy, Hannah!'

Hannah was immobile. The doctor got out of his chair and approached her. She backed away into the haven of Cassie's dimpled knees.

'All I want to do is see what pretty tonsils you've got.' Hannah was immune to his flattery. 'Can I have a look at your tonsils?' He was getting impatient.

Hannah shook her head vehemently. Cassie wondered if she knew what tonsils were. Most patients never had a clue what doctors were talking about most of the time. Either they used terms no one else had ever heard of or the patient was in such a panic they paid no attention anyway.

'Will you open your mouth for me?'

Hannah made a slight concession: she parted her lips very slightly.

'That's a start,' said the doctor. 'Now a little more.'

46

But Hannah was not to be won over so easily. Cassie admired her. This was how to treat the medical profession!

'Hannah!' scolded Lynda. Hannah closed her mouth tight again.

Cassie felt the tension rising. There was a lot at stake here. The doctor was intent on not looking a fool and Lynda had to show that she had some vestige of control over her daughter. With a child's sure instinct, Hannah knew that the doctor and her mother were scheming against her. It was so unfair – you feel ill and all you want to do is stay at home with your mother and have nice, sweet-tasting medicine, and they take to the doctor's and you have to do horrible things like open your mouth and be poked and prodded – or so Cassie imagined Hannah thought.

'Never mind,' said the doctor. 'Let me just listen to your chest and put this little strip on your forehead.'

Hannah relaxed. The forehead thermometer intrigued her as it was like dressing up. The stethoscope was also non-intrusive. She submitted ungraciously.

'There's nothing on her chest,' he said, 'although there is a slight temperature. I'd just like to have a look at those tonsils. Can you open your mouth, Hannah?'

She shook her head so violently that her ponytail swung from side to side.

'I need to look at your tonsils to find out what's wrong with you!'

Don't let him, thought Cassie. At that moment the phone rang. The doctor ignored it.

'Hannah!' exclaimed Lynda. 'Do as the doctor tells you.'

'Come on, now, Hannah,' said the doctor. 'Don't be naughty.'

Hannah scowled at him contemptuously. Cassie felt her body tremble with dislike and fear.

'Hannah, this is silly!'

'No!' Hannah cried, and as she did so the doctor was in there, forcing apart her lips with his fingers and peering inside. It was at that moment Hannah was violently sick again.

'I feel better now!' Hannah declared.

'I'm sure you do,' Lynda said, strapping her into the car. 'Though I'm not sure how the doctor's feeling.'

'At least he said he was sure it was nothing serious,' Cassie reminded her.

'Yes, he did,' Lynda agreed. 'He also said it was probably only a virus and to take some Calpol to bring down the temperature. Doctors! For virus, read "don't know". But it's a relief, anyway. I'm all in, now. Exhausted. Hannah, Hannah, Hannah!' she lamented. 'What do you do to me?'

Cassie glanced behind her at Hannah, who was now sleeping peacefully, her head skewed to one side. The drama was over. Cassie, too, felt exquisitely tired, though whether that was the belated effect of her workout, she didn't know. Just as you needed exercise to get properly tired, she supposed you needed the odd crisis to make you appreciate tranquillity.

Either way, she knew she would sleep well that night.

Chapter Four

There was a knock on the office door. 'Come in,' Jane said.

It was Jodie, and she relaxed. Of all the interviews with full-time staff, this was the one she knew she would find easiest. Jodie was only nineteen, and brimming with enthusiasm. Jane had deliberately saved her till last as a treat. The other interviews had been predictably stressful, but Jane knew they were a necessary investment of her time if she was to succeed here and she had made a thorough job of the getting-to-know-you chats.

Siobhan Murphy had been curt, on her guard, even defensive. It clearly rankled that she had been passed over for the job. Jane had expected her to start looking for a position elsewhere and was perturbed to discover that she had no such plans. She knew she would have to exert her authority over Siobhan, only she resolved to do it in a kindly fashion. Kendra, the receptionist, had been voluble but had actually said little. Jane quizzed her on her absence record and discovered she was prone to back problems, digestive disorders and painful periods.

Garth was the only one of the full-timers who had been entirely at ease. He was a walking advertisement for fitness, and in that way good for the club. She imagined that female members might flock around him as he combined his physical attractive-ness with a rather intimate, personal manner. At first she was a little concerned that he was trying to befriend her, or even flirt with her. It annoyed her that he felt he could do that — she was his boss, hadn't he realised that? — and she had felt herself getting quite hot under the collar, so to speak. But then she guessed that that was probably his manner with all women. She decided to reserve judgement. For now she needed someone like Garth on her team.

Jodie came in, her ponytail swinging gaily. She was the only trainer to look good in sunflower yellow. She hesitated until Jane offered her a seat at a right angle to her own, so that the desk did not form a barrier.

'As you know, I'm having these little chats so I can get to know you all and find out about your ambitions and interests in the health industry,' Jane opened. 'You can set the agenda. I see from your records you've been here a year. Are you happy with the way your career has progressed?'

'Oh, yes!' Jodie said. 'This is, like, the best place! Because it's dead friendly, and the staff are really, really nice, and with us not being that big, you get to know the clients, and it's great to be able to use the facilities for free, and I really get on with *everyone!*'

Jane couldn't help smiling: she loved the girl's enthusiasm. 'And do you have any career aims?' she asked Jodie.

Jodie smiled. 'I suppose so. I haven't really thought.'

'Because with your cheerfulness and openness I get the impression you could go far.

'Can I tell you why I'm so cheerful today?'

'Go on!' Jane liked Jodie and was happy just to listen to her. 'It's Darren.'

'Darren Hughes?' Jane called him to mind. He was one of the part-timers, on occasional day-release to complete a sports-science degree. It was likely — and even desirable — that Jodie should take up a similar qualification. Perhaps Darren had mentioned the idea to her. She smiled encouragingly.

'Yeah, Darren. He asked me out last night. Like, I have had a crush on him *this* big.' Jodie gesticulated with her arms. 'He is *so* gorgeous. And I know he's a colleague and all that and I promise it won't interfere with my work in any way and I'm so excited I just have to tell everyone.'

Jane was flattered that Jodie felt sufficiently at ease to tell her this. It boded well. Yet it was a pity someone so promising should get sidetracked by a relationship. 'Have you known Darren long?'

'Only for the last three months since he joined. He was the last new trainer before all the trouble started.'

'The trouble?' Jane enquired. She was still not entirely clear in her mind why the previous owner of the former Sunnybank Health and Fitness Centre had sold up. She could see no harm in pumping Jodie for information: she seemed keen to talk.

'Well, I suppose I shouldn't be telling you any of this, but since Trudy's gone now, there can't be any harm in it. You see, the club was losing money. We didn't get the number of clients we needed and there were days when hardly anyone came through the doors. I used to get a bit bored, to tell you the truth. I'd just be standing there most of the time watching Sky Sports on the monitor. But Trudy didn't mind that. She never bothered how hard we were working. It was easy to get time off. If you rang in sick, she'd be, like, "Don't come in until you're better, we don't want you spreading any germs." Some people were off for days. Or she and Siobhan would go off for these long lunches. Not that Trudy ever did any work here to speak of. She just came in and hung around. Do you know her?'

'Know her? Why should I?'

'Oh, I thought everyone knew Trudy Thompson. She's the wife of Charlie Thompson!' Jodie said, with a flourish.

'Charlie Thompson?'

'Manager of Sunnybank FC. They were promoted to the third division last season.'

'Oh.' Jane had never taken an interest in football.

'Yeah. The Thompsons were rolling in it. But Trudy was always really generous and that, and gave us bonuses on our birthdays and took us out for drinks. We'd close up the club early if it was a staff birthday and kick out the clients.'

'I'm not surprised the club didn't make a profit.' Jane remarked.

'And that was the whole point!' Jodie exclaimed. 'Trudy ran the club to make a loss. It was something to do with taxes. I don't really understand how.'

Now this was interesting. Jane was beginning to get to grips with the dynamics of the club. Trudy could afford to be an indulgent employer if her aim was simply to offset tax. She would have made herself very popular among her staff, no doubt. Hers would be a hard act to follow.

'And then of course it all ended when she ran off to Portugal,' Jodie continued.

'To Portugal?'

'Yeah. She left Charlie. It was ever such a scandal. There was a rumour she had a bloke over there, or she was just fed up. She used to love the tanning beds. Maybe she just wanted a permanent tan for free.'

Jane nodded thoughtfully. 'How did the staff take all of this?'

'We never stopped talking about it, obviously. Siobhan was a bit gutted and, of course, everyone was worried for their jobs, and even though we were pleased Fit Not Fat bought us up, we were scared of redundancies. Kendra reckoned they'd bring in all their own people. Like you,' she added candidly.

Jane nodded in acknowledgement. 'I think they're stopping at me. I'm happy with the staff here and I have no intention of getting rid of anyone. In fact, my plans are to expand and eventually take on more staff. The bigger the branch, the greater job security and opportunities for us all.'

'Wow! So I could, like, get promoted?'

'You certainly could. I was wondering whether you'd like any areas of responsibility of your own. That would be a start.'

Jodie looked at her wide-eyed. 'Jane, do you know what I'd like to do? Put up posters and that. To make the place more interesting. You could focus on a different exercise every month, or a competition. Could I?'

Jane was delighted. Jodie was showing initiative. 'Definitely. Plan out some posters and run them past me.'

'Oh, yeah! Did you know I got an A in my art GCSE?'

'You can put it to some use.'

'Cool! Like, this is such a brilliant day. First Darren, and now this. It's like everything good is happening at once. I can't wait to go home and tell my mum. I still live at home, see, but I get on dead well with her. We're more like best mates, because she had me when she was only twenty-one so she's quite young. Listen to me. Am I babbling or what? Is there anyone else you want me to get?'

'No. But you can remind the full-timers I want to have a few words with them all later on this afternoon. Just about the plans for the club.'

'Sure. No problem.'

Jodie bounced up from her seat and made for the door. Jane watched her with pleasure. If she could have invented an ideal member of staff, it would have been Jodie. Her bright personality would buoy up everyone. Yet some of what Jodie had said disturbed her. The staff would have to get used to a more rigorous regime than in the past and Jane had to accept that she would not be popular to begin with: she knew she would find that hard. She was the sort of manager who wanted to be loved. She knew other colleagues from Head Office who simply enjoyed ordering people about, or who saw their staff as numbers in a game of logistics. That seemed immoral to her. The health industry was all about people, and a happy staff spelt a happy club. Yes: she could see that she had her work cut out at Sunnybank.

When Jodie arrived back in the gym she saw that Kendra had left her post at reception and was whispering to Siobhan and Garth. She wondered if something was up. Luckily as she approached them they continued to whisper so they couldn't have been talking about her.

'But what I want to know is *why* she asked me how I saw my career developing. Does she think I'm not doing enough out in reception? I don't think she realises how stressful it is. People arrive all at once demanding locker keys and what-have-you, then the computer crashes and I have to keep written records and everyone likes to have a little chat – no wonder I can't digest my lunch properly!'

Siobhan looked sympathetically at Kendra. Jodie understood they were talking about Jane. She had been at work for long enough now to know that you always had to slag off the boss, even if you liked her. But Jodie didn't feel like slagging off Jane. She had enjoyed her interview, and was thrilled that Jane was so keen on her idea of brightening up the gym with posters. Instead she just listened to the conversation.

'I wouldn't let her catch you in here talking to us, Kendra,' Siobhan said. 'She'll think you've got time on your hands. But don't worry, I'll cover for you. I think we're all going to have to watch out for each other. What did you make of her, Jodie?'

Jodie blushed. She didn't want to badmouth Jane but neither did she want to alienate herself from her colleagues. Also she had a feeling that she had been indiscreet in her interview and was inclined to cover up for herself. 'She . . . she knows what questions to ask,' she said.

Siobhan agreed and Jodie was relieved. 'You're right, and what's more, I think she's got her own ideas for this club, and it won't matter what we say to her. Someone like her is just using Sunnybank as a career move. She'll be up and out of here before six months are over.'

'Then you'll be made our manager,' Kendra said loyally.

Now it was Siobhan's turn to blush. 'That's as maybe,' she said. Then she turned to Jodie. 'What's this I've been hearing about you and Darren?'

'We're going out!'

'Lucky Darren,' Garth said. Jodie glanced at him. He was also dead good-looking – not her type, though. He was like a film star – all muscles and dark, smouldering eyes – but she liked her men cute. Darren was cute: a good body, a baby face and blond hair to die for. And that laugh he had, which chuckled and rippled and turned her legs to jelly. Garth sometimes flirted with her, but he flirted with everyone. You had to if you looked like that. Some of the clients had asked her if he was gay, but he wasn't. Actually it was Siobhan who was gay but nobody ever talked about it, except Trudy in the old days. Siobhan liked to keep that part of her life quiet, which was fine with everyone. She was a private person, anyway. That was why Trudy had confided in her.

'And the other thing,' Kendra said, 'did you know that Tina who takes Pilates asked to miss a couple of classes to go to her sister's baby's christening in Leamington Spa, and *she* gave her a hard time about it? She let her go, but told her not to ask for something like that again.'

Everyone looked severe at this evidence of Jane's lack of charity. Even Jodie felt that that had been a bit harsh of her, but on the other hand, what about all the people who were expecting to do Pilates? Life could be difficult sometimes. No, it wasn't! She was going out with Darren Hughes. She was in charge of posters. Energy and optimism zapped through her body. Life was brilliant and she was the luckiest girl in the world!

*　　*　　*

Jane was looking forward to addressing her key personnel. She did not feel nervous although she knew her appointment was not universally popular. However, she had sufficient faith in her public persona to know that it would carry her through. She was also prepared for things to be tough for a while – in her job, as in her workouts, she liked to feel the burn. Yet Jane also had a touching faith that good would always prevail and she knew she meant well. She also knew she had prepared and rehearsed her presentation several times, and Head Office had confirmed their approval of her plans.

Her main objective, though, was to fill her staff with the same enthusiasm that fired her. She was convinced that enthusiasm was the fuel of any successful organisation. At least, it was her preferred fuel. She had been at work since seven that morning, bright-eyed and bushy-tailed, opening up to welcome the early risers, and had decided to stay on till late, and felt not in the least bit tired. Jane was still raring to go, on top form, in overdrive. She liked herself best like this. The meeting was going to be a triumph. She was buzzing with energy and determination.

It was early in the evening when she was able to get her full-time staff together in the fitness-assessment room. There was hardly enough room for them all. Jane stood by a flip-chart jammed up against a wall. Kendra sat by the table adjusting her glasses, Jodie was cross-legged on the floor, and Siobhan, her hair pulled back so severely it seemed to tighten the skin of her forehead, was perching sideways on the exercise bike. Garth displayed himself by the door, standing at ease. It was hot in the fitness-assessment room and the neon light created an unwelcome glare. Jane hardly noticed. She was living in the moment: all of her attention was concentrated on what she was about to say.

'As you all know, the fitness industry is booming. But we must not be complacent. Fitness International has just acquired a club in the area and that's serious competition. So it's my intention to embark on an expansion programme to make Sunnybank Fit Not Fat the foremost provider of health and fitness in this section of north Manchester.' Jane's cheeks were flushed. 'So here is my five-point development plan. One: a membership drive, consisting of advertising, special promotional offers and a survey of existing inactive members to bring them back to the club. Two: a community outreach programme in which we send our class instructors to other groups, schools, churches, synagogues, local clubs to raise our profile. Three: getting funding from Head Office for a café on the premises. Four: competitions with prizes for our regular members, to create incentive. Five: eventually to increase profits so that we can buy the wasteland next door and build a pool.'

Jane stopped: she needed to give her staff time to recover. She surveyed them all to see how her words had affected them. Jodie looked as if she was about to break into spontaneous applause, Kendra looked worried, Siobhan seemed unimpressed and Garth gave her a long, lazy smile, which unsettled her and made her feel as if she was playing a silly game. She felt herself bridling and becoming hotter than ever. She pulled herself up short. She would not lose her equilibrium. She still had to talk for a little longer about the details of her plans and the philosophy behind them. After another ten minutes she reached her conclusion.

'OK, that's it. Are there any questions?'

'Yes,' said Jodie. 'Will we able to afford a pool?'

'With Fit Not Fat behind us, I'm certain we can.' Jane smiled at her. Oh, if only they were all like Jodie!

'Where are you intending to build the café?' Siobhan asked. 'There's no space in this building.'

Jane felt herself tense, knowing the answer would not be popular. 'We're going to convert the staff rest room. But don't worry, I can get a Portakabin for you all to use when you're off duty, in the first instance.'

'But this membership drive,' interrupted Kendra. 'Don't you

think we're busy enough as it is? You should see the queue for lockers at peak times. I'm thinking if it gets too busy it will put people off because they won't be able to use the equipment.'

'Then we shall have to invest in more equipment,' Jane countered. She could feel her stomach tightening. Being under scrutiny like this was much more testing than simply giving a presentation. She was conscious of hostility in the room and for the first time began to question herself. Were her plans over-ambitious? Had she bitten off more than she could chew? Her staff's decidedly muted response disturbed her more than she had anticipated. Doubt gripped her. Should she have taken this job in the first place?

Of course she should! She was filled with new determination, pulled herself up to her full height and looked around comba-tively.

'What kind of competitions do you have in mind?' Garth asked her.

Jane felt flustered. 'Well . . . say, the fastest time a distance is covered on a rower? Or a mock Tour de France on the bikes? I'd welcome suggestions. Do *you* have any ideas?' There was a note of challenge in her voice. She had to show Garth she was his equal. Moreover, she had to convey that she was not in the least bit attracted to him. She felt her chin jut out and she assumed a somewhat masculine stance.

'I'll think about it,' said Garth, grinning at her. Why, oh, why was she blushing?

'I don't think the survey of existing members is a good idea,' Siobhan interrupted, her arms folded tightly across her chest.

'Why not?' Jane asked.

'I don't see why you're bothering with old members if it's new members you want to attract.'

Jane tensed. She was uncomfortably aware of Siobhan's antagonism and put her question down to resentment. She answered her more abruptly than she had intended. 'Old members bring in new ones. They talk to their friends and family. If they feel we meet their needs, our reputation grows.'

Siobhan did not meet her eyes but glanced at her watch in a manner Jane thought rude. She wondered if she should say more to justify her views but told herself that she was the boss and Siobhan would have to abide by her judgement. Then she thought that unthinking obedience was not what she wanted from her staff, but their hearts and minds. Yet it was important to exert her authority from the off. At the same time, she wished Siobhan liked her. 'What do the rest of you think?' she asked.

Jodie smiled at her encouragingly, Kendra looked blank, and Garth said, 'Do as you think best.'

Jane was grateful for his support and allowed her eyes to meet his for a moment. 'I'll draft a suitable form for the survey and give it to Kendra for typing within a day or two. Jodie and I will work together on the competitions. I'll keep you all posted about progress with the café and outreach work. That's it.'

Siobhan and Kendra left the office together and Jane knew they would be talking about her as soon as they were out of earshot. It made her distinctly uncomfortable. She wondered just for a moment if she was really cut out to be a manager. Yes, you are! she told herself.

'That's brill, Jane!' Jodie said, as she got up off the floor. 'I'm really excited. I've got to go and check the ladies' loos now.' Jane watched her go. Garth was left. She felt uneasy. While she was certain that Jodie liked her and Siobhan certainly didn't, she couldn't tell with Garth. What was worse, she wasn't even sure what she thought of him. She began to dismantle the flip-chart.

'You have some pretty impressive ideas,' Garth commented, watching her.

'Thank you,' she said, wondering if he was being patronising, but his tone was frank. She dared to glance at him.

He was perched on the table, watching her in a friendly way. 'Don't be put off by Siobhan,' he said. 'She's still sore she didn't get the job. It's understandable. She did all the work for Trudy, who just sat on her backside and watched us all. She's one of life's victims.'

Jane finished with the flip-chart and stood by the door. Garth seemed to be offering his tacit support and she was glad. She knew he shouldn't be dishing the dirt on Siobhan like that, but was pleased nevertheless that he had. Siobhan's coldness had hurt her, and his support was a balm.

'But what about you?' She asked. 'You applied for it too.'

'It was more for a laugh than anything else. People expected me to have a go, so I did. I'm glad I wasn't successful as I don't intend to stay here for ever.'

Jane was momentarily disappointed, then realised that that might be for the best. 'Why? Do you have other ambitions?'

He nodded. 'There's a number of things I'd like to try. I've been thinking of working freelance as a personal trainer, or going into sales of health products.'

'Such as?'

'Food supplements, vitamins and minerals. I've always been interested in that side of fitness. You'd be amazed by how many of our clients come here to lose weight and starve themselves thinking their workout will be more effective, when in fact it's vital they eat properly to achieve the best results. They put themselves through agony and don't bother to find out what a sound, balanced, vitamin-enriched diet could do for them.'

'Absolutely!' Garth was talking her language. 'Why don't you write something about this and we can produce a flyer for the clients?'

'I might do that,' he said. 'although it's a relatively new field for me. I'm just looking into it. I'm investigating a herbal supplement that's supposed to work wonders. L8, I think it's called. It boosts energy as well as the immune system.'

Jane was interested: she could do with something like that.

An energy-boosting herbal supplement might help her drink less coffee. 'You must tell me more about it,' she said.

'Do you want to arrange a time when we can meet up?'

She was on the alert again. She didn't like the way he'd said that. There was something insinuating in his manner — or maybe not. Perhaps he was just being friendly. If only she knew. She was rather out of practice with men — that was the price you had to pay when you concentrated on your career. 'Perhaps when I'm less busy,' Jane said, reserved again. 'Right,' she said briskly. 'I must see to the wages.'

'Sure,' he said. 'See you,' and left.

Jane watched him go, a little regretfully. He had been nice to her, and she had liked that. But on the other hand she felt instinctively that she couldn't trust him. Or was that just because he was a man? Perhaps she couldn't trust herself. And at that awkward notion she stopped her thoughts in their tracks and decided to *do* something, to keep busy. But first she would try to assess how the meeting had gone.

Now that it was over, she was utterly drained, but couldn't stop replaying all the comments that had been made. Her head was throbbing and she felt alternately hungry and nauseous. As the tension ebbed away, she felt empty and in need of something — what? A hug? A debriefing session? A double vodka?

Jane pulled herself up: this really would not do. The wages for the part-timers needed to be made up, and she must not get behind on her self-imposed schedule. How could she live with herself if she wasn't on top of things? She had every intention of working late tonight, and she would do so. She would see to the wages, write a few letters, ask Jodie to pop out to Tesco's and get her a sandwich, and look at the figures for the day.

It was a quarter past ten when Siobhan let herself in to the stone-built, terraced house. The murmur of the television set informed her that her mother had not gone to bed and was waiting for her. She went straight to the back room, and as soon as she opened the door Kathleen Murphy was out of her easy chair. 'Shall I make a brew?'

Siobhan nodded. There was nothing she wanted more. As her mother busied herself in the kitchen she slumped into an armchair and watched the news in a desultory fashion, her mind blank. Before too long Kathleen reappeared with a tray of tea-things and Siobhan smiled at her. 'Have a good day?'

'Fair to middling,' Kathleen replied.

'Any messages?' Siobhan's eyes strayed to the telephone on its own table by the back window. It stood on a lacy mat, as did all the other ornaments in the back room. Kathleen felt it was a sign of good breeding to put things on things; besides, it saved the furniture. There were no tell-tale scraps of paper beside the telephone.

'No one for you,' her mother confirmed.

So her summons was not going to come today. That would have been just too convenient. Siobhan did not want to stay at Sunnybank while all these plans and alterations were taking place. The club she knew and loved would turn into the limb of a corporate monster, and she didn't think she could bear to see it. She never liked change at the best of times. Some of the happiest times she had ever known had taken place at Sunnybank.

'Not a good day, dear?' her mother asked sympathetically.

Siobhan raised her eyebrows expressively. Kathleen already knew that she loathed Jane and that she was convinced the club was poised to go downhill. Her mother had been as devastated as Siobhan when Jane was appointed. As Siobhan gave details of Jane's development plans Kathleen tutted and frowned. Her sympathy made Siobhan feel both better and worse: better to know that she was not alone, and worse because it confirmed her suspicions: Sunnybank could never be the same again.

Complaining about Jane's youthful inexperience was like drinking from a poisoned chalice.

'If I were you,' her mother said, 'I'd think of moving on. I've always thought you could do better working for the council.'

'Maybe,' Siobhan said, but would not meet her mother's eyes. It wasn't time to tell her yet. She would be sad enough when the time came, and there was no point in extending the misery. Siobhan could not take a new job because she wouldn't be in the country long enough. Any day now the phone call would come; if not today, then tomorrow. It was the only thing keeping her going.

Perhaps, she thought, sipping her tea while her mother's attention strayed back to the television, she should ring Trudy herself although, in some way she didn't fully comprehend, that would spoil things. She felt sorry for herself. She didn't know how she was going to stand another day at that pathetic club. In the old Sunnybank days, there had been a buzz and the club had had a family atmosphere. They had all joked and gossiped and on the nights when the customers were few on the ground, Trudy would shut up shop and decamp to the pub. Trudy had a natural charisma – she was a people person, unlike Jane, who was a theorist. Trudy cared, and Siobhan had allowed herself to think that she might care a little more for her than she did for the others.

Right from the start Trudy had chosen her as her confidante. She picked Siobhan's brains about the rest of the staff. She confided in her. When Siobhan had taken the huge step of telling Trudy about her sexuality, Trudy could not have been more understanding – in fact, she seemed almost pleased. She had taken her back to her house on Holcombe Hill and regaled her with wine, and they had talked and talked. She knew Trudy had respected her confidence and that no one else at Sunnybank had ever found out. Trudy had thought that it was something to be kept quiet; and Siobhan agreed passionately with that as she hated the idea of anyone gossiping about her or trivialising the most important issues of her life. She was hardly able to express how she felt about a whole range of things, not because she didn't have the words but because she *felt* so much. That was why she was such a private person, naturally close, self-effacing. But she had opened up to Trudy, and had never regretted it.

Trudy had made Siobhan feel special, in a way that nobody else had. She had nurtured her and listened to her. She had confided in her, knowing that Siobhan was as steadfast as a rock. Siobhan was the only who knew about the troubles in Trudy's marriage – in fact, she was almost certain she was Trudy's best friend. She wasn't part of her social circle, naturally. Trudy's husband was chairman of the local football club, a keen Rotarian and she moved in entirely different social circles from Siobhan. Trudy was caught up in a constant round of dinner parties, charity bashes and coffee mornings. She told Siobhan all about them, which made her feel special, splashed by glory.

Siobhan was probably the first person to know that Trudy walked out of her marriage. She knew before the Sunnybank Health and Fitness Centre was put on the market that its days were numbered. She had driven Trudy to Manchester Airport at five a.m. one bitter Tuesday morning when the ground was still frozen underfoot and the sky was clinging perilously to night's darkness, and had sat drinking coffee with her as men with commercial cleaning machines had edged around them. Trudy had promised her faithfully that she would send for her as soon as her purchase of the leisure complex in the Algarve was complete. Siobhan would help her run it – It would be in weeks – months, at the most. Siobhan had decided there was no point in moving from Sunnybank. Why court even more change? As it was, she would have to prepare her mother for losing her, although she had done nothing as yet. She could not bear to hurt Kathleen, yet she would have no authentic life if she didn't leave home and start afresh.

Once Trudy had gone through the departure gates Siobhan was surprised to discover her eyes were brimming with tears. She didn't like saying goodbye to anyone, let alone her closest friends. Perhaps that was it. She didn't have many friends, but those she had she valued immensely. In caring for them, she found herself, and in putting their interests first, she had purpose in life. Her own needs were few: she enjoyed keeping herself fit, playing golf, going to the cinema. Yet she sensed that she was biding her time.

It wasn't so much that she was jealous of Jane – she had applied for the managership simply so that she could keep things at Sunnybank the way she liked them. Had Jane been a different sort of person she might even have tolerated her. Instead she felt a profound antipathy towards her: it was the way Jane made out that she knew what was best for everybody, and her assumption that they would all just to fit in with her plans for her own career. She came over as if she knew the club better than Siobhan did, but Siobhan had been there at its birth. She hated the way Jane dressed – prissy girlie power suits, stilettos, for goodness' sake. She despised her naïvety and desire to impress everyone, but most of all she hated her for not being Trudy Thompson.

But there was not long to go. With every day that passed, the odds that Trudy would ring shortened. Then she would have to explain to her mother that the best opportunity to date in her career had opened up. Kathleen could come for frequent holidays. Siobhan would be able to walk into the stupidly named Fit Not Fat, march into Jane's office and hand in her notice. Then her prison sentence would be over.

So there was hope. Tomorrow was another day.

Chapter Five

———◦◦◦◦◦———

This is like treading grapes, Cassie thought, as she maintained a steady rhythm on the stepper. The thought pleased her. She was transported in her imagination away from the gym to an Italian vineyard, where she and several others, barefoot, pounded succulent grapes, releasing sweet, fragrant juices in the Mediterranean sun. Slowly she returned her mind to the gym and checked the clock on the stepper. She had nearly completed her ten minutes. Unbelievable! In just over four weeks she had mastered this machine. She glowed with a sense of achievement and glanced at her reflection in the mirror. She looked authentic – a genuine member of the exercising classes. Her new Adidas leggings certainly helped. So what if they were size sixteen? She was on her way down the scales.

And that was an odd sensation. The nurse at her local surgery had offered to monitor her progress by weighing her once a week, and each time Cassie had gone, she had shed a pound or two. At first she had felt a mixture of surprise and disbelief – she didn't feel any different. Perhaps the scales were in a mechanical conspiracy with the exercise equipment at the gym: she worked hard on one machine and another showed a loss. Then she noticed that her clothes were looser: a sweater she had not worn for years because it made her look pregnant fitted. The endemic indigestion was conspicuous by its absence. She was sleeping better.

Her consciousness of the changes swept through her now and added zest to her movements. Yes, it was the harmony of woman and machine. What she loved about the exercising in the gym was that it took every bit of her concentration. This stepper, for example. She couldn't pretend it was easy. In fact, that was the fun of it. If you weren't going to collapse in a heap you had to have strategies. Like taking your weight on your arms and leaning on the bars. She snatched at the towel hanging on the side of the machine and wiped her forehead.

The gym was busy today. Over in the far corner two men were doing something or other with the weights. One was watching the other decide which pair of weights to select. They looked serious. It amused her how men had the gift of making everything they played at look deadly important. Finally the man with the hairy legs in the black shorts began lifting, making the familiar grunts and groans that Cassie associated now with the gym. Men who exercised liked you to know how hard they were working. Women, on the other hand, liked to know how hard *you* were working. Often she had seen women running next to her sneaking a surreptitious glance at the clock on her treadmill.

The cardio equipment was in the middle of the gym – rows of steppers, treadmills, cross-trainers and bikes. Around the walls was the resistance equipment. As far as Cassie could see all you did was sit on it and move very slowly. She couldn't wait to graduate to it. At first the machines reminded her of a torture chamber but now she thought of it as an adult's playground – you had a go on one thing, then you got bored, and had a go on something else.

She'd also begun to recognise the regulars. The cliché about gyms was that they attracted beautiful, Lycra-clad people who didn't need them in the first place. At Fit Not Fat this was patently not true. The clientele were a motley crew. There was the old bloke with white hair, white shorts and a Manchester Marathon T-shirt who spent hours on the treadmill, a beatific smile on his face. He was an exception: everyone else looked as if they were having a dreadful time. There were young men in glasses pedalling away on the bikes reading trade magazines to divert themselves. There were women of her age rowing frantically with grim determination. A young man doing sit-ups on the mats actually looked as if he was in pain. It was like a vision of a medieval limbo, with lost souls condemned to cycle, run, row and march endlessly. And yet while you were working out, people would come over to you and say the most positive things. 'Keep it up – you're doing great!' 'You're working hard today.' 'It's worth it in the end.' It was the spirit of the Blitz.

Also Cassie had become increasingly aware of people's bodies. They were so varied – backs pitted with old acne scars, pale thighs dimpled with cellulite, brawny shoulders, tanned midriffs, protruding stomachs, washboard stomachs, non-existent bosoms, bosoms that shook and wobbled almost independent of their owners. The human form was infinitely different.

If she became bored watching the other exercisers, there were always the TV screens positioned around the gym. There were twenty-four-hour news channels, sports channels, good old BBC and music channels. Cassie found herself drawn to the music. On the trainers' advice she had brought some headphones from home, plugged then into the cardiotheatre and often worked out to MTV. She was beginning to feel as though she was developing a personal relationship with some of the presenters. The pop videos were three concentrated minutes of pure fantasy, and Cassie found herself posing on beaches, dancing suggestively in darkened nightclubs, standing on the roofs of countless buildings, the wind blowing through her hair, moving through the countryside on motorbikes or in fast cars, or splashing in pools and diving through translucent green water to end up in a plastic sexual encounter. Well, they passed the time.

Finishing her stint on the stepper, she moved over to the water fountain and helped herself to a drink. She noticed one of the trainers smiling encouragingly at her and she smiled back. It was the girl called Siobhan. She was in the gym most afternoons. 'How're you doing?' she asked Cassie.

'Fine. I've lost nine pounds!'

'Great!' Siobhan responded.

Cassie wondered at herself. She was talking like a seven-year-old keen to impress the teacher. *Look at my work, Miss! Very good — you can have a gold star.* She wondered if her change of lifestyle was infantilising her. It was a thought. However, it was not a sufficiently powerful thought to prevent her babbling on to Siobhan. 'Have you any views on hypnotherapy?'

'Hypnotherapy? What for?'

'Losing weight. My friend Lynda wants to recommend someone to me. She says he can help sustain my motivation.'

'Hmm,' said Siobhan. 'Well, I suppose there's no harm in it.'

Siobhan's doubt extinguished Cassie's enthusiasm. The other day, when Lynda had caught sight of a Mars bar wrapper shoved at the back of the glove compartment in Cassie's car, she had tried to talk her into going to a hypnotherapist. Cassie had been tempted: after her first month, she knew her motivation needed a boost and was willing to give anything a try. Now she wasn't so sure. In the cold glare of the gym lights, it seemed a silly idea. Still, it was good to know it was there if she needed it.

'Well, on to the recliner bike now!' Cassie announced.

'Good for you,' said Siobhan. Cassie noted she was not a great conversationalist. A pity, as she was feeling chatty today. She strolled over to the bike, adjusted the seating, and began pedalling. Her calves ached, her thighs hurt and she wondered if she would last the usual twenty minutes. Don't look at the clock, she told herself, otherwise you'll see what a long time you have left. She looked at the clock. Fifteen minutes to go. Quick! Think of something else. Dinner tonight. The Peasants' Revolt.

Terry's last article. The car needing servicing. She tried to focus her concentration on the current pop video and was assured that the five blonde seventeen-year-olds walking along a cliff's edge would always love her, but rejecting their advances she looked straight ahead (not at the clock, Cassie, not at the clock!) and saw that a young man had come over to the resistance equipment opposite her and was reading the instructions beside it. She took the liberty of studying him in that dispassionate way she had learned in London when travelling on the tube. You adopted an expressionless stare and pretended not to see the person opposite you while covertly imagining who they were and why they were there and whether, in the event of a nuclear holocaust, you would end up creating the next generation with them. In this case Cassie decided against it. He had a good pair of legs, though, and nice taste in sports gear – neat grey shorts and a Ralph Lauren T-shirt.

What intrigued her about him was that he looked as lost as she had a few weeks ago. He was having some difficulty in setting up the equipment. He was almost certainly a new member, still learning the ropes. As it happened Cassie was reaching the end of her programme and threw him a sympathetic glance. Once she had come to a stop and had towelled herself dry, he spoke to her. 'Do you have any idea how to work this thing?'

'Sorry, not a clue. I haven't been on that one yet. It's for developing chest muscles, isn't it? I've seen other blokes use it. Nasty thing, if you ask me, but I'm sure one of the trainers will help you.'

They both looked over to where Siobhan had been, but she had gone.

'Seems like no one's around,' the young man said, somewhat redundantly.

Cassie grinned, high on endorphins. 'Are you new? Though you don't look as if you need to exercise – I mean, it's not as if you're overweight. But of course I shouldn't say that because everyone needs to keep fit. It's an insurance policy for the future. Keeps the cardiovascular system in good nick. And every organ of the body benefits. You'd be surprised. I'd keep it up if I were you.'

Cassie took the liberty of talking in this knowledgeable way as the man was so obviously younger than her, by ten years or more. He had a boyish, pleasant face and seemed interested, though. She was encouraged. 'Yes – I can't tell you how much better I've been feeling since I started coming here. I try to make it three times a week. Mostly I succeed. You see, I have gallstones – small lumps of cholesterol in the gall bladder. When they get stuck in the neck of the gall bladder they cause incredible pain and there can even be further complications. But you don't want to be hearing about my insides. Why have you joined?'

'I find exercise helps me wind down after work.'

'Really? And what is your line of work?'

'I'm a GP.'

Cassie turned scarlet. But the GP was smiling, not in the least offended. 'I'm so sorry,' she continued, knowing she should shut up but finding herself unable to, 'preaching at you when you know better than me. Tell you what, you can lecture me on the Albigensian heresy and then we're equal – I'm a lecturer in medieval history. Cassie Oliver.' She offered her name as a way of making peace.

'David Richmond.'

Just then the door of the gym opened. Cassie was expecting Siobhan to return, but instead the manager walked in. She occasionally did a stint in the gym, and Cassie was a little afraid of her. She was in the habit of criticising Cassie's technique.

'That's Jane, the manager,' Cassie explained. 'She'll give you a hand with the chest expander.'

But David didn't reply immediately. Cassie glanced covertly at him and smiled to herself as she saw the way in which he was studying Jane. At first she thought he knew her from somewhere then realised that what she had witnessed was a look of frank appreciation. It was true that Jane was a pretty girl, and David had the same air of freshness and enthusiasm that she radiated. Never one to spoil a romance, Cassie made her farewells and went over to the water-cooler but glanced at David as he talked to Jane. Very interesting, she thought.

Now it was time to return to the real world: there was a lecture to prepare for the next day. Relishing the exquisite sensation of exhaustion flooding her body, Cassie made her way back to the ladies' changing area. Opening the door she saw immediately that a class had just finished: a number of women were in various stages of undress, conversing together. Cassie offered a shy smile and began to take off her T-shirt. As she did so, she tuned in to their conversation. It was gripping.

A well-preserved woman in leotard and leggings was holding court. 'So I knocked at her door. When she greeted me, she said, "My vision's gone!" Naturally I had to calm her down and I thought, it's a migraine, only *she* said, "No, I've had migraines and I know what they're like. This is different. How can I describe it? There's a thick black line running across my eye." So I took her straight to the eye hospital, and do you know what they said?' She paused. 'It was a virus.'

'A virus?' responded her fascinated auditor.

'Yes, a virus. It took months for her sight to come back and even now her vision's fuzzy – the way it is when you're using eye-makeup remover.'

A woman in bra and pants put down the hair-dryer she was about to use and took up the baton. 'My friend Moira began to have this pain in the chest *and* down her left arm. Well, you can imagine what she thought it was, especially because there's a history of heart disease in her family. Her husband drove her straight to A and E. And they said it was a virus – it had got into the wall of her lungs.'

A wiry grey-haired woman continued, 'My cousin had a virus

that made his muscles go into spasms. His left leg locked and they had to get the paramedics.'

Cassie was agog. In medieval times the same women would have talked about the work of the devil; these days, it was the work of a virus. They spoke in tones of reverence, fear and relief it wasn't them. Yet Cassie was no better — she felt compelled to listen, hoping for even more bizarre stories. But the women had stopped now and were discussing the details of their latest diets. This was far less exciting. Nothing bored her more than hearing what other people ate or, worse still, denied themselves the pleasure of eating. Although it was true that she was cutting back, she had not said a word to anyone. She couldn't see why it should be of interest to them. Or perhaps she didn't want to commit herself publicly to eating less. She had to allow herself a get-out clause by pretending she wasn't dieting so that if she was caught eating something forbidden, no one would stop her.

Maybe Lynda was right about the hypnotherapy, or perhaps she wasn't. As a historian, Cassie could always see two sides to every question. She had promised Lynda she would think about it and she had kept her promise. She was still thinking about it. And that it was all she was prepared to do right now. Because the trouble with this exercise thing was that it made you very, very hungry.

Exercise was not the only thing that made Cassie hungry. Even worse was preparing course materials for the department's new Internet distance-learning site. She had her misgivings about teacherless learning and her heart was not in the task. Her mind was wandering too, back to the couple of slices of toast she had had when she came back from the gym. After eating them she decided she would compensate by missing her planned evening meal, which was so meagre anyway that it would have disappointed a Spartan. But she was hungry, and feeling just a little sorry for herself.

When she heard her doorbell ring she was delighted. Anyone, even the man to read the meter, would be a welcome distraction. Her unexpected guest was Terry and she didn't hide her pleasure when she opened the door. She was rewarded by his smile of gratification. Her life was looking up.

Cassie launched into a tirade about the distance-learning project while Terry made himself at home, carrying two plastic bags full of things into her kitchen. Cassie followed him, in full rhetorical mode. 'There is this complete refusal to admit that learning in isolation is a poor alternative to learning *with* people. As if students *like* being alone! *No one* likes being alone!'

'I don't,' said Terry. 'Which is why I'm here. We haven't had a meal together for ages. I'm getting withdrawal symptoms.'

'And then there's the question of intellectual property. To whom precisely does my material belong? To me? To the university?'

'Are you hungry?' Terry asked her.

'Ravenous. And what I want to know is, am I selling myself down the river with this project? I have a good mind to contact the union and—'

'Come here,' Terry said. The warmth from his hands travelled into hers, then up her arms and dissolved her tension. He was smiling at her. 'Why don't we eat first and talk later? Then you can use me as your sounding-board, if you like. Only it's Saturday night and you shouldn't be working.'

Cassie appreciated his concern for her. And he was right — she was getting obsessed with this particular problem, and needed to let go, which seemed an attractive proposition, especially with Terry in the house. 'OK. I'll stop working. But I can't eat much, as you know.'

'Terry looked at her critically. 'Mmm. You've lost weight.'

'Nine pounds!' Cassie announced.

'That's probably enough,' he said. 'You don't want to look haggard. Anyway, see what I've got in here.'

Terry began to remove various items from the carrier bags. There were some savoury pastries, a bag of rocket salad, dressing, and something cold in a plastic box that looked as if it had just come out of the freezer. Cassie touched it to confirm her suspicions.

'Home-made ice-cream,' Terry explained. 'I had fun with that.' Finally he took out two bottles of wine, a Semillon Chardonnay and a Sauternes.

Cassie was watching with mounting horror. 'But you know I can't eat those sort of things.'

'Maybe not all the time,' Terry said reasonably, 'but tonight you can.'

'And what's so special about tonight?' she asked.

'It's our five-month anniversary,' he replied.

Cassie couldn't hide her surprise. The five-month anniversary of what? He made it sound as if they were married already when all they had been doing was seeing each other, although admittedly they had certainly been seeing a lot of each other. She didn't understand his need to label things and date them. Unless it was his way of taking control of what was going on by defining it in his terms. Yes, that was what he was up to. She was beginning to see what game he was playing. And, what was more, he was making himself necessary to her, subtly insinuating himself into her affections. The dinner he had brought over was a Trojan horse. If she ate it, she would be totally at his mercy.

Cassie had kept meaning to think about Terry but, what with work and the gym and that cowardice when it came to relationships, she had put it off. If she didn't take a stand, they would soon be sleeping together (she had certainly been tempted by the idea) and then what? The trouble with Terry was that he was so damn nice you couldn't just sleep with him. You would have to marry him or something. Marriage made Cassie just a little nervous. Her parents had been happily divorced for years.

'Cheer up,' he said as he uncorked the wine. 'We can have a drink while I put this together. I can understand the problems you have with distance-learning but there are some people who have no choice. Do it for them. Surely any kind of learning is better than none. This tart is full of onions but if we both eat them it won't matter. How do you light your oven? I can never get it to work.'

'You need to use matches,' Cassie said, still a little pre-occupied. He seemed so comfortable in her kitchen, yet she was feeling increasingly uncomfortable at the prospect of eating forbidden foods. She was shaken by the discovery that her willpower was so weak. Today, dinner; tomorrow, Terry and a full-blown relationship. She could see it all happening.

'I'll tidy up,' she told him, and went back into the living room to close down her lap-top and remove her papers from the dining-table. She took her glass with her and sipped the wine abstractedly. The alcohol was making her light-headed, reckless, and she felt as if events were overtaking her. She was glad. She had suddenly decided she liked Terry very much, after all.

Before too long he had laid the table and presented dinner to her. With relish she attacked the onion tart, took a large helping of salad and cut herself a huge chunk of the cheese and onion bread Terry had magicked from somewhere. It was all immensely satisfying. There were no rumblings from her gall bladder. She had never enjoyed food more in her life. She was living for the moment and deeply appreciated having someone to look after her. She glanced up at Terry, who was also savouring his food. Their eyes met and there was no need to say anything. There never is, thought Cassie, when things are going well.

After dinner, with the sweetness of the ice-cream still singing in her mouth, they settled together on the floor, their backs propped against the *chaise-longue*. Terry had his arm round her.

'This distance-learning project,' Cassie began.

'I think you can learn more close up,' Terry said, and proceeded to clear Cassie's mind by a practical demonstration of what he meant. As he did so Cassie became aware that Terry's hands were testing her new body. There was less of it, and it was stronger, fitter. Feeling good about herself made her more enthusiastic about this side of their relationship. She wondered how much she had been put off sex in the past because she had felt unattractive.

'Cassie,' he murmured. 'We ought to sleep together.'

'"Ought" suggests a moral duty or an obligation to—' The rest of her sentence was stifled by his kiss. She attempted to struggle free.

'Why not?' he asked her. 'Don't you like me?'

'Of course I like you,' Cassie replied. 'I like you very much. *Very* much. But sleeping together is a big step – at least, it is for me.'

'And for me,' said Terry. 'Don't for one minute imply that just because I'm a bloke I'll have sex with anyone. That's insulting.'

'Sorry. It's not that I'm frightened this is too casual, it's the opposite. I think we're getting serious. I'm not sure I can do serious. I want to be absolutely sure we're doing the right thing. And if I sleep with you now, am I doing it because all the other changes in my life are affecting my judgement? And wouldn't you want me even more if I was a stone slimmer?'

'What on earth has your *weight* got to do with it?'

'Maybe not my weight, but my health. Shall we hold on until I know what's happening with my gall bladder? I want to be sure.'

'I'm sure,' Terry said.

Cassie felt unaccountably nervous. It was difficult for her to admit even to herself what was going on. Once she slept with Terry, she felt it would be for keeps. Then, either way, she was taking a risk. If the relationship failed, she would lose everything. If it succeeded, she would be settling down and giving up on the illusion of eternal youth, which you maintain effortlessly in your twenties, with a little more difficulty in your thirties, and only with determined naïvety on approaching forty.

She kissed him. 'I'm not rejecting you,' she said. 'Let me sort myself out first.'

'I'll help you,' said Terry. 'You are a bit of a mess.' He proceeded to straighten her clothes and she was grateful to him for not making a scene. She knew she was mad to push him away. Why had she done it?

Once he had gone she asked herself the question again. Away from Terry, she could think more clearly. Was she scared of commitment? Possibly. Was she worried about settling down? Possibly. It was a curtailment of freedom. Did she feel unable to live with someone else? It would certainly take some adjustment. Why was she so faint-hearted? Was it because she was an academic? She had trained herself to think carefully and cautiously about everything, that was for sure.

She wandered into her kitchen and smiled. Terry was certainly not perfect. He had left her all the washing-up. He had also left the container of ice-cream in the freezer and she looked at it longingly. Since she had already sabotaged her eating regime, what harm would there be in finishing it? Only a sharp memory of the pain she had suffered with her gallstones stopped her.

She closed the fridge, pleased with her willpower and disappointed that she was so mean to herself. Only it wasn't her fault, it was Terry's. If he liked her so much, what was he doing bringing round and leaving precisely the sort of food that would harm her? Did he not want her to get well and strong and fit and lean? Did he like only the old Cassie? And why was she asking herself all these questions? Usually it was only at the time of year when she was setting examination papers that she thought in question marks. Now it was becoming habitual. And Cassie knew that as soon as she started thinking, she stopped acting. If she began to question why she wanted to carry on going to the gym three times a week and eating as little as possible, she would stop doing it.

The art of success lay in not thinking – that was it! Cassie resolved not to think about Terry and not to think about why she was increasingly attracted to the fit, healthy life. She would just go for it. And if she couldn't control her thinking, she knew just what to do about it.

'Clench all of the muscles in your right leg. And then let go. Good. Now all of the muscles in your left leg. And let go. You'll feel that warm, soothing sensation of relaxation travelling up both your legs and you'll feel heavy, very heavy . . .'

If you say so, thought Cassie. She was determined to reserve judgement and remain open-minded about this experiment in hypnotherapy. The man himself seemed on the level. When she had come to his office for the first time a few days ago he had impressed her with his businesslike air and qualifications. Certificates from seemingly illustrious bodies decorated the walls with testimonial letters from satisfied clients. Two had made a definite impact on her. The first was from a man who had succeeded in changing the habits of lifetime and had lost four stone, and the other from a woman who was scared of commitment; she had attached a photo of herself on her wedding day. The hypnotherapist himself had questioned Cassie carefully, told her he would not take her on if he felt he couldn't help her but, thank the Lord!, *had* felt he could help her, and had arranged this first session. That was why Cassie was spreadeagled in his armchair, trying to relax with all the effort she could muster.

'Now clench your abdominal muscles . . .'

Well done, thought Cassie. 'Abdominal' was a hell of a word to pronounce correctly but as a decent professional hypnotherapist you had to attempt it otherwise you would end up having to say something coy and patronising, such as 'tummy', or 'stomach', which was only slightly better, but . . .

'The warm, liquid feeling of relaxation is moving up your spine and dissolving all the tension located there. Now clench your right fist . . .'

Cassie did, and it was a relief because she was finding it increasingly difficult to relax. How could you relax in a stranger's office? It wasn't that she didn't trust him, he seemed a thoroughly nice man, with his sympathetic smile, in his early forties, wearing a suit. It was more that she didn't like surrendering her mind to anyone. Independence of thought was the habit of a lifetime. He had explained to her that all he would be doing was harnessing the power of her subconscious mind by reprogramming it with the thoughts her conscious mind chose to have. So she had colluded with him in scripting the session. He was going to tell her that fruit and vegetables and grilled fish and chicken were attractive and desirable, that working at the gym was her reward at the end of a busy day and that she should visualise herself svelte, fit, healthy and happy. Fair enough. Harmless, really, if it worked. The relaxation was necessary, apparently, to release the powers of the subconscious. Cassie had been assured that she would be aware throughout of what was going on, and she would not be given any thought that she herself had not requested.

'Loosen your tongue and open your jaw slightly. Good. Let your forehead slacken and relax.'

Cassie's body felt languid and heavy; her mind was razor sharp. What was he going to do next? How odd to lie here with her eyes shut in somebody else's chair knowing its owner's eyes were open and that he was watching her. Beyond his voice was the trickle of a miniature artificial fountain on a cabinet and pan-pipes music. The tune was familiar and vaguely irritating.

'Now you are walking along a path and come to some steps. Slowly and effortlessly you begin to descend them. You find the first step – good – then carry on down to the second.'

Cassie was quite enjoying this. She was trying to visualise the steps. Were they stone? Did they have moss peeping through the cracks? Or brick, perhaps – yes, she would prefer red brick. Perhaps a brick or two was loose. Which reminded her that her own front doorsteps might need repointing soon. That was the trouble with old property. There was so much more maintenance to consider. In a year or two she would have to think about getting the exterior of the house painted but it might be more than she could afford unless she skipped a holiday abroad and—

'You have reached the bottom . . .'

Damn! She had let her mind wander. What a waste of a hypnotherapy session! Cassie reprimanded herself sharply and made herself pay attention. She half expected to have her knuckles rapped by the therapist but luckily he could not know what she was really thinking. The idea delighted her. Cassie was at her happiest when she could be subversive.

'. . . And you find yourself on a deserted beach, with the sun going down just beyond the horizon, casting a warm, rosy glow over the water.'

Would it be rosy, though? A *rosy* glow over the water? Would it not rather be golden, because of the sand? Or maybe the beach was shingle. She would have to wait and see.

'All is peaceful, deserted. You take off your sandals and feel the fine grains of warm sand between your toes.'

Oh, no, I don't, thought Cassie. When she was a small child and her father insisted on taking her to the beach at the weekends on which he visited her, she hated taking off her shoes and socks because the sensation of the sand on the soles of her feet made her feel that the world was breaking up. Mentally Cassie covered her feet in large, crusty brown hiking boots,

Terry's hiking boots, the ones that skulked behind his front door. That was better.

'And now you sit down at the water's edge, and let the sand trickle through your fingers.'

Forget the sand!

'You feel peaceful, more peaceful than you have ever felt in your life. The last rays of the sun caress you like a blessing.'

The internal rhyme was too much for her. Cassie felt as if she was in a Patience Strong verse. Had she taken leave of her senses? Had she voluntarily delivered herself to this man, whom she hardly knew, to be brainwashed? Well, she had nothing against brainwashing as long as it was intelligent brainwashing, and if it worked . . . if she returned to her self-imposed eating regime with renewed vigour. She had her inner critic in a half-nelson now and would hold it there until it begged for mercy.

'You feel sleepy and lie back on the beach.'

Dangerous, she thought. A deserted beach? God knows who's lurking just beyond it! And it would be chilly if it was evening. Perhaps she was resenting the beach because when the hypnotherapist had asked her before the session what her favourite place was, she had said Manhattan, in a plush penthouse apartment overlooking Central Park. He had told her that wasn't suitable for a creative visualisation as it wasn't a *natural* environment. She had negotiated by suggesting a roof garden but he hadn't been impressed. Cassie reprimanded herself again. He was coming to the important bit now. She began to pay close attention.

'On a table in front of you, you see a tempting array of food, juicy apples, glistening segments of orange, and round, tender grapes. You take one, put it in your mouth and enjoy the exquisite sensation of flavour bursting in your mouth . . .'

He ought to have been an advertising copywriter, she thought.

'You think with loathing of the food you used to eat, toast dripping with butter, obscene slabs of chocolate, pies, curries . . .'

Cassie felt hungry.

'And you think instead of the new Cassie, slim, healthy, capable of anything, the person you know you can be.'

It was an appealing vision, one that Cassie had conjured up for herself. Never having been anything but dumpy all her life she had wondered frequently what it would be like to be slim. Now that her gallstones were quiet, she suspected that her motives in attending the gym were not quite as healthy as they had been. Or, rather, that she was killing two birds with one stone: she would cure herself, then reinvent herself. For the first time in her life she hoped to experience vanity.

And then the hypnotherapist was taking her back along the beach, up the steps and telling her to wriggle her toes, her hands and slowly come back to his room and open her eyes when she was ready. It was a great relief to be back in control.

The therapist beamed at her. 'Well?' he asked.

Cassie didn't want to be rude. 'Lovely,' she said. 'I feel so relaxed.'

He switched off the pan pipes, and Cassie could hear the rush of traffic outside. 'I've made a tape for you,' he told her. 'You should listen to this every day, but not when you're tired as you don't want to fall asleep while it's on.'

Cassie nodded, got up and went over to his desk where she wrote a cheque. They made polite conversation and an appointment for a week's time. She took her jacket from behind the door and bade him goodbye. And then she was out in the street.

She slunk away from the consulting rooms, feeling ever so slightly guilty that she should have stooped to hypnotherapy. And yet it made a strange kind of sense. She had to subjugate her mind to the needs of her body. That was the turn her life was taking. The hypnotherapist was a nice man and obviously believed in what he was doing. The problem was, Cassie didn't.

She hoped he wouldn't be too upset when she rang up to cancel the appointment she had just made. She reckoned she wasn't the type to benefit from hypnotherapy. Having to relax just gave her a headache. She was happiest in the gym, she thought, *doing* something. And eating succulent, fresh fruit, juicy apples, glistening segments of orange, and round, tender grapes.

Chapter Six

Jane replaced the receiver, grateful for small mercies. A part-timer from Middleton's Fit Not Fat could cover for a couple of days. She herself would have to man reception as Kendra had been off for a while and might not be back until the end of the week. Darren was away, too, and Adam, another part-timer, had not turned up yet. Siobhan, who was only back today, was fairly certain he'd come down with the bug, too.

Drat that bug! The odd thing was, it seemed to affect everyone in different ways. It upset Kendra's stomach but made Siobhan lose her voice. Darren had a splitting headache, apparently, while Adam had been complaining of a temperature last night. Jane was highly suspicious. She had noticed at Kearsley Gate that a number of the staff treated illness as a way of extending their holidays. Everyone seemed to feel entitled to a certain number of days on the sick, almost as if it was written in their contract, and the women were generally worse than the men.

Jane had to admit that she didn't feel too good herself, but *she* was here. In her case, she knew her illness was self-inflicted. A little too much wine before bedtime had disturbed her sleep. She had been wide awake since four a.m., tossing and turning, going through the Fit Not Fat figures in her head, then counting sheep while reaching for the paracetamol. She had dozed for a while, then was jolted by her alarm clock, suddenly alert, her mouth dry, her throat tight. She downed as much coffee as she could manage, got in the car and zoomed to work. Work was her cure-all.

Here, in her office, she still felt the thrill of being in command. It excited her that there was so much to do, and it was only frustration with staff absenteeism that was a problem. The job was every bit as wonderful as she had hoped it would be. Already, in six weeks, she had effected a transformation. Jodie had put up posters everywhere; Jane had sent out a membership survey and was eagerly awaiting replies; she had arranged a meet-the-members coffee morning for the coming weekend; and had selected designs and materials for the coffee shop. She was living and breathing Fit Not Fat. This was as it should be.

Of course, there was still some tension with the staff. She knew she was being observed and her every movement charted. It surprised her that neither Garth nor Siobhan wanted to move on, but Jane accepted the situation. Garth was unfailingly pleasant, sometimes almost too pleasant, and Siobhan . . . Well, Siobhan *was* a thorn in her side, that was true: she oozed resentment. Jane ached to make the situation better. She could see that Siobhan was a good worker and fundamentally trustworthy. If only she could harness her loyalty.

Just then, as if on cue, there was a rap at the door and Siobhan entered. Her greeting smile was brief and enigmatic. She had the post with her. There were a few unopened envelopes addressed personally to Jane, and other, opened correspondence for her inspection. Siobhan placed it all on the desk, her eyes not meeting Jane's.

'Are you feeling better?' Jane asked, glancing over the correspondence.

'Yes, thank you.' She cleared her throat. 'There are quite a few cancellations of membership,' she remarked.

'Cancellations?' That did not compute. Jane pulled the letters to her and leafed through them. Siobhan stood by the desk, expressionless.

'Take a seat, Siobhan. You're spooking me.'

Siobhan sat down.

What she had said was true, Jane saw. There were two, three, four — in all, eight cancellations of membership. Jane's inactive-membership survey had reminded these people that they were paying monthly subscriptions to a health club they never attended, so they had decided to cease payment immediately. She could have kicked herself. Why on earth hadn't she predicted this? 'Have you read these?' she asked Siobhan.

The other woman nodded. Jane could swear that the hint of a smile was playing around her lips.

'I should have seen this coming. And there'll be more, won't there?'

'Only about fifty per cent of our membership attends the club regularly,' Siobhan said.

A shiver ran through Jane.

'Did you read the letter from Mrs Halstead?' her second-in-command continued.

Jane leafed through until she found it.

Dear Fit Not Fat,

I am writing to inform you that I am cancelling my member-ship of your club. I joined Fit Not Fat six months ago only on the insistence of my husband who felt I ought to get in shape. Until receipt of your letter, it had been a fairly simple business to put my sports bag in the car and create the impression I was coming to the club. My husband, who is not particularly observant, was satisfied that I was looking trimmer, although this was entirely due to the new wardrobe I had been steadily acquiring while he thought I was sweating it out doing abdominal crunches. Unfortunately he caught sight of your letter identifying me as an inactive member and we have had words, most of which are not repeatable. He has now insisted that I should have a personal trainer come to the house. Do you have any recommendations? Male, naturally.

With regards,

Jane put her hand to her mouth.

'They'll be requesting your attendance as a witness in the divorce courts.' Siobhan said.

Jane caught her eye and saw that far from seeming critical, Siobhan was vastly amused. In fact, she had never seen her look more cheerful. She didn't seem disposed to blame Jane at all. It was a relief, and made her ignominy less.

'Who shall we recommend? Garth?' Siobhan suggested.

Jane attempted a laugh. 'I really think we should ignore the letter . . .' She thought for a moment. 'I don't suppose there's any way of getting some of these members back?'

'No. They'll just start paying subscriptions to Weight Watchers and not turning up there.'

Siobhan's wry comment made Jane try humour too. 'Or maybe the effort of thinking about working out was making them break into a sweat and burning up the calories. For some people just belonging to a health club makes them feel ten pounds lighter. It's a bit like going to church. You feel holy even if you don't pray while you're there.'

'It's the image you create, I suppose. If you go to the gym, other people think of you as fit so you believe you are.'

'That's right!' Jane could hardly believe it. Here they were, she and Siobhan, having their first decent conversation since she had started. Of course, it had taken a monumental failure on her part to occasion it, but it was almost worth it – no, it *was* worth it.

Siobhan carried on: 'These cancellations wouldn't have gone on paying for much longer, anyway, and we'll always be able to attract new members.'

'That's very true,' Jane said. 'Which reminds me. I've arranged to visit the Tuesday Afternoon club at the church hall to speak to the over-sixties. The date's in the diary.'

'That's original,' Siobhan said. 'I'll get my mum to go along.'

'Does she live locally?' Jane said, delighted Siobhan had volunteered this much personal information. It was a first.

'Yes,' Siobhan said.

'Near you?'

'With me.'

'Oh.'

Jane backed off. It didn't need much sensitivity to see that Siobhan did not want to talk about her mother. Jane wondered why. Perhaps they did not get on. Perhaps her mother was too involved in her own life to care much about Siobhan's. Perhaps she made her feel inadequate in some way. You could never tell what went on in other people's families. 'I'm clocking off early and having a night off,' she volunteered. She hoped Siobhan would relax enough to offer some information about herself too. In all the time they had worked together she had said hardly anything to Jane about her private life. Fine: that was her prerogative. But it created a distance between them, and that was a pity. More than anything, Jane wanted Siobhan's support – and, better still, friendship. Yet getting to know her was as difficult as scaling the north face of the Eiger. Unwilling to give up, she continued to talk about herself, hoping Siobhan would follow her lead.

'Some of my mates are coming round tonight, Gina and Liz. They're up from London. We've been friends since we've been at school. Gina writes features for magazines and Liz is an accountant. Well, when I say they're my friends, they are, but they're not my best friends. I've known them a long time, though. I do have other, closer friends but Becky's working in London and Emma's in Liverpool with Guy. And there are other people from various clubs I've been at, but do you find it's harder to make friends at work? Close friends? I do. For a start, there's never the time, and . . .'

Jane felt as if she was drowning. She was desperate to establish a friendly rapport with Siobhan.

'Do you have friends out of work?' she asked.

'Yes,' Siobhan said.

'Male? Female? Do you have a boyfriend?'

'No,' Siobhan said. 'Sorry I can't stay and chat. I've got to check the temperature in the sauna.' She left the office.

She doesn't like me, Jane thought, and felt the edifice of her self-belief shake a little. Siobhan's hostility ate like acid into her image of herself. It was so painful to know that someone didn't like you. Why? What had she done wrong? Taken the job Siobhan had applied for, true. Maybe it was all jealousy. It was so much easier to conclude that someone didn't like you for that reason. Jane bit her lip. She knew she should not need Siobhan's affection: Siobhan was her employee, and friendship wasn't part of her employment contract. And yet it would be so much easier if they got on. But no: Siobhan's stiffness should not be a problem — *was* not a problem.

Jane acknowledged that her Achilles' heel was that she took things too personally. She needed to develop a harder edge. And how could she do that? It occurred to her that she hadn't trained for at least three days — far too long. A session in the gym at lunchtime would make her feel more positive, less vulnerable, in control. She always had her training gear in the office and she could easily be spared for an hour. What was more, a bout of intense physical activity would help her fight off her hangover and help her sleep tonight. Her mind made up, she turned with resolve to the rest of the correspondence.

It was mean of her, Siobhan knew, to feel glad that Jane had cocked up so magnificently, but she couldn't help it. It vindicated everything she had ever thought about her. Siobhan felt ineffably right and superior. It was blindingly obvious to anyone who knew anything about the health industry that half the paying membership had simply wanted to forget they were members. Jane's reminders had been precisely what they didn't need.

Yet at the same time Siobhan was conscious that the débâcle was partly her fault. She could have prevented it. She should have warned Jane that mass defection was the likely outcome, and stopped her sending out those letters. Her conscience pricked. However, as much as she disliked Jane, she had no desire to crow over her discomfiture to their colleagues: it was enough that Jane had proved herself a fool and that Siobhan had received a postcard from Trudy that morning.

She wrote up the sauna temperature on the chart by the door and prepared to go out to reception to check if she was booked for any assessments. The postcard pictured the coastline at night strung with lights, and on the reverse Trudy explained that the Portuguese conveyancing system was extremely complicated and painfully slow, but that as soon as the premises were legally hers, she intended Siobhan to come over and start planning the club's facilities. Not wanting her mother to see the card, she had taken it in to work with her and it was now in a zipped compartment of her sports bag. Siobhan decided she would treat herself to it again at lunchtime, although she knew the contents off by heart. It was her passport out of Sunnybank.

Jane was at the computer, working on some exercise plans for distribution in the gym. She was irritated by yet another knock at the door. It was Garth.

'Yes?' she said, just a shade abruptly.

'Sorry to disturb you. I was wondering if it was OK if I went home this afternoon.'

'Why?'

'Not feeling too good.'

Not Garth too! Jane tried and failed to hide her exasperation. 'Is it the bug?' she asked tartly.

'I don't know. I'm just a bit shivery and aching. But if we're still short-staffed I'll stay on. I'll take some paracetamol. I'll be fine.'

'No, if you're ill you'll only pass it on. You go home.'

Only Garth didn't go home. He took the seat opposite Jane and made himself comfortable. 'Thanks,' he said. 'I won't if I can help it. I can see what pressure you're under. At the moment there's only the girl from Middleton in the gym, but she seems to know what she's doing. You can relax a bit. I've just popped out for my coffee break. Can I get you a coffee too?'

As usual with Garth Jane felt a little uneasy, and couldn't understand why. She had never gone for that male-model look. For all she knew, he was gay. What suggested it was that he was so clean, his hair so immaculate, his gear so well chosen. But he had natural advantages too: his jaw was square and his eyes were dark and sensitive. His lips were just a shade too full and made you stop and consider them. Garth knew he was good-looking too.

'A coffee would be nice,' she conceded.

Within a few moments he was back, and placed a black coffee carefully on her desk. Although she knew she should get rid of him, she felt like a little distraction. His thoughtfulness, suspect as it was, warmed her.

'Are you feeling well?' he asked her.

'Yes, fighting fit.' She ignored her throbbing head and dry mouth.

'That's a relief. We couldn't cope if you weren't here.'

She sipped her coffee, aware that she was being flattered but quite enjoying it.

'Siobhan seems a little better,' he continued. 'Her throat's her weak spot. She's been a bit low lately, I've thought. She's taking it hard that she didn't get the job. Trudy Thompson virtually promised it would be hers. The trouble is that Siobhan doesn't have much of a life outside the club, which makes it difficult for her to cope when problems arise.'

'I know what you mean,' Jane replied. 'You've got to have a break. I'm seeing my mates tonight.'

'Are you going into town?'

'I don't know what we'll end up doing.'

Garth grinned at her. Perhaps he wasn't gay after all. Jane felt a little hot. 'Because if you do go into town, there's a new bar behind Deansgate.'

'Do you mean Space? I've heard it's good.'

'It is. I hang out there when I'm not here.' Garth had a disarming, unaffected laugh. It was his best feature. 'But, hey,' he continued, 'the club's looking good. You've certainly sorted out the cleaners. Some of the members were saying what an improvement there was in the club's appearance. There've been quite a few enquiries about new memberships.'

Jane had not known this and was cheered. The day wasn't quite so bad after all. 'Really?'

'Definitely. And the ad you placed in the local paper has also produced a response. I was looking after reception this morning and took three calls from people who wanted to look round our facilities.'

Jane beamed at him. Perhaps she was being hard on Garth. He was genuinely big-hearted, and cared about the club.

'A lot of us are happier now,' Garth continued. 'Trudy had a policy of divide and rule. In the club the word is that you're fair. That's important. And don't let Siobhan get you down. She's difficult to get on with at the best of times, and now she's biting everyone's head off, although it's not surprising . . .' He let his voice drift away.

Jane was not going to question him further. She didn't approve of gossip.

'She's a hard worker, though,' Garth went on, unabashed. 'And so are you. Just make sure you attend to your own needs. And speak to me if you ever want any vitamin supplements or similar. Now, drink your coffee before it gets cold. I'll go and check the gym.'

He grinned at her again, conspiratorially. Jane smiled back. She was glad of his support and found him surprisingly perceptive. Perhaps she was feeling a little overworked. Lucky that she was going out tonight. She opened her drawer and reached for the paracetamol.

When Jane entered the gym at lunchtime it was reasonably quiet. Two middle-aged women in black leotards and shorts, their hair and nails immaculate, were walking side by side on treadmills, having a pleasant conversation. A young man was cycling while reading a John Grisham novel. Another woman was taking a break, reclining on the leg press and listening to her Walkman. Over on the stepper she recognised another good attender – Cassie Oliver. Garth had told her she was a university lecturer. Jane had been interested in that. She seemed to be working hard: her cheeks were red with effort.

Jane was a little concerned to find no instructor in the gym and made a mental note to find out why after she had completed her workout. Just then Garth came in with a new water container, and began to substitute it for the one that was nearly empty. It took him a moment to realise that Jane was there. 'Hi,' he said. 'Are you training this lunchtime?'

'I am.' Jane felt uncharacteristically self-conscious. She wondered why. Perhaps it was the way he gave her that assessing look, the way his eyes travelled up and down her body. It annoyed her. She lifted her chin defiantly. 'It's my lunch hour.'

'Just make sure you don't overdo it,' he said, paternal now.
'I won't.'

He strolled away and she watched him pick up some members' personal programmes. She couldn't decide whether she liked him or not: on one hand, he was loyal, caring and remarkably attractive: on the other, he was too loyal, too caring, too attractive. Far too attractive for his own good and hers. Not that he would present her with a problem: Jane did not have time for involvement right now. Men were just a distraction and perhaps she resented Garth precisely for that reason.

Glancing out of the window, she saw Jodie, who had come in for the late shift and looked a little down, Jane thought. Surely Jodie didn't have the bug too. Cheerful little Jodie who was keeping them all entertained with her romance with Darren. Once, Jane had had to have a word with her about not embracing in front of the clients in the gym. She had been mortified and promised she would never be so indiscreet again. Jodie had chosen Jane as her confidante, so Jane knew all about their first date at the cinema, how easy he was to talk to afterwards, and how he had taken her out to eat, insisted on paying *and* bought her a red rose afterwards. No one had ever bought her one before! Jane had also learnt how well he was doing at college, how the rugby team he played in was top of the league, how special he made her feel, how well he got on with her mother and that he had bought two gorgeous shirts from Paul Smith.

Jane ascended the treadmill just behind the steppers and began to walk. She made a note to herself that if she began to feel light-headed, she'd stop. She was aware that one should not train if one was feeling ill, but the rhythm of the treadmill was making her feel better. She settled her eyes on Cassie, who was still sweating it out on the stepper. Jane could see that she had lost a considerable amount of weight, and that she looked different. Her face had more definition and she didn't look as wide as she had before. Jane wondered if she would like to feature in an advertising campaign for Fit Not Fat – perhaps she had some particularly unflattering 'before' pictures . . .

She pressed on the control panel to increase the speed of the treadmill. Now she broke into a run and all her concentration was focused on summoning the energy for her sprint. Only when she had finished her two minutes at high speed did she fall back into a jog and contemplate Cassie again. She was the sort of new member they needed to encourage: she took her exercising seriously. In fact, Jane wondered whether to have a word with her about overtraining. Some of the new recruits believed mistakenly that the harder and longer they worked the better it would be. They didn't realise that muscles needed to rest and recuperate for maximum benefit.

Later, when they had finished on their respective machines, they approached the water-cooler at the same time. Jane insisted Cassie go first. Cassie looked at her, frowning, unable to place her. 'I'm Jane Wright, the manager here. It's my lunch-hour so I'm fitting in my training now.'

'I knew I recognised you,' Cassie said, 'but I always think of you in a suit. Not that you look at all bad in your leggings.'

'And you don't look bad yourself. You've lost weight, haven't you?'

Cassie grinned. 'Almost a stone.'

'Well done!' Jane almost envied her. There was nothing like that feeling of having improved yourself. It was almost worth having a problem like that in order to solve it. Yet she must give her a word of advice. 'I've watched you working out. Remember that you should always feel comfortable at the end of a session. If you're light-headed or dizzy, you're overdoing it.'

'Point taken,' Cassie said. 'I don't think I'm overtraining. I'm full of energy when I come out of here. I'd like to say I felt ten years younger but I didn't feel this good ten years ago.'

'Are you here to lose weight?' Jane knew virtually all her female membership were here for that reason. For most the fitness element was simply a cover. The men were just as vain, but it was muscle definition they wanted.

'Only as a by-product,' Cassie said. 'I came here as part of a lifestyle overhaul. I was diagnosed with gallstones and the consultant said . . .'

Jane's attention swerved. She was allergic to discussion of illness.

'I was wondering,' she said, when Cassie had finished, 'whether you'd like to feature in our club newsletter as a successful loser.'

'A successful loser? Isn't that an oxymoron?'

'An oxymoron?'

Jane and Cassie looked equally confused.

'A contradiction in terms,' Cassie explained. 'A loser, by definition, is not successful.'

'Ah!' Jane said. 'All I meant was that you'd been successful in losing weight. So think about it and let me know.' Jane followed Cassie's eyes over to the leg press where the woman using it seemed to have stopped working and was lying with her eyes shut.

'Oh, and I hope you're coming to the members' coffee morning this Saturday. It's a new idea – your chance to say what you want from the club and what improvements you'd like to see.'

'This Saturday? Sure! Love to.'

Jane was pleased. She needed a good attendance. Feeling better by the minute, she moved over to the stepper. She was now ready for the most intense part of her workout.

She liked interval training. She got on to the machine and set it to a level with which she was comfortable. Then as soon as her body adjusted she increased the speed until her legs could hardly maintain the pace. Her knees were weak with the effort. She remained defiantly upright, scorning the chance to lean on the side bars. Sweat coursed into her eyes and she blinked it away.

Just when she knew she couldn't keep it up a moment longer, she switched the machine back to the initial level. Relief cascaded through her. She kept up a steady, comfortable rhythm, secure in the knowledge that she had activated her fat-burning mechanism and that those fat cells were burning away even though it seemed she was hardly making any effort. Then, just as she was allowing herself to feel complacent, she forced herself to turn up the machine again even higher. Shocked, her body threw itself back into a frantic pace. Every atom of concentration was channelled into keeping going. Jane counted the seconds to steady herself. And then, just when she thought she would collapse she switched to the easier level. Now she felt as if she was burning up, and wondered again if she really was feeling one hundred per cent. But she didn't care: triumphing over her body and its weaknesses was such a stimulant it would do as a substitute for good health.

Twenty minutes later Jane came down from the stepper, her legs refusing to carry her. She held on to the machine and waited for the gym to stop spinning. Euphoria set in as she realised how hard she had just been working. She had probably lost a pound or so too. Although she knew better than anyone that body weight was an inaccurate and unreliable way to measure fat and that the body-mass index was infinitely preferable, there was nothing like the lift you got from standing on old-fashioned scales and seeing that you'd lost weight. Jane did so, and was pleased to see that she was just under eight stone ten. Now she must shower, change and get back to the office.

It was half past three. Jane had just finished interviewing a new yoga teacher. Alone again, she allowed exhaustion to wash over her. Maybe her workout had been a little too vigorous. No matter. It was done now, and that was good. She closed her eyes. It hit her that she had skipped lunch, which would never do. She decided to find Jodie and ask her to fetch her a sandwich from the petrol station.

Jane summoned all her energy, left her room and went to the gym. Jodie was not there. Siobhan said she was in the changing room checking the lavatories. Jane made her way there and, sure enough, found Jodie replacing loo rolls. 'Not the nicest job in the world,' she remarked sympathetically.

'It's all right,' Jodie said.

'I wondered if you fancied a break and would run over to the garage to get me a sandwich.'

'If you like.'

'Jodie, are you feeling OK?'

Jodie turned slowly to look at Jane. Her face was haggard and her eyes lifeless. Her ponytail hung limply and her shoulders seemed to sag.

'Jodie, you haven't got the bug, have you?'

'The bug? No.'

'Has anything happened?'

'Nothing in particular.'

Jane knew she was lying. Her body language gave her away. She ran through all the possibilities. Darren had dumped her. She had dumped Darren. He was seeing someone else. She was seeing someone else. She was pregnant. He was – no. Luckily the ladies' changing room was empty. Jane guided her away from the loos and sat her down on a bench. She put an arm round her in a sisterly fashion. 'Come on, now, you can tell me about it.' Jodie said nothing. Jane waited. She knew that sometimes it wasn't easy to talk. Then she heard Jodie swallow.

'I just don't know what he sees in me. I know it can't last. I mean, look at me. I've got a figure like a boy and my face is so ordinary. He's only going out with me because he took pity on me. I'd made such a fool of myself chasing after him he felt morally obliged.

'Whatever happened to make you think this?'

'Nothing. I've just been putting two and two together. There's Darren studying for a degree and him being so fit, and then there's me. God, I'm so *disgusting!*'

'Nonsense! You're incredibly pretty and most women would kill for a figure like yours. Darren's the lucky one. Are you sure nothing's happened?'

'No. And sometimes even the job gets me down. It's so repetitive—'

'I'll arrange a change of responsibility—'

'— so repetitive and you see people train and they do ever so well and then they stop coming and when they return a few months later they've undone all the good work. And these competitions I've been running, what good do they do? The same people win all the time. So all I'm doing is encouraging the people who don't need encouraging – they're obsessive enough. And all the people who need motivation are put off trying. And next week it's eight years since my gran died.' Jodie allowed a few tears to escape.

Jane gave her a hug. 'Come on,' she said. 'This isn't like you. You're normally so cheerful.'

'Don't accuse me like that! I can't help it!'

Jane was aghast at her anger. Just then Siobhan entered.

'Not you too!' Jodie muttered.

'Is it that time of the month, Jodie?' Siobhan enquired.

'No. Yes. Oh, I don't know. You all think you know me so well and you don't, none of you. Not even Darren. Especially Darren. What kind of sandwich, Jane? Will egg do?'

'Egg will be fine.'

'I'll take the money from petty cash.'

In a fury, she stormed out.

'Jodie's always been like that. She has particularly bad PMT. You missed it last month because she took some leave owing to her then. Poor kid.'

'Isn't there anything the doctors can do?'

'Apparently not. The pill doesn't suit her.'

'Well, at least I'll know next time. We don't leave her alone with the clients when she's like this, do we?'

'Why do you think I asked her to check out the changing rooms?'

'Good. Oh dear. Well, I'd better get back to the office, then.'

'I'll cover in the gym.'

Siobhan vanished again and Jane got to her feet. It was hard enough managing the staff without having to deal with their illnesses too. She shivered as she walked along the corridor and wondered whether she too was suffering from PMT. All she knew was that she would be glad when the day was over. Gina and Liz would be bound to buoy her up, and even if they didn't, she could indulge in the comfort of a large glass of dry white wine.

Jane resolved that she wouldn't have too much too much to drink, even though she wasn't driving. There was work in the morning. She had only bought three bottles of wine so that her friends could see that she was hospitable, and up for a good time.

She had not seen Gina and Liz for a while. Both of them had been working in London and were now coincidentally back in the north, Liz permanently as her fiancé was working in Bolton, and Gina just for a fortnight's holiday. It was strange, Jane reflected, that they had kept in touch. Theirs had never been an equal relationship. At school she had always looked up to them and had been no more than a hanger-on to their clique. She remembered them well because she had studied them carefully: Gina was a bit of a swot but knew how to let her hair down; Liz was the wild one, boy-crazy and rebellious. In the last few years they had changed dramatically. Liz had settled down, was taking her final accountancy exams and was looking forward to her wedding; Gina was a successful journalist, spiky, assured and challenging. Jane had changed just as much. She had been a bit of sheep, it was true, trying desperately to be just like everyone else. Now she was a leader, the manager of Fit Not Fat. And that felt good.

She decided not to have a drink before Gina and Liz arrived. She didn't want them to think she was a lush. She wasn't; she just enjoyed her drink and used it as a means to relax. It was considerably quicker than yoga. It helped her unwind and turn off; she knew it was important to let go and dismissed thoughts of Garth, Siobhan, her aching limbs, Garth – no, she'd dismissed him already. So she would dismiss him again. There – he was gone. She kicked some magazines under the settee, plumped up the cushions and closed the window, which she had opened earlier to let in some fresh air, and as she did so she heard the sound of a car engine slowing.

In a few moments they were at her front door. Everyone squealed with delight to see each other, and exclaimed that Liz's short hair really suited her, that Gina looked more glamorous than ever and that Jane had lost weight. The compliments having been evenly distributed, they settled down for a good night in. 'I've borrowed my parents' car tonight,' Gina said, 'so only the smallest glass of wine for me, and that's it.'

Jane filled Liz's glass almost to overflowing. She sat with her on the settee and watched Gina curl up in the armchair. She had her hair pinned up with a large butterfly clip, and wore a long black dress. Jane realised why she had hero-worshipped Gina for so long. 'How's London?' she asked.

'Incredible,' Gina replied. 'I'm living in a flat in Dalston – that's the wrong side of Islington. It's not convenient for the tube but I prefer to take taxis everywhere. It's just as quick.'

'And, really, when you work out the cost of running a car, it's probably just as cheap,' Liz added.

Jane took a large sip of wine.

'Yes,' said Gina, 'I'm sure you're right, and I still have a great social life, not driving. That's the best thing about London – it's the centre of everything. I don't think I could bear to have not left home.'

Jane gulped some more wine.

'I expect it's important for you to be there,' Liz answered. 'You need to establish contacts. As for me, I'm happy to come back.'

'Well, you would be, wouldn't you?' Gina chaffed her. 'Are we invited to the wedding? When is it? And are you getting married in a church or what? Have you chosen the dress?'

Liz described the dress, the cake design, the church, the little hotel where they were having the reception, told them the date, assured them they would be receiving invitations and ran through everyone else on the guest list. Jane's mind drifted. Perhaps she ought not to have asked Siobhan so many questions about herself – had it come over like an inquisition? Did Garth like her? Did he *fancy* her? Ridiculous. She didn't fancy him, not one bit. Not remotely. She finished her wine. As she did so she felt a lightness in her chest and excitement zapped through her. The drink was taking effect. She was happy.

'And what about you?' Gina asked her. 'How are *you* doing?'

It was her turn now. When three people were talking it took some time for the conversation to focus on the third, she understood that. Now Gina and Liz seemed genuinely interested in her. She basked in their attention. 'I've been in my new job for six weeks now and it's going well. Sunnybank Fit Not Fat is only a small club, but the challenge is to expand in the face of competition. Fitness International is opening up near to us, so it's a matter of attracting new members, building profits, maybe even acquiring land. It's my first major opportunity to prove myself.' Jane was alight with enthusiasm.

Her friends entered into the spirit of it. 'How many people are you in charge of?' Gina asked.

'Four full-timers, six part-timers and another six freelance teachers. That's not to mention the maintenance staff. It's quite a responsibility, especially as my second-in-command applied for my job and didn't get it.'

Gina gave a long, low whistle. 'That can be tricky,' she said. 'Are health clubs as bitchy as newspapers?'

'I don't really know,' Jane said candidly. 'Siobhan – she's my second-in-command – isn't bitchy, just cold and distant. I know she doesn't like me. I'm sure she's criticising me all the time.' She refilled her glass and topped up Liz's.

'It's resentment,' said Liz, and proceeded to analyse the situation and compare it to her workplace. Jane listened avidly. It was good to get this off her chest. Gina and Liz were great mates – God, had she missed them! She was so glad they were here. She took a handful of nuts and washed them down with some more wine.

'She sounds like a cow,' added Gina, summing up their discussion of Siobhan. 'I don't see how anyone couldn't like you. But you make me glad I work independently. Dealing with features editors can have its downside, though. Did I tell you the trouble I had with my Mel C interview?'

Mel C had always been Jane's favourite Spice Girl. She liked the Spice Girls. And Take That. She had loved Take That – and all pop music, the cheesier the better. And rock, and club and trance. Everything, in fact. She loved all forms of music. It soothed the soul. It made you happy. Fascinating to hear that Gina had not only met Mel C, but also Russell Crowe and Richard Branson. And Kate Winslet and Fergie.

She must have poured herself a small glass of wine last time as it had gone very quickly. It was a long time since she had enjoyed herself so much. That alone justified another glass. And she would drink gallons of water before she went to bed. At least she wasn't aching any more. In fact she felt great, on top form. 'And there's this other instructor,' she told them. 'Garth. Phwooar! Not that I fancy him, but there you go. I mean, men aren't on the agenda right now. But he's eyecandy, know what I mean?' Jane was confident she was sounding more like Gina every minute.

'Lucky you,' said Gina. 'I love nothing better than muscles on a bloke. Nice rippling muscles, tight bum.'

Jane laughed loudly.

'Come on,' said Liz. 'You're as bad as the blokes who talk about girls in terms of their figures.'

'It's about time we exacted our revenge' Gina rejoined.

Jane laughed again and noticed Gina helping herself to a little more wine from the second bottle. Encouraged, she topped up her own glass. It was brilliant to listen to Gina and Liz's witty conversation. She loved them and knew they understood her. There was a delicious moment of silence, when they savoured the pleasure of being together.

'So, how are your parents?' Liz asked her.

'Fine, just fine,' Jane said, reached for her glass and gulped some down. 'And yours?' she said. 'And yours?' she said to Gina. Then she laughed because it was so funny that she'd said the same thing twice. 'And yours,' she said, for the third time, then realised she was being slightly ridiculous. Time to sober up. Time to prove she could be as articulate as anyone even when she had drunk – well, not a whole bottle of wine, probably, but it was a small bottle anyway because of that dimple-thing at the bottom.

'The truth is,' she said, falling back on to the settee, holding her glass carefully, 'that it's not always easy, running a club. I wouldn't say that to everyone, but I know I can say this to you. I love you guys. I don't know what I'd have done without you because it's lonely at the top. Really lonely. Like, I sit in my offish – office, and there isn't anybody else there. And you don't know what they're thinking, I mean, I don't what you're thinking. I think. Oh, God, I'm not really drunk, but just very tired. I didn't sleep much last night. So if I sound a bit inco-inco—'

'Incoherent?' Gina suggested.

'That,' said Jane. 'What I want to say is, it isn't always easy, running a club. And I want to say that I don't fancy Garth — I don't trust him, you see. And it's important to wind down and relax and not think about work all the time. I'm not going to have any more wine. I have work in the morning. I bet I'll sleep all right tonight. I love my job. It's the best thing that's ever happened to me. This is like — this is like my celebration for getting the job. And here's to you, Liz, on your engagement, and you, Gina — you're doing so well. We're all doing so well.'

Liz stood up. 'Shall I put the kettle on? I fancy a coffee.'

'Sure,' said Jane. 'But I'm warning you, it's a tip in there. I think I should have a coffee too, or just some water. Yes, some water.'

Jane trusted she didn't sound as silly in real life as she thought she did in her head. But she was tired now, and much as she loved Gina and Liz, she wanted them to go so she could sleep. Then in the morning she would give up drinking for a while — detox, that was it, she would detox, flush out her liver.

She didn't remember much about the rest of the evening. Someone put the wine away and she might have drunk a lot of water. Gina said something about an argument with her sister, and Liz said they must do this again soon, maybe go into town and live it up a little. Jane was sure she agreed to that. And kissed them goodbye and just had enough energy to take off her makeup and stumble into bed and guessed she would have regretted some of the things she'd said had she been able to remember what she'd said.

And fell asleep.

And woke in the morning vowing never to drink again.

Chapter Seven

As Cassie opened the door of the ladies' changing room she paused to savour the exquisite feeling of having just completed a workout. There was nothing like it in the world. It was composed of justified exhaustion, virtue and the knowledge that she needn't come back to the gym for forty-eight hours. Although that was a pity. This was a place where Cassie could escape the complexities of her life, and the demands that others made on her. It was a place where she looked after herself. Bliss.

It was also a place where lots of other people looked after themselves and she was aware of the atmosphere of intense self-absorption. Her fellow exercisers were profoundly concerned with their own bodies, nobody else's. They called it a club, thought Cassie, but the only relationship you formed was with yourself.

And, thinking that, she was about to walk past the smaller of the two studios when she noticed movement inside it and saw a trestle table laid with cups of coffee. She frowned, puzzled, and then remembered it was the meet-the-members' coffee morning. She hesitated, and Jane arrived. 'Are you joining us?' she said brightly.

Cassie said she was, and decided that a cup of coffee (black, no sugar) was not such a bad idea. Jane frogmarched her to the trestle table and poured it for her.

'I'm glad you could come. We want to get feedback from as many of our members as possible. This is your chance to say how you want the club to be.'

'Thank you,' said Cassie, her mind blank. There was a longueur in the conversation, and Cassie decided that she had nothing in common with the manager of the health club. Time to indulge in small-talk.

'I've done my workout for the day,' Cassie said. 'I'm off to the theatre tonight.'

'The theatre?'

'Yes. Terry was given some free tickets. And then we'll find a decent bar, no doubt.'

'Careful with your alcohol intake, Cassie! You'd be surprised how many calories there are in a glass of wine.'

Does she think I'm a lush? Cassie thought, offended. Just as she was about to move away, David joined them. Cassie was pleased to see him. Since their first meeting they had often exchanged a few words in the gym. She considered him her first Fit Not Fat friend and imagined that he found this coffee morning as ridiculous as she did. It was highly artificial: the fifteen or so people there were reflected several times in the studio mirrors, and the trainers were keeping themselves to themselves, standing in a knot over by the mats. A soft-rock tape was playing over the loudspeakers.

'Hi, David!' Cassie said chummily.

'Hi,' he said, in reply, but his eyes slid to Jane. Aha! thought Cassie. I know your game.

'David Richmond,' he said to Jane. 'Do you remember me?'

'Yes,' said Jane. 'You joined a few weeks ago. I hope you're happy with the club.'

'Oh, yes.'

Cassie recognised that she was a spare part, and knew she

ought to move away, but something stopped her. Partly she was curious: David's interest in Jane was obvious and Cassie wanted to see how she would react – her emphatically professional exterior did not suggest someone open to romance, and she was hardly the flighty, flirty type. Also Cassie felt a little piqued that she had lost David's attention so, because she wasn't wanted, she decided to hang around. She'd be damned if they could dispose of her that easily.

Jane went on to explain about the forthcoming changes in the club. There was to be a coffee bar, apparently, competitions, prizes, new classes and possibly even a swimming-pool. David seemed riveted by her account of the new pricing structure, including large discounts for frequent attenders and off-peak users. He fed her with questions and, Cassie noted scornfully, wore the simper men affected when they were besotted with the woman they were talking to. It was a little-boy smile, a puppy-dog look.

And what of Jane? She was responding, Cassie was sure. She adjusted her hair self-consciously and would not look him directly in the face, then suddenly did, smiled and looked down. He edged closer to her as she spoke; she did not back away. They spoke of *t'ai chi* and *astanga* yoga but the words were the least important part of what was going on. Then it got personal. He asked her where she lived, deftly probed into her family circumstances, mentioned that he had only just moved into the area, had a small flat and had joined Fit Not Fat partly to get to know people. He smiled at Jane. Jane smiled at him. Cassie was mesmerised.

'What do you do for a living?' Jane asked him.

'I'm a GP,' he told her.

Cassie noticed a change in Jane's demeanour. She seemed taken aback. 'Oh,' was all she said.

'I'm at the Beech Road Practice.'

'That's nice. But, look, I must move on. I want to speak to as many members as possible.' Her smile had a frozen quality now. She held out her hand, which David shook. Cassie was certain he held hers a fraction longer than was necessary.

He watched her depart with a curious expression on his face. Then he chuckled to himself, and glanced at his watch. 'I must be off,' he said. 'I'm on call this afternoon. I'll most certainly see you around.' He grinned at Cassie with frank good nature, and disappeared.

She finished her coffee, and couldn't help contrasting the comradely way he had bidden her goodbye with the smouldering look he had given Jane. Which was as it should be. She was much older than him and fully occupied with Terry. Yet it left her feeling nostalgic for a time when men she met had tried to chat her up. They had been few and far between, even when she was younger – her size had excluded her from flirtation. Now her age did. Cassie, whose disposition was essentially sunny, did not recognise the hollow ache in her chest as jealousy mingled with regret.

As she went to replace her coffee cup on the table she was greeted by Garth. 'Hello!' he said.

'Hi,' she told him. 'I'm on my way out.'

'Are you going to the gym?'

'No. I've been.'

'You're doing well, aren't you? I can remember when you first started here and we had all that trouble on the stepper.' He chuckled.

Cassie appreciated his interest and was flattered that he remembered. 'And now I'm on level six.'

'Six!' he said, and whistled under his breath. 'But I'm not surprised. I've noticed how regularly you attend. It's going to pay off in the end. You've already lost quite a bit of weight.'

'A stone,' Cassie said, proudly.

'It looks like more. And it suits you.' Cassie felt breathless. Was he paying her a compliment? She expected him to move away but he didn't. He stood there in companionable silence, which he broke by asking. 'So what's your line of work, then?'

'Actually I teach. At the university.'

'The university! I'm impressed. You must be very clever.'

'Don't be ridiculous! Just because I have reams of useless information about the Middle Ages doesn't necessarily mean I'm clever.'

'The Middle Ages? Hey – you won't believe this, but history was my favourite subject at school. The Middle Ages! When they had those tournaments, that was the Middle Ages, wasn't it?'

'Sure was,' said Cassie. 'The lists. A knight sat on his horse and tried to knock the other bloke off with his lance. And gave a favour to his lady beforehand.'

'What sort of favour?' Garth asked.

'Oh, a love token – a handkerchief, something like that. It was part of the tradition of courtly love. Very often a knight would fight on behalf of a married woman – the Queen, even, as in the story of Lancelot and Guinevere, only that business backfired.'

'So this Lancelot and Guinevere, they lived in the Middle Ages?'

'No, they're characters in a myth, but the story was popular at the time. It had significance. It captured the *Zeitgeist*. One theory was that the medieval courts were full of bored married women and young men who didn't have the wherewithal to settle down with a wife and establishment of their own.' Cassie came to: she was lecturing Garth, one of the Fit Not Fat trainers, on medieval sociology. She needed to get a life. She blushed.

'That was interesting,' he said. 'The trouble with this job is that you never get to have any intelligent conversation. Particularly when I hang out with Darren and Andy. We only talk about sport. I'm not knocking sport, but there's only so much to say about it. I try to watch documentaries on the telly, but I much prefer hearing you talk. You bring what you say to life.'

Do I? thought Cassie, delighted. She began to reassess Garth. She had noticed from the start how good-looking he was and, in some way she didn't understand, it disqualified him from her attention. He spent most of his time in the gym, glancing in the mirrors or staring at the TV monitors, but maybe he just lacked stimulation. Perhaps there was more to him. 'You ought to read history books,' she ventured.

'Suggest some,' he said.

'I will, next time I'm in the gym.' She grinned at him, he grinned back, and Cassie felt herself flood with embarrassment. This was all very silly. She was a grown woman. 'Have you worked here long?' she asked, trying to normalise the conversation.

'More or less since the club started as the Sunnybank Health and Fitness Centre. In fact, I applied for the position of manager here.'

'Is it hard to work under a new boss?'

'Not at all. I respect Jane and feel she's doing a far better job than I could ever do. But I'm looking into other ways of developing my career. 'I'm investigating food supplements. I'd like to give nutrition advice, and maybe study the subject at college. Have you heard of L8s?'

'No.'

'A friend told me about them. It's a food supplement that increases your absorption of essential vitamins and minerals so it boosts your energy and immune system.'

'Gosh!' said Cassie, to cover that she hadn't been listening to him but considering how very good-looking he was. There was something of George Clooney about him, or a young Sean Connery, or . . .

'I might be able to supply some to you.'

'Great! Well, keep me posted.'

'I will.'

Just then, Jane offered them a plate of Danish pastries.

'Oh, I shouldn't,' Cassie said.

'I know what you mean,' Garth agreed. 'You feel as if it would sabotage your work in the gym. Leave it and have some fruit when you get home.'

Cassie was delighted to have him bolster her will-power and take such a personal interest in her. Now that was what you called a trainer! She picked up her sports bag and said goodbye to Garth and Jane. There was a spring in her step and she felt ever so slightly light-headed. It was either caffeine or lust.

The marking she had to do during the afternoon prevented her thinking any more about the morning, and indeed, there was very little to think about. Nevertheless, it was difficult to concentrate on the legacy of the Lollard knights with so many changes going on in her life. Difficult, too, to sit down for long. Cassie had noticed that she no longer enjoyed being still for long periods of time. That was another change. Before, her legs had been simply the lower half of her body, usually tucked under her when she sat on a settee or an armchair. Now, nearly two months after starting at Fit Not Fat, she had discovered their usefulness in getting her from place to place.

She consulted the clock on the mantelpiece and decided she had done enough work for the day. She had promised Terry she would go with him to the Studio at the Royal Exchange as he had been given the job of reviewing a new production there. She might as well go and get changed.

In her bedroom she took off her jeans and experienced an illicit thrill that they were now too big on her – illicit, because vestiges of political correctness still troubled her: she ought not to be so pleased about losing weight. Her goal had been, purely and simply, to deal with her gallstones. The weight loss was a by-product. And yet human nature was such – Cassie's nature was such – that the weight loss loomed larger than the gallstones. We only worry about ill-health, she thought, while we are unhealthy.

Once we are well, we consign it to oblivion. Until fate catches up with us again.

She examined her profile in the mirror. Yes, her shape had changed, and people had begun to notice. Not her students, who only saw her as the disseminator of vital information, and treated her with sycophantic deference. Most of them rarely looked at her – in lectures their heads were bowed, as they apparently scribbled down every word she said. Or maybe not.

Her colleagues, however, were another kettle of fish. The men with whom she worked had said nothing directly, but talked to her now in a different way, noticing her. They looked faintly surprised, and one or two even appreciative. Cassie was annoyed and flattered in equal measure. It was galling to be seen as a sex object, but gratifying too. The women were naturally more outspoken. Most had asked her how she had done it. Cassie became aware of the common female delusion that there was an ultimate solution to losing weight. The others had complimen-ted her in vague hyperbole – 'You look fantastic/brilliant/incredible' – which implied lack of belief that it was really Cassie they were looking at. She sensed that their admiration was laced with envy, and the discomfort that comes from a change in the ranking. She was sad that women still responded in that way, but delighted that she was the cause.

Cassie wondered too whether *she* now saw life differently on account of her weight loss. She spent an embarrassingly large amount of the day thinking about her lifestyle change, whether to go to the gym or not, whether to have fruit for lunch or a sandwich without butter, and she had stopped avoiding mirrors. Instead she paused in front of them as she did now. There in front of her was a reasonably attractive woman, still slightly large but large in a shapely way. It interested her. She was still detached from the new Cassie and often experienced a faint shock when she caught her reflection unawares.

Yes, losing weight *was* making her see life differently. She had begun to notice men more – that is, as *men*. Where they were concerned, Cassie knew she was an *ingénue*. She had never had crushes on pop idols or film stars – it had seemed pointless as she knew they would never reciprocate. At university she had simply accepted the men who had presented themselves to her, teaching herself to see only their good points. Now, at the grand old age of thirty-nine, she was beginning to choose.

The professor of linguistics was attractive in a brooding sort of way, with his craggy eyebrows and sulky mouth, but would probably not be very good company. The junior lecturer in philosophy had attractive curly hair and a baby face, but never knew his own mind. She lunched with a physics lecturer, who had an engaging smile and amusing taste in ties. But usually Cassie confined her fantasies to the gym, where acres of male flesh were invitingly on display. She would notice an impressive torso here, or a neat pair of legs there – funny how they never all seemed to come together on the same man . . . although, come to think of it, they did on Garth. And to think he was interested in medieval history too! She tried to remember whether he was on duty on Monday evening, when she was next due to visit the gym. He had seemed to enjoy her conversation, although, she thought quickly, he probably saw her as a mother figure – no, not so much a mother figure as an older sister, or perhaps (who knows?) a type of Mrs Robinson from *The Graduate*. She smiled at her vanity, and proceeded to get dressed.

She was walking along Cross Street with Terry. 'It's amazing, really,' she continued. 'I can run on the treadmill now for about ten minutes at a stretch. I walk for about five minutes to break myself in, then go like the clappers. You get into a rhythm after a time. This morning I managed to keep going for eleven minutes forty seconds. I burned up eight-seven calories.'

She glanced at Terry. He didn't seem interested, which

annoyed her because her fitness regime had become her all-consuming passion. In fact, he looked rather preoccupied, his hands thrust into his jacket pockets, his shoulders hunched and determined. Be like that, then, she thought.

They reached the Royal Exchange and climbed the steps. Cassie attempted to run up them and did, almost. Terry was a few paces behind her. The entrance to the Studio was to the right. They threaded their way through the crowds waiting to see the Shakespeare production at the main theatre, and Terry gave their tickets to the young man dressed in black at the doors leading to the Studio. Once inside, he walked over to the bar to get their drinks. Cassie noted that she and Terry comprised approximately 30 per cent of the audience. This did not bode well.

'What's this play about again?' she asked him.

'Apparently,' he told her, after a swig of his lager, 'it's a one-act meditation on the meaning of the legend of the Holy Grail in the twenty-first century. It's set on a building site in Beswick.'

They made their way into the interior of the theatre, a small oblong space with several rows of free-standing chairs facing a compact, bare stage. As minimalist as the production seemed, Cassie still felt the excitement of being in a theatre and knowing that some proper grown-ups were going to emerge shortly and act out a story for her. And, lo and behold, the play was about to begin.

A woman walked in with several plastic carrier-bags full of rubbish, put them down and began to remove various items from them, old stockings, McDonald's wrappers, empty shampoo bottles. Her face was expressionless. Then a male actor entered, wearing a suit, carrying a briefcase, and asked her when the next bus to Swinton was. In response she gave him a plastic Spider-man toy, which he examined carefully in silence as the lights focused on it. Then, slowly, he removed his clothes while the woman engaged in a long monologue about her life. She had been born in Highbury, had moved to Richmond, then Kew. She worked for a while in Moorgate then married and settled in Margate until she emerged in ancient Carthage and was consumed in a vast fire. Meanwhile the naked man at her side stretched upwards yearning for something. In the background 'How Much is That Doggy in the Window?' played.

Cassie looked sidelong at Terry. His face was impassive. There was a blackout and the stage was empty. A few stirrings from the other members of the audience denoted the end, and there was a little applause.

'Hmm,' said Terry.

They left the auditorium and headed for the bar. Sensing that Terry was none too impressed, Cassie decided, just for the hell of it, to defend the drama they had just witnessed. 'I can see where they were coming from. Those bags of rubbish contained the detritus of commercialism, and the bus that never comes – very Pinteresque! – is about never feeling we reach completion, and the nakedness is . . . a statement of our fundamental humanity? And Spiderman was a sort of Nietzschean Superman!'

Terry smiled at her, amused. 'Do you want to write the review?'

She ignored him. 'And do you not think that the complete absence of anything like a Holy Grail shows our spiritual emptiness?'

They found a table at the back of the foyer and settled down. Far from trying to fight with her, Terry looked happier than he had all evening and was evidently content to let her witter on. Cassie was quite enjoying herself. 'And what's more,' she continued, 'not having the Holy Grail *in* the play means we're free to find our own Holy Grail, whatever that might be. So the play is ultimately empowering.'

'What's your Holy Grail?' Terry asked.

Cassie thought for a moment. 'Happiness. But happiness is a cop-out, because it's actually the *result* of a successful quest for the Holy Grail. I suppose I want some status in my profession, fun, lots of it, enough money, oh, and health. Health is a prerequisite because without it you can't enjoy anything else.' Cassie found herself getting carried away by her own rhetoric. 'Don't you think that health is really everyone's Holy Grail? We all want to be cured of our illnesses. We want to be whole again. And the preoccupation with health, these days, is just a substitute for religion. In medieval times, since everyone died relatively young, what mattered was dying well. Now we try *not* to die by being as healthy as we can. Not looking after your health is the biggest sin there is. Look at how smokers are treated now – like social lepers. Fat people are lectured to and preached at. Doctors instruct you how much it's safe to drink, and woe betide you if you overstep the limit.' She drained her Chardonnay in a gesture of defiance. She sought Terry's eyes to see how her lecture was received. He was still smiling, but she had a feeling he hadn't heard a word she'd said. 'Terry,' she asked, 'are you OK?'

'Yes,' he said. 'Cassie, will you marry me?'

At first Cassie thought it was a joke, but one look at Terry disabused her of that notion. He had clearly summoned all his courage to ask the question. Cassie panicked because she didn't know what to say in response. Then she was angry because he hadn't prepared her, then inexpressibly moved, then angry again, decided to treat his request flippantly and then realised that would be the worst thing she could do. She remained silent.

'Well?' he prompted her.

'I wasn't expecting this,' she parried.

'I thought not,' he said. 'I reckoned I'd surprise you.'

'What brought it on?' she asked.

'I suppose I'm pretty certain that I want to spend the rest of my life with you. I know we suit each other. You know we suit each other. We've known each other long enough to be sure of that. I can't imagine life without you – and we've both admitted what we feel for each other.'

'But marriage!' Cassie laughed awkwardly.

'Why not? I've nothing against marriage. Just because it didn't work out for your parents doesn't mean it won't work out for us.'

'But the statistics—'

'Sod the statistics. Live dangerously.'

Cassie laughed again, even more uncomfortably. She felt cornered. It was hard to say no to Terry, and there was a fifth column within her that tempted her to say yes, and to hell with it. She lifted her drink and examined the contents.

'And anyway,' he said, 'it's not as if we're spring chickens any more. I reckon it's time to settle down.'

No, it's not! thought Cassie. Not for me, not now. She could hardly breathe.

'So what do you say?' he cajoled.

'I say we should carry on as we are for a bit longer, until I'm more sure of what I want to do.'

'Do you?' he asked. His voice was flat.

'Now I know what you're thinking . . .' she added, lamely. Slowly he shook his head. Cassie wasn't certain what he meant by that. She could feel a vein throbbing in her neck.

'I can't do that, Cassie,' he said.

'Can't do what?'

'Go back to how we were, having a pointless, meandering relationship. I love you, and I feel all the wrong things that go with loving someone, like possessive, selfish, obsessed—'

Cassie smiled. 'I'll still let you feel all those things without marrying me.'

'No – what I'm saying is you have a choice. We either marry – we commit – or we go back to being friends, with the understanding that I'm free to try to find someone else and you are too.'

Terrible prospect! But he was blackmailing her! If she didn't agree to marry him he would leave her. Terry leaving her was worse than her marrying him. It was Scylla and Charybdis all over again. Remembering her Classic-Civilisation A level calmed her a little. The academic Cassie took over and began to argue. 'No, Terry. It needn't be one or the other. You're right, we do love each other. All we're arguing about is the label we're putting on commitment. You say it has to be marriage. I say to choose to be together each day is enough. Maybe we could think about living together.' This was her sop, her compromise.

'No,' he said, after a long pause. 'You're still holding something back by doing that. You're saying you're not prepared to make a public statement of how you feel. You're giving yourself an escape route. *I* don't need an escape route.'

Cassie was feeling desperate again. 'Look, just please give me time! What you've done is not fair. You've thrown this at me. You can't reasonably expect me to give you an answer without having a chance to consider. All I'm saying is, let me go away and think about it. Look, wait until my hospital appointment. Let me see what's going to happen with my gall bladder. Give me till then, and I'll decide once and for all.' She smiled coyly at him. 'And then I'll have lost another half stone.'

'So why is that important?'

Suddenly Cassie was aware of a gulf between them. Why didn't he understand how important it was? And, furthermore, how could she begin to explain it?

'It just *is*, right? It's something I want to do. I've never looked good until now. I want to see what it's like.'

'You look good to me,' he said.

At one side of the ring stood Terry, at the other her burning desire to reinvent herself. He didn't want her to change: as he had admitted earlier, he was possessive and selfish. She wanted to change. He didn't realise how profoundly dissatisfied she was with herself — or, at least, how profoundly dissatisfied she had become with herself recently. 'I need to look good for myself,' she countered.

Terry looked quizzical. She hated the way he could make mincemeat of her ideas with just a lift of his eyebrows. Was what she had said so preposterous?

They were silent for a while, alone in the bar except for the barman polishing glasses and two actors lounging on a bench.

'Well, what's it to be?' Terry asked her.

Cassie was exhausted, and sick of this. 'Give me time – a couple of weeks.'

'Until then,' he said, 'we'll cool it. We'll just be friends, as we were before.'

Cassie saw she had no choice. He had put himself in a position where he could call the shots. Sadly, she agreed to be friends. It occurred to her that she would be lonely. Still, she thought, there was always the gym.

Chapter Eight

It had been a good week right up until this afternoon. Jane had been briefing Siobhan and Garth in her office about the outreach programme when the phone had rung. She had answered it, annoyed at being interrupted, and was jolted when she heard her mother's voice. They were passing through, she said, and would love to take Jane out to dinner. Was she free? Good. They would meet her in Est Est Est at eight.

Jane had not seen her parents since she'd started at Fit Not Fat. There hadn't been any time – or, rather, she'd ensured that there hadn't been any time. Now, hearing her mother's voice, she felt guilty. What kind of daughter was she that she avoided her own parents? And she was an only child at that, all they had. She tried to summon up some pleasure at the idea. 'My parents,' she said to Garth and Siobhan, 'they're coming over.'

'That's nice,' Garth said.

Siobhan said nothing, and Jane felt a spurt of envy. Siobhan lived with her mother and was always getting things from the shop for her, taking her places, and no doubt criticising Jane to her. Siobhan was close to her mother. Then, insanely, she wondered if that had held Siobhan back in her career. Jane was lucky in that her parents had set her free to make her own way. Well, that was one way of looking at it. Now, feeling slightly vulnerable, Jane wanted more from Siobhan than that stony expression. No chance. As ever, Siobhan looked as if the last place she wanted to be was in the office with Jane. Thank God for Garth! He seemed to have an innate gift for knowing how she was feeling. She could almost read sympathy in his smile. Or was that just her imagination?

She had other reasons to be grateful to him too. He had interposed himself the other day when David, the GP, had approached her in the gym for a friendly chat. He had suggested that Fit Not Fat should advertise in his surgery and that Jane herself should bring round some fliers. Maybe, he'd said, he could take her for a drink afterwards.

Jane was torn. It was a superb publicity opportunity, but she had a profound dislike of doctors' surgeries. Since moving here she had not even registered with a GP. She could send Jodie, but that might feel like a snub and he was trying to help her. And the drink was even more problematic. Jane liked David: he was attractive and funny; she could almost imagine getting to know him a lot better. But she had no time for a relationship at present, *and* he was a doctor, which she found off-putting, only she hardly knew why. In the event, she didn't have to give him an answer. Garth had appeared out of nowhere and sidelined the conversation.

Now David was the least of her worries. In a few hours she would be with her parents. And, worse, she wasn't drinking. How on earth would she be able to put up with them without alcohol? On the whole, though, she felt better without the booze and her sleeping had regulated itself. But in the last day or two she had felt slightly odd and today her throat felt tight. Her voice was croaky – but she liked that: she thought it made her sound sexy. She felt a little warm, but that was because of the heating in the club. And the slight trembling in her muscles was caused by the dread – no, anticipation – of seeing her parents again.

*   *   *

They were waiting for her at the bar, and Jane wondered what on earth she had been worried about. After all, they were her parents. Her mother was a neat, smart woman in her sixties but looked ten years younger. Her hair was well-cut so its greyness looked fashionable. Her pale green suit made her look girlish. Her father was twice her mother's height, rangy, spare and almost awkward with energy. They were the sort of just-past-their-prime couple who drew people's eyes. He looked distinguished, while she was still attractive, full of fiery energy. They had magnetism. Jane knew she could never live up to them. Perhaps it was her inadequacies that had soured their relationship, or that they were all so busy. Jane's father ran a car showroom and never seemed to be away from it; her mother worked part-time as a PA but was also secretary of the local branch of the Women's Institute, helped in an Oxfam shop, went to art classes, was learning Italian and jogged every evening.

Jane hugged them with real feeling. From this moment on, she thought, we'll get on perfectly well. It was while I was trying to establish myself in my career that there were tensions. Now it will all be different. She couldn't wait to tell them about Fit Not Fat, about her staff, her plans for expansion, the progress with the café, her trip next week to the over-sixties club, the success of the advertising campaign, and she might even confide in her mother about David. His interest was flattering, after all. The fact that her parents had arranged this meeting signified their interest in her. Didn't it?

'Shall we have a drink first or go straight to the table?' her father asked.

'Let's go straight to the table,' Jane said.

The restaurant was lively that evening. The waiters were joking among themselves and a family party at a nearby table was celebrating someone's birthday. Jane enjoyed the bustle and realised she was hungry. She grinned at her mother, who was studying the menu. So was her father. No response. Better luck next time. The wine waiter came over and her father suggested a Merlot.

'Not for me,' said Jane. 'I'm driving.'

Her father nodded approvingly, but went ahead and ordered the Merlot, with a bottle of sparkling mineral water. He had forgotten that Jane preferred still, but that was because they had lived apart for so long. The ordering completed, he sat back, looking pleased with himself.

'Well, darling, how are you?' her mother asked.

'Wonderful,' Jane said.

'That's nice. Did you know Auntie Irene has been poorly? It turned out to be a middle-ear infection. She said at first she discounted the symptoms – she just had a feeling of fullness in her ear, and buzzing, you know, but then her ear felt damp and there was a yellowy liquid coming out of it. So she went to the doctor and by that time she was in a lot of pain. The doctor said the eardrum looked perforated. I was there at the time so I took her in the car and went back with her to help her with Charles. His spondylitis isn't much better. He has to sit doubled up, you know. They're considering surgery. Who would have thought this would be the result of his back pain? It makes you think – it could happen to anyone. I gave their house a quick spring-clean and popped over to Tesco's so they wouldn't run short. It's lucky your father and I are never ill, are we, Jeremy?'

'Never ill,' he said. 'Runs in the family.'

Jane's throat throbbed so she reached for her water and sipped it. She felt unaccountably guilty, as if she was letting the side down.

'But Mrs Woodward next door has been diagnosed with a goitre! It was terrifying, Jane. She developed a lump in her neck and you can imagine what she thought. But after a thyroid scan and ultrasound they realised what it was. She was relieved, but it wasn't pleasant, I can tell you. I picked her up from hospital after the tests, took her home and put the kettle on. She was so glad I was with her as she was in a lot of discomfort. Ah, good! The starters have arrived.'

Jane prayed her mother would stop talking about illness. It put her off eating. Perhaps she ought to try to change the subject. 'I've been choosing tiles for the café,' she said.

'That's nice,' her mother replied. 'Do you remember when I chose the tiles for Auntie Rita's bathroom and found them half the price at Tiles Direct, and she was prepared to pay an extortionate price at Luigi's? She certainly thanked me for that. They were sea blue, with a splash of white. Did I tell you, Jane, that your father and I are entering a half-marathon on behalf of the NSPCC?'

'Really? That's wonderful.'

'Yes – there aren't many couples in their early sixties who could do that. We're hoping you'll sponsor us. I've brought some forms and perhaps you could put them up around Fitness International.'

'Fitness International?'

'Your club, dear.'

'My club is Fit Not Fat,' Jane said.

'Oh, dear. Well, they're very similar. We obviously want to raise as much money as possible. The local press has picked up on the story and someone is coming round to interview us on Monday evening, and take some pictures. I shall have to get my hair done. Now, Jeremy, you be sure to be home from work.'

He nodded.

'Because your father is incorrigible! He works every hour God sends. Last night he didn't get home until ten o' clock,' she said proudly.

'There was an important sale under way.'

'That's what he says!' Jane's mother laughed. She prodded him in the ribs as if he were a prize bull. 'Lucky I keep myself busy, too. How's your work, dear?'

Jane took a deep breath. There was so much to say it was

hard to know where to begin. 'I think things are going well. There are still teething problems. My second-in-command is still dissatisfied and—'

'Ah, good! Here are the pizzas and Jane's chicken. Make sure mine's the one with anchovies, Jeremy.'

Jane waited until the food had been served. 'So, as I was saying, there are lots of ideas around. On Tuesday I'm visiting an over-sixties club to spread the word and—'

'There's a coincidence. I went to our senior citizens' Wednesday club to talk to them about Oxfam. It was a great success. We got four new volunteers and everybody said I was wonderful. The speaker the previous week had bored them rigid. They said I was very lively and they never believed me when I told them that at my age I was still in paid employment! I told them age was all in your mind. Sometimes I feel I'm as young as you, Jane. Do you remember when I went to your school parents' evening and your French teacher wouldn't speak to me because she thought I was your older sister?'

'I remember that,' Jane's father put in. 'Good pizza. I'm glad I decided to book here. Client recommended it.'

'Well, you eat up,' her mother said. 'Do you know? He gets so carried away at work sometimes he forgets to eat!' She beamed at him. 'Some weeks I hardly ever see him, he gets home so late.' She seemed quite pleased about this.

Jane cut up some chicken and wished she could work as hard as her father.

'He did sixty-three hours last week!'

There was a silence as they all chewed. Jane knew her mother was always full of herself. People were always telling her how lucky she was to have such a talented, lively mother who did so much for others. Last year she had been nominated for Prestburn Woman of the Year but was beaten by a cancer survivor who had cycled the coastline of Great Britain. She was most put out.

Jane put some chicken into her mouth and found it hard to

swallow. What was wrong with her throat? Surely it couldn't be an infection. When she was younger she used to catch throat infections regularly and there had been the glandular fever just before her A levels. Jane's mother had been wonderful, dashing to school to pick up homework, liaising with the doctor, and providing Jane with round-the-clock care. It had been her finest hour as a mother, her sisters had said. Jane had vowed never to be ill again or, if she was, never to let her mother know about it.

'The other thing I have to tell you, Jane, is that your cousin Belinda, who's working in Sydney, has got engaged!'

'That's lovely,' Jane said.

'We might even go out there and stop over in Singapore. I've always wanted to visit the Far East, and I'd hate to miss her wedding. I love weddings.'

Was there something unspoken in the air? Jane felt another twinge of inadequacy. But, then, if she were to get married, it would be yet another arena in which her mother would triumph. She had the oddest sensation, as if her chair and the floor were shrinking. Then she was being pushed and buffeted by invisible forces. Or perhaps she was feverish. Quickly, so that no one would notice, she raised her hand to her head and felt her forehead. Unsurprisingly, she was hot.

'I saw Gina and Liz the other day, Mum,' Jane said. 'Do you remember them?'

Her mother frowned. 'Your school friends? Nice you should still keep in touch. And it's strange you should mention that as Susan and I were thinking the other day it would be fun to arrange a school reunion of Prestburn girls' grammar. I've already rung the school to see if they could open it for us one Saturday. What do you think, Jane? Wouldn't that be a splendid idea?'

'Yes.'

'I think so too. So interesting to find out what everyone has done with their lives. I love nothing more than hearing about other people.'

Jane played about with her food so that her parents would not notice how little she had eaten. For some reason she had no appetite but found her eyes drawn to her father's glass of Merlot. Normally she avoided red wine, but now it teased and enticed her. How much better she'd be able to cope with just one glass. Stone-cold sober, she was assailed by all these awful thoughts about her mother – how she never thought of anyone but herself, how she was hell-bent on admiration, how Jane didn't like her very much. Which was blasphemy, because it was tantamount to not liking herself very much. Terrible thoughts, and then with mounting horror she watched her mother lift the bottle of Merlot and pour herself some, and the dregs into her father's glass. Nothing for Jane. That's it, she thought. As soon as I get out of here I'm having a drink.

'Your cousin Sandra's baby is delightful, Jane, but he's teething. Sandra was convinced he was coming down with something but I explained to her what it was and babysat one evening so she and Trevor could go out. No one should be expected to put up endlessly with a crying baby. They needed a break. So they went to the cinema and I stayed with the baby. It's easier for me – he cried all the time but naturally it didn't upset me as much as it would them.'

Jane hardly listened to her mother's monologue. She was trying to calculate how quickly she could escape. She had done her duty, and needed to get away, best of all with some friends, to talk or not, but certainly to drink. Because she had been dry for nearly a fortnight, which was proof positive that she did not have a drinking problem. Quite simply, she had a parent problem for which the remedy was drink. 'Excuse me,' she said to her parents. Her mother continued explaining something to her father.

Jane slipped into the ladies'. Maybe it was her fault. Maybe she should make allowances for her parents. Maybe she was expecting too much from them. She got out her mobile and dialled. When Liz answered, Jane apologised for interrupting her but wondered if she and Gina were up for a night out. To her delight, Liz seemed interested. Robert was away and she and Gina were fed up with Friday night TV. Jane suggested Space, having remembered Garth's recommendation. They agreed to meet in an hour. The night was young.

Jane tidied herself and returned to her parents. They were deep in the dessert menu. Once they had chosen, she explained that while she had been in the ladies' Liz had rung and asked her to join them in town, because Gina was returning to London soon. Her mother said it was a pity as she had so much more to say. Another time, Jane told her. Guilty and elated, she kissed her parents, and told them once again how well they were both looking. She glanced back as she left Est Est Est and saw her mother search for a waiter to take their order.

Freedom, she thought.

'A double vodka with Slimline tonic,' Jane told the barman. She followed him greedily with her eyes as he turned to get her drink. Why was he being so slow? She had driven straight from the restaurant to town, miraculously finding somewhere to park her car behind Kendal's. Space, as Garth had suggested, was a good place to be. It was loud, noisy and full of the right sort of people, young men in narrow black designer specs, women with almost perfect figures.

The bar itself was, as the name suggested, an empty space, with a metallic bar, metal tables and a bare wooden floor. It was the crowd that gave it a buzz. Gina and Liz had not arrived yet. Music drummed in the background, a counterpoint to the excited chatter from the self-consciously fashionable, and made Jane's ears buzz and vibrate. Her vodka, arrived and she paid for it hastily, then drank with the intensity of the parched traveller at the oasis. With it, she stationed herself near the door to wait for her friends. She decided there and then that she did not want to

talk to them about her parents. It would make her seem pathetic
– and she was just so glad to be away from them that the last
thing she wanted to do was think about them. All she wanted
was to be swallowed up by the music and frenetic conversation
surrounding her. She sipped some more vodka. Bliss.

There they were! Gina and Liz, were sitting on a red velvet
window-seat. How could she have missed them? Eagerly she
made her way towards them. They were deep in conversation.
Gina was wearing leather pants and a top that exposed her
midriff; Liz was more demure, in a short, navy dress that
shouted, 'Expensive!' For a moment Jane felt as if she would
let the side down – it was the residue of what she had
experienced with her parents, the sense of being not quite good
enough. But no – they were her friends. With them she could
relax and let go. She drained her vodka, and greeted them. 'Hi,
you two!' She kissed them both. 'Can I get more drinks?' She
took their order and returned to the bar. Already the vodka was
uncovering a different Jane, carefree, happy, in control. She
watched the barman put her order on a metallic tray, which she
carried carefully to their table. They took their glasses, and in a
moment Jane was hip to haunch with Gina, into her second
double vodka.

'How are you?' Jane asked.

'Never been better,' Gina said. 'I had a phone call today.' Her
voice suggested that Jane should enquire further.

'A phone call?'

'From *City Girl* – you know, the magazine. They liked my
sample column, and want to take me on.'

'That's fantastic!' Jane said, genuinely pleased. This was
wonderful news for Gina. She lifted her glass in a toast. 'To
us,' she said, 'and all our successes.'

'Present and future,' Gina added.

They clinked glasses.

'So, how much are they paying you for the column?' Liz

asked Gina. She had a habit of seeing everything in pounds and pence.

'Four hundred a week initially, so I'd better get writing.'

'Writing about what? You told me before that this was a dating column but you're not seeing anyone,' Liz teased. 'What are you going to do? Make it up?'

'Make it up?' Gina put on a look of mock-horror. 'My dear! Everything I write is absolutely true. It just might not have happened to *me*, that's all.'

'You're not going to write about me and Robert, are you?'

'Not in so many words. But if I do, you won't be out of pocket.'

Jane envied the way Gina and Liz were able to bait each other with such deadly accuracy. She knew that if she made a barbed remark its subject would be mortally offended and never speak to her again. Her philosophy was to be nice to everyone. It meant she took a back seat in situations like this.

'No, seriously, Gina, you're not in a relationship right now. I bet you'll end up writing one of those sad columns about a girl crippled by inadequacies, unable to get her man,' Liz joked.

'Me? Unable to get a man? Well, let's see. Find me a single man I ought to be in a relationship with. There are plenty here.'

Liz surveyed the crowded bar. 'OK. See those two guys over there? The little one with the black specs and black jumper. He looks like the advertising-agency type. Make something happen with him.'

Gina sized up the situation. She rose to her feet and walked over to them. She picked up a menu by their side and stood reading it. Jane was horrified and delighted. Trust Gina to have the confidence to do something like that. She envied her courage and felt swept away by her friend's recklessness. Gina had now finished reading the menu and smiled dazzlingly at the guy in specs, then said, 'Thank you,' and kissed his cheek. She sashayed back to their table. 'That should do it,' she said.

She was right. Jane noticed that both men were taking a more than casual interest in them. Gina, meanwhile, would not even glance at them. Then, as if on cue, she looked up, met the eyes of her target, and smiled so suggestively that Jane was embarrassed. Within a few moments both men had arrived at their table. They started to engage in the usual banter. The man in specs pulled up a chair beside Gina; his friend took up position between Jane and Liz.

'Don't tell me,' Liz shouted over the music, 'you work in advertising.'

'And you're a clairvoyant,' he remarked smoothly.

Liz cast down her eyes demurely. Jane racked her brains to think of something smart and witty — or just smart *or* witty — to say to him, but drew a blank. It hardly mattered: she was too late. He had engaged with Liz. She was the odd one out. Of course, it was all a game, and Liz was content with Robert, and Jane didn't fancy the guy at all — was that a paunch overlapping his trousers? — but, still . . . No one liked being the person left out, the one who was not selected. Jane drained her vodka and wondered if she should suggest another round.

The guy in specs pre-empted her and offered them all a drink. Jane was about to ask for another double vodka but Gina intervened: 'No, sorry. This is strictly a girls' night out.' My friend Liz is celebrating an eight-stone weight loss. You should have seen her a year ago — talk about the *Titanic*! Jane here has just recovered from hepatitis B and needs to take things very slowly. But have my card,' she passed it to him, 'and ring me. After a night out with just the girls and their hormones I could do with some testosterone.'

The men retired, puzzled. 'He'll ring me,' Gina said. 'And I promise I'll let you both know what happens. And all the readers of *City Girl*. But forget them. Let's talk about us. Let's talk about Jane. How are things at work?'

'Oh, yes,' she said. 'Brilliant. Fantastic. Pretty exhausting, of course, as I'm still working long hours, but that will settle down when I've got things running my way.' And Jane realised now that she loved her job, her friends, Space, Manchester, everyone and everything.

'It must be tough,' Gina said, 'managing people. I'm glad I don't have to do that.'

'The trick is to keep your distance,' Liz remarked. 'Shall I get in some more drinks?'

'Yes, please,' said Jane. 'A double vodka with Slimline tonic for me.'

Jane watched her go. Liz looked so self-possessed and sure of herself. Perhaps she ought to consult her about the Fit Not Fat figures.

Gina interrupted the flow of her thoughts. 'You've not said that much about work, Jane,' she said. 'I suppose it's all a bit bewildering to begin with, as you've got to get to know the system and the people.'

'Sure. I reckon I'm getting there. The next stage is to double the membership, buy the adjoining wasteground and build.'

'Then invade Austria,' Gina commented.

'So what's wrong with being ambitious?'

'Nothing at all. Just don't kill yourself in the process. You never seem to be away from that health club. Remember to look after yourself.' Gina gave her an affectionate squeeze.

Jane was piqued. Gina was such a hypocrite, telling her to take it easier while she was probably always at her computer thinking of new angles for features. For one fleeting moment she wondered if this was Gina's cunning ploy to get her to slow down so she could race ahead in the career stakes. Then she dismissed such an unworthy thought. Gina was her friend and nothing like her mother. And they were out on the town and having a brilliant, memorable time. Liz returned with the drinks and Jane reached eagerly for hers. This is medicinal, Jane thought, aware of the buzzing in her ears and the pain in her throat, which was only there when she swallowed. She swallowed again. It was hard to hear Gina and Liz above the hubbub but it didn't matter. She didn't need to hear what they said. She loved them anyway. They understood her. They shared a philosophy, which was . . . which was . . . That nothing much mattered except living for the moment and having the courage to exploit each minute to the full.

'You know,' she shouted at her friends, 'nothing much matters except living for the moment and having something or other.'

Gina grinned at her and Jane wondered if she might have had just a little too much vodka. But that was fine, she needed to relax and let go. Waves of sound washed over her, music and laughing and Gina and Liz's chatter.

'Oh, wow,' said Gina. 'just look at who's walked in!'

'I didn't know men like that actually *existed*,' Liz echoed.

Jane attempted to follow the direction of their eyes. She guessed a local celebrity had arrived, and she tried to work out who it might be from the knot of men standing by the entrance. But it was no celebrity. It was Garth. She was just about to claim him when she stopped herself. A wonderful, perfectly formed plan entered her mind. She was thrilled with her own invention. Here was her chance to make Gina and Liz notice her.

'This one's for me,' she said, and rose unsteadily to her feet. With extreme concentration she wove between groups of drinkers and made her way towards him. Just before she reached him he noticed her and his face broke into a smile of recognition. Jane hoped her friends had not seen that. 'Hi,' she said to him, trying to adjust her smile so that it was controlled yet provocative. She suspected it was just a stupid grin.

'Jane – what are you doing here?'

'Nothing special. Will you take me home?'

'Why? Is something wrong?'

'No,' she said, clinging to his arm for support. It was rock-hard, strong, and safe. 'I just want to go home with you.' Garth placed an arm round her waist. Jane glanced over at Gina and Liz, who looked eaten up with envy. It was all going brilliantly. Now she gazed up at Garth, who smiled down at her, and Jane thought that she might like him very much indeed and what was wrong with living for the moment? So what if he was her employee? No one at Fit Not Fat needed to know. This was simply between him and her — and Gina and Liz.

'I haven't got a car with me,' Garth told her, 'but my place is near enough to walk — it's not far from Piccadilly.'

'Can we get a taxi?' Jane wasn't sure if her legs could carry her even to Piccadilly.

'Sure.'

'I'll just say goodbye to my friends.'

She made her way back to Gina and Liz. Gina made a motion as if she was fanning herself. 'We're going back to his place,' Jane told them. 'Pass me my coat.'

'Take care, Jane, you don't know him,' Liz warned, placing a restraining hand on her arm.

'That's what you think,' Jane said, enjoying the mystery. 'I'll ring you tomorrow.' She reached for her glass and drank what was left at the bottom. 'See you when I see you. And don't worry about me.'

Garth was standing by the entrance. She took his arm proprietorially as the bouncer pushed open the door for them both to exit into the chilly night air. She leant on him as they walked towards Deansgate where there was a row of taxis. The next thing Jane knew was that she was in the back of a black cab with Garth, swaying against him as it did a U-turn and moved off towards Piccadilly. She felt Garth's arm round her waist and had to suppress the desire to laugh. She was being very silly and she knew it. But then, on the other hand, she was stranded: she couldn't possibly drive home, and spending the night on Garth's floor was probably sensible, especially as she was so tired.

It was so kind of Garth to look after her, and it was a funny trick to play on Gina and Liz. She would ask Garth if she could ring them on their mobiles when she got to his flat. Garth was lovely, nice to look at, kind, he understood her, he wasn't Siobhan and he wasn't her mother or her father, just Garth, with full lips that made you want to look at them and see what it felt like to kiss him. And he was someone to hug, who hugged her back, with big, strong arms.

And then she rested her head on his chest and fell asleep.

At first Jane was aware that her mouth was dry and sticky. Then she realised that she had slept with it open, closed it and swallowed, which hurt. The discomfort brought her to consciousness. In an instant she was fully awake.

She was not in her own bed. Her heart racing with alarm, she tried desperately to work out where she was. A light, airy bedroom with white vertical blinds, shut now. A crisp white sheet over her with a navy check duvet, which had fallen to the floor. Garth's room. But where was Garth? Quickly Jane reached for the edge of the sheet and pulled it round her. She forced herself to recall what had happened last night.

She had left the bar with Garth, and her head full of vodka. Gina and Liz had been impressed and worried. So far, so good. Then they had got into a taxi and she had snuggled up to him. Jane's eyes widened at the thought. Had there been a kiss? There might have been. She could only remember his powerful body and the scent of a sharp, modern male fragrance. He had paid the taxi driver and taken her into his ground-floor flat, in a block near Piccadilly, across the road from Argos. It was bright and clean, and she had sunk gratefully and gracelessly on to the sofa. He had come to sit by her. Then what? How had she got into the bedroom?

Her head throbbed as her mind took her inexorably towards

the next step. There had been another kiss, she was sure of it. Who had begun it? She didn't know. The next thing she remembered was telling him that she was very thirsty and needed a glass of water. He had fetched her one. She had knocked it over. He ran back to the kitchen for some kitchen towel. Then she was attacked by a wave of nausea. He was all concern. He took her to the bedroom.

Then what? Her mind was blank. If anything had happened, she had no memory of it. Her body *felt* as if nothing had taken place, and she saw with relief that she was still wearing her bra and knickers. She had a searing pain in her head, that uncomfortable tightness in her throat and her mouth tasted foul. Garth was nowhere to be seen: she had full use of his bedroom. It was possible, and likely, that he had put her to bed and spent the night on the settee.

As the enormity of what she had done dawned on her, Jane trembled with humiliation and self-hatred. Yet again she had drunk far too much and let herself go. Even if she and Garth had not slept together, she had destroyed her authority as effectively as if she had danced naked in front of him. *Had* she danced naked in front of him? She couldn't rule it out. Could he blackmail her? No, he would never stoop so low, not Garth. But how could she retrieve this awful waking nightmare of a situation? She didn't know. She knew nothing except that her head hurt, her limbs ached and she was desperate for water.

She looked around the room, taking the opportunity to study it fully since its owner was not there. It was light and simple. There were white fitted wardrobes with mirrored doors, the bed, some weights lying on the carpet and a desk with computer screen on it. Under the desk were plain, unmarked cardboard boxes, sealed with masking tape. One wardrobe door had been left ajar, and there, too, Jane noticed more boxes. She wondered if he had just moved in. Her clothes had been placed neatly over the back of the chair by the desk. There was the distant sound of traffic and she could hear movement in another room. She flinched at the thought that Garth would see her like this, in his bed in her underwear, with her makeup smudged and her face puffy. There was a hesitant rap on the door.

'Jane?' came Garth's voice.

'Yes?' she croaked.

'Can I get you anything? Coffee?'

'Do you have some orange juice?'

'Sure.'

Jane shot out of bed and examined herself in the mirror. She looked dreadful. She hurried into her trousers and top from the night before, feeling as dirty, decadent and disgusting as it was possible to be. She coughed in an attempt to clear her throat but it was no use. She was a mess, and deserved it all. She adjusted her hair and wiped the excess makeup from her eyes. There was another rap at the door.

'I'm decent,' Jane said, feeling that nothing could have been further from the truth.

Garth entered, with a tray on which stood a jug of fresh orange juice and a single glass. He looked as if he had recently come out of the shower. He was wearing cream-coloured combats, a white T-shirt and his hair was still damp. 'How're you feeling?' he asked.

'Not good.' Jane found she couldn't look at him. This would never do. He was her employee, for goodness' sake. She forced herself to meet his eyes and smile. 'I presume nothing *happened* last night,' she said, her voice husky.

'No.' Garth chuckled. 'You weren't well. I just helped you into bed.'

'Well, thank you very much for looking after me.'

'No problem.'

'I shouldn't have had so much to drink. I'm not really used to it. I've never been a heavy drinker. One drink, and I'm anyone's — no! I mean, one drink, and I do things I regret. As we all do, sometimes.' Jane attempted to recover her dignity and coughed again to clear her throat. She sounded dreadful. Most women, when they were losing their voice, sounded sensual and sexy. She resembled Marge Simpson.

'I understand,' Garth said. 'It can happen to anyone. Lucky I turned up.'

'Yes, it was,' Jane said, grasping at this preferable interpretation of events. 'I was feeling rotten, and there you were. I was desperate to get home but I felt I couldn't leave my friends.'

'And you weren't in any fit state to travel home alone, with that cold coming on.'

'Absolutely! So you brought me back here and let me stay the night.'

Garth nodded, and Jane appreciated him more than ever. Far from taking advantage of her, he was even colluding in a story to save her face. She drank her orange juice, which lubricated her throat and enabled her to make polite conversation. 'You have a lovely place,' she said. 'Have you moved in recently?'

'Fairly,' he said.

'Mind if I have a look round?'

'Be my guest.'

Jane poured herself some more juice, then walked with it out of the bedroom and into the main living area. It was cool and spacious, with pale walls, curiously bare. There were more mirrors, designed to give the illusion of space. She noted the cream leather settee, a slate grey coffee table, a drinks cabinet, a wide-screen television and a window overlooking the courtyard where an artificial fountain played. 'Gosh. I'm envious. I'd love to live in a place like this.' She blushed as she realised the implication of her words. 'I mean, I'd love to move into the city centre. There's more going on – but, then, it's not so convenient for work.'

As she talked she wondered how Garth could afford a place like this when she couldn't. She knew exactly how much he earned, and it wasn't a lot. Still, it was possible he had inherited money, or had been saving. He was a little older than her and had been working for longer. The most unlikely people had a lot of money stashed away.

Suddenly there was a ring at the door and Jane froze, but it was only a courier carrying another large box, which Garth signed for. He whistled as he took it into his bedroom. Of course he was under no obligation to explain what it was — perhaps some clothes from a mail-order company or an Internet site? — but Jane was dying to know.

He emerged from the bedroom, smiling at her. 'Sorry about that,' he said. 'Look, do you want breakfast or what?'

'No – nothing to eat. In fact, I'd better be getting home. Shall I ring for a taxi?'

'Don't bother, I'll run you to your car. I'm on the midday shift this morning.'

'I'd be very grateful.'

Jane was glad they had established their relationship on the old footing. And yet it wasn't on the old footing. Her indiscretions had forged a link between them. It was as if some dotted line connected them. And yet the horrible truth was that he wasn't her type. What was wrong with her that she should fling herself at him?

This was what was wrong with her: she should have never drunk so much. From now on, she would forgo alcohol and work harder than ever. Nothing quite felt so tempting at that moment as work: cool, dispassionate, hard work. Garth picked up his keys. 'Shall we be off?'

'Yes,' she said. 'Lucky it's the weekend. I feel dreadful.'

'You need a rest,' Garth said, tenderly, it seemed to Jane. 'You work very hard. Promise me you'll spend most of the weekend in bed.'

'I will,' said Jane. 'Thank you.'

'I haven't done anything to deserve your thanks.' He paused.

Jane wondered if he was flirting, and realised, with a sinking heart, that he had every right to. She had been an utter fool. 'Come on. Let's be going,' she said.

'Are you sorted?'

She picked up her bag and jacket from the side of a chair. 'I am. Let's go.'

Chapter Nine

'It's heaving in here,' Lynda said. 'It's like the sales at Marks and Spencer!'

This happy thought seemed to reconcile her to having given up her free afternoon to accompany Cassie to the hospital for her check-up, but it did little to reassure Cassie. She had hoped to be in and out quickly. Although she was fairly sure that the consultant would be pleased with her weight loss and four-month-long lifestyle change, there was no saying what his decision would be. She had played over all the possibilities in her mind. 'I'll think we'll take out your gall bladder just to be on the safe side.' Or 'You can keep your gall bladder for now, as long as I can see you every three months for the rest of your life.' And so on.

She and Lynda joined the queue for the desk where Cassie had to announce her arrival. The hospital's central lobby reminded her of an airport concourse, and the reception desks, labelled with consultants' names, rather like check-in counters. Cassie ruminated on this discovery: she was as nervous of flying as she was of anaesthesia; both seemed unacceptably risky. And airports processed you in the way hospitals did: departure lounge, departure gate and the aeroplane itself, compared to arrivals, consultants' waiting area, the nurse, then the consultant

– usually a man just as pilots were still generally men. Your life in *his* hands.

As ever, it calmed her to be analytical. In fact, she told herself, hospitals were fascinating places. She thought about all the people in them and the way their lives had collided at moments of personal crisis, hundreds of dramas playing themselves out, with the last act in the operating theatre. In her case, she hoped not. And yet perversely, fearful as she was, and so tense that she had been in and out of the loo all morning, there was something about hospitals that cheered her.

What was it? That there was a relief in facing the worst? No. Rather it was the way that people rallied round others to resolve a problem. Whereas striving for success often brought out the worst in human nature, adversity brought out the best. The hospital authorities had refurbished Outpatients to make it as bright and cheery as possible – a bit like painting the condemned cell in pink and yellow – and the administrative staff behind the reception booths and the orderlies pushing trolleys full of patients' notes were as smiling as aeroplane stewards. At any moment she expected to be offered a drink with a tiny packet of peanuts. Which, now she came to think of it, was rather a good idea. She might suggest it to the hospital management.

She reached the booth where she handed her appointment card to the receptionist, who was predictably cheerful. She turned and rooted through a trolley until she found Cassie's notes, checked her address and, directed her to another waiting area, where she must sit until her name was called.

Lynda followed her and they took seats along a corridor opposite a painting of mountains and a lake. 'Thank you for coming with me,' Cassie said.

'Don't mention it! I know how nervous you're feeling. It's awful going to the hospital by yourself. When Dad had that pain in his stomach we all went to A and E with him. It turned out to be a blockage due to constipation – do you remember?

It was a nightmare weekend as Hannah developed thrush in her mouth as well. Then I came with Auntie Myra after she'd had her fall. We were scared she'd had a stroke but the soles of her slippers had worn away and that was why she tumbled down the stairs. Then when Candice from Admissions found a lump in her breast we—'

'Lynda, do we have to talk about illness?'

Lynda looked taken aback. 'Not if you don't want to.'

'I don't,' Cassie said. 'How are your children doing at school?'

'Josh's reading's picked up this term and the headmistress told us at the parents' evening – we didn't get to speak to his teacher as she was off with a frozen shoulder – that he was above average in maths, although he missed the tables' test when he was off with a tummy-bug. It's been going round Hannah's class too. It's much worse for the little ones because they don't know when they're going to be sick. I remember the time we had both of them in the back of the car—'

'I think I'll stop you there,' Cassie said – Lynda was as bad as a retired army general for recounting tales of battles lost and won.

They jumped when a nurse called loudly, 'Cassandra Oliver!'

'That's me!' Cassie said, and they rose to follow another orderly into the recesses of the hospital. Cassie felt her heart pound. She was being led further and further away from safety and the outside world. People sat along corridors looking uncomfortable and resigned.

'If you just sit here until you're called,' said the nurse.

Cassie wondered why no one ever explained what you were waiting for or how long you would sit there. It increased anxiety exponentially, and underlined the authority of the consultant and his minions: he had you at his beck and call.

Lynda was looking about her, orienting herself. You felt compelled to do that in a hospital. First, you looked around to see if anyone was *really* ill, and tried to guess what might be wrong with them – since Cassie's consultant was a general surgeon, it was impossible to narrow down what her fellow appointees might be suffering from. You tried to work out how many people were likely to be seen before you, and thereby calculate the possible waiting time. Then you glanced at the posters about the room, tried to regulate your shallow breathing, and discovered it was impossible to concentrate on anything – no one was reading, few people were talking – and tried desperately to distract yourself.

'Lynda,' Cassie said, 'how did you feel when Merton proposed to you?'

'I thought, about time too.'

'Hmm,' said Cassie.

There was a pause.

'Why?' asked Lynda, sniffing something of interest.

'No reason.'

'Who's been proposing to you, Cassie? Not Terry? Terry! Well, *mazeltov*! When's the wedding?'

'Hold on, I haven't said yes.'

'Explain, please.'

'It's a big step. I'm thinking about it. Well, OK, I haven't been thinking about much else. It's just that I can't see why we couldn't just carry on as we have been doing, with freedom, and space, and things like that.'

'Don't you want children?' asked Lynda, as if she was questioning someone from another country.

'Not at my age. Which takes away a reason for getting married. At least, I think I don't want children. As a university tutor I get to see what they turn out like in the end.'

'Do you love Terry?'

'Oh, yes, sure, but you don't have to marry someone because you love them.'

'But what about security, and waking up in the morning with someone and making decisions together and not being lonely?'

'Well, I—'

'Cassandra Oliver!'

Cassie jumped at the sound of her name, and turned to see another nurse standing in the doorway of a consulting room. Immediately she rose to obey the summons, and followed the nurse into her den, feeling the walls close in on her.

The nurse asked her to confirm her name again and also asked for her address to check it against her records. It occurred to Cassie that she had missed her last chance of escape — had she pretended to be another Cassie Oliver of a different address she could have got away scot-free. But it was not to be. Already the nurse was asking for her specimen. Shamefacedly Cassie fumbled in her bag and brought out a bottle wrapped in a brown paper-bag and handed it over as if she was involved in some drugs deal. As the nurse went over to the sink to do whatever nurses did with other people's wee, Cassie looked everywhere but at her. 'Fine,' said the nurse. 'Now, if you'll just hop on the scales.'

Why was it people always asked you to *hop* on to the scales? Did you weigh less on one leg? Disobediently Cassie *stepped* on and waited to see the needle move to somewhere around the thirteen-stone mark. It didn't. It gave up at eleven stone. Cassie was astonished. She felt dislocated, as if she wasn't herself any more. Where had the rest of her gone?

'Oh, that's good!' said the nurse, who was quite buxom. Did Cassie detect a note of envy in her voice? 'You've lost two stone. Mr Ali *will* be pleased!'

Cassie felt mutinous. She hadn't lost weight to please a man, even if that man was a consultant surgeon. She had lost weight initially because she was scared of having her gall bladder out, and she had continued to lose weight because . . . because it was impossible to stop once you'd started. Everyone praised you, your clothes swam on you, you felt brave, you had will-power, you saw yourself re-entering the human race — or at least that segment of the human race that cared about image, which was the bulk of it. Where would it all end?

After a few more formalities the nurse took Cassie back outside. Those had been just the preliminaries. The man himself would see her shortly.

'Well?' asked Lynda.

'Nothing. That was only the nurse. I have to wait again before I see the consultant.'

'Cheer up. It shouldn't be too long now.'

This was probably true, although time had become meaningless to Cassie. Lynda had opened her handbag and was reapplying her lipstick. Illogically Cassie resented that. Opposite her were a middle-aged man and woman: he was entertaining her with some anecdote that made her smile from time to time. Cassie assumed they were married: they had a sort of comfortable familiarity. Just then, imagining Terry by her side, someone who belonged to her, unlike Lynda, whom she had just borrowed, she wondered whether she should have greeted his proposal with more enthusiasm. Marriage, after all, was specifically formulated to encompass sickness as well as health. Sitting here in the hospital reminded her of what really mattered. Marriage was two people sticking together through thick and thin. Terry had offered to be by her side for ever. Had she been a fool to hold him off like that? When this appointment was over, whatever the outcome, should she ring him, and tell him yes, she would marry him?

'Cassandra Oliver!' This time the sound of her name dispersed all thoughts of Terry to the far corners of the earth. The Day of Judgement had come. After this a wedding ceremony would be plain sailing.

Lynda squeezed her hand. 'Good luck,' she said. 'Lie back and think of England.'

'Shut up,' Cassie said, and smiled, ingratiatingly, she hoped, at the dapper Mr Ali.

She entered his consulting room and he shook her hand as if they were meeting at a dinner party. He had a firm, smooth hand, and Cassie did not trust him an inch.

'And how have you been getting on?' he asked her.

'Fine. Wonderful. I haven't had a day's illness since I last saw you. Fighting fit.'

'Hmm.' Mr Ali consulted her records. 'That's a good weight loss.'

'Yes! I've been working out at the gym. Three times a week. Bikes, steppers, treadmills – you name it, I've done it. And I don't eat fat. Well, hardly ever.'

He smiled at her approvingly. She was winning. She eyed the door and wondered how soon she could escape.

'I just need to have a look at your tummy.'

Tummy? The word made her feel six again. Was he being patronising or trying to calm her by reverting to baby-talk? Cassie hitched herself up on to the consulting table and lay down on the paper cover. Mr Ali came at her, beaming, smug with power. His head was two feet above hers. Her midriff was exposed to public view. The nurse who had weighed her earlier stood in one corner of the room (in case she bolted?). Mr Ali put his cool, unsympathetic hands on to her stomach and *felt*. Cassie hated knowing that he had more information about her than she had, information that was literally at his fingertips. He pressed gently and Cassie waited breathlessly for his verdict.

'OK,' he said. 'You can sit up now.'

Cassie did, eagerly.

'I don't think I need to see you again.'

'Sorry?'

'You're discharged. As long as there isn't any recurrence of your symptoms there's no need to do anything.'

Cassie wanted to hug him, or at least give him a high five. No, she wanted to hug him. He was the best consultant surgeon in north Manchester – no, in the North-west, in England, the world, the universe. He was a charming, utterly delightful man. In fact, it was a pity that he would never see her again. Her life would be the poorer for not having the company of such a distinguished and wise physician. She grinned at him, as happy as a condemned man given a last-minute reprieve.

'So that's it,' she said, still not trusting her luck.

'That's it.'

'You mean I don't have to have my gall bladder out?'

'Not at present, no.'

'Because I never wanted to waste NHS resources in the first place – I'm perfectly healthy, really. No, that's great. Right. Well. Thank you very much. Can I go now?'

'Yes.' He really was one of the most charismatic men Cassie had ever met.

She went to the door and bade him farewell.

'Remember,' he said to her, 'you still have gallstones.'

'I will,' Cassie promised.

And she was out, free, no longer ducking and diving to avoid the surgeon's knife. Her life could carry on just as it had before. Except it couldn't. Because she couldn't imagine not going to Fit Not Fat, would never eat fatty foods again *just in case*, and she had to make up her mind about Terry.

Lynda brightened when she saw her. 'Are you OK?'

'Never better! I'm discharged.'

'Wonderful!'

'Come on!' Cassie said, and taking Lynda by the arm, marshalled her out of the waiting area, out of the Outpatients lobby, into the bay where taxis disgorged their passengers, and on to the road where Cassie had parked her car. The cool air and the soothing sounds of traffic elated her still further. She prattled on to Lynda, recounting the tale of her few brief moments with the consultant.

'What are you going to do to celebrate?' Lynda asked her, at a break in the monologue.

Cassie consulted her watch. It was a quarter past three. 'I'm not sure. I said I'd see Terry later tonight, but I have all this free time.'

'Shop,' said Lynda.

'I've been to Sainsbury's this week.'

'No, I mean *shop*. Get yourself something new to wear. Something sexy.'

'Come with me,' Cassie said.

'I'd love to but I can't. I have to get the children from school.'

So, reluctantly Cassie drove Lynda to her house and thanked her over and over again for coming with her. Lynda's idea had taken root. Cassie decided she would hit town and buy herself something to wear for this evening. It seemed the right reward for all her hard work.

As she drove into town she became increasingly demob-happy. She was not a patient any more. She was restored to full human status. She felt as frisky as a kitten and young again – no longer fair, fat and nearly forty, but fair and thirty-something, a different kettle of fish altogether. Kittens? Fish? Mixing metaphors was hardly important at a time like this. She was more cheerful than any order of animal you might care to mention.

She drove into the multi-storey car park and found a space easily. It was evidently going to be one of those days when everything was going to fall smoothly into place. She was soon in Market Street and revelled in the bustling commercial atmosphere it exuded. Here were shantyesque stalls with traders selling witty novelties and Manchester United tea towels – how wonderful to live in Manchester and be able to lay claim to such a successful football team! And look at the tired but happy shoppers resting on the thoughtfully provided benches! The smell of the burgers they were eating was the bass note of the symphony of Market Street, and the cries of the mother disciplining her offspring added to its human comedy. The eagerness of the *Big Issue* sellers, and the determination of the

Socialist Workers to change the world delighted her. She admired the courage and creativity of the boy who walked past her covered in piercings. She looked at the urban flowers — empty McDonald's milkshake containers, crushed Coke cans, tiny cigarette stubs — scattered on the pavement and thought how wonderful it was to be in a city, in the midst of everything, to feel part of the beating heart of humanity, to be alive, and the man in the Rasta hat turned on his ghetto-blaster and demonstrated — just for her delight — a mechanical dog.

She made her way to Evans and looked in the window, wondering what she wanted. And then she paused. Would Evans' sizes fit her any more? What size was she now? It was possible she might find something to wear in a normal shop. Then it occurred to Cassie that she didn't have a clue where to start. As an outsize woman, her choice of clothes shops had been strictly limited. There were Evans, Rogers and Rogers, Ann Harvey, she knew them all, but now she was excluded from them, ejected from the Garden of Eden. She had to compete in Top Shop and Dorothy Perkins along with the rest.

She went to Dorothy Perkins first, and tried on a pair of grey trousers in a size sixteen. She had suspected they might be a little tight, but they were not. In fact, there was room around the waistband. Astonishing! Cassie went back to where she had found them and took a fourteen. She eased herself into them gingerly and attempted to do up the buttons in the front panel. It was a stretch but she succeeded. She was in a pair of trousers that were size fourteen.

It was a moment to be savoured. She could not remember a time when she had been a stock size. Fourteen. It sounded positively girlish. She examined herself in the changing room mirror and saw that the trousers fitted too tight, to justify a purchase now, but they would probably be fine in a month or so. Amazing. Weird. Cassie gave them to the assistant and stepped out of the shop, elated and feeling traitorous. She had defected from the safe world of big women, who shopped at Evans, made jokes about their size to hide their vulnerability, and comforted the rest of the world by being larger than everyone else. Cassie had been happy to be fat, was happier still to be slim, yet felt perversely that she had lost something more than her weight. A badge of political correctness? A barrier? A protective layer? A figure that stuck two fingers up to the money-making image-conscious fashion industry? But, hey, why worry? She was size fourteen!

She entered Next. It was an Aladdin's cave of sensory delights. She examined trousers, blouses, and then remembered Lynda's words: 'Buy something sexy.' Sexy? Cassie thought first of fishnet stockings and suspenders but realised this was not what her friend had meant. She wondered whether she ought to buy a short skirt. Now that she was somewhere between a fourteen and a sixteen this should be relatively easy. She sorted through the rail of black skirts. Curiously, it was not so simple. There were one or two eights, legions of tens, a sprinkling of twelves but sixteens were like gold dust, and even fourteens were thin on the ground. Cassie began to realise that it was only the very large and the very small for whom clothes shops catered. She was now an in-betweenie, neither one thing nor another. Neither Next nor Evans, an ex plus-size refugee. She was a little sorry for herself, and eventually decided to try the sole skirt with any chance of fitting her, the size fourteen. Feeling daring, she picked up a creamy silk blouse to go with it.

Once in the changing room she put on the skirt. It was too tight around the hips and would ride up revealingly when she sat down. The blouse was a sixteen and fitted — just. The buttons fastened but the material stretched suggestively over her bust, emphasising it dramatically. It had a plunging neckline that almost dissuaded Cassie from buying it, until she remembered Lynda's words again. Perhaps they had the skirt in a sixteen. Cassie left her cubicle and was about to ask the girl at the entrance to the changing rooms if she could run out and get a bigger size. At that moment she saw Garth.

For seconds she couldn't place him – he was wearing a smart business suit, which threw her – but then an image of him in his sunflower yellow sweatshirt came to mind and she knew exactly who he was. He turned then, saw her, and smiled in recognition. Cassie grinned back, delighted to have the attention of someone like Garth in such a public place. She hoped everyone was watching. To make things even better, he came over to her. 'Hi,' he said. 'Out shopping?'

It was obvious that she was, but Cassie felt she could hardly expect intellectual acuity as well as such breathtaking male beauty. 'I sure am. It's a treat – I've just had some good news.'

'What news?'

'I've been discharged from hospital. I don't need to have my gall bladder out. It's mainly thanks to the gym,' Cassie said, giving credit where credit was due.

'Fantastic,' said Garth. He was smiling at her almost protec-tively, it seemed to Cassie. They were positioned between a rail of blouses and a stand with bracelets and earrings. She hoped people might think Garth was her husband or lover. She smiled up at him almost flirtatiously. 'That is good news!' he said. There were laughter lines at the corners of his mouth. Cassie supported herself with one hand on the blouse rail.

'I like what you're wearing,' he said, his eyes on her cleavage. She resolved instantly to buy the blouse.

'Have you got a lot more shopping to do?' he asked.

'Not really. I'm just killing time.'

'Kill some with me. I'm after a coffee. Do you fancy one?'

'Yeah. Why not?' Cassie felt herself redden. 'I'll just get changed.' Not believing her luck, she went back into the changing room.

Standing in her bra and knickers in the cubicle, Cassie wondered what had prompted Garth's invitation. He was being matey – it was impossible that a man like him should fancy her, despite the weight loss: she was probably at least ten years older than him. And with his looks he could take his pick of the entire female population. She had better stop being silly and go back to worrying about Terry. This was only a pleasant interlude – the sort of interlude, she thought to herself, that a married woman couldn't, or shouldn't, have. Which was something to be thought about later. Now she would live for the moment.

She took the blouse to the till and looked around in case Garth had changed his mind, but he was still there, lounging by the sale rail. Cassie fumbled with her credit card at the till, stealing glances at him. For reasons she would have to analyse later, their relationship seemed to have altered. Acknowledging each other out of the gym suggested a friendship that extended beyond it. And she might as well admit to herself that she found him very attractive – who wouldn't? It made her feel special, too, to have won his friendship. Please, please, thought Cassie, silently addressing him, don't sit me down with an espresso and tell me all about your girlfriend. Let me hang on to my fantasies a little longer. She joined him at the entrance to the shop, and together they walked down to the Exchange Arcade.

They took a table outside the coffee shop facing Cross Street. Cassie insisted on paying. 'This is my thank-you,' she said. 'If it wasn't for your encouragement, I might have needed an operation after all.'

'Don't mention it,' Garth said. She insisted he had a pastry too and he chose one sprinkled with sultanas. He had a mocha, and she an espresso. Cassie realised it was going to be up to her to make the conversational running. She must spur him on as he had her in the gym. 'What are you doing in town?' she asked. 'I noticed the suit.'

He looked down at himself. 'Yes,' he said. 'I've been seeing clients today.'

'Clients?' Cassie was puzzled.

'I've started L8 counselling,' he told her, between forkfuls of pastry.

For a moment Cassie thought he'd said Relate and had difficulty imagining him solving marital disputes – it was more likely he would be the cause of them. 'Sorry?'

'Don't you remember I told you I was looking into selling L8s? Here, help me finish this off. A little won't do you any harm.' He brandished a forkful of pastry at her and she took it in her mouth. Perhaps it was the sugar rush that made her suddenly feel so light-headed.

'L8 is short for di-enzyme co-provamol L8. It's a nutritional supplement. It releases extra energy from your food and boosts the immune system. It was discovered by a homeopath living and working in Africa. There are signs that it melts cholesterol too. I've just completed my training and I'm qualified to sell it.'

'So it's something you can get over the counter?'

'Not exactly,' he said. 'L8 comes under the umbrella of alternative medicine. It's still being tested in the USA but in some European countries it's freely available. All the signs are that it really delivers.'

'But what about side effects?'

'It's a naturally occurring substance. The side effects are minimal. There are well-documented cases of Africans eating the plant extract containing it and living for well over a hundred years. I've arranged to go to a conference shortly where scientists are going to pool their knowledge so far. It's the next wonder drug. It slows ageing too.'

'That sounds like hype to me.'

'No,' said Garth, in mock-earnestness. 'Really I'm eighty-six.'

They laughed. Cassie was glad to see he had a sense of humour. It reminded her of Terry. But forget Terry – he had an annoying habit of popping up where he wasn't wanted.

'So are they very expensive, these L8s?'

Garth nodded ruefully. 'Yes, because at present they have to be imported. Sixty pounds for a thirty-day supply. But the price will drop when the formula can be manufactured artificially.'

'And they work?' Cassie was dubious.

'They work,' Garth said. 'Trust me.' Then he smiled at her, a long, fond, lingering smile.

It took Cassie's breath away. She had seen men look at women like that in romantic films. But this was crazy. There was no way he was interested in her in any way but as a prospective client for L8s. He was trying to sell her something, that was all. 'I'm not interested in L8s,' she said, testing him.

'I thought you wouldn't be. Intelligent women like you are trained to be sceptical, and that's good! Anyway, you don't need them. You're doing well enough without them.' Again, that look. It stopped Cassie in her tracks.

'I've been watching the History Channel,' Garth said next.

He'd remembered their conversation at the coffee morning! Cassie tried and failed to hide her pleasure.

'Yeah, I have,' he continued, 'but it's mainly about the Second World War and stuff like that. Not so much on the Middle Ages.'

'That's because they didn't have many TV cameras then!' she said brightly.

He laughed. Garth had a disarming little boy's laugh, an infectious chuckle, that made a woman feel she was witty, in control and capable of giving pleasure.

'I'll try to find you something to read, but to be honest, I find it hard to think you're really interested in history, when there are so many other things to occupy you. Women, for a start.' Cassie was fishing.

'Women? Sure. But you'd be surprised how difficult it is to find the right one. I work with a lot of women who care about their figures but that's it. I want more than just good looks. It's hard to put into words what I mean.'

'You mean you want depth, commitment, a meeting of true minds.' Cassie was engrossed, her chin propped on her hand.

'Yes! You've put it very well. Like, there are other things that matter – caring for each other, give and take.'

Cassie nodded assiduously. 'I bet women throw themselves at you,' she said.

'Just the other night,' Garth said, almost to himself, and changed the subject. 'Are you in a relationship, Cassie?'

She paused before answering then chose her words carefully. 'Kind of. Not exactly. I suppose you could call it an open relationship at the moment.'

'So you're free to go out with other people?'

'I think that's how he sees it.' She knew she was being dishonest but, boy, did it feel good. Never in her life had she been naughty. Frumpy Cassie had not been tempted to stray. At last she had an opportunity to be thoroughly wicked. 'I'm not really into commitment – I think,' she added hastily, remembering her earlier deliberations in the hospital.

There was a moment or two of silence as they watched two teenage girls walk through the arcade, both talking on a mobile phone.

'This is nice,' Garth said. 'Our coffee bar at Fit Not Fat will be finished soon. We must do this again.'

'Yes,' said Cassie, sorry that this stolen half-hour was coming to an end.

'I was only having a break from my counselling. It's my day off from Sunnybank, and I've got several more appointments. Quite a few of my clients are interested in L8s as it helps weight loss. The effects can be quite dramatic. It has appetite-suppressant qualities and increases energy levels.'

'It aids weight loss?'

'Sure.'

'You know, I might be interested in it.'

'Don't let me put any pressure on you.'

'No, no, you're not. But perhaps we could talk about this again.'

'Yeah. Soon.'

They stood up and, to Cassie's surprise, he put out his hand to shake hers. She responded to his strong, friendly grasp. Did he hold her hand for just a little too long, or was it her fevered imagination?

' 'Bye,' he said.

Cassie, and one or two other women, watched him depart. Her mind and pulse were racing. What had all that been about? He had given definite indications that he liked her—*her*, Cassie Oliver, old enough to be his mother! Well, maybe not mother, perhaps elder sister, or junior aunt, certainly his teacher. And Garth, Fit Not Fat's senior trainer, no less! She strode down the arcade and into the square oblivious of the *Big Issue* sellers and some music students trying to supplement their loans with some high-quality busking.

Life was very, very odd. Cassie had always imagined that her fate was to end up with second-rate men. Nice men, but men with flaws — pot bellies, big egos, hairy backs, whatever. How would she react if she was propositioned by a first-rate man? Would her prudishness vanish in a puff of smoke? If someone like Garth wanted to go to bed with her, would she discard every inhibition? Every scrap of pride?

She had always thought her body, its pleasures and needs, was the least important part of her. Intellect mattered, ethics mattered, but the body was a lower priority. Perhaps this was an idea she had developed from the medieval philosophers she'd read. But no, much medieval Christianity was concerned with humiliating the body — flagellation, hermits' cells — precisely because church leaders were aware of the power of the body and its appetites. The body mattered.

Only I'm not a medieval Christian, Cassie told herself. I think I'm pagan through and through. She stopped by St Ann's Church, uncertain where to go next.

Manchester was busy now and she glanced at her watch. It was five o'clock, and she had not arranged with Terry where to meet. In her present state she hardly felt as if she could see him. Although she had done nothing, she wanted to come down to earth and reassemble herself. How long would that take? At least twenty-four hours. She decided to try postpone their evening out.

She found a spot with a good signal and dialled his number. 'Hi, Terry. Excellent news! I've been discharged. No operation for me!'

'That's fantastic, Cassie.'

'Look, I'm ringing from the middle of Manchester – I've been shopping and I'm all in. Can we postpone our celebration till tomorrow?'

A silence. At first Cassie thought the network had disconnected them and she checked her phone to make sure.

'You were going to give me your decision tonight,' came Terry's voice.

Cassie prickled with embarrassment, hating herself. 'I know, but so much has gone on today, I find I'm still not ready to—'

Now the phone really was cut off. Cassie swore inwardly and tried to reconnect. She reached the answering service. Wherever she tried to ring him, the result was the same. She presumed he had switched off his phone. All the euphoria drained from her. She had taken one liberty too many. Terry had gone. She had lost him. As soon as she thought that, the absurdity of it hit her. Terry would never leave her. She was being uncharacteristically melodramatic. Even if he had left her, she could get him back. Cassie without Terry didn't make any sense. He would recognise that, surely.

She tried his number again. Still that same, soulless, computerised Stepford wife telling her to leave a message. Perhaps we both need time to calm down, Cassie thought.

Chapter Ten

There were four or five tired-looking people huddled by the door of Fit Not Fat when Jodie approached at seven in the morning, keys in hand. They were the earlybirds. Jodie enjoyed seeing the contrast between their just-got-out-bed selves and the dynamic business people they turned into after half an hour in the gym and a makeover in the showers. They greeted her and she unlocked the main doors, turned off the alarm and switched on the interior lights.

While they were changing, she opened up the gym and turned on each piece of equipment. Then she got the music system going as the first earlybird entered the gym with a cursory nod and made for one of the bikes. Jodie knew it was OK to leave the gym, so she skipped upstairs to the jacuzzi to test the chlorine and PH levels.

She was feeling much happier although, oddly enough, things in her life had taken a turn for the worse. Well, not so much in her life as in Darren's. Yesterday afternoon while he was playing rugby someone had landed on top of him and he had fallen awkwardly and hurt his ankle. He was sure it was a torn ligament but the doctor would confirm that this morning. He had rung her to cancel their date, but Jodie had asked him if he'd like her to pop round and see him anyway. Yes, he had said, in a small, pathetic voice. Her heart had gone out to him. Men were so sweet when they were poorly. And when she arrived at his flat he was clearly making an effort to be brave for her. She had appreciated that. He managed a tight smile before he grimaced involuntarily. He had propped his foot on a stool and Jodie could see the swelling. When she went to stroke his ankle she must have touched it too heavily because he groaned with the pain.

She asked if there was anything she could do for him. Nothing, he had said. Except he hadn't eaten so maybe she would put some chips in the oven and fry some eggs. Oh, and fetch him the remote from the coffee table so he could change channels if he needed to. And bring him over his mobile as he was expecting some calls. She did all that gladly because, of course, he could hardly be expected to move. She noticed that every time she passed him on her errands he was wincing with the pain but trying not to show it. However, television was a good distraction because she spotted that when she was not there, cooking in the kitchen, he didn't look as if his ankle bothered him at all.

After he had had supper she suggested to him that they should go to A and E at the local hospital to get his ankle X-rayed. To her surprise he looked horrified, but immediately offered another brave smile and said, no, he didn't think it was bad enough. Jodie had pointed out the doctors could rule out any serious damage and the nurse would bind it properly for him. No, he said, he could wait till the morning. When she suggested it for the third time he got quite angry, and she could see how important it was for him to be brave in front of her. She dropped the idea of hospital and suggested instead that he take some heavy-duty ibuprofen. Darren had said that lager would be just as good, and cajoled Jodie to go down to the off-licence and get some in. She did that willingly enough. Later on he got quite amorous but even while he was kissing her, he said, 'Ow!'

occasionally, or 'Careful not to go anywhere near my ankle!' When she had left him to go home, as she was on early shift, he hadn't wanted her to leave, and she had felt torn. However, she knew that Kev and Jimmy would be back from the pub soon and they could help him if necessary.

When she had got home she had told her mother all about his injury and how much pain he was in, and described how brave he was being. For some reason her mum found this funny and said, 'Just like your dad,' except her dad had never injured his ankle. Still, she wasn't going to puzzle over that. It was cool to be needed by Darren and, secretly, she was glad he had injured himself, as long as he got better quickly, and even though she knew he had to see the doctor today she was feeling good. She couldn't see the point of taking those evening-primrose oil capsules Siobhan had got her. They looked too big to swallow anyway.

When she got back to the gym she was pleased to see Jane there in her workout gear, about to ascend a treadmill. 'Are you feeling better?' she asked her.

'Yes, much!' Certainly Jane's voice was almost back to normal. Jodie had been quite worried about her. She'd been fighting a throat infection for a couple of weeks and Jodie reckoned she hadn't given it a chance to get better. She had been working all hours, filling in for absentees, liaising with the decorators in the café, studying the latest fitness research. As Jane began to run Jodie could hear sounds that suggested the work-men had arrived to carry on with the installation of the café kitchen. It was going to be state-of-the-art, apparently, with Italian coffee machines and a juice extractor. Jane had chosen a tiled floor and marble tables, elegant but ultra-modern. Jodie couldn't wait to see it all finished. No other health club nearby would have anything like it. The suddenly she had an idea. What they ought to do was hold a competition to publicise the opening – say, the person who clocked up the most steps on the stepper would win free coffee for a year! It was a brainwave! When Jane had finished her workout Jodie explained her idea. Her boss smiled encouragingly. 'Say free coffee for a month, maybe. You get to work on it.'

'I can print something out on the computer today. Oh, but we're short-staffed. No, we're not — Garth's back today. But Darren's off, of course, and Marcia's put her back out.'

'It's OK. It doesn't have to be done right away,' Jane said. 'By the way,' she paused and wiped her forehead with her towel, 'Garth's had quite a bit of time off recently. He's used up nearly all of the holiday time he had owing to him. Any reason that you know of?'

Jodie tried to recall the conversation they'd had in the Portakabin the other day. 'He said it was some kind of business. I don't know what business. He doesn't tell us much about his private life. Not because we don't ask him!'

Jane seemed pleased by that, Jodie thought. 'So he doesn't tell you much about his private life,' she repeated cheerfully.

'No. Do you mean about his girlfriends and that? He doesn't say much to me and Siobhan. I don't know what he tells Darren and Andrew, but I think his friends aren't really from Fit Not Fat. Of course, women are crazy about him. Quite a lot of the clients make eyes at him. He's a bit old for me.' Then a light went on in Jodie's mind. Did Jane fancy him? How could she find out? 'I don't think there's a woman in his life right now,' she continued. She tried to think of a subtle way to find out if Jane had feelings for him, an indirect comment that might lead to her boss admitting more than just a friendly interest in her senior instructor.

'Do *you* fancy him?' Jodie asked Jane.

'Jodie! Don't be ridiculous!' Jane tossed her head angrily.

Ouch! thought Jodie. But she was reluctant to dismiss the idea. How cool would it be if Garth and Jane got it together!

Jane began to walk slowly but steadily on the treadmill,

warming up. Jodie was about to move away but Jane called her back. 'Jodie, I was thinking last night. How would you like to give a talk and demonstration to an over-sixties club? I booked myself to do it this afternoon but a number of other things have come up. It's quite straightforward. Just the usual spiel about exercise-is-good-for-you and a bit of chairobics.'

'Oh, wow!' Jodie was thrilled to be asked, but then recalled the staffing situation. 'I'm down to do two tours and assessments this afternoon. And there's no one in the gym.'

'Can I cover for you?'

That was dead kind of Jane, but Jodie felt obscurely relieved that she couldn't go and do the talk. Being a trainer was one thing, but standing in front of a group of people and talking to them was another. It made her a bit jittery just thinking about it. 'No, Jane. You go. I reckon you'd be really good at it. You inspire all of us at meetings so I'm sure you'll inspire the over-sixties too. Why are you giving them a talk, anyway?'

'Public relations. It gives Fit Not Fat a good name, and the over-sixties have children, too. The more impact we have in the community, the more we'll be thought of as *the* premier club.'

Jodie nodded earnestly.

Jane continued walking then unexpectedly stopped the machine. 'You said you found me inspirational,' Jane said, half smiling. 'Does that go for all of you?'

'And Garth!' Jodie said mischievously.

'Forget about Garth! What about the others? What about Siobhan?'

Now Jodie felt uncomfortable. Most of what Siobhan said about Jane was unrepeatable. She thought Jane was using Sunnybank to climb the Fit Not Fat career ladder. She had told them over coffee that Jane was only in the business for herself; in fact, she was one of the coldest, most selfish people she had ever met. That if the opportunity arose, Siobhan would be out of there. In the pause, while Jodie was collecting her thoughts, Jane began again. 'Because I've noticed she's not been attending meetings. She always has a reason, I know, but I get the feeling all's not well with her. And when I pop into the Portakabin, she always seems to be on her way out.'

'Yeah, well . . .' Jodie began.

'Is anything on her mind?'

Jodie squirmed. What ought she to say? Her desire to tell Jane the truth fought with her overwhelming need to put the brightest possible gloss on everything. The latter won. 'No! She was in a brilliant mood yesterday. She'd had a letter from Trudy – she showed it to us. There was a picture of her on the beach. She had an amazing tan. Siobhan was talking about going out there for a holiday. I think that's a very good idea.'

'And why is that?' Jane persisted.

Help! thought Jodie.

'Well, to tell you the truth, she *has* been rather down lately and it's difficult to help Siobhan. She isn't someone who asks for pity. She's always there for you if you're in trouble but she'll never admit to being in trouble on her own account. Even though she's hard to get to know, and I can see why people wouldn't like her, *I* like Siobhan.'

'I don't think she likes me,' Jane said.

Jodie was desperate to reassure Jane that she was wrong, even though she was right. Today Jodie wanted everyone to be happy. 'I'm sure she does like you, really. I think it was a disappointment to her, not getting the job. And it does take her a long time to make friends. She was even a little bit reserved with me when I started. Also I guess she's missing Trudy. She loved Trudy. Not in that way!' Jodie knew she was blushing. As much as she loved passing on information she knew that Siobhan's sexuality was her own affair. She tried to recover her poise. 'I mean, love in the sense that she was her best friend – Trudy was married, although she left her husband but you know all that. What I mean was, Trudy used to take her out for lunch and that.'

'Do you think I ought to take her out for lunch?'

'Yeah! That's a brilliant idea! Why don't you?' Then Jodie nudged Jane. 'Look, it's that doctor again. He's started to come nearly every day. He's really into it.' Jodie watched him make for the weights. Day by day he was developing a more toned body. Jodie couldn't help wondering if there was a reason — some woman, maybe? That was why most men ended up in the gym.

'I'd better get changed now,' Jane said. 'And the competition's an excellent idea. You get on with organising it.' She left, casting a cursory glance at the doctor, who was also watching her depart.

Jodie sighed. She was so lucky to be able to work for Jane. She was great. Jodie had already begun to copy some of her mannerisms, quoted her at home and had privately decided that when she was Jane's age she would like to be a manager too. In fact she would like to *be* Jane. But that was in the future. Now it was time to start cleaning the rotary torso machine before the day began in earnest.

Jane parked her car, checked her watch, and saw that she had five minutes before she was due to walk through the doors of St Bede's church hall. Good — she needed the time to prepare herself. When she had first decided to go out into the community to preach fitness and raise the profile of Fit Not Fat, old people's groups featured as just one on a list of many local organisations — charity committees, youth clubs, the mothers' union. She had presumed she'd be able to farm out this talk to someone else. Yet due to persistent staff absenteeism and a deplorable lack of forward planning on her part, *she* had to do it.

It wasn't that she didn't like addressing people — in fact, public speaking was one of her strengths. It was so much easier to believe in yourself when other people were giving you approving feedback so she always gave her all when she had an audience, no matter how great or tiny. It was just that . . . these were old people. Like her parents – maybe that was it. No, it was more than that. Jane frowned and looked unseeingly through the car windscreen at a broad, empty, rain-spattered, tree-lined street. It was that old people were . . . old. Sick. In fact, they could keel over at any minute. At one time it was suggested to her that she might like to train as an infants'-school teacher, and the real reason she had told the careers adviser that she wasn't interested was that little children got ill and might throw up. She liked working with people who could control their bodily functions.

Jane pulled herself together. If these old people were well enough to come to a club, they shouldn't be that decrepit. And they would be bound to have a qualified first-aider on the spot. She was doing them a favour – this was like charity work, in a way. She would be brave. She would sparkle at them, cheer them up, show them how they could improve the quality of their twilight years. Resolutely, she got out of the car and locked the door.

St Bede's church hall reminded Jane of her old school hall: there was a stage at one end, long, tall windows on one side and a vaguely institutional smell composed of disinfectant and damp. To make the comparison even more apposite, she noticed children's paintings pinned to the wall, evidently from Sunday school. All around her were graphic depictions of the ten plagues of Egypt – boils, locusts, insects, the slaying of the firstborn and more besides. She shuddered.

None of this seemed to bother Jane's audience, who were milling around, exchanging news and occasionally shooting her curious glances. Meanwhile an elderly gentleman in a Paisley jumper was explaining to her the arrangements for the afternoon. Jane half listened to him and glanced at a cosy semi-circle of chairs facing a desk from behind which she would address the over-sixties. She noticed there was a microphone, which she thought unnecessary in such a compact space. However, it was possible and likely that all of her audience were considerably hard of hearing. They needed all the help they could get.

Within a few minutes Jane was standing behind the mike, flanked on each side by the president and secretary of the club and gazing into a sea of grandmas and granddads. Everyone was smiling at her in much the way her own grandparents used to when she was small and was about to recite her twice times table. They were encouraging her because they didn't want her to feel nervous. Her eyes roved over tight white perms, lacy blouses, smart blazers and shining bald heads. No one looked particularly ill, although there were one or two suspiciously fragile ladies in the middle, one caked savagely with rouge. Her gaze came to rest on a sharp, motherly, reassuringly healthy face. She addressed her opening remarks to its owner.

First came the basic information. She explained the cardio-vascular system to them, the advantages of joint flexibility and how important it was to take a little walk every day. She noticed that the people in the front row were drinking in her words but several isolated individuals towards the back had shut their eyes. Jane hoped they were only asleep. Her chosen lady, however, was nodding knowledgeably. The back row – as back rows every-where – were a little disorderly, nudging each other and passing the odd comment. Jane tried to make eye-contact with them. She explained how if you don't use certain muscles they become unusable.

'You can tell my husband that,' one of the women on the back row announced.

'Ee, Ethel, you are a one!' said her friend. Jane decided to ignore her.

She proceeded through the importance of adequate nutrition and remembering to consult your GP if you wanted to undertake any programme of exercise. She described to them in glowing colours the life of a fit senior citizen, able to play with grandchildren and go for gentle country walks. Then she asked if they would like a demonstration. There was visible interest, except from a few more infirm individuals, who shook their heads. 'If at any time you feel uncomfortable or out of breath,' Jane said, 'please stop. Don't feel obliged to join in — it really isn't compulsory. And if you feel at all faint, sit down immediately.' She hoped she wasn't putting them off but at their time of life you couldn't guarantee what would happen if they were over-enthusiastic.

Jane's warning came as a relief to some of the women, who retreated to the back of the room to watch. Meanwhile the men pushed the chairs to one side and began rolling up their sleeves and flexing their biceps.

'First of all to warm up we'll try some marching on the spot.' Jane demonstrated and was joined by some women stepping carefully while a few men began running, while making comments about National Service. She wasn't sure, but she might have seen the back row attempting the can-can.

'Good,' she said. Then she darted among them distributing weights. 'These are very light, and at home you can substitute a can of beans. So if you just take one in each hand . . .'

Already the men were swinging them above their heads.

The women seemed amused at the idea of weights. 'Ee, love, I don't want to be developing muscles in the wrong places at my age!' one said.

'I wouldn't mind some muscles in the right place,' her friend reported, and all of the back row chuckled.

'Stop it, Maisie!' said Jane's protectress. 'You're embarrassing the young girl.'

The weights caused great amusement.

'Well, I don't know, this is a lot easier than I thought,' another woman said. 'It makes you think. All those blokes on telly, grunting and groaning. It's just for the show. Men always like you to think they're making an effort.'

'OK,' Jane said. 'Time for some chair exercises.'

They abandoned the weights and went over to the chairs. One man attempted to lift a chair with just a hand around one leg. A few of his friends tried to copy him.

'No,' Jane said. 'I mean you sit on the chairs.'

'That's more my style,' a woman said. The men seemed a little disgruntled. Soon Jane had all her audience back on chairs and she took them through some movements intended to improve joint flexibility.

'Does this burn up many calories?' asked a woman in a red jumper.

'Hark at her,' said a voice from the back row. 'As soon as we serve tea she'll be the first one at the biscuits.' There was a ripple of laughter, but Jane saw the woman shoot a furious glance at her heckler.

At the conclusion of the session everyone looked pleased. They gave Jane a round of applause and the president thanked her then invited her to stay for tea. Jane knew she ought to get back to Fit Not Fat and, indeed, had some invoices to look over. Yet something instructed her to stay. As much as the elderly made her nervous she exulted in being able to overcome it. She accepted the invitation. Anyway, since they had all survived her exercise session, they probably weren't going to drop dead that afternoon. Some members gravitated to the back of the hall where the kitchens were, and Jane found herself surrounded by a number of grateful people.

'I did enjoy that. It's important to keep fit.'

'Physical jerks, we used to call them.'

'You're very young to be running your own club.'

'Make way, Jess. I'm bringing her tea.'

Soon Jane was presented with a cup of tea and a biscuit.

'Does she eat biscuits?' came another voice.

'Yes, thank you,' Jane said, and bit into the bourbon. A number of people still hovered about her.

'Excuse me,' said a little lady, with glasses hanging from her neck on a chain, 'I've got arthritis. What exercises can I do to get rid of that?'

'I don't think you can get rid of it, but have a word with your doctor. He'll be able to advise you.'

The women began to talk among themselves.

'Who is your doctor, Eileen?'

'Dr Patel.'

'He's lovely, he is. He's only young, and he's got bedroom eyes. I'd do anything he tells me. He cured my heartburn.'

'I don't like them young 'uns. Give me Dr Khan any day. You can tell he's been around and he knows what's what. He was wonderful with my ingrowing toenail and Alfred's hiatus hernia. And he made short work of Valerie's piles.'

'Now, when I came out of hospital Dr Brandon rang me up, he did, to see how I was getting on. What do you think of that? That's what I call a doctor. He rang me at home, he did. I don't rate Khan and Patel half as highly as Brandon.'

They were talking of their GPs as if they were film stars or even football-team managers, Jane thought. She guessed this was because doctors loomed large in their lives. It can't be easy getting older and being confronted with your own frailty and mortality.

'But what do you think of that young Dr Richmond?' piped up another lady.

Jane swerved round to listen.

'The one who's just started? He's a kind man. Horace saw him with his angina.'

'A lovely man. Young for a doctor, but very reassuring, I'll grant you that.'

'I wouldn't mind being reassured by him! He's like one of those telly doctors.'

Jane eyed the speaker, a white-haired, rakish-looking woman in brown trousers, which were baggy at the knees, and a long, mustard-coloured men's cardigan. Suddenly she turned to Jane. 'Now look here,' she said to her, 'what do we want to exercise for at our age? I've slaved away all my life and now I'm looking forward to a bit of a rest.'

'You'll get your rest in the grave,' came a croaky voice. No one paid any attention.

'They say to you don't smoke, don't drink, don't eat too many calories so you'll live to a ripe old age. Well, I'm buggered but I'm eighty-three now and I've reached my ripe old age and I've done with all that. Had me first cigarette last week, and I've started drinking stout again. I feel a lot better for it.'

'You've got a point, you know,' said another woman. 'They keep telling you this is bad for you, and that's bad for you. Now, when I were a lass we was fed on suet puddings to nourish you, and good old roast beef, only now they're saying it gives you mad cow disease and clogs up your arteries. And me dad told me never to touch a drop of alcohol – they were teetotal, my folk – but now red wine is supposed to make you live longer. When I was in the ATS we were told smoking relieved your nerves, and now it's a sin. Oh, yes – you had to go to work on an egg, and then they turned out to be full of cholesterol, and butter's good for you, and then it's marge, and then it's butter again. These experts know no more than I do. That's why I don't give a toss what anyone says any more. Pour me another cup of tea, Mary.'

Suddenly Jane felt all her conviction slipping away from her.

'A little of what you fancy does you good,' someone else said.

'And a lot of what you fancy does you even more good.'

Jane thought inexplicably of Dr Richmond, and then she felt someone propelling her by the elbow towards the back of the hall to join the main group of club members. 'You don't want to have them going on at you,' her guardian said. It was the lady who had been nodding at her during her talk. 'I know who you are,' she said. 'My daughter works at Fit Not Fat. Siobhan Murphy.'

Jane was surprised, then delighted. It occurred to her that befriending Siobhan's mother was an excellent way of getting into Siobhan's good books. 'What a coincidence! She didn't tell me you were a member. I've left her in charge today, although I'm sure she could do this sort of thing just as well as me. Siobhan lives with you, doesn't she?'

'Yes, that's right.'

Jane picked up on the same reticence to talk that charac-terised Siobhan. It made her a little nervous and unsure what to say next. She found herself deleting, one by one, all the questions she would most like to ask. Had Siobhan come to terms with the new management? Was she looking for a new job? What was the best way to get round her? What did she do with herself in her spare time? Was she in a relationship? And, most importantly, was Siobhan beginning to like her?

Just as she was deciding instead to make some inane comment about the weather their tête-à-tête was spoilt by a dapper gentleman with a tonsure. 'Very nice talk,' he said to her. 'Now, I've got a question for you. Would you recommend I start taking these new pills I've been reading about lately? Those L8s?'

'L8s?' Jane had not heard of them.

'Aye. L8s. They slow down the ageing process by reducing the rate of biochemical reaction in the body. It's the same stuff pregnant elephants produce, or so my daughter tells me. She's started taking them and she wants me to have a go.'

'Very interesting,' said Jane. 'I'll have to look into them.'

'Not that I reckon I need them,' the man said. 'Fit as a fiddle, me. And I will be to the day I die. And after that.' He wandered away.

'Nice meeting you, love,' Siobhan's mother said, and left her too.

Jane deliberated whether to have another biscuit or make

tracks. She decided on the first option, and collared one or two people to tell them about the club. Gradually the members left in their uniform buttoned-up coats and plastic rain-hats. Eventually Jane noticed she was holding up the two or three members detailed to look after her. 'I really ought to go,' she told them. 'Thank you for letting me come to speak. I've enjoyed myself.'

On the way out, she realised it was true. The afternoon had been a kind of oasis in her packed day, her frantic week. And to think some of them knew David! There was a coincidence. She thought a little more kindly of him, and could see why some people might even find it attractive that he was a doctor. He was attractive despite being a doctor. But Jane stopped her thoughts in their tracks. She couldn't be trusted around the opposite sex. Her idiocy with Garth mocked and haunted her; since then she had abjured both alcohol and men. Instead she had worked harder than ever. She had also avoided Garth – it had been easier to retreat into her professional shell.

Shortly she was back at Fit Not Fat, happy to see that it looked the same as it had when she left it. With builders around, you could take nothing for granted. She entered the building, bustled along the corridor and opened the door of her office. Siobhan was sitting at her desk and jumped.

'What have I caught you at?' Jane said jocularly.

'Nothing. I was just filling in an exercise programme.' Her voice was tight and defensive.

'Good.' Jane took off her jacket. 'I had a great afternoon. I met your mother. She's like you in many ways. You must ask her how she thought I went down. Some of the members—'

'Jane, you had a call while you were out.'

Something in Siobhan's tone alerted her that it had been an important one, and. Jane had a fleeting sense of impending calamity, though she couldn't have said why.

Siobhan cleared her throat. 'It was Sarah Curtis from Head

Office. They're sending some people round to have a look at the club.'

'Why? Did she tell you?'

'Yes.' Siobhan coughed. 'It seems that they're not satisfied with the figures and—'

'What figures?'

'Hold on. The profits, basically, and they're worried about the competition from Fitness International. They want to assess the club's viability. She was saying that in order to maximise group stability they might need to rationalise the number of Fit Not Fat clubs and—'

'So you're saying they're thinking of closing us down?' Siobhan was impassive, like a statue. Jane put out a hand and leant on the corner of her desk to steady herself. 'So they're coming to inspect us, and if they don't like what they find, they'll sell up?' Still no response from Siobhan. Jane's stomach was hollow and her ears were ringing. She felt as if she'd received a physical blow. If they closed Fit Not Fat, her staff would be out of work, her clients would be without a club, and she would have failed publicly. Her copybook would be blotted. She would be unemployable. The manager who failed to turn a club round. Jane Wright, the no-hoper. But it wasn't just her, it was all of them. If Fit Not Fat closed, Jodie would be smeared, so would Siobhan, for all her tight-lipped passivity, and Garth, Darren, Andy, Marcia, even Kendra in reception. She was weak with fright, and a tidal wave of despair threatened to engulf her. 'When will this inspection be?' She asked Siobhan, in a tiny voice.

'Sarah didn't say. In a few weeks or so.'

Jane took a seat. 'If only it was in a few months. We've been working so hard to recruit new members. And when the coffee shop is finished, more and more people will be dropping in. It isn't fair.'

Siobhan stood there, a silent witness to her distress. And

then, as if from nowhere, Jane felt herself fill with determination. Ever since she was little, her response to imminent failure had been to try harder. If anyone could pull through this crisis, it would be Jane Wright. She would fight with every ounce of effort in her body. She would not let Fit Not Fat close down. She owed that to everyone, as well as to herself. This was her chance to be a hero, to save them all. This would be her finest hour. She had been made for this moment. She imagined herself glowing with an incandescent light.

'Siobhan,' she said resolutely, 'we can't afford to lose a minute. We'll impress the hell out of Head Office. I'll formulate a plan. I'll speak to all the staff.' She glanced at her second-in-command. Siobhan had still revealed nothing of what she was thinking. This would not do. Jane remembered her conversation with Jodie earlier that morning. 'And I'd like to take you out to lunch next week,' Jane said, 'to discuss our plan of action. And other things. I need you, Siobhan.'

Siobhan dropped her eyes but did not say no. That was a beginning.

'OK,' said Jane. 'You can go back to the gym. I need time to think.'

Siobhan left, and Jane was alone. She was still buoyed up by her resolve to fight back. Scenes from old British war movies came unprompted to her mind. She was like the about-to-be-victorious commander planning an escape from Colditz. Or a police detective on the heels of the prime suspect. Only there was so much to do and no time to waste. Suddenly everything imploded. Could she do it? Was she capable? Had she bitten off more than she could chew?

There was a knock at her door. 'Come in,' she said, pulling herself together.

It was Garth. Seeing him helped her regain her composure. She could not make a fool of herself in front of Garth again. 'I've just heard about the inspection,' he said, his voice all concern.

Jane nodded. She hoped he wasn't going to be nice to her. She had to stay in control at all costs.

'If there's anything I can do . . .' he added.

'I'll take your offer into consideration,' Jane said, with all the dignity she could muster.

'Look,' he said, 'I have a suggestion.' He perched familiarly on the edge of her desk. 'You're going to be under a lot of strain in the next few weeks. You're going to need to look after yourself.' Jane felt herself crumbling. She never knew how to react when people were kind to her. She felt for one awful second that she would burst into tears and bury her head in his chest – if only because it was the nearest chest to hand. She took a deep breath and steadied herself. Luckily when he spoke again he sounded businesslike. 'I've recently started selling a new food supplement – in my spare time. It's called L8. It boosts your energy by maximising the nutrition you get from food. It promotes well-being and positivity. I can let you have some at a reduced rate, if you like.'

'L8s?' questioned Jane. They sounded familiar. Perhaps she had heard someone recommend them.

'Clinical trials are under way in the States, but already there are some incredible results. Forget Prozac. I take L8s myself and I've never felt better. I just thought they might help you through this.'

'Thank you, Garth. You really think they'll have an effect?'

'Bound to. I wouldn't offer them to you otherwise. You're the health expert, not me. Only I think I've stumbled on something here, and I want to share it with you. I'm just as keen as you that Fit Not Fat survives.'

He was talking her language now. Her indiscretion was forgotten. Garth could help her after all. She would sample the L8s and deploy him as she saw fit. Perhaps he could seduce Sarah Curtis, she thought, in a moment of insanity. She felt her resolve return and smiled at him. 'Do you know? I think I'll take you up on these L8s. How much did you say they were?'

'Only sixty pounds for thirty days. I promise you'll see an effect immediately.'

'You're on,' Jane said.

Chapter Eleven

Cassie had brought her Walkman to the gym and was listening to the tape she had compiled for her workout. Lots of Bruce Springsteen, some upbeat reggae, Abba, and truly inspirational songs such as 'I Will Survive', for the recliner bike, 'The Only Way Is Up', for the stepper, and 'Staying Alive', generally. At that moment, however, she was not listening to the music.

Another thought about Terry had struck her. Perhaps he had gone away because if he saw her his resolve would break, and he would fall in love with her all over again. That would dent his male pride, so he had opted to get as far away from her as possible. This was a cheering thought, which fuelled her and she picked up speed on the treadmill. She tried to imagine him in a Roman trattoria, for she had had it on good authority – a mutual friend – that he was in Rome reviewing restaurants for a Euro-feature in a Sunday supplement. Was this a coincidence, or had he begged the features editor to let him go – the latter-day equivalent of joining the foreign legion? She could see Terry now, sitting at a pavement café in front of a plateful of pasta, with wild mushrooms, his favourite, and a bottle of Frascati. Was he thinking of her? She sincerely hoped so. It was unthinkable that he should stop caring.

She sagged a bit, and her speed dropped. It pained her to

think of Terry so far away. Then anger set in. How ridiculous of him to cease all contact with her just because she had asked for an extension on her decision! Imagine if she treated her students like that every time they were behind with an essay! Preposterous! His withdrawal was a sort of passive aggression, not what she would have expected from easy-going Terry. Was this the male menopause? Was he having some sort of post-feminist crisis with his masculinity? She made a note to consult her friend who specialised in Gender Studies. What hurt her most was that Terry had rewritten the script of their relationship without her consent. *He* was supposed to be the tolerant, urbane, dependable one; *she* had the right to be difficult. *She* needed humouring, *he* was there for her. Now he was in Rome and she was in Fit Not Fat.

Cassie pushed down the uncomfortable idea that in some way she was responsible for this new turn of events. Since he had escalated the crisis by absconding, she had become the victim. He had overreacted while she was only human. He was being emotional, she, level-headed. And guilt, like a hump-backed beast, skulked in a cellar in her mind. When she was ready she knew she would admit her responsibility in this dreadful mess and eat humble pie. But not yet. It was childish, but she wanted to get her own back. In the meantime, she spent every available hour at the gym.

At the gym, she didn't have to analyse the situation. Moods washed over her, but her focus was the machine she was on. All the time she knew she was doing herself good, and in some obscure way punishing Terry. She broke into a jog to 'Waterloo'. She would not give errant Terry one more moment of her precious time.

The door to the gym opened just behind her and Cassie turned her head to see who had just come in. It was not Garth. She felt a blend of relief and disappointment: relief because she was trying to avoid him when she was hot and sweaty, and disappointment because she had decided that she would allow herself the luxury of having a crush on him. It was as innocent as the feelings her fourteen-year-old niece harboured for Boyzone's Ronan Keating. In fact, Cassie felt as if she had got to know Ronan Keating quite well in the past few months from the countless times she'd seen him on music videos – coincidentally, there he was now, looking wistful on a park bench. A nice boy, and not bad-looking, reminiscent, in fact, of Darren, who was on duty now. He was standing in front of Sky Sports listening to an interview. Cassie didn't think much of him. He didn't interact a great deal with the clients unless they were friends of his. She'd also seen him ogling the TV screen when the likes of Shania Twain and Britney Spears were on in a way she found rather objectionable.

And yet here am I, she thought, obsessing about Garth purely for his body. It was appalling to contemplate. Cassie ran harder. If Terry had been at home, this would not have happened. But she felt entitled to her little game, and it would be as well to see Garth out of her system before Terry returned. One way of looking at it was that Garth kept her coming to the gym – he was responsible, albeit unknowingly, for the last seven pounds she had lost. And Terry would be the beneficiary, for Cassie could not imagine a future without Terry in it. Forget Terry! she screamed internally. She pushed herself to run faster than ever until she could run no more. Then she dropped her speed.

She took that opportunity to check her reflection in the mirror. Her cheeks were red with effort, but she was a normal size now, not buxom, not dumpy, but normal, average, the sort of figure you'd pass in the street. No one could call her fat. Not that she had minded being thought of as fat before, but now that she was not fat she felt the full horror of having been fat. She was constantly in flight from fatness, burning calories, flushing her system with water, avoiding food, thinking thin, and sharply conscious of all the women she knew who were still slimmer than her. She had become aware of a latent competitive streak. She had begun to peek at other people's speeds and gradients on the treadmill, and tried to row faster than the person next to her. Why? To prove something. To prove what? That she was better, stronger, fitter.

With her dispassionate, scholarly eye, Cassie could see the absurdity of it all. Just as you always felt you could do with just a little more money, you always needed to be a pound or two slimmer, or run just a little faster. There was never a point at which you could say, 'I've done it, I'm there, I've arrived.' The pursuit of fitness was a life sentence. It was endless self-improvement because if you stopped you regressed. Before, she had never exercised and it wasn't an issue. Now she measured herself by the number of times in the week she went to the gym. Her eyes sought out mirrors so she could monitor her appearance. As her body became healthier, her mind seemed increasingly diseased. Her addiction to physical perfection – hers and Garth's – was out of control. And, like any addict, she was powerless to resist.

She recognised all of this with her usual detachment. She could see that her character was changing, and she had just watched it change. She had been playing dice with Terry. She had spent her savings on clothes. She thought about Garth in lectures and during seminars. She experienced an illicit thrill every time the scales showed that a pound had vanished into the ether. This was her new life – dreadful, yet she could justify it. It was for health reasons. Health. The word wielded immense power. It was the mantra of the western world. Health. Today, when people felt powerless to stop the global suffering pumped through their television sets, they turned their backs on others and focused on themselves. A supermarket sold a brand of food called Be Good To Yourself –, not Be Good To Others. Because of health. Health, as Cassie had told Terry, was a new religion. So, OK, she was the high priestess. The gym was where she and her fellow worshippers assembled, watching themselves in the mirrors on every wall.

And then Cassie felt her mind dissolve: she had had enough of clever comparisons. She was just glad to be here with the music playing, her muscles working and all the purposeful activity, and the possibility of Garth in the vicinity because never in her life had she consorted with someone so unbelievably gorgeous. She'd fancied what would happen if she invited him to the Department of Medieval History on some pretext. She'd imagined other things too, less academic, or at least, attempted to imagine them. She'd guessed sex with him would be like sex in movies, an aesthetic as well as physical experience. She would never find out so she was free to imagine all she liked.

She looked down at the clock on the treadmill and saw she had only a minute to go. She began to walk, enjoying the sensation of coming to a rest. The exhaustion stilled her mind and filled her with virtue. All that mattered was that, in a moment, she could step off and gulp down some chilled water.

She stopped and wiped her forehead with the side of her hand. It was gratifyingly damp.

Back in the changing rooms, several women were sitting around in various states of undress reminding Cassie of Seurat's bathers on the beach. Perhaps they were exhausted from their efforts at the high-impact step-aerobics class that was just over. Two were sitting on a bench, another leant against the mirror, her back towards it. Two more stood by the lockers. Another, a woman rather older than Cassie whom she had only seen once or twice before, was peeling off her Lycra leggings.

'I don't know why we bother,' one woman said.

'It's not as if it's good for you,' said her friend. 'Remember Judith? You've not seen her for a bit. Did her back in during a class. And Rosemary? Turned the stepper up too high. She was off work for weeks.'

'And Pam damaged her knee. But she was lucky, the surgeon was able to repair it by keyhole surgery. And then he sent the video to her, as a kind of keepsake. Her ten-year-old son likes to watch it over breakfast.'

'Hmm,' said her listener, taking off her hair bobble and shaking out her damp hair.

'You won't injure yourself if you exercise properly,' said the older woman. Cassie noticed how all the women looked daggers at her: she was robbing them of the one solid gold excuse they had for not turning up at the club. 'It's important to warm up and stretch your muscles then cool down afterwards to disperse the build-up of lactic acid. And most exercise only needs small movements to be effective.' She turned to Cassie. 'Hi,' she said. 'I've seen you around in the gym. I'm Anita.'

'Hello,' Cassie said, amiably. 'Cassie Oliver.'

'I've noticed you working very hard.'

Cassie warmed to her immediately. 'Have you been coming here long?' she asked, as she opened her locker. The other women were now giving them the silent treatment. This made her realise she had sided with the class goody-goody, but there was some satisfaction in doing so.

'Just a couple of days,' Anita told her. 'I used to go to Fitness International. I've been working out for longer than I care to remember – I won't see fifty again.'

Cassie felt it was politic to trade compliment for compliment. 'I'd never have guessed. I'd have placed you in your early forties.'

Anita smiled. 'I work at it.'

Cassie smiled back, intending to work at it too.

'So how often do you come here?' Anita asked.

'Three times a week,' Cassie said proudly. 'Four if I can manage it.'

'Me too. And then on my rest days I do some *hatha* yoga, or go for a gentle run around Heaton Park.'

'Impressive,' Cassie said.

'I like to keep active.'

Anita rooted through her sports bag, bringing out various massage oils and talking as she did so. Evidently she was one of those women from whom conversation bubbled continuously. 'I've noticed you mainly use the CV machines. They're good in some ways but you really need to step up your resistance work, and not just because building muscles can prevent osteoporosis. The muscles act as shock-absorbers so you're less likely to injure yourself. And resistance work increases your metabolic rate, and helps burn fat more effectively.'

Cassie began to worry that perhaps Anita was right. Ought she to get her programme changed? She would do anything to burn fat, anything. Put it on the funeral pyre, and burn, burn, burn!

'Because these instructors are very young, straight from college some of them, they lack experience and the advice they give you isn't always the best. You really need to read up for yourself about fitness.'

For various reasons, Cassie felt inclined to defend them. 'Surely the more recently you've been in college, the more up-to-date your knowledge?'

'I suppose. But the trainers at my old club often gave bad advice and even taught exercises incorrectly. Many times I'd have to explain to people they were doing their side bends wrongly. And the trainers were just standing there, having a good old gossip. Sometimes I wonder if this place is any better.'

'Oh, it is,' Cassie said. 'They take good care of you here. Since I started coming I've lost over two stone.'

It was out before she could stop it. She was boasting about her weight loss just like the sort of brainless female who valued herself only in pounds and inches, and the fewer, the better. But those words, 'I've lost over two stone', were music to her, and they were generally admired by her listeners.

'That's *very* good,' Anita said. 'You've done well. Not many people stick an exercise regime out. They train for two or three weeks then make excuses to themselves. What diet have you been following? Weight Watchers? Slimming World? Cabbage Soup? F-Plan? Hip and Thigh? Judith Wills? Jenny Craig?'

'Just a boring old low-fat diet,' Cassie informed her.

'Well, good, but you must be careful. The danger of conventional dieting is that you miss out on vital nutrients. Not many people know what a balanced diet really is, or what the right food can do for you. Take radishes—'

'No thank you,' said Cassie. 'Can't stand them.'

'Take radishes. They contain cancer-curing ingredients. And sprouting grains might, too. I have a collection of them on my window-sill. They need constant watering. Of course, I also take plenty aloe vera, which has helped my eczema as well as my flatulence. Then carrots prevent strokes and courgettes are generally very cleansing. The trick is to try to eat a variety of different-coloured foods every day. Did you know that stuffed mushrooms stop brittle hair?'

'Do you rub them in?'

'For boosting your immune system there's nothing like a glass of water with sunflower seeds. The time you spend planning your daily menus can add years to your life.'

'I hear what you're saying,' Cassie said, 'but most women don't have that time. Isn't it easier just to take vitamin pills?'

Anita placed a hand on Cassie's arm. 'So you might think. But do you know? The other day I was examining my stool and saw a whole, undigested vitamin pill. It'd passed straight through me. That's why I take *liquid* food supplements now, along with my cod-liver oil in the morning. It makes a real difference. I don't feel so tired. I don't need to take an afternoon nap any longer, or at least, I can confine it to a five-minute power nap, normally at around two fifteen in the afternoon, when my energy levels drop. I like to position my feet a little above the rest of my body so I don't get puffy ankles. Fluid retention can cause all sorts of problems, you know. That's why I try to take particular notice of how much water I pass. I have a measuring jug by the side of the—'

'Well! Is that the time? Look, I must jump into the shower. Er . . . I'm meeting someone in the café.'

'Yes, they've done a good job with it, but they really ought to improve the juice bar. Did you know that fresh onion and garlic juice effects the condition of your blood whereas prunes, of course—'

Cassie did not wait to hear about prunes. She took her towel and shower gel and vanished. What a weirdo! Examining her stools? There were more pleasant ways of passing the time. Still, it wasn't surprising that the health club attracted its fair share of freaks. You had to feel sorry for them. She was glad that not all of her life was devoted to the pursuit of well-being – thank heavens for her forthcoming lecture on the Black Death! Yet as she scrubbed herself vigorously she recalled what Anita had said about the aloe vera and courgettes. Would they go well together in a soufflé?

She was glad to see that when she came out of the shower the changing rooms were empty. She glanced at her watch and got dressed, then applied a little makeup. Just a couple of weeks ago she had had her hair restyled and everyone said it made her look years younger. It was in a short bob now and she could either tuck it behind her ears or separate some strands and arrange them so that they partly obscured her eyes. It was a style favoured by some of her students. She hardly recognised herself: she was a new creation, assured, attractive. Now all she had to do was grow into this new image.

This new image. Now, *image* was an interesting word. Was it linked with imagination, suggesting you could make yourself into whatever you wanted to be? Cassie hoped so. She wanted her image to be smart, slim, sophisticated, sexy. Could she believe in herself enough to act that way? Was it advisable? Because an image was not *real*, not part of the fundamental personality of an individual; it was a construct. People such as actors, models, even academics who relied on their image often lost touch with their true selves. To become your image is to lose, in some senses, the essential source of you-ness. But do we *have* a core identity? Do we not constantly invent and reinvent ourselves? The new Cassie mused for a while on the mysteries of the human personality and precisely how she was going to reinvent herself as a sex goddess.

On her way in that afternoon Cassie had noticed that the café had opened. It was only right that she should patronise it. With her sports bag in one hand and her sweater over the other arm, she went in, inhaling the aroma of freshly brewed coffee and new paint. She ordered an espresso, eyeing disapprovingly the glass-fronted display cabinet containing a selection of cakes. Call this a health club? Perhaps it was the management's way of keeping their client base: they worked out, pigged out, then needed to work out again. Ingenious. But Cassie was not tempted by the cakes: she thought of herself now as someone who could take or leave chocolate. She had learnt how to flirt with food rather than eat it. You pretend you're going to eat something when you haven't the slightest intention of doing so, and get a vicarious thrill from thinking about eating it — fewer calories that way. Once her coffee had arrived, she took it to a table near the emergency-exit door and sat down.

They had done a good job with the café, she had to admit. The tiled floor gave it a continental air, and the marble-topped glass tables were elegant and unpretentious. Even the coffee compared well with Starbucks'. A glass partition gave a view of the corridor and the squash courts opposite. On the two walls were numerous posters, advertising a two-for-the-price-of-one membership deal, a bring-a-friend day, nutrition advice and a number of other competitions. They were certainly pushing the club, Cassie thought. She imagined that this was the work of the young manager, Jane Wright, whom Cassie found rather terrifying in her unremitting enthusiasm. Jane was so full of energy that Cassie felt drained when she smiled at her.

Her eyes were locked on the corridor. It was possible – likely? – that Garth might appear. If he did, would he see her? Cassie realised she was being ridiculous but enjoyed sitting there, buoyed by hope. Having a crush was so rejuvenating. What made it all the more enjoyable was that she could tell no one; it was her guilty secret. It was wonderful to feel so dissolute. She finished her espresso. Should she have another?

Just as she was deliberating on that and deciding that the Black Death lecture needed revision, she saw David Richmond enter the club and glance into the café. He saw Cassie and broke into a grin. In a moment he was by her side. 'Nice, isn't it?' He gestured at the café.

'Not bad at all,' Cassie said. 'Have you come in for your workout or just to have a peek?'

'Well, you know . . .' David said, somewhat awkwardly, and pulled up a chair by her.

'Can I get you a coffee?' Cassie asked him.

'No. I'd better – oh, what the hell? Yes, what sort of coffee do they . . . ? A *latte*?'

Cassie rose and went to order, casting surreptitious glances at him. All was not well with David. He might be a GP but Cassie could tell that he was the one who needed looking after. She brought over the coffee and settled down again. The sound of footsteps in the corridor made both of them jump and glance to see who it was. Anita. They slumped back in their chairs.

'How's life treating you?' Cassie asked him.

'Not too bad. And you?'

'Not too bad either.'

There was a prolonged silence, during which Cassie recalled

the last time she had spoken at length to David, which was at the coffee morning. He had been showing a noticeable interest in Jane. It occurred to her now that things might have developed. She rather hoped they had, except he hardly seemed as cheerful as a man lucky in love should be. His gaze kept wandering to the corridor. Was he hoping to see Jane as much as she was hoping for a glimpse of Garth? The situation struck Cassie as laughable – at least, in her case it was laughable. She decided to presume on her status as older woman to question him further.

'You seem a little out of sorts,' she commented.

'So, what would you prescribe?' He attempted a smile.

'Tell me what's wrong first.'

He sighed and shrugged. 'OK. I was hoping to see Jane – Jane Wright, the manager.'

Cassie nodded, in her best bedside manner.

'I think I upset her yesterday. I was around when they were delivering some stock for the café. I offered to give her a hand and we saw to the cakes and other perishables. She seemed glad of my assistance – and it was a chance to put these into practice.' He flexed his biceps. 'Anyway, we hit it off, or so I thought. It turned out she'd heard some patients of mine talking about me the other day. She was teasing me, and I reckoned I was getting somewhere at last. And look, Cassie, I'm not slow in these things – I was a medical student for seven years and you know what that means. I suggested dinner. I said I thought she'd been looking a bit stressed lately and it might do her good to get out of the club and spend some time with someone who knew a thing or two about blood pressure. And that was it. She froze, and was gone in an instant. What did I say? I know I should drop it and move on but I can't. There's something about her . . .'

'You mean the way she comes over and turns up the level when you're rowing?'

David gave a disarming laugh.

At that moment Cassie would have done anything to bring

them together but she, too, was mystified by Jane's behaviour. 'Was it the mention of blood pressure? Maybe she's phobic about it. A friend of mine won't ever have hers taken. One look at the sphygmomanometer and she's on the floor.'

'That's unlikely for a fitness instructor. The health industry is her life, as much as health is mine.'

'The funny thing is,' said Cassie, 'I'm convinced she likes you. I've seen the way she looks at you.' He perked up, she was pleased to see. 'Maybe you ought to confront her, state your feelings and ask what her problem is. Be assertive. Go for it. Find her and tell her you want to get to know her better. Get in there. Secretly every woman likes a man to be forceful. That's what we fantasise about. The man who finds us irresistible and tells us so to our face. I wasn't going to tell you this but in fact I also—'

'So you're saying I should just march into her office and tell her she's coming out to dinner?'

'Well, give her a chance to let you know what's on her mind.'

'Hmm.' David was suddenly lost in thought. So was Cassie. It intrigued her that Jane gave such mixed signals. She had often watched her when she was training and had amused herself by imagining what she got up to out of the gym. It was hard to think of her doing anything that was not involved with physical fitness. Did she ever just lounge about in front of the telly with a packet of biscuits and a crossword puzzle?

'I think I'll do as you say,' David said reflectively. 'I can't believe I'm so obsessed with someone. I've got to see it to the end. Wish me luck.'

'I know how you feel,' Cassie said meaningfully.

David shot her an odd look. 'Thanks for the coffee. My round next time.' And he was off.

Cassie wondered why she always ended up footing the bill when she had coffee with a member of the opposite sex. One day, she thought, someone will treat me to something. She picked up her bags and made for Reception, where she handed her locker key to Kendra. Only it wasn't Kendra at Reception, it was Garth. 'Hi!' she said, as a blush stole across her face.

'Hi yourself,' he said, pleased to see her. Cassie held on to the edge of the counter to steady herself. 'I haven't seen you around for a while.'

'Oh, I've been here,' stated Cassie. 'Have a look at my attendance card!'

'I believe you.'

There was no one else in Reception. Cassie knew she ought to go but could not bring herself to do so. This was crazy. What had happened to her? 'How are you getting along with your L8s?' she asked, grasping at straws to prolong the conversation.

'Brilliantly. Word of mouth alone does the job. Our manager's taking them now, and Kendra. I'm covering for her while she takes an aerobics class.'

'Kendra? She always goes on about hating exercise.'

'Not any more.'

'Oh, come on,' Cassie said. 'I don't believe in your L8s. It's like all that alternative medicine. If you believe it works, it does. People pay so much for their various pills and potions that they have an investment in them working. And energy is such a nebulous thing. Just thinking positively can give you energy. Aren't you capitalising on people's naïvety?'

'Does it matter if they feel better?'

'Yes, it does. It means you're a cheat.'

'But I'm not cheating them. L8s work. Try some and see.'

This was fun. Challenging Garth like that had struck sparks from him. Cassie was breathless with febrile excitement. 'I might,' she said. She was aware that she probably had a silly grin plastered all over her face and that he was almost certainly laughing at her, but it didn't matter.

'Well, OK. I'll get you some. Tell you what, are you busy tomorrow night?'

Breathe in, breathe out, Cassie told herself. 'Nothing I couldn't cancel.'

'Cool. Meet me here at eight when I come off duty. Perhaps we can have a drink and I'll explain all about them.'

'No promises, mind.'

'Can't I even promise you a good time?'

Cassie heard herself give a silly, nervous laugh. She was pathetic. *Worse* than a fourteen-year-old. And yet for the first time he had said something to her that was indisputably flirtatious. It was as unbelievable as the Turin Shroud. *Could* he fancy her? There was an insane possibility that he just might. This was almost as bad as being propositioned by one of her students. Yet, now she thought about it, there had been the odd cases of male tutors dating female undergraduates, although it was frowned upon. Who was to say that thirty-nine-year-old Cassie couldn't date a younger man who wasn't one of her students? No one.

As she was trying to think of a witty rejoinder David reappeared, looking considerably more cheerful. He was clearly bursting to tell her something.

'See you tomorrow,' Cassie said to Garth, giving him one last smouldering look.

'See ya,' he said.

She and David walked out towards the car park. 'You won't believe this,' David said, tossing his car keys into the air. 'We're going out – and she asked me!'

'Congratulations!' Cassie said.

'Hold on – now I'll explain what really happened. I knocked on her office door and walked straight in. She was on the phone. She looked taken aback to see me, which wasn't surprising since I hadn't waited for a response. It was clearly an important call and I felt a bit of an idiot, standing there. She was speaking very intently. Then she put her hand over the receiver and asked me if I'd accompany her to the Fit Not Fat managerial dinner. Of course I said yes. Then she spoke some more. She was apologetic after that, said that she was put on the spot by Head Office asking if she had a partner for this bash, and for various reasons she needed to say that she did. She hoped I didn't mind. I said not at all. She explained that it was just a one-off, and she appreciated the favour. I reckon she's using me as a male escort, but I've got to start somewhere.' He was grinning from ear to ear.

Cassie hardly heard him. There were much weightier matters on her mind, like what on earth should she wear tomorrow evening? Should she drive, or walk? And what had he meant in promising her a good time?

'*Ciao*,' said David.

'You too,' Cassie said, and strode off to her car.

Chapter Twelve

It was so large that Jane had to break it in two before swallowing it. She placed one half of the pink L8 on the back of her tongue, then downed it with a gulp of water. It was too early to say if the pills were doing her any good, but she needed all the help she could get.

Life had become unbelievably hectic. There were times when the pace was all too much for her and she felt an enormous scream building up inside. At others she was conscious of a raw excitement and realised she needed stress – she was the sort of person who thrived best when they were busiest. Every moment brought a new challenge, and she was constantly having to think on her feet.

Take yesterday. When Sarah had rung to confirm that the annual managers' dinner had been brought forward, she had asked her if she was bringing her partner. 'But of course you're not,' Sarah had said. 'I'd forgotten, you're single.'

'Actually, no,' Jane had said. 'I *shall* be bringing someone.' It was lucky that just then David had burst into her office. The Fates were with her for Sarah's comment had smacked of bitchiness. Moreover, the managers' dinner was an opportunity for her to show them how confident she was. She had to go in there with success written all over her, and having a trophy boyfriend on her arm would add to the effect. Not for one moment could she admit the possibility of Fit Not Fat closing. It was up to her to generate that belief and convince everyone, by osmosis, that Sunnybank Fit Not Fat represented the future of the fitness industry in north Manchester.

Perhaps the L8s were having an effect after all, she decided, and felt a rush of feverish energy. Good old Garth. He had his uses.

The next challenge was Siobhan, with whom Jane was going out to lunch. Her mission now was to win over Siobhan once and for all. With Siobhan behind her, everything would be easier.

Tensed to expect her, she still jumped when Siobhan rapped at the door. Her deputy was dressed in a grey trouser suit with a long jacket. She wore her hair down and Jane noticed it had a natural, not unattractive wave. However, her wide forehead was as prominent as ever: it bulged aggressively above a face devoid of makeup. Altogether she looked as ill-at-ease as a child in school uniform for the first time. Jane hoped mateyness would dispel the artificiality of the situation. 'Right. I think everything's in order. Kendra knows where we are in an emergency. I've reserved a table at the Birtle Arms. I have to say I'm ravenous. I haven't eaten since seven this morning. I'll just switch on my voicemail. I'll drive – my car's round the back.'

Jane heard herself babbling but made no attempt to stop. Anything was better than the stony silence Siobhan carried around with her like an invisible shield. She ushered her out of the door and together they walked through Fit Not Fat, Jane glancing into the studio and the gym as she passed them. Siobhan looked straight ahead, a prisoner led by her warder.

Soon they were on their way out of Sunnybank, driving towards the green belt of quasi-countryside beyond Bury. 'I was on the phone to Head Office this morning,' Jane told Siobhan. 'I managed to squeeze some more details out of them about the inspection. Sarah will be coming, along with one of the auditors and the northern director. I told you the management dinner has been brought forward, didn't I? That's an opportunity for me to create a high profile for us and see if we're the only branch under threat. I think one of our strongest defences is that we have all this wasteland at the back of the club. If I can persuade Head Office to part with some cash, we could expand and build a pool. Then we really could give Fitness International a run for their money. Meanwhile there's a lot to do as it's vital we make the best possible impression. Unfortunately that means being on top of paperwork and high standards of cleanliness as well as everything else. Is MTV back on in the cardio studio? Can we afford two new Cybex trainers? Have you had a word with Jodie about her handwriting on some of the posters? 'Feel the burn' is all very well but she must make sure that 'burn' doesn't look like 'bum'.

Siobhan nodded. Jane was sure she had been listening to every word she had said, but it was impossible to know what was going on in her mind. Her expression was as impassive as ever. Jane decided to ask her a direct question. 'What do you think our chances are?'

'It's not really for me to say.'

Jane took a deep breath to hide her exasperation. This lunch was going to be harder work than she had anticipated. How on earth was she going to get Siobhan to open up? If she wasn't going to express an opinion or even pass the time of day, an hour or two in her company would be hellish.

She put the car into second gear as they drove up the steep hill to the Birtle Arms, past defunct cotton mills and bumpy fields with bored sheep. Jane turned into the car park and found a space. She and Siobhan got out and stood admiring the view. The whole of Bury lay beneath them, a hotchpotch of houses, factories, monolithic blocks of flats and a worm of motorway with a constantly moving stream of traffic. Beyond it was the cloud-smudged horizon of outlying hills, the Peak District, the Pennines. It was a relief to be outside and feel the breeze fan her face, a breeze, Jane soon realised, that brought with it pinpricks of moisture: it was drizzling again.

They entered the pub and made their way to the dining area in the conservatory. Jane was glad to see that they were being ushered to a table with a view – of the car park. Siobhan took a chair facing her, and they sat down to peruse the menu.

Jane decided immediately on the salmon salad and debated with herself about wine. Since her night with Garth she had hardly touched alcohol. She had limited herself to just one glass of something on alternate evenings. Last weekend, at the pub with friends, she had deliberately driven there in her own car to stop herself drinking. Well, she was driving today, so she would order a bottle of wine and limit herself to one glass with the meal. Siobhan could have the rest. Hopefully the booze would succeed where Jane had failed in loosening her tongue. 'Do you like wine?' she asked Siobhan.

'Not if I'm working.'

'Well, you're not working now.' Jane called the waitress over. 'The Chilean Chardonnay, please.'

Siobhan ordered home-made cheese and onion pie with chips, and Jane cast a cursory eye over her figure. Siobhan was perfectly trim, one of those annoying people who could eat anything without putting on weight. Jane wasn't sure if she was another because she'd had never dared to experiment. She actively controlled her weight as she did every other aspect of her life. The waitress wrote down their order and left them. Jane smiled at Siobhan, who gave a half-smile back. In the background there was piped music, the clink of cutlery on plates and the indistinct hubbub of other people's conversation. The more Jane tried to think of something suitable to say, the more impossible it seemed for her to come out with anything that hit the right note.

'It's raining again,' was all she could think of.

'Yes,' Siobhan said.

'Call this summer!'

Siobhan gave a little laugh.

'It's nice here, isn't it?' Jane continued. 'I've been here a couple of times with my mum and dad.'

'I've never been here before,' Siobhan said.

And they were going to have another hour or so of this! Jane's limbs ached with the effort. Was Siobhan a moron or what? Then she hated herself for her unkind thought. The waitress came with the wine. Jane tasted it, pronounced it perfect, and watched the golden liquid pour into their glasses. 'So,' she said, taking another gulp of wine. 'Alone at last.'

Siobhan didn't answer that. Jane tried again. 'I like your hair down,' she said. 'You should wear it like that more often.' Siobhan blushed at that, and Jane wished she hadn't been so foolish as to comment on her appearance. She drank some more wine, which encouraged her to speak frankly. There was no point in beating about the bush. 'I haven't invited you here to talk about the inspection, Siobhan. The reason we're here is that I want to get to know you better. I know it can't have been easy to have me come in as your boss and I want to say I appreciate that and I think you've been really generous in the way you've supported me so far and worked with the situation rather than against it.' She sipped some more wine. 'If there's anything I can do to help you in your career, you just have to ask.'

'Thank you,' Siobhan said.

'How do you see it developing?' Jane asked her.

Siobhan fumbled with her glass. She didn't meet Jane's eyes. 'I haven't given it a great deal of thought.'

'I really do think you're management material. You have such a clear mind, you're very organised and you know your stuff. You're popular with the clients too.'

'Thank you.'

'Would you think of moving from the area? Or are you tied here? Would you not want to leave your mother?'

'I'll have to, at some time.'

'I guess. She's sweet, isn't she?' Immediately Jane saw how patronising that was. She tried to correct herself. 'But sharp too, like you. I could tell after a time that you were her daughter. I bet you're very close. Do you have any brothers or sisters?'

'I have an older, married brother.'

'With children?'

'A little boy of two.'

'And what about you? Is there any man in your life?'

'No,' said Siobhan, her eyes down.

As Siobhan said that it occurred to Jane that it was a silly idea: someone as self-contained as Siobhan wouldn't want one. But surely she didn't spent all her off-duty hours with her mother.

'What do you do in your spare time? Do you go to the cinema, watch TV, see friends? I'm not being nosy, I just want to get a picture of you.' Jane felt her embarrassment mounting. She drained her wine-glass and poured herself a little more Chardonnay. 'Or are you like me? I have to admit I put work first. I do have a few close mates and I keep up with some old school friends. They're doing well for themselves. Sometimes they make me feel inadequate in comparison. I think that stems from my schooldays when I could never do maths. Even now I struggle a bit with the accounts. Do you have a good head for figures?'

'Not bad,' said Siobhan.

Jane proceeded, increasingly reckless. 'So, go on, what are your hobbies? Mine's drinking,' she said, as she helped herself again.

'I see the girls on the hockey team. I give my mother a hand in the garden as she's a bit stiff these days. But nothing much else.'

'Have you always lived in Sunnybank?'

'I was born in Radcliffe so I've never really left the area. I did work in Leeds for eighteen months in a council leisure centre, as you know.'

Jane did know, and she regretted that this lunch seemed to be turning into an interview. Was it her fault? Siobhan's fault? Absently she refilled her glass and went to top up Siobhan's. Siobhan had hardly touched hers.

Siobhan's discomfort was spreading like an infectious disease, and Jane wished she was anywhere but the Birtle Arms. Battling through sub-zero temperatures in the Antarctic? On the gynaecologist's table? With all the stress she was under, Siobhan's self-imposed distance was threatening to become the last straw. She knew she was becoming increasingly desperate. Should she burst into tears? Perhaps not now, not in the middle of the Birtle Arms. Thank God for the wine.

She returned to their one-sided conversation. 'I'm taking these new L8s,' she said brightly. 'Has Garth told you about them?'

'He has mentioned something.'

'He tells me it'll help me cope with stress, and I only hope it's true. I think he must believe in them as apparently he's been bulk-buying them from a friend abroad. Quite a lucrative earner, I should think. Better than training, anyway. Have you always wanted to work in the fitness industry?'

'I suppose so. It was something I felt I could do, something that I enjoy.'

'Did you ever have any other ambitions?'

A laugh escaped Siobhan. 'Well, when I was a little girl I wanted to be an engine driver.'

'An engine driver! Hey, I bet that was because of your older brother. Maybe you were copying him. I bet you looked up to him.'

'I probably did, come to think of it.'

'You were lucky, having an older brother. I was – I am – an only child. I always wanted a brother or sister. I was lonely, I reckon. I know it's supposed to make you self-reliant, being an only one, but I can just remember evenings with no one to play with. Maybe it would have been all right if my parents were different, but they've always been very busy. Look, I don't want to give you the impression they neglected me – that wasn't it at all. But it was like –' more wine '– it was like their lives just carried on on one level, and mine on another, and I felt like shouting, "Hello, it's me down here," and it was like nothing I did could attract their attention. And now I find I resent them, which is so wrong because they were good parents, but one day I'll make them notice me. Or does everyone hate their parents? I bet you don't. Your mum's nice. Look, we can get a taxi back. I know I've drunk too much to drive.'

Jane noticed Siobhan was acting differently now. She sensed that she was listening to her, really listening. It was as intoxicating as the wine. 'And in a way, Siobhan – yes, this is what I wanted to say all along – I think of the club as my family, my real family, so it's not just a matter of making a profit for me. Fit Not Fat can go and hang itself for all I care because I want you all to like me, and you most of all, Siobhan. You see, I don't want to keep my distance. I want to be the sort of manager who's more like a friend. A sister. I believe in teamwork, and I want to be seen as a team leader, that's all. Please don't think I'm out to get you. Look, here's lunch.' Jane topped up her glass again as the waitress delivered their food. She wasn't ready to eat yet. There was so much more she felt she had to say. She lifted her fork to emphasise the points she was making. 'You see, for me, work *is* my life. Sure, I have friends at home, and Gina and Liz, but we're not as close as we used to be. And look, I don't have a boyfriend either. You know, you're a very good listener, Siobhan.'

Jane punctuated her monologue with forkfuls of salmon. 'That's why relationships at work mean so much to me. You end up spending longer with your workmates than the people you live with. You get to know them better. They become your significant people. They matter. You matter most of all. I know that we're all under pressure and that it's easy to rub someone up the wrong way unintentionally. As long as you realise I've never meant to upset you – I like you, Siobhan. And I can see you're basically quiet and want to keep yourself to yourself and that's fine by me. But I just want to feel you like me too – and I'm sorry if I've given the impression that I've been prying today. I know my questions have sounded nosy, but I can be clumsy sometimes. What I mean is, in other words, I'm interested in you. Can we be friends, do you think?'

Siobhan gave a small cough. 'Well, I have a friend. I was going to tell you—'

'No, I don't mean your best friend – I just want you to think that we get on. Am I making any sense here? I know we're very different but that's just why I think we'd make the best team. So how about it?'

Siobhan's reply was hesitant, but noticeably warmer. 'I'll try. I was going to tell you that my mother enjoyed your talk.'

'Did she? Good! I have to tell you, I loved the over-sixties. They seemed much more willing to have a go than many of the class members of Fit Not Fat. And there was I thinking they'd all drop dead on me! I've always felt uneasy around old people. And ill people. The whole illness thing panics me. Like your whole body is out of control and threatening to give up on you. Do you think there are people who actually want to be ill? Half our staff seem to be off with one thing or another. I'm never ill. It's a sign of weakness, isn't it, to be ill?'

'I don't think so. You can't help catching flu.'

'Well, I don't know about that. I mean, if you're determined not to. Ha – and another thing, Siobhan, I'm going out with a doctor!'

'I thought you said you didn't have a boyfriend?'

'I don't. But you know David Richmond, one of our new

members? He's been chatting me up. I think he's a bit of a hunk. But it spooks me, the fact he's a doctor.'

'Why?'

'Working all the time with people's diseases – but it's not really that. Like, how would you feel if you went to bed with someone who knew all about your insides?'

'Is that a problem?'

'Oh, I don't know. It's just the way that doctors make out they know everything. But David's all right. He's more than all right, but the point is, I can't afford to have anyone in my life right now. Not with the inspection pending. He's coming with me to the managers' dinner. If he wasn't a doctor . . . I mean, sometimes I just can't be trusted with men! You'd never guess what I did the other day. Oh, God, I can't believe I'm going to tell you this.'

'You don't have to.'

'No, to be honest it's a relief. I met Garth in town a few weeks ago. I'd had too much to drink – it all gets to me sometimes – and I asked him to take me back to his flat and I ended up in his bed. Look – nothing happened, nothing at all. But how embarrassed was I! Don't tell David. If I had to go to bed with anyone, it would be David. Because maybe there are even some advantages to someone knowing all about you and your body. Why am I telling you all this? Really we should be talking about the inspection. The inspection. Right. The in-spection. Perhaps we should put on some kind of show, or—'

'I think tomorrow would be a better time to plan it out.'

'Yeah, you're right. I'm glad we're friends, Siobhan. I'll take your advice because I need your help. And when it's all over I'll get you a title – something like sales adviser or deputy manager – you just tell me what you want, what will help you. I know that the old manager, Trudy Thompson, trusted you. I can see now why she did. You're a rock, Siobhan. We've got a future together.'

'Jane, there's something I must tell you.'

'Fire away.'

'I . . . I don't intend to stay at Fit Not Fat much longer.'

Jane stopped eating. 'But . . . why?' She felt her drink-induced euphoria slip away.

'Trudy Thompson has offered me a job, in her new leisure club in the Algarve. I told her I'd take it on. I'm waiting to hear from her that it's all gone through, and then I'm going over. I don't know whether you'd like me to hand in my notice officially, but . . .'

'Oh, Siobhan! No, stay with us. Forget that – I can see you'll want to go. I appreciate you telling me. Oh, damn. Just when things were beginning to improve.'

'I don't want to leave you in the lurch, but you've got to understand about Trudy. We've been through a lot together. I came to Sunnybank when I left Leeds. There was a lot on my plate then and . . . and Trudy helped me through that. So I feel I want to stick with her. I'm probably her closest friend.'

'How much longer will you be with us?'

'I don't know. Maybe for another month, maybe more. I'll let you know. I feel better now this is in the open.'

'Sure. But I'm disappointed. You should have told me before, but I can see why you didn't. At least there are no more secrets between us. It seems I've told you all of mine.'

'Don't worry,' said Siobhan. 'I won't tell a soul. I'm an expert at keeping secrets.'

It was just as well, thought Jane. She was dimly aware of having done it again, having got drunk and disgraced herself. Just as well, really. It was a warning about the managers' dinner. At all costs she must keep sober, especially as she would have David by her side. She didn't want to give him the wrong idea. Or was it the right idea? It hardly mattered. She needed to sober up as soon as possible.

'I'll order coffee,' she told Siobhan. 'Gallons and gallons of it.'

The few people working in the gym didn't need any supervision. Gerry, lifting weights, had been training since the club first opened. On the treadmill Faye was half-way through the same routine she did four times a week. Cassie, who had obviously invested in some state-of-the-art designer sports gear, was working the stepper while glancing at her profile in the mirror. Lynda was lying on the mat, her eyes closed. On the TV screens an immaculate presenter read the news, someone scored a goal, a Latin-style crooner gyrated his hips and *The Jerry Springer Show* played on in dumb show.

So Siobhan was free to think, and the subject of her speculation was Jane. She wasn't as tough as she made out. That much was hardly surprising. What was surprising was just how soft she was. She was lonely, scared of the inspection and relied on drink to unwind. It never occurred to Siobhan to criticise her for this; in fact, she was glad, not because she was the stronger but because she was needed. Siobhan loved to help people and collected lame ducks. Other people's vulnerability attracted her. It had drawn her to Trudy. It was now affecting her feelings for Jane. She did not like Jane in *that* way, as she did Trudy, but she could see now that Jane needed her and, knowing that, her hatred had dissolved. She had only disliked the supremely competent Jane. This new Jane, trying desperately to control her life and her own mutinous emotions, demanded her loyalty and affection. What she had said about Garth would most certainly remain their secret. It reflected well on Garth that he had said nothing, but then, he could be as reserved as Siobhan. She had sometimes wondered if he was gay too.

Half an hour ago Siobhan had popped her head round the door of Jane's office. She had fallen asleep, her head resting on the desk, her cheek flushed, her hair disordered. Siobhan wanted to make her more comfortable, but instead went back to the gym. It saddened her that just as she had discovered that her new boss was not so bad after all, she had had to reveal that she was leaving. There was a poignancy to it, which made her all the more inclined towards Jane. Yet it was not as if she was leaving immediately: she would certainly not leave until after the inspection. It was ironic that, for weeks, the knowledge that she was defecting was the only thing that had helped her survive. Now she felt almost traitorous, having this escape route.

Siobhan could imagine herself talking to Jane at some time in the future. She might explain how her relationship with Trudy was more than just friendship – at least, it was for Siobhan. And Trudy had left her husband. Why, when no other man was involved? In those days Trudy had clung to her and they had become more intimate than ever. Siobhan had not dared to do or say anything, knowing that it was up to Trudy to take things further, if indeed she wanted to. So she had waited, understanding that Trudy's decision to live and work abroad had been primarily to give her time to think. She had said so. And she had looked Siobhan in the eyes. 'And when I'm ready, I'll call you.' She had said that too. Then they would be partners in every sense of the word. If Siobhan could tell Jane all of that (how *do* you talk about your feelings?), Jane would understand immediately and let her go.

And yet Siobhan had not heard from Trudy. There had been the postcard, true, followed by that letter with the photograph, and Siobhan had written back, but as yet she had had no reply, and she did not feel she could do any more. Her present life was just a waiting room.

The door to the gym opened and Jodie came in with a new member. 'Hi, Siobhan. This is Anita – she's here for a one-to-one.'

'Would you like me to supervise?' Siobhan cut in. Jodie's

tone had said it all. Her PMT had returned, and in that state she shouldn't be let near the clients.

'OK,' Jodie said. 'If you want.'

Siobhan glanced at the new member's programme, and then at the new member. She seemed in reasonably good shape already. She carried a large bottle of water, a towel and wore a sweatband around her forehead. Siobhan wondered if she had come from another health club. 'Have you belonged to a gym before?' she asked her.

'Yes.' Her reply was abrupt; shifty, even.

Siobhan was intrigued. 'Which one?'

'Fitness International.'

Their rival. Siobhan was pleased. 'Didn't you like it there?'

'They suggested I leave,' she said. 'Anyway, let's not waste any time. I've been in once or twice before today as I wanted to get to work as soon as my membership took effect. The truth is I do know what I'm doing. The controls on your treadmills are the same as the ones I'm used to.' She climbed on to one and began her workout. Siobhan observed that her mouth was tight with determination and her eyes had a manic glint. Every so often she increased the inclination of the treadmill without slowing her pace. It occurred to Siobhan that she might be training for a specific event – a marathon? Her stamina was exemplary. The other members in the gym had noticed too and were throwing her uncomfortable glances. Anita seemed oblivious to them all, lost in the pounding rhythms of her own body.

Forty minutes later, at the end of her run, Siobhan approached her again. 'You must be shattered,' she remarked.

Anita shook her head. 'Oh, no,' she panted. 'No, I'm fine. Got to run. Love it.' She took her towel and wiped her head. 'And I eat well. I had a baked potato three and a half hours ago, an organic orange two hours ago and a small square of chocolate an hour since.'

'What are your targets?' Siobhan asked. 'Are you training for anything in particular?'

'No. Just . . .' she mopped at her chest '. . . like everyone else. To get . . .' she filled her lungs '. . . fit. To keep my resting heart-rate low and guard against osteoporosis. To achieve the correct ratio of muscle to body fat. I'm currently twenty-five per cent body fat, which is good. I have a body-fat monitor at home so I can check.' She took a swig of her water. 'Important to replace fluid,' she said, 'and detox the system. Time for my resistance work. And then a turn on the stepper.' She gave Siobhan a brief smile and made her way to the leg press.

She's keen, Siobhan thought, but at that moment Cassie approached her and began to chat about her workout. As she did so her eyes strayed to the trainers' rota pinned to the wall. Lynda joined them and, attracted by the company, then Jodie appeared, dark shadows under her eyes. 'You don't look too good,' Lynda said.

Jodie shrugged. ''S nothing.'

'Now that won't do,' Cassie chaffed her. 'This is a health club and you're supposed to set a shining example to rest of us!' Jodie glared at her.

'Are you sure there's nothing wrong?' Lynda persisted.

Siobhan felt obliged to explain. 'Just that time of the month. Jodie suffers from bad PMT.'

Silence. The quiet bonding of women. An acknowledgement of the rhythms of female bodies that sometimes fits so awkwardly into the rest of female lives.

'I'm sorry I teased you,' Cassie said. 'I was out of order. Forgive me.'

'Listen, Jodie, you don't have to suffer, you know. I used to have dreadful PMT until I started taking vitamin B6. And I made a discovery.' Lynda paused for dramatic effect. 'PMT is a hormonal imbalance, right?' Her audience nodded. 'Well, *I* think it stands to reason that it's an excess of female hormones.

So what I used to do is make sure I was with men at the time – to absorb some of their testosterone.'

'And how, precisely,' asked Cassie, 'did you do that? No – I don't want to know.'

'Just being around men can help. It's common sense, really. Look, it worked for me. I used to force myself to sit in the same room as Merton when I felt at my most irritable. Sure, he suffered, but I felt better.'

Everyone laughed, even Jodie.

'He'll cheer you up,' Jodie's mum said, as she dropped off her daughter outside Darren's flat.

'I guess,' Jodie said.

She looked up at the three-storey house where Darren lived on the top floor with his flatmates, and took a deep breath. She had almost cancelled this evening. In all of their brief relationship she had never let Darren see her in this mood, when PMT permeated her like a noxious mist, distorting everything. Her love affair with him was too precious to risk. She was only here tonight because of what Lynda had said. It was clutching at straws, maybe, but if it worked, it might change her life. She had rung Darren earlier in the day to say she was a bit down and asked if she could see him that evening. He had sounded pleased and told her she was welcome to come round and watch the United match with him; he added, with meaning in his voice, that he would be alone. She would certainly get her fill of testosterone.

So here she was and, as yet, there was no change. The world and its cares were still pressing in on her, Darren's house seemed shabby, even squalid, with its tatty, overgrown hedge, and the uneven stone steps leading up to the front door, where even in the dark you could see that the paint was peeling. The bell rang with an annoying rasp, and she waited impatiently until Darren appeared.

He grinned at her and pecked her on the cheek. 'Come on, it's just beginning.'

She followed him up the stairs and into the living room where United and Spurs were waiting for the kick-off. Her eyes were drawn to the screen. She didn't mind watching the odd game of football, although she'd been brought up on rugby – her father was a fanatic – but she felt rather restless tonight: it irritated her to have to sit still and watch something. She sat down on the settee with Darren, who put an arm around her shoulders and nuzzled against her. She tried to respond because she remembered what Lynda had said about getting as close to him as possible, but almost gagged at his not-quite-fresh masculine aroma then reminded herself that some women found male sweat a turn-on. She glanced at his profile to check that he was still attractive to her, and, yes, she could see that he was good-looking, his chin still had that perfect definition, his eyes that cute expression that melted her. Now those eyes were trained on the TV screen, but she wasn't going to be unreasonable: it was an important match. She was only here to get better. She snuggled closer to him, hoping for some beneficial effects while her eyes strayed around the room.

It was a tip. Old clothes were strewn over the chairbacks and a dirty pair of football boots sat on newspaper under the table. The detritus of the evening meal had not yet been cleared away. There was even an opened can of baked beans sitting there – had someone been eating them straight from the tin? The glass in the window was cracked – she could see this because no one had bothered to draw the curtains. The window-sill had not been wiped for ages, the carpet was littered with crumbs and fluff, and the corner of an old magazine peeped out from under an armchair. The room was sordid, disgusting even, yet all the electronic equipment was clean, modern and huge – the wide-screen television, the video-player, cable set-top box, the Dream-cast console, the music system. It was as if a Dixon's showroom and a condemned bedsit had collided in a time warp.

Jodie felt uncomfortable. The springs on the settee were sagging and she had to support herself by leaning on Darren, whose bones were digging into her.

'O-o-ohh!' Darren exclaimed.

Jodie had missed whatever had happened. The game was in progress again.

It was no use. She couldn't just sit here. She was restless — the untidiness of the room pricked and vexed her and, as tired as she was, she had to be on the move. 'I'll tidy round,' she said.

Darren had not heard her — he was caught up in the game. She extricated herself from his embrace, took some plates from the table and carried them into the kitchen. No one had bothered to wash up and the sink was full. The work surface was covered with toast scrapings. It was all thoroughly disgusting. She paused and wondered whether she could be bothered to start fighting her way through all of this mess. But if she didn't do it, who would? That was what her mother often murmured as she scrubbed the bathroom. I'm turning into mum, Jodie thought. The idea depressed her.

She turned on the water and waited until it ran warm, then squirted fluorescent green washing-up liquid over the soiled plates. Men! It was so unfair. Everywhere they went they created chaos — they just didn't know what an effort it took to keep things civilised and clean. They left a trail of destruction behind them — they didn't think about other people.

She scrubbed viciously with a scabrous scourer at a crusty plate. Resentment trickled through her veins turning her blood to acid. Darren had known she was coming round and he hadn't even bothered to wash up. He was only thinking of himself, always and only of himself. Sure, he had treated her well in the beginning, but that was just to hook her. Now he was sure of her he took her for granted.

'Yes!' he screamed from the living room. 'We're one up!'

'Sodding bastard,' she said to herself, and prayed that Spurs would score.

And then she realised that she was being disloyal to him, to her own favourite team, and alone in the kitchen, she felt remorseful, repentant and filled with self-loathing. It was all her fault that she'd got herself into such a state. She was such an incompetent. She was ugly, fat, spotty, revolting – yes, it was she who was disgusting and incapable of coping with everyday life. It wasn't a crime that Darren hadn't washed up. He chose to live like this. It was Jodie who was neurotic, at the mercy of her hormones, mean, bitchy, horrible, horrible. It calmed her to call herself names. She lashed herself mercilessly.

She could see it clearly now. She was a failure. Everybody else knew what they wanted, they were card-carrying members of the human race. She was a misfit, clumsy, stupid, bad-tempered. Nobody loved her. She didn't deserve anybody's love. She would sneak out of the flat when Darren wasn't watching – it was the kindest thing she could do – and lose herself somewhere. The dirty plates were noble compared to her.

She went to the living room to take one last look at him. And yet, if Darren was to look at her now and say he loved her, or do something to make her feel wanted, she might just stay. She paused on the threshold, but he was immersed in the game. She had never felt lonelier in her life.

'Hey, come 'ere, Jo,' he said.

Too little, too late. She hesitated between going back to join him, and leaving. In the end, it was only Lynda's theory that nudged her into staying. She sat down on the settee. There had been an injury. A player was writhing on the field while the others stood around watching. Suddenly Darren lunged at her. To her amazement, he kissed her passionately. A moment ago she had been in the kitchen and her hands still smelt of Fairy Liquid. Now he was coming at her from nowhere, it seemed. Didn't he realise she needed to be in the right mood? That she needed to be prepared? She was in shock as his tongue explored her mouth and his hands found their favourite places. She neither pushed him away nor responded. He didn't seem to notice. She pulled away. 'Hey? Wha – Oh, right – they're playing again. Cheers!'

Now Jodie felt worse than ever. She had moved from beating herself up to loathing Darren. He was insensitive, selfish, boorish, and she couldn't imagine what she had ever seen in him. He had been treating her like some inflatable sex toy, unaware of what she was thinking or feeling. He was a beast, hell-bent on his own gratification. She was filled with the desire to wound him in some way and entertained brief but exciting fantasies of plunging a knife into his chest, cutting through yielding skin and splintering hard bone, or bashing his skull with a hammer, seeing the shocked look in his eyes, watching his blood spatter the carpet – not that anyone would notice, with all the mess.

She pulled herself back to reality. She would never commit an act of violence, but she had to speak out. 'What's up with you tonight? You hardly seem to know I'm here.'

He looked at her, baffled. 'The match is on!' he said.

'I can see where your priorities lie,' she said coldly.

He pulled a face, then went back to watching the screen. She was furious and determined to get a reaction. 'You make me sick,' she said.

'Sssh,' he said. 'Yes! Two–nil! Go, go go!'

'I wish I'd never come round!'

'But we're winning two–nil.'

'*Listen to me!*' she screamed. Darren looked at her, as surprised as if she'd suddenly sprouted wings.

She stood in front of the TV screen, obscuring it. 'I come round here because I'm feeling low, and you don't bother to prepare for me in any way. You don't ask me how I am, all you care about is the football, and then you lunge at me and stop as soon as someone scores and I'm sick of it, I'm sick of you, and I'm not going to be second best, even though I'm know I'm the most horrible person ever to walk this earth, and that you hate me. I know you do. And I deserve it.' She was crying tears of rage and self-pity.

'Wha—'

'See? You can't even think of anything to say! You don't talk to me! I know we're supposed to be having this wonderful relationship, and what is it? For you it's just sex, or it would be if I let it. You never talk to me, you don't know the least thing about me. It's always me making allowances for you, keeping the peace, doing and saying the right thing, making this relationship work. And you don't do anything. And I'm pissed off.'

'Are you feeling all right, Jodie?'

'Yeah, I am.' And she burst into tears.

Darren adjusted his position on the settee so he could see round her to the screen. It was half-time. He stood up, approached her gingerly and put a hand on her heaving shoulders. 'Are you sure you're feeling all right?'

'Yes – no – I get PMT and . . .'

'PMT? Oh, right, like it's your hormones.'

'And everything gets out of control.'

'So you didn't *mean* any of what you said?'

'And I just don't know what to do to get rid of it.'

'So you can't help it. Hey, relax, baby.' Darren started to kiss her. It was OK, then. For a moment, he had been worried. He'd thought she was getting at him, but it was just because she was a woman and got these moods. They were all like that, irrational, because of those hormones. You just had to let it pass, ignore it, and sweeten them up. He tried to calculate whether he could get her to the bedroom and out again before the second half. His hands found her bra strap. There was no resistance.

To Jodie, nothing made sense any more. She had said everything that was on her mind. He ought to be furious with her, but instead he was carrying on as usual. She couldn't decide whether this was a good thing, or whether it was tragic. Were men and women always destined to misunderstand and hurt each other? Was romance an illusion? Was her relationship with Darren no more than a combination of his lust and her foolishness? She cried as he undid her bra. 'Hey, Jodie, it's all right. I'll only go as far as you want me to.'

'It's not that,' she said. He was encouraged and felt for the zip on her jeans.

'No, stop it,' she said. 'I'm not in the mood.'

'It'll make you feel better,' he cajoled.

Jodie doubted it. And, besides, she'd promised her mother she'd never do anything unless she was on the pill. And if she was going to sleep with Darren, it would be when she felt better. Now was the wrong time.

'I think the second half is beginning,' she told him, and wriggled out of his clutches. 'I'll see if there's any beer in the fridge.'

He was disappointed and his hang-dog look made her feel a little ashamed. Maybe it was she who was selfish. Or maybe not. She didn't know what to think any more. All she knew was that she was drained, defeated, lifeless and in need of some lager too. Lynda's theory had failed to work.

Jodie made her way to the kitchen. Well, at least Darren was still talking to her. If United won, as looked likely, he'd forget all about her outburst. Short-term, there seemed to be no problem. But, long-term, Jodie knew she would have to tackle her mood swings. She would have to talk to someone. Jane, perhaps, or Cassie. She was a university lecturer and Jodie felt an exaggerated respect for her. Because she was either going to lose the PMT, or lose Darren, and the worst of it was she didn't know which she'd prefer.

Chapter Thirteen

———❦———

Fit Not Fat was bathed by the dying glow of the setting sun. Even the brash brick exterior seemed softened. The light that blazed out from the gym and the studios stained the ground outside, and Cassie noticed the building all the more because she was walking to it: she had left her car behind. She told herself that this was because she hadn't been to the gym that day and needed the exercise.

As she approached the club the excitement she had carried with her all day liquefied into nervousness. She was about to go out for a drink with Garth. Repeat. *She was about to go out for a drink with Garth.* There was no saying what would happen although, of course, the most likely outcome was that he would not be there, having forgotten about her, or had left a message saying that something – or someone better – had come up. Cassie had been aware that she was courting disappointment in taking Garth up on his offer, but something had driven her on. *Carpe diem*, she told herself. Seize the day. Everything sounded more respectable in Latin, even her lustful imaginings.

Naturally he was not in the lobby, and one of the part-timers was at the desk. Cassie had to explain that she wasn't going into the gym but meeting someone. Standing in the club with no intention of working out made her feel even more guilty, and she began to read a leaflet of shopping tips for those losing weight. I do that, thought Cassie. And that. And that.

'Are you right, then?' Garth had come up behind her.

Cassie recovered her composure. 'Yes,' she said.

'You look nice,' he said.

Cassie wanted to believe him, although she couldn't quite. She had spent ages deciding what to wear, tried on virtually everything in her wardrobe and come out finally in a pair of black trousers and a black polo-neck she had bought recently from Wallis. She looked more like a scene-shifter in the theatre than the vamp she wanted to be.

'I thought we might go into town,' Garth said. 'There's nowhere decent to drink round here.'

'Sure,' Cassie said, aware that so far she had been speaking in monosyllables, letting Garth take control of the situation. That in itself was a novelty. She agreed when he said he would drive, and pointed out that she didn't have her car with her. She followed Garth out to his discreet silver Honda Civic, slipped in beside him and into a parallel universe, in which almost-middle-aged university lecturers were courted by drop-dead gorgeous fitness instructors. She laughed at all Garth's pleasantries as they proceeded swiftly into the centre of Manchester. Their subjects of conversation: her lecture that day; her holiday plans – a tour of French castles; his holiday plans – skiing that winter; the conference she was shortly to attend in Gothenburg; his preparations for an inspection at Fit Not Fat by Head Office. Before long Garth had parked near the Bridgewater Hall and they were walking in the direction of Deansgate Locks. Cassie noted that as yet Garth had said nothing about the L8s, the flimsy excuse on her part for this evening out.

He led her to a bright, noisy bar near the Comedy Store. There were booths along a side wall and luckily a couple was in the process of vacating one. Cassie slipped in and Garth left her there to get some drinks. This gave her the opportunity to orientate herself.

There were a few tables, lots of standing space and lots of people, younger than her, standing in it. It occurred to her that she might be in a student venue and her eyes roved around the bar hoping she wouldn't recognise anyone. No: the clientele here was wealthy, well-dressed and chic, as well as young. She scanned the crowds again and realised she was one of the oldest people there. She felt simultaneously out of place and supercool, defying, as she was, the march of the years. If only the music wasn't quite so loud.

Before long Garth returned, and took a seat on the other side of the table. Not as intimate as side by side, she thought, but all the better for feasting her eyes on him. 'So how's business?' She raised her voice so she could be heard above the music.

'Pretty good. I'm selling L8s as fast as I can get them.'

'Sorry? What was that?'

'Business is good.'

'I was wondering, where do you get your supplies from? Is the stuff manufactured in Britain?'

'Abroad.'

'Do you need a special licence or something?'

'That part doesn't concern me. It's tricky to explain. My partner sees to it, anyway.'

So he had a partner. Business or romantic? She had to find out. 'Who exactly is your partner?'

'An old friend.'

Cassie was relieved. He meant a business partner. So far, so good, but she was starting to feel that her chances of getting to know Garth better in this venue were pretty slim. The background noise was such that they could only converse in brief bursts, shouting to each other as if they were forty yards apart. So Cassie gave up, and tried to look sophisticated as she sipped her wine.

She looked around again. She guessed no one would be able to hear much of what anyone else said. Maybe that was the point. It was the image that mattered here: the pose was everything. At one time Cassie would have felt excluded because of her size, but not now. There were even women who were clearly in the thick of things and considerably larger than her. But they were younger.

Was this to be the final irony? That she had lost weight only to discover that she was too old for it to count? Of course, she knew she wasn't too old for anything that really mattered, but she was too old for fashion, too old to represent the *Zeitgeist*. Having a good time in public was a privilege that belonged to the young. She was a fish out of water. It was sad, and terribly unfair. Surely she deserved more after all her hard work at the gym. Again her gaze rested on Garth. Perhaps life wasn't so unfair after all. Was his foot nudging hers?

'What do you think of this place?' he called over to her.

'Nice. A bit noisy, though.'

'Yeah.'

Garth was quiet again, happy to look around. Cassie cast covert glances at him, until he looked at her and smiled. It was a long, slow, deliberate smile and did strange things to Cassie's lower regions.

'Shall we go?' he said.

Cassie nodded, and they left.

It was a blessed relief to be out in the cold and able to converse at a normal volume. She scuttled along by his side until they reached the car, hoping their evening was not over.

'I didn't bring any L8s with me,' Garth said, 'but I've plenty at my flat, which is near here. Why don't we go back there and chill out for a bit?'

'Sure,' Cassie said, her heart soaring. One advantage about being an older, assertive woman was that one could go back to a man's flat without feeling vulnerable. If things got sticky she could always put him to sleep by explaining the origins of the Wars of the Roses.

*   *   *

He lived in a ground-floor flat in a courtyard of apartments close to Piccadilly. Somehow that did not surprise her: she had always imagined him in this slick urban setting. His living room — with its pale walls, the mirrors designed to double the space, the tang of expensive aftershave — was perfect. She sat down carefully on his cream leather sofa and he went to fetch some L8s.

She noticed the absence of books, and the stark lines of his slate-grey coffee table then spotted herself in a mirror, perched awkwardly, her shoulder bag flung untidily at her feet. Hastily she rearranged her hair so that her face was partly concealed by it. No, she looked like a scarecrow. She decided to tuck it behind her ears. Far too severe. She brought out a lock and fiddled with it, glanced at herself again, and realised how dreadful her posture was. She made herself sit up straight, which had the effect of making her bust all the more prominent. Good.

At that moment Garth entered with two cartons of pills. Cassie sprang to her feet.

'Here they are,' he said. He gave them to her for inspection. She read the legend on the box and Garth vanished again. When he returned he was carrying a bottle of tequila. 'Fancy a shot?' he asked.

Since she wasn't driving she could afford to be interested, in a detached, scholarly way, in what tequila and red wine did when mixed together. She knocked back the contents of her glass in one, felt a little light-headed, and sat down.

Garth came to sit by her. 'Interested?' he asked, his eyes on the pills.

'Oh, I don't know. Part of me feels it's silly not to give them a try, but a bigger part feels it's a lot of mumbo-jumbo. Sorry.'

'Don't be. That's one of the things I like about you. You're not afraid to speak your mind. Most of my clients are fairly desperate people and believe everything I tell them.'

'So are you admitting that L8s are a con?'

'No. I wouldn't sell them if they were. Don't think that of me, Cassie.'

He looked a little hurt and she hastened to reassure him. 'I can tell you're convinced of their merits. And I never had you down for a con artist.'

'How *do* you think of me?'

Christ! she thought. How do you answer that? Sex on legs? My fantasies personified?

'I think you're an excellent trainer,' she said cautiously, 'and as a person, not quite what I expected.'

He laughed, somewhat hollowly. 'You mean you thought I was an airhead just because I look good? It's OK, everyone does. I'm used to it. Good looks can be a curse, too. The women I know are never interested in me as a person.'

Cassie was fascinated. Look how far feminism had come! Ten years ago, or even five, it would have been a woman speaking in just that way. Garth was articulating the cry of the dumb blonde. Only he was a bloke – a bloke who yearned to be taken seriously. Perhaps he was attracted to her precisely because she was older, more discerning, more likely to see beneath his veneer of physical perfection. It was all falling beautifully into place. 'No, Garth, I *am* interested in you as a person, otherwise I wouldn't be here,' lied Cassie.

He smiled at her. 'I know, because you're not really interested in the L8s.' They both laughed, and he swung one leg over the other and sat back on the settee. God, he was gorgeous! Cassie regarded his full lips and the jut of his chin, the well-defined shoulders and the merest suggestion of muscles pushing against his mohair sweater. Then, as if from nowhere, some music played. It was laid-back rap, chilled but suggestive. Garth drank his tequila. 'This is nice,' he said.

Cassie nodded. She wondered where this evening would end.

'Hey, maybe we could go out and eat later,' he suggested

'If you like,' she said, a little disappointed. She looked around the flat again, saw white walls, mirrors, several Garths, from the front, rear and side elevations, and many Cassies making jerky gestures as she spoke, still a little plump, really, her hair untidy, her cheeks flushed. The silence was getting to her. And now that he had said he wanted her to take an interest in more than his body, she owed it to him to make a stab at some intellectual or educational conversation. Hopefully that would turn him on.

'Your flat is lovely and yet it's fascinating to think that seven hundred years ago there would have been no aesthetic appreciation of this minimalist style of décor. People liked gold, bright colours, blues, yellows – which surprises us today because we think of medieval art as dull, but that's only because the colours on the paintings that have survived have faded over time. There's a restored medallion of Our Lady in the cathedral at—'

'Tell me a little bit about you.'

'Me?' Her stomach lurched. Surely his comment was mildly suggestive. 'Well, I think you know everything about me, everything that matters, that is.' And it was true. In supervising her fitness routine, Garth, knew that she could now manage level seven on the stepper for five minutes at a time, and that she had started some resistance work and . . . Cassie found herself talking more and more unguardedly, about the way she used to be, and the way she was now, about the changes that seemed to be taking place in her every day. 'And what people never tell you when they encourage you to lose weight is that it changes more than just your body. You relate to everyone in a different way. Or, rather, it takes time for your image of yourself to catch up with the external changes. I feel I have to get to know myself all over again. I think that's why, I turned Terry down. Did I tell you about Terry – my partner, my ex-partner? He's gone to Rome without me, but it's my fault. I made him go. Maybe I deserve to be lonely.'

'I know about loneliness too,' Garth said.

Suddenly Cassie's crap-detector went on red alert. She looked at him narrowly. He was acting, she was sure of it, yet his physical beauty was having a hypnotic effect on her. She guessed he was someone who acted a part because he lacked self-knowledge; she had met similar types before. Now Garth moved towards her. Her heart pumped faster – maybe this was all the cardiovascular work she needed. It was about to happen, the scene she had been concocting in her mind night after night. She prayed that she would not be disappointed.

'Teach me something, Cassie,' he murmured.

His kiss was exquisite: his lips were soft in texture, hard with latent power; his hand went to the small of her back and remained there while he explored her mouth and her reactions to his kiss for precisely the amount of time that one ought to do these things. Then he broke away to look at her.

Cassie's mind was in overdrive. It had happened: he was offering himself to her. She didn't have a clue why, because despite all her silly fantasies, a man as young and nubile as Garth ought not to want to sleep with her. Utterly bizarre. But did she want to sleep with him? Silly question.

'Shall we stay here,' he asked her, 'or move into the bedroom?'

She just had to get away from those mirrors. 'The bedroom,' she said.

She followed him through the living room and into the short corridor leading to it. The wardrobe doors were mirrored. She watched him close the vertical blinds. Then he lifted his T-shirt over the top of his head to reveal a chiselled midriff with a flat stomach that tapered down, taking Cassie's eyes with it. Sitting on the bed, she watched him unbutton his trousers, one, two, three, and he wriggled slightly so that they fell to the floor. He stepped out of them and quickly removed his socks. His black pants bulged invitingly. Cassie took in the fine dark hair lying smooth on his legs, the turn of his calf muscles, his firm, broad feet. She looked up again at his whole physique, and past him to the woman on the bed, hunched, looking lustful and terrified, hair worse than ever, and it occurred to her that this woman ought also to take off her clothes.

Garth stood there, waiting for something. Cassie was thinking at the speed of light. She could not possibly take off her clothes because her bra straps were held together with safety-pins and her briefs were two sizes too big and sagged horrendously. And losing two stone was all very well but her breasts had gone all dangly and her stomach still protruded, would always protrude, and it was fretted with stretchmarks. The skin on the inside of her thighs had wrinkled since the fat had departed.

Was it possible to make love with your clothes on? Possible, but not very comfortable. No, she would have to strip. It was what Garth was waiting for her to do. She pulled off her sweater, and glanced at him for his reaction. His eyes were focused a little way above and beyond her, and she was puzzled until she saw that in the mirror on the wardrobe door was the reflection of a mirror that presumably hung on the wall above the bed. In it there was a further reflection of Garth's firm, naked body and Garth looking at it. She clutched her sweater like a security blanket. He was turning himself on by looking at himself.

Any further intimacy was impossible. Making love to some-one with a perfect body was arguably the least sexy thing you could possibly do — by comparison you felt hopelessly inade-quate. But it wasn't even that: the fun of sex was the squidgy bits, the unexpected pot belly, the imperfection that made someone unique, the demonstration of vulnerabilities, the sharing of two bodies that were not quite perfect to make something that was pretty damn good. The point about Garth was that to feel good he didn't need anyone else. He was Narcissus, in love with his own reflection. She was just an accessory, a spectator. A spectator sitting with her sweater in her hands. She put it back on.

'Cassie?' He looked puzzled. 'What's wrong?'

'Sorry. No can do. I'm not quite the libertine I thought I was. Old habits die hard. I've been too deeply ingrained with all those sermons about the seven deadly sins. Lust is a killer. It's ten Hail Marys and a cold shower for me.' She took a last, lingering look at that unbelievable body and a thought occurred to her: she didn't want him to feel rejected. 'It's nothing personal,' she said. 'I mean, who could resist you? Well, me, actually, but I'm just a crusty old history lecturer.' She glanced up at him. His face was closed. 'I'm sorry if I've led you up the garden path. To tell you the truth, I thought it would be the other way round. But it just goes to show. I know I'm talking nonsense but that's just because I'm as embarrassed as hell. Look, why don't you pop your clothes back on and I'll make us a cup of tea?'

Cassie scurried out of the bedroom and wondered how to salvage this situation so that she and Garth could still be friends – she could not possibly stop going to Fit Not Fat, not now. She would have to buy some L8s – a small price to pay – and explain again to him that her inadequacies had scuppered their night of romance, not his deficiencies. She hoped he would believe it, and guessed that he would: Garth did not strike her as the type of man who would doubt himself.

'Maybe another time,' he said to her, when he came into the kitchen.

'No hard feelings?' she asked him.

'None.'

'I think what it is, you know, is Terry. I'm not over him. I was kidding myself when I thought I could forget about him. I'm so sorry for giving you the wrong impression.'

'Don't mention it.'

'Believe me, there's nothing wrong with you. Nothing at all.'

'I know,' he said.

'But I tell you what, I'll take some of those L8s. It's payday today. I'll give them a fair trial, see if they do me any good, and I'll let you know.'

'I'll get you some,' he said, and went out into the living room.

He paused before he opened the cupboard where he kept a reserve supply of L8s. He was just a little shaken. This had never happened to him before. He had been certain Cassie was just his type. He had picked her out from the day she'd started at the gym. His only reservation was that her fitness programme might change her too much. If anything, he had preferred her before she had lost weight. He disliked women who pranced about obsessed with their own appearance – or, rather, they did nothing for him. That wasn't how he got his kicks. He ran his hands down the sides of his thighs. No, he liked women who could reflect himself back to him. That was what sex was all about. He felt most authentic when he was most admired. He cheered himself up by looking in the mirror again, running his eyes over his perfect proportions, the swelling muscles in his arms. It was enough simply to be himself; it always had been. Since he was a small boy he had attracted the admiration of women, his doting mother, his two aunts who took him to the photographic competitions, numerous girls at school, too many to count. When he was little, he had taken it for granted. It wasn't until he was fourteen that a pattern emerged. It started with the girls' games teacher, who had taught him a few new things to do with his body one night in the sports hall after athletics' practice.

Perhaps she had been responsible for his preference for older women. Certainly he appreciated their undisguised admiration, their gratitude, their desire to hold on to him. They loved him almost as much as he loved himself. They tended to have a bit more about them than younger women, such as healthy bank accounts and a propensity for giving presents. Younger women made him a little uneasy, although he was unable to say why. He recalled the night Jane had thrown herself at him, but he could have never made love with someone as naïve as her. And she certainly was naïve. She was completely taken in by his best-mates act – fortunately. No, young women weren't for him. Nor were men, although he'd been approached by a few, and had experimented once or twice. No, there was nothing like the sort of woman who couldn't believe her luck in getting him. An older, shop-soiled woman, worshipping him like a devotee in a temple.

Garth had moved seamlessly from woman to woman, until Cassie. Not that it really mattered. She was only to have been a diversion anyway. The best was yet to come. Garth knew never to leave himself unprovided for. He was raking it in with the L8s and there shouldn't be long to go before he was out of here – before the shit hit the fan.

The thought cheered him, and restored his equanimity. He took the pills and went to give them to Cassie.

All Cassie had in the fridge at home were four tubs of fat-free *fromage frais*. She scooped them all out into a bowl, mixed them, and told herself to pretend it was rice pudding or custard made with full-cream milk. She sat at her kitchen table spooning it resolutely into her mouth.

She had made a spectacular mistake. But what had it been? Turning Garth down, or getting herself into that position in the first place? Like the historian she was, she assembled all the evidence in her mind, replaying scenes of Garth undressing, her acute embarrassment, the vacuous, self-regarding way he had looked at himself in the mirror, his cool demeanour afterwards. She could blame herself neither for her determination to have a big adventure, nor for declining when she realised that Garth was weird – in the way he was so narcissistic and in wanting her. In the world of sexual attraction like stayed with like. Phenomenally good-looking people hung out with other phenomenally good-looking people. Average people like her found other average people, like Terry. And no matter what you did to yourself – lifting weights, pounding the treadmill – you couldn't hide the fact that you basically belonged to one group or another. She had been mad, allowing herself to pursue Garth. Perhaps she should ring Fitness International and see how much their membership was.

The *fromage frais* had gone, and her cat jumped on to the table to lick out the bowl. Cassie stroked him absently. It was time to think about Terry. Or, rather, it was time to think about how to get Terry back. Lynda had promised to keep her ear to the ground and let her know as soon as he arrived back in Manchester. Then what should she do? Ring him? E-mail him? If she did, what should she say? 'Terry, will you marry me?' sprang to mind as tears pricked her eyes.

They brought her up short. Cassie was not sentimental and felt obliged to ask herself dispassionately what was going on. Was she turning to Terry because she had been disappointed in other quarters? In that case, she didn't deserve him. He was far too good for her. But what she had experienced in Garth's bedroom was not so much disappointment as a coming-to-her-senses. She had been on a trajectory in which her pursuit of the body beautiful had turned into a pursuit of Garth's body beautiful. Both had turned out to be pointless. As any medieval philosopher could have told her, the things of the flesh are temporary, even illusory. Or, in other words, since joining Fit Not Fat she had been drawn into a world where the state of your body mattered more than the state of your soul, where the heart was an organ that pumped blood around your body, and not the seat of your affections. Or, to put it yet another way, the gym was like a drug, she was hooked, and she'd stopped seeing straight.

Now, in this moment of clarity, she could consider Terry again. She thought about when she had first met him, and how she was immediately comfortable with him, as if he was a long-lost brother. They saw eye to eye on almost everything. Then there had been that alarming but not unpleasant discovery that she had other feelings for him too, which had been reciprocated. As it developed, their love was not so much a towering inferno as the steady glow of an old-fashioned coal fire, that flared up nevertheless when stoked.

Before Terry, Cassie realised now, she had felt incomplete. And feeling complete had given her the *chutzpah* to think Garth might find her attractive. This was crazy but true. To put it more crudely, she wanted to have her cake and eat it. Now it was time to grow up. A future without Terry was unthinkable and unless she took the initiative it loomed ahead of her. She had better act soon. Maybe it was too late already.

She debated about what to do. Given her academic duties, flying to Rome was not an option. Neither could she propose by electronic mail, nor even by telephone. She would have to waylay him the moment he returned, speak to him face to face and try to explain how she had temporarily lost her sanity.

'Geoffrey,' she said, to her cat, 'do *you* think he'll have me back?'

The cat contorted himself and began to wash his genitals.

'I never get an intelligent answer from you,' she said. 'I don't know why I bother talking to you in the first place.'

Cassie knew she was alone with this one. No one could help her approach Terry and confess how wrong she'd been. And the worst part was, she would have to wait an unspecified amount of time before she could speak to him. How could she make it pass quickly? Nothing that involved money as the L8s had cleared her out: she had bought a whole box from Garth in an attempt to ensure his loyalty. Well, she thought, no point in wasting them. She reached down for her bag, took out the box, and prepared to start the course.

Chapter Fourteen

———◦◦◦◦◦———

Jane drummed her fingers on the desk. She had got in at seven that morning to go through the notes David had given her on nutrition and fat reduction, and had rewritten them so that they could be used as literature for her clients. She had read up on the latest research project on the benefits of interval training and resolved to send Siobhan on a course. How else could she occupy her time?

She did not feel in the least bit tired, despite waking at five thirty that morning. It was not anxiety – she was positively looking forward to the managers' dinner. She would make sure she collared Sarah and talked up her staff, and mention the fund-raising they were doing for the local maternity unit. And ask Sarah to present the cheque – that would get her on their side. Another brilliant idea! These days, she was constantly having ideas.

She suspected that this frenetic creativity might be due to the L8s, which were definitely having an effect on her – a welcome effect. Admittedly there were side effects too: she slept little, and strange moods of wild elation, followed by numbing despair, swept through her unpredictably. Occasionally she found herself trembling, as she did when she'd drunk too much coffee. Still, that was not an altogether unpleasant feeling. Set against that was the energy that zapped through her every hour of the day. L8s also had the highly desirable effect of taking away her appetite: her stomach felt as tight as a nut while waves of electricity charged through her veins. She worked out more effectively yet noticed that she dehydrated more easily – she was drinking gallons of water. Still, water was good for you. And, best of all, L8s lifted her mood – they made her feel capable of anything. The mere thought of them convinced her that it was possible to triumph tonight: she would make Sarah and the rest of them see that Sunnybank was the jewel in Fit Not Fat's crown. Jane Wright could do anything she set her mind to.

Or could she? She experienced a wave of nausea, panic and conviction that she had left something vital undone, because so much was going on in her life. Life was a race – or, rather, the inspection was a race, and afterward she could relax a little. But not now. Success. What a lovely word it was. Sibilant, seductive, perfect. It would be hers. To Jane the tightness in her stomach and the dryness in her mouth were evidence of her determination that everything would turn out all right. She was full of plans these days, exciting, visionary plans. And she had so much energy – gallons, litres, hogsheads of it. The L8s liberated something in her.

On the other hand, she felt most peculiar. With the mood swings she was almost as bad as Jodie. And it was vitally important that she get a grip of herself, keep calm, and stay in the driving seat. With immense effort she pushed the turmoil of her conflicting emotions down to some dark place inside her and shakily poured some water from the bottle on her desk into the glass by it. She would live from one moment to the next, starting *now*. Except that the L8s made her feel it was impossible to live in the moment, as this moment so rapidly became the next, so that she was always living in the next moment, and the next, and the next, and she had to remember to ring Liz and chase her up about the pool feasibility study she'd offered to do, and ask Siobhan to present an analysis of the membership numbers and check that Garth had tracked down a new *astanga* yoga teacher and write the morale-boosting speech she planned to give her staff, and all of this without any alcohol at all, not one drop, at dinner tonight.

Siobhan pushed the stationary bike to one side so she could vacuum underneath it. She hoped the two regulars who were lifting weights at the other end of the gym would not mind the noise, which drowned both MTV and her troubled thoughts. She focused on the intricacies of the vacuuming operation and told herself not to think, suppose or speculate, because thoughts could affect emotions, and emotions were always best kept out of the workplace. She turned off the vacuum and edged the bike back into position. At that moment Jodie came in.

'Do you need a hand?' she asked Siobhan.

'You could scrub down the mats.'

Jodie winced. 'It hurts to bend down. I started this morning – that's why I'm late in. I have the most awful cramps. Like someone's tied a metal band round my stomach and is pulling it tighter and tighter.'

'Have you taken anything for it?'

'I have some pills. But you know I don't like taking pills. It's the thought of swallowing them.'

'There's always soluble painkillers.'

Jodie gave Siobhan a pathetically grateful look, but Siobhan knew she wouldn't take her advice. Jodie was obstinate like that. She guessed it was her age, or lack of it. Also, she knew Jodie was the sort of person who brought her indispositions to work in order to attract a little bit of mothering.

Kendra however, loved to shock them with all the dramatic details of her illnesses. There was the time when she had woken up from the anaesthetic during her D and C, the time when she had had a polyp removed and watched the whole procedure, and the unforgettable occasion when she swallowed a chip that stuck in her throat and was rushed into A and E. She was just about to have a general when she was sick over the anaesthetist. Kendra was not very popular at Fit Not Fat.

But Siobhan was happy to give Jodie all the attention she craved. It stopped her thinking about herself. 'At least you're through the PMT,' she told Jodie.

Jodie gave a rueful smile. 'Did I tell you I made an absolute exhibition of myself at Darren's? I went round to see him when I was in the thick of it and I was so irritable I started to clean round even though he hadn't asked me to, which was daft, wasn't it? Then, would you believe it? *I* got angry with *him* for letting me, and I had such a go at him – this bit will make you laugh – because he was coming on to me and I wasn't in the mood. Poor bloke. All he wanted was to watch the match in peace and have a bit of a cuddle. But the evening turned out like World War Three.'

Siobhan thought privately that Jodie had been rather kind to Darren in her interpretation of events. She found him a charmless individual, but was reluctant to draw any firm conclusions, as she suspected her dislike of him might stem from some silly homophobic remarks she had overheard him make. Still, it wasn't her place to interfere with Jodie's relationships. Siobhan knew that people had to make their own mistakes.

'I felt such a fool afterwards, Siobhan,' Jodie continued. 'Last night, when I was feeling a bit better, I took him round a bottle of wine to say sorry. He was dead nice about it. And dead understanding. He reckons most women are ruled by their hormones. Men are different – they're more on the level all the time. He said he'd never imagined that having a steady girlfriend would be easy. He's realistic like that. God, I feel wretched today.'

'Do you want to go and have a rest? Or a cup of tea?'

'No. I couldn't drink a thing, I feel so sick. But it will go away. I might just put my trainers on and have a walk on the treadmill while it's quiet. That helps sometimes. It's Jane's dinner-dance tonight, isn't it?'

'That's right.'

'And is it true she's taking one of our members with her — that dishy doctor who comes in?'

'Yes.'

'Who asked who? Is she going out with him, do you know?'

'I'm afraid she hasn't said a word to me about it.'

'Oh, I just wondered,' Jodie said. 'And, Siobhan, did you see that notice out on the wasteland at the back of the club? I spotted it as Mum drove round to drop me off. It says, "Sold." And it had the name of some property company on it.'

'Sold!' Siobhan was alarmed. That was the area where Jane had hoped to put the pool. This was not good news. 'Has Jane seen it?'

'I don't know. She won't be in till later. I'm just popping out to get my trainers.'

Siobhan was not superstitious but couldn't help reflecting that the storm clouds were gathering over Fit Not Fat. Apart from her own concerns, this development would be a blow for Jane. The viability of the club depended on her expansion plans, and this sale had happened just before the inspection. She would make light of it, for Jane's sake, but she was not happy.

No, she was not happy, but it was her firm intention to keep the cause of her disquiet to herself. She would simply have to ring Trudy again, tonight or in a day or two's time. Nothing the maid had said last night had made much sense. Of course, this was only because her English was poor.

Siobhan had decided to ring Trudy because the uncertainty was getting to her. She felt she wanted to know once and for all what was happening. It was disconcerting to see her mother pottering around happily, ignorant of what her daughter was cooking up. Jane's questions about the complex in Portugal were embarrassingly impossible to answer. Trudy's silence was increasingly worrying. So yesterday evening she had taken the bull by the horns and rung her.

The phone had made those subterranean gurglings it always did when connecting with abroad. The maid had answered and Siobhan had not understood a word she said. 'Can I speak to Trudy Thompson, please?' she interrupted.

'No. Sorry.'

For one awful minute Siobhan imagined the maid had been given orders not to put her through. 'Is she in?'

'No. At the hospital.'

The hospital? Siobhan went cold. This explained everything. Trudy had not contacted her because she had fallen ill. She prayed it was nothing serious. If it was possible, she decided, she would fly out there immediately. She had enough money for the airfare. 'What is wrong with her?' Siobhan spoke slowly and clearly.

'Sorry? I no understand.'

'What is wrong with her? Is she ill?'

'She is at the hospital. She not back for weeks.'

'Is she sick?'

'Sick? Please?'

'Please tell her Siobhan Murphy rang. Siobhan Murphy. Please ask her to ring me.'

The maid had difficulty in pronouncing her name.

'Look. Do you know which hospital she is at?'

'She is at the hospital. Sorry. Goodbye.'

Siobhan replaced the receiver, her pulse racing. All the time she had suspected something was wrong, and her forebodings had been justified. It was vital she got a clear picture of what was going on. Yet laced with her panic came relief that Trudy had not abandoned her. She had been prevented from contacting her because she was ill. Please God it wasn't a breast lump, or something equally sinister. It was hell not knowing. Hell, too, not being able to tell anyone. Except Jane. Yet Siobhan felt uneasy even at the idea of telling Jane. She failed to see how Jane could help her, and she was reluctant to burden people with her personal problems. No: the only thing to do was to wait, and ring again, perhaps this time with a Portuguese phrasebook beside the phone.

When Jane arrived at the President Hotel she saw David immediately. He was standing just to the right of the reception desk and his face lit up when he saw her. Jane found herself responding to his obvious pleasure and felt glad that he was there. Having him by her side was like bringing a part of Sunnybank Fit Not Fat with her. He took both her hands and kissed her cheek. They studied each other and Jane thought how good he looked in his dress suit. His hair looked different, shorter and cut close to his head. 'Thanks for making such an effort,' she said.

'Don't mention it.' She found his smile infectious, and on another occasion, at another time, who knows what might have happened? But the last thing she could afford was to let herself be distracted from making a good impression tonight. David was her accessory, and he'd promised he understood that. Fighting her own desire to retreat to the bar with him and a have a large glass of wine, she became enthusiastically business-like.

'Let me explain who's who,' she said, as she took her coat to the cloakroom. 'The people I must try to impress particularly are Sarah Curtis, human resources, and Colin Ricketts, northern manager. They're coming to inspect the club in ten days. Most people at the dinner are the other managers from the region. I know some of them, but company policy, I'm afraid, is to set us in competition with each other. I've got to keep my cards close to my chest when it comes to talking about Sunnybank – rumour has it that several clubs might be for the chop so I can't let anyone know about our plans. You understand? And we've had a minor setback. I was hoping to convince Head Office to let us build a pool next door, but I've found out the land has been sold. My friend Liz is trying to get more information.'

'You're shaking, Jane. Are you cold?'

'Just a little keyed up – I guess it's when I think about the inspection.'

'Because you're worried your job's on the line if Head Office don't like what they find?'

'Certainly not. The club's going to come through this with flying colours. No more talk about jobs being on the line, please. It's time to make our grand entrance.'

David offered her his arm, and Jane took it, grateful for the support. Together they walked towards the Cadogan suite, where dinner awaited them.

The room was grand and high-ceilinged, with tall windows giving out on to the night sky. The tables bore sunflower yellow napkins and gold and white helium-filled balloons, and cham-pagne flutes were laid out in rows on a temporary bar. Jane handed one to David, and took a glass of orange juice for herself. There was a hubbub of noise, which almost drowned the string quartet. She found herself scanning the crowd for familiar faces and spotted Sarah and Colin. Sarah was standing by the bar stubbing out a cigarette. Colin was with a woman Jane did not recognise, presumably his wife.

David raised his glass in a toast. 'To us,' he said. 'That is, to Sunnybank Fit Not Fat.'

'To Sunnybank Fit Not Fat,' Jane echoed.

Colin and his wife approached them. 'Jane!' he said. He shook her hand vigorously and introduced his wife, Andrea.

'And this is David,' Jane replied smoothly. 'My friend and the club's consultant health professional.'

'So, how goes it?' Colin asked.

'Wonderfully well,' she said. 'We're looking forward enormously to the inspection. You'll see quite a few changes since Fit Not Fat took over the club.'

'I'm sure we shall. I hear you're working on plans to get us to finance a pool.'

'A pool? Well, it's true that I've been looking into that, but of course there's a lot to weigh up. Pools attract families, which means children, and Sunnybank's atmosphere is more adult. Its strength is that it attracts a different sort of client base, sophisticated, wealthy, able to afford subscriptions set at an appropriate level.'

'Yes, we're certainly a classy outfit,' David added, 'Exclusive. Very exclusive.'

Jane appreciated his support and shot him a grateful look.

Colin sipped his champagne and hailed a passing waiter, who was carrying some canapés. He helped himself to a handful of fried chicken goujons. Colin's love of food was legendary, and evident in the way his shirt strained over his corpulent middle. Jane experienced a twinge of dislike for him, which was immediately eclipsed by her recognition that this man was necessary to her. She had to impress and please him. Just as she was trying to think of a flattering pleasantry, Colin swallowed what he was eating and stabbed his finger in her direction. 'Fitness International,' he said. 'They've opened up *very* near you, haven't they?'

'Yes, and a number of their members have joined us in recent weeks,' Jane replied.

'And is your café doing well?' Colin continued.

'I can't tell you the number of people who've just walked in off the streets, stayed for a drink and then enquired about membership.'

'Yes,' added David, 'it's *the* place to be seen in Sunnybank.'

'But see for yourself, Colin. Have lunch there when you come for the inspection. Who else will be with you?'

'Sarah, and Greg Black, the accountant.'

'Inspections can be very stressful, can't they?' Andrea's voice was all concern.

'For some,' Jane said.

'Andrea is a freelance stress-management consultant,' Colin explained. 'Excuse me.' And he was gone, his attention caught by someone more important than Jane.

Andrea did not react to her husband's disappearance. She returned to the subject of stress. 'All inspections are difficult. I know because I've done a lot of work in schools, you see, giving workshops prior to Ofsted inspections. It's the psychological element of being judged,' she continued. 'It robs us of the freedom to make mistakes. The quest for perfection is one of the main causes of stress.'

She was making Jane nervous. Nothing stressed her out more than hearing about stress. It was rather like someone telling you that you didn't look well when you were feeling perfectly all right. You began to wonder if you were ill after all.

'Most stress is self-imposed, you know?' Andrea continued, 'It comes from the drive for success, the desire to be all things to all people. What I do is get my clients to analyse and recognise the patterns of stress they create for themselves then get them to let go of their destructive habits, such as working too hard, then drinking too much to relax. Many of my clients come to me with burnout, or if they find it difficult to cope with redundancy.'

Jane felt increasingly uncomfortable and tried to think of a way of extricating herself from this conversation.

'I give therapeutic massage too,' Andrea continued. 'I've trained in reflexology. Most reflexologists work through the feet but the *chakras* can also be affected by pressure points in the hand. Let me demonstrate.' She took Jane's hand and worked it, pulling her fingers, pressing into her palms. 'Stress can be a killer, you know. It weakens the immune system thereby opening the door to all sorts of conditions. It's so important to relax. Yes, just as I thought. Your nerves are in shreds. I guessed as soon as I saw you. Are you getting adequate nutrition? I can feel an imbalance somewhere in your cardiovascular system. There's a knot here — ah, that's better. You should have a full body massage too.'

'Why?' asked Jane. 'Do you think I'm tense?'

'Enormously, you poor thing.'

'Well, you're quite wrong, because I've never felt better in my life. Oh, look, David! There's the manager from Kearsley Gate — we must have a word.'

She pulled him away, furious with Andrea. She hated people who gave you information about yourself you hadn't requested — in fact, it was the height of rudeness, like saying to someone they were overweight or needed a haircut. She was an awful woman. And fancy unsettling her like that when she felt rather like a goalkeeper facing a premier-league football team all shooting at her net. She couldn't afford to let up. Relaxation was the last thing she needed. In fact, what she could do with right now was an extra L8, to prevent her flagging later. She excused herself to David and hurried out to the ladies'.

She carried the pills with her at all times, although she had never before taken more than the dose Garth had recommended. But L8s were only a herbal supplement and surely an extra one would do her no harm. Jane broke one in half and swallowed both parts. She smiled at herself in the mirror and went to rejoin David. 'Did you enjoy your hand massage?' he asked her.

Jane laughed dismissively.

'I know what you mean,' David said. 'The unscientific theorising that goes with massage and reflexology amuses me too. Some people will believe anything. Or perhaps in these work-mad days people feel so guilty at taking time out for pleasure that they have to pretend it's some kind of medicine. So smelling something nice is called aromatherapy and having someone tickle your feet is reflexology. And you do yourself as much good slobbing out in front of the TV as you would in deep relaxation. As long as you switch off from time to time.'

'Quite,' Jane said. 'But we all need different amounts of relaxation. I need very little.'

'Maybe you *think* you need very little.'

Jane ignored that. 'As I was saying, I think a lot of these alternative practitioners are cranks. Like you said, they're not scientific. And I'm sure the only reason they've been so successful is that they're not as frightening as conventional doctors. When they treat you it's just a matter of massage, essential oils and laying their hands just above your body. Real GPs are scary.'

'You're not frightened of me, are you?'

'Oh, no! Heaven forbid! Anyway, I'm never ill. Why don't we pretend you're not a doctor tonight?'

'So what would you like me to be? A construction worker, an estate agent, an airline steward?'

It was then that the master of ceremonies announced dinner was served. Jane took David by the arm and led him towards a table. 'Let's eat,' she said.

On her left was the new manager of the club in Altrincham, and David was on her right. Next to David was Sarah, from human resources. She had already engaged him in conversation. Jane's other dinner companion was talking to his wife on his left. She was thus left alone to study the menu. There was a choice of black pudding or mushroom pâté for starters, a main course of steak and kidney pudding or a country vegetable pie, and sticky toffee pudding for dessert. It looked as if they were all going to be Fat Not Fit. Jane supposed that in the fitness industry when you wanted to relax, you were as unfit as possible. But she had no appetite and would gladly have eaten nothing, She turned to David. Sarah was talking to the man on her other side now. 'Enjoying yourself?' she asked him.

'Sure.'

'Do you think I'm doing OK?'

'Brilliantly. Can I pour you some wine?' David reached for the bottle in front of them.

A moment of indecision. She would feel much better if she had just a little – but could she stop at that? And she had not asked Garth about mixing the pills with alcohol. But surely just one glass would not do anything terrible. If she felt bad, she'd stop immediately. If she took it slowly, surely there could be no harm. The truth was she couldn't last another moment without some alcohol. And, besides, everyone else was drinking.

'OK,' she said. She watched the cool, golden liquid fill her glass and took a sip, then another, and another. Already she felt much better. If anything, the L8 increased the effectiveness of the alcohol, and she began to feel insanely happy. She moved her leg towards David's. 'I'm so glad I brought you,' she said.

'I'm glad I'm here,' he said.

Then she turned brightly to the couple on her left and asked all about the club at Altrincham.

The service was slow, and Jane had finished her wine before the food had arrived. Solicitously David poured her some more. Jane could see no reason to stop: she was feeling more assured, more confident, more certain by the minute that she was having the time of her life. 'It's wonderful here, isn't it?' She said.

'Pretty good. You look flushed. Are you OK?'

'Fine. Sometimes alcohol affects me like that. I'm not really used to it.'

The conversation crashed around her like waves and she shivered. She experienced a moment of dissociation from the hot, noisy dining room, the advancing waiters and waitresses with hundreds of dishes of black pudding and pâté, the elaborately laid tables, and the oppressive scent of flowers from the vase in front of her. The dissociation moved swiftly into pure paranoia. What was really going on here, she suspected, was that they were all out to get her. She had to stay on her guard. She attempted a smile, but to no one in particular as David was making conversation with Sarah again.

A waiter arrived with the first course. Jane chose the pâté and looked at the unappetising slab of grey sludge in front of her with its twist of orange on top. She began to spread it on a finger of toast while listening to the Altrincham manager discuss the pros and cons of raising subscriptions. She bit into it. It tasted of nothing. It was important, she thought, to join in the conversation so no one would suspect a thing.

'Raising subscriptions?' she said to him. 'I should imagine you could do that in Altrincham. You're catering for the Cheshire set there. But if I were you I'd do it in stages. Increase the premier membership first so you can justify yourself by saying that off-peak is still the same. Then what you could do is break down off-peak into two categories, and so on, until you've sneaked in an overall price increase. Or the other thing you could do is sugar the pill with special offers – vouchers for hotels, discounts for using other Fit Not Fat clubs. And you could launch the offer with a local sporting celebrity to create some extra publicity. Ring me at Sunnybank and I can explain more as it's so noisy here we can't talk. Have you met David? This is David, my partner.' She linked her arm in his. 'He acts in a consulting capacity to us. I'm sure he'd help you too – if I can spare him.' She removed her arm and studied his face. 'We must do this again – go out to dinner, I mean.' She kissed him. 'I'm so happy,' she said. And she was. The moment of terror had passed. Now she was riding high on a wave of euphoria.

She raised her glass to her lips again, then put it down. She was shaking again and thought that the alcohol might be responsible. What if someone noticed? Suddenly she was cold, then warm again, and optimism exploded inside her like fire-works. 'Hi, Sarah! We're so looking forward to the inspection! I just know you'll be amazed at what you find! We have – this is true – the best staff in the North-west, in the country probably, in the *world*. I've never known anyone as efficient as Siobhan, and so well informed about fitness. And Garth is training in nutrition consultancy and young Jodie is management material if ever anyone was. I'm telling you this because as head of human resources you need to know these things. Sometimes it's easy for you to get out of touch – no criticism intended – because you have so many branches to overlook. My advice to you would be to have a rota of visits and monthly meetings with managers to discuss staff development. I'll help you set it up if you like. Because a club is judged by its instructors. Everyone likes the personal touch. I know I do. Someone to take care of you and only you, although I wouldn't know what that was like. I guess you feel safer, Sarah, when you're being self-reliant. You feel as if you can't get hurt. Because as soon as you let someone else in they'll tell you that you need to slow down and you're probably frightened to slow down because if you did you'd be no one. That's probably why you went into human resources. I can see things clearly these days. Shall I tell you why? It's all got to do with Garth – oh, look, there's Colin! He must be coming over to do the hospitality bit. How's it going, Colin? Just look at that paunch you're developing! Come round to my club and I'll soon get that off you. Only joking.'

Jane took a deep breath. She was amazed at how witty and perceptive she was being this evening. In fact, she seemed to have silenced everyone. They were stunned in admiration. She had never been in better form. She sat back and luxuriated in her success as the waiters brought round the main course.

'Are you feeling OK, Jane?' David asked.

'Why are you asking me that?' she retorted angrily.

'You don't seem yourself.'

Jane ignored him and attempted to eat some of her dinner. It was tasteless, all of it. Instead she began to compose in her head the speech she would give when Fit Not Fat awarded her the trophy that didn't exist yet for the manager of the year. What a night that would be! At the end of her speech there would be rapturous applause and a band would strike up with Tina Turner's, 'You're Simply The Best'.

A lovely idea. Jane sang the song softly to herself. To her pleasure, everyone at the table turned to listen.

'Jane, are you sure you're OK?' David's outline seemed rather fuzzy. Perhaps he needed glasses. He stood up. 'Excuse me, everyone. I know Jane is on a new medication for a mild thyroid condition and it doesn't seem to be agreeing with her. Would you understand if I took her home?'

There were mutterings of concern around the table. Jane laughed loudly at David's crazy sense of humour. She had never thought he was a practical joker. Maybe this was his way of getting her alone – not that she minded: he was lovely and in truth . . .

Before she knew it she was leaning on David's arm being shepherded across the ballroom. Once in the lobby he sat her down on a *chaise-longue* by the entrance. Every time someone came in through the revolving door a welcome blast of chilly air washed her face.

'Jane,' he said, 'I had to take you out because you're not behaving normally.'

'Because I'm very tired,' she told him. She wanted nothing more than to put her head on his shoulder and go to sleep. She moved towards him and took him by the hands so she could do that.

'Jane, listen. What's wrong? You didn't have that much to drink. Are you on any medication?'

Suddenly Jane came to her senses. What was she doing out here in the foyer? Was she on any medication? Only the L8s and they didn't count. 'No.'

'Have you been sleeping well?'

'No. I never sleep. I'm never ill.'

'I'm going to take you home and insist you don't come into work for at least a week. You need complete rest. Otherwise you'll burn out.'

'OK,' she said. Really, he was being very silly. He'd forgotten there was an inspection in ten days' time. Afterwards she would have a rest. But she might cut down on the L8s.

'Jane, did you hear me?'

'Yes,' she said. She snuggled up to him. He was lovely and warm. He made her stand up, spoke to someone in a peaked cap and then they were in a taxi. She gave him her address, and the next thing she knew, they were outside her flat. Then she came to.

'I'll take you into your flat, Jane. Which one is it?'

'It's OK,' she said. 'I'm fine now.'

'Yeah. Right.' David followed after her as she went up to the first floor and unlocked her door. She realised it would be rude not to let him in, and winced when she saw the state of her living room. She noticed David give it a cursory glance. 'I'm going to make you a hot drink – some herbal tea. Unless you can't stand the thought and you just want some water.'

'Thanks for bringing me home,' she said. 'You can go now.'

'No. I'll stay a bit if you don't mind.' He cleared some tops that needed ironing off a chair and sat down.

Jane's head was pounding now. What had she been saying over dinner? All she could recollect was that she had been trying to be helpful. 'David? What happened to me?'

'You just seemed to get a little over-excited,' he said to her.

'Do you remember what I was talking about?'

He rubbed the back of his neck awkwardly. 'Not exactly. But you were giving Sarah some advice on how to do her job, and you did make a comment about Colin's paunch.'

'I didn't!' She was shocked.

'Don't worry. They could see you were out of it. I covered up for you. Then you started serenading us with Tina Turner.'

'I *what?*' Jane went cold. She had half recollected doing that but thought she had dreamed it. 'Oh, no. I've blown it, haven't I? I've really blown it.'

'Don't worry. I'm sure they—'

'Just get out. I need to be alone. I've got to get my head round this. Don't just stand there – go!'

And he did.

Chapter Fifteen

Damn, damn, damn, damn, damn. Nothing in the pantry except tins of fat-free soup, low-sugar baked beans and all the cooking ingredients Cassie had used once and then forgotten – a jar of allspice, dried tarragon, thyme and three jars of curry powder. And in the fridge nothing except skimmed milk, sugar-snap peas and broccoli. She bit her nails anxiously as she tried to think if anywhere in the house there was something she could binge on. And yes – miracles do happen – she remembered that upstairs, at the back of her wardrobe, behind her winter shoes, was a large box of Black Magic given to her by a grateful postgraduate student three months ago and stashed away for just such an emergency as this. So, superfit Cassie took the stairs two at a time and emptied her wardrobe to get at the chocolates.

Now, as she returned downstairs she came up with the necessary righteous justifications for what she was about to do. First, just a few chocolates wouldn't harm her, and now that she had learnt the art of self-denial, she *would* be able to stop at just a few. Second, she deserved them as a reward for losing two stone. Third, she couldn't bear the tension of waiting for a call from Lynda to tell her that Terry was home. And by way of a footnote, there was no art in giving up chocolate if you didn't remind yourself of what you were missing, the student who bought her the chocolates would *want* her to eat them, she had to test her gall bladder because it might have got better all on its own, and the chocolates ought to induce that familiar but not forgotten sensation of mindless torpor when all problems were subsumed in the peculiar and rich satisfaction of eating them.

Ignoring the lecture notes strewn over the dining-room table, Cassie tipped back her chair, scrabbled at the Cellophane packaging, opened the box, and discarded the layer of crinkly paper. She took a coffee cream. It was interesting how her desire to eat seemed unrelated to her appetite. She wasn't hungry, it was just that she wanted to put something into her mouth. Come to think of it, she hadn't suffered much from hunger lately. Rather, she had been full of a wild energy that had turbo-charged her workouts, sent her jogging along the corridors at the university and even prevented her sleeping, so that she was able to catch up with her paperwork and amaze the history faculty. She put this down to anxiety, or the L8s, or a mixture of the two. But no matter how hungry you weren't, it didn't put you off chocolate.

The coffee cream was disappointingly plastic, not as good as she remembered, so she sampled a caramel, then raided the bottom layer for all the caramels, and started on the caramels with nuts. She bit into the brazil, but the resulting crunch did nothing to dissipate her memories of cavorting with Garth. The guilt was dreadful, even after ten days. It had occurred to her that perhaps the theories of the medieval church about women were correct. There *were* only madonnas and whores. And, after her recent escapade, she was just a faint-hearted whore. How could she look Terry in the face, knowing what she had been up to? And there was another dilemma. Should she tell him what she had done? Cassie believed in honesty and it had always been the lynchpin of their relationship.

She moved on to the strawberry creams and the other soft centres. She was feeling nicely stuffed and sick now. Still her head was buzzing with random thoughts: the chocolates were not as effective a narcotic as she had hoped. Perhaps she hadn't given them a fair trial. She popped a toffee into her mouth. And then there was that sinking feeling as she felt something hard in the elastic toffee adhering to her teeth – yes, a filling. It was a divine punishment. Since she was alone, Cassie felt in her mouth and took out the whole sticky mess. God, she was disgusting!

And then it hit her. What the hell had she been doing, pigging out like that and sabotaging all her hard work? Suddenly she was gripped by panic. She would get fat again. Terry wouldn't see her at her slimmest. She had reversed her progress towards perfect health. She had consumed hundreds of calories in one sitting. Her hands were shaking.

Nothing for it but to go straight to the gym. Well, not straight to the gym. Cassie knew she had to wait for an hour or so after eating so that she would not get a stitch. As she had been back quite a few times since her night with Garth, she had got over the embarrassment of seeing him, and she could hardly join Fitness International before Fit Not Fat's inspection. She valued old-fashioned loyalty, and hoped Terry did too.

Lynda's call was a welcome distraction. She confirmed that Terry wasn't back yet, then Cassie spent some time reassuring her friend that the L8s weren't doing her any harm. The side effects were minimal and safely disregarded. To be honest, Cassie was partly attempting to convince herself. She had become rather fond of her L8s. Then they chatted about the shenanigans in the modern-languages faculty. Gossiping restored Cassie's equilibrium: thinking about others provided respite from her own problems.

In a few moments she was flinging her leggings and T-shirt into her sports bag and lacing up her trainers, with the strange mixture of enthusiasm and reluctance that she experienced whenever she prepared to go to the gym. She locked her front door, feeling that she was locking up her problems behind her. Then she was in the car, key in the ignition, and speeding off on the now familiar route to Fit Not Fat. And she was through the double doors, handing her card to Kendra at reception, into the changing rooms, and finally into her sanctuary, the gym. It was bliss to be back in this straightforward place where all she had to do was work her body and ignore her tangled emotions. Oh, how she loved the bright lights, the trashy music, the sunflower yellow tracksuits of the trainers, the men lifting weights and the way everybody looked as if they weren't enjoying themselves. Because she wasn't enjoying herself much either.

She began to jog on the treadmill and soon got into a nice rhythm. She noticed Anita set the control panel of the treadmill next to her, and carried on, increasing her pace. It felt good and bad all at once. She glanced at Anita again. What was that woman doing? She had adjusted the treadmill so that it was at a precipitous incline. She was marching up it, beads of sweat escaping her headband, glistening virtuously on her forehead. Cassie's running seemed pathetic in comparison. Still, not to be outdone she set the machine to a higher speed and ran until she thought she would burst. She visualised those chocolates evaporating into pure energy, fuelling her pounding legs. When she could run no more, she slowed back into a jog. Anita was still climbing mountains beside her.

Cassie could not compete. Instead she made for the recliner bike, and gave herself a rest as she pedalled at a low level. She could see herself in the mirror opposite, red-faced (good!), her knees pumping up and down. Jodie was reflected in the background, Cassie's favourite trainer. That was partly because Jodie was the first person she had met at the club, and partly because of her youth. Jodie was talking to that boyfriend of hers, Darren. Cassie watched them idly, unable to hear what they were saying, but reading their body language.

He was grinning and there was a swagger in his movements. Jodie smiled less certainly then looked at the floor, and he gave her a puzzled glance. He moved towards her; she stayed stock-still. He placed a hand on her shoulder; she looked up at him now and said something. He looked immensely surprised, then laughed. After a while she laughed with him. Then his eyes strayed to one of the TV screens on which a golf tournament was being played out. Jodie turned round to put some cards away in the cabinet and Cassie turned up the intensity on her bike and resolved to burn away at least the strawberry, orange and pineapple creams.

Later she staggered off the bike desperate for some water. She saw Jodie standing aimlessly by the door, lost in thought. Although Cassie had been looking forward to telling her all about this heroic workout, she now suspected that Jodie was the one in need of a sympathetic listener.

'Are you all right?' Cassie asked her.

'Oh, yes, sure.' She grinned unconvincingly.

Cassie was certain now that something had upset her. She determined there and then to help her. She owed her a favour. Over two stones' worth of favour. 'You know, Jodie, I'm pretty fed up too. You don't fancy having a coffee with me? Are you able to take a break from the gym?' Then, daringly, she added, 'You can tell me what's troubling you.'

Jodie looked taken aback, but pleased. A little nervous too, Cassie thought. She hoped she wasn't coming across as too intimidating.

'I'm off duty in half an hour,' Jodie said.

'Fantastic.' Cassie grinned at her. 'I'll meet you in the café when I'm changed. No one would want to be near me in the state I'm in now! In half an hour, then?'

'OK,' Jodie said.

Her hair still wet from the shower, Cassie carried her sports bag into the café and saw that Jodie was already there, her chin propped in her hands, thoughtful. Now Cassie was certain that all was not well. Jodie was the same age as her students, and sparked off her latent maternal feelings. She could feel herself slipping into problem-solving mode. She tried to recall what she knew about Jodie. Over the months that Cassie had been coming to Fit Not Fat, she had noticed the girl's moods varied. Some days she was all good humour; others she looked as if all the troubles of the world were on her shoulders. Cassie suspected that Darren might be the culprit. Now, no doubt, all would be revealed. She bought Jodie a mocha, herself an espresso, sat opposite her, and could feel herself turning into Dr Oliver, student counsellor. She had on her listening, concerned face. Jodie responded with a pathetic little smile, and Cassie couldn't help but be flattered that Jodie had chosen to confide in her so readily.

'Nice coffee?' Cassie asked.

'Mmm. You should try some.'

'Too rich for me,' Cassie said.

'I love coffee with chocolate in it,' Jodie said. 'Lots of chocolate.'

Cassie felt guilty. She knocked back her espresso in one. The café was almost empty – a pity, she thought, as its neat, tiled floor and marble-topped tables made it so pleasant. Jodie illuminated it in her yellow tracksuit, but again Cassie became conscious that the girl was not herself. Her eyes travelled aimlessly around the café; she fiddled with a stray tendril of hair; she looked for all the world as if she was trying not to cry. It's all right, Cassie wanted to say to her, you can have an extension on your essay.

'Do you want to talk about it?' Cassie prodded her. Silence. She continued carefully, 'I could tell you were feeling down when I was watching you in the mirror in the gym.'

Jodie breathed out audibly, evidently trying to control herself. 'So you saw him? Did you hear what he said to me?'

'Sorry, no. I had my headphones on.'

'Yeah, well.' Jodie was quiet for a bit. 'It's nice how they've done the café, isn't it?'

'Come on, spit it out, Jodie.'

'Oh, look, it's nothing really. Just man trouble.'

'Men are always trouble,' Cassie said sincerely.

'No, they're not, they're lovely! It's me, really. I'm too sensitive.'

'Oh, dear! That can be a problem. Tell me how you're too sensitive.'

'Yes, well, you saw me talking to Darren before, didn't you? But I'd better start at the beginning. Did you know we've been going out for four and half months?' She paused so that Cassie could reflect on this impressive statistic. 'This afternoon we were chatting and he was telling me about this ex-girlfriend of his he bumped into the other day. She's had her hair cut, apparently. He said it looked gorgeous, and she'd lost a lot of weight. But it was the way he said it, like he still fancied her – you know that smooth voice guys use? So I sulked a bit to show him I was hurt, and he was, like, I didn't mean anything by it, and there wasn't a law about him not fancying other girls, which made it worse, because it just confirmed what I was thinking. And then he laughed and said it was probably my PMT again. You see, I suffer from dreadful PMT. He's had to put up with me in the most appalling moods. Only it isn't time for my PMT yet, so it couldn't have been. So now I'm wondering if my PMT isn't getting worse, and I don't want the doctor to put me on anything, because I'll feel like I'm ill, and I'm not ill. But my moods are messing up my relationship.'

'Hold on, hold on. So there are really two problems here. Darren implied he might fancy someone else, and you suffer from PMT.'

'Well, yes.' Jodie looked a little more cheerful. Cassie always liked to bring an analytic slant to her counselling sessions. It helped the students get things into perspective.

'So which do you want to deal with first?'

'Darren?'

'OK. Darren. Now, Jodie, do you ever fancy other boys?'

'Of course I do, only I wouldn't tell Darren in case he was hurt. It doesn't do to be honest all of the time.'

'Do you really think so?' asked Cassie, fascinated. 'But never mind. So, what you're really doing is accusing Darren of not caring whether he hurt you or not. He was quite happy to tell you that he might fancy someone else.'

'I suppose I am.'

'So do you think you're being over-sensitive, or just reasonable?'

'What's the date today? The twelfth? Well, I could be a bit over-sensitive, but not that over-sensitive because my PMT doesn't really get going until the fifteenth.'

'Jodie,' said Cassie, feeling her way very gently, 'say Darren had mentioned his ex-girlfriend on the sixteenth?'

'I'd have told him where he could get off. I'd have said if he fancied her so much he had no right fooling around with me. I would have said she was welcome to him and his stinky rugby socks and filthy sink and sick sense of humour.'

'Bravo!' Cassie said. Jodie looked surprised. 'So this PMT you suffer from, what are you doing about it?'

'Not a lot. I don't like swallowing pills.'

'Shame. You should try these L8s Garth's flogging. They'd soon sort you out. But carry on.'

'Siobhan says I should take extra vitamins but . . . well, perhaps I will. And I know things might get better if I tried the pill again but then if Darren found out he really would insist I went to bed with him.'

'So you're not sleeping together?'

'Not yet. The time hasn't been right.'

Cassie was more and more certain that Jodie ought to finish with him. But, then, she would think that. She, Cassie Oliver, had recently become adept at finishing with men. But the art of counselling was to get the counsellee to see the solution to their problem themselves. 'OK, Jodie. Darren has upset you, but you're not sure whether to blame him, or yourself for being over-sensitive.'

'Yeah! But the more I think about it, the more I can see it's probably my fault. Like you said, it's natural for him to fancy other girls. I'm just daft because of my PMT. It does my head in.'

'Whoa!' Cassie held up her hand and stopped her. 'Do you know anything about history, Jodie? Did you know that in Victorian times men thought women were ruled by their wombs, which floated about their bodies doing all sorts of harm, making them mad, in fact? All women were deemed unreasonable, fragile and in need of the guidance of a strong, assertive male. Utter bollocks, of course. It was a convenient theory to keep women in their place. Surely we've moved on since then. Your PMT doesn't make you mad. It just makes you emotional. And there's nothing wrong with being emotional. Nothing at all.'

'But those female hormones. They—'

'Hooray for female hormones, that's what I say. They make you kind, thoughtful, loving, responsive – we'll forget just now about the excruciating period pains and sore breasts.'

Jodie stared at Cassie, amazed.

'The real trouble here, Jodie, is that Darren doesn't have enough female hormones. Or, in other words, you're normal and he was insensitive.'

'I know what you're saying but I really *do* have terrible PMT. And when I do, I hate him, Cassie. And then when it's gone I love him to bits. That can't be normal.'

'Oh, yes, it is. Has there ever been a man who deserves to be loved all the time?'

Jodie looked uncomfortable.

'And think about this. Another thing women do by their very nature, whether it's genetic or through social conditioning I really don't know, is keep the peace. We go around dodging men's tempers, propitiating them. We oil the wheels of relationships and keep them running smoothly. What your PMT does is stop you making concessions all the time, that's all. Because you feel rotten, you hope some bloke will take care of you, but he doesn't because he's so used to you taking care of him so you get resentful. That seems reasonable enough to me. No, there's nothing wrong with you.'

'So are you saying I haven't got PMT?'

'No, but I'm saying PMT has its uses. It gives you a reality check. It tells you whether you really like the way Darren treats you.'

'He can be a bit selfish sometimes.'

Cassie was silent.

'And his place is a tip. You should see the state of his bathroom.'

Cassie continued silent.

'And he teases me in front of his mates, which I can't stand. And he makes jokes about Mum. And I thought he would be, like, the cutest boyfriend ever, but he's boring sometimes. And he makes out I'm so lucky to go out with him.'

Cassie waited.

'But if I throw him over I'll be suicidal when I get my PMT back.'

'There are lots more fish in the sea.'

'That's what my mum says.'

'A wise mother,' Cassie supplied.

'No, I can't finish with him.'

'But, just remember, you always have that option,' Cassie said.

She noticed there was light in Jodie's eyes again. It hardly mattered whether she chucked Darren or not. The mere fact she realised she had it in her power to chuck him was enough. Just then the glass doors of the café opened and in came Garth. Cassie waved to him, glad that the tension between them had dissipated because she had something to ask him. She beckoned him over to their table. 'Can I get you a coffee, Garth?'

'Sorry. I've only popped in to help Jan empty the till.'

If he was a little brief with her it was hardly surprising, given their history. 'Before you go, Garth, a question. The L8s. Do you know what's in them?'

He paused by their table, grinned at Jodie and answered: 'Sure. I thought I told you. Some North American plant.'

'North American? I thought you said they came from Africa originally.'

Did Cassie detect a momentary hesitation? She could hardly be sure because Garth continued as suave as ever.

'They contain both plants – there are so many ingredients it's hard to remember them all.'

'So *anything* could be in them!' Jodie exclaimed. 'You're not really taking them, Cassie?'

Cassie nodded but resolved to stop immediately – until she found out once and for all what was in those blasted pills. Or, rather, she'd finish the box she was already dipping into. Who knew what damage she would do to herself if she stopped the course half-way through? 'Cheers, Garth,' she said, and watched him go over to the till and flirt with a delighted Jan. Funny how she felt no attraction whatsoever to him now.

'I've got to be getting home,' Jodie said. 'Thanks ever so much for talking to me. You've made me feel loads better.'

'Any time,' Cassie said, and meant it.

Cassie entered the seminar room. No one had opened the vertical blinds so the waiting students were sitting in a shadowy half-light. Some were slumped on the conference-style table in the middle of the room; others sat with their heads drooping. The faces Cassie could see looked terrifyingly blank, as if someone had surgically removed their owners' brains. There was a smell of dead cigarettes, musty clothes and rotting trainers. Cassie's arrival did little to disturb the morgue-like atmosphere. There was just a shuffling of papers and some tentative smiles from the female members of the group.

Cassie found student torpor comforting; at times like this it seemed to her that the older you got the healthier you were. Young people always looked half dead; it was generally the forty-somethings you saw jogging at night along rain-lashed streets or cycling fit to bust through Heaton Park in a vain attempt to cling to their vanishing youth. In fact, she decided, they had got it wrong: to be convincingly young, you had to be permanently hung-over or suffering from advanced sleeping sickness. Like her students.

She took a seat at one end of the table and placed her files and folders in front of her. She noticed as she did so that her hand was shaking. Discounting Parkinson's disease she wondered again about the L8s. It would be a pity if she had to stop taking them as in other respects they suited her well. At the faculty meeting yesterday she had been unstoppable and even accused her head of department of not pushing hard enough for funding. She dismissed thoughts of the meeting. Time to focus on the Black Death.

'Did you manage to get most of the reading done?' she asked her students conversationally.

One or two looked shocked at the idea. A girl, however, said, 'Gruesome!' This was generally held to be a wise remark as it was greeted by nodding. At least they knew what the Black Death was. There was still hope.

'OK. So the question on the table today is, do you think the changes that took place in the social structure of late fourteenth-century society were caused by the Black Death, or might have happened anyway?'

Everyone thought about it and decided to keep their opinion to themselves.

'The Peasants' Revolt, for example. In what ways might the Black Death have contributed to that?'

One student raised his hand. 'I thought we were doing the Angevins,' he said.

'Next week,' Cassie told him. 'How did the Black Death affect the supply of labour? Helen? Claire? Iris?'

'Did people die?' asked Iris.

This was harder work than level eight on the stepper, Cassie thought. 'OK. Since you thought we were doing European history, can you tell me about the interface between the Black Death and religion? The flagellants, for example? The pogroms? What on earth is wrong with you lot? Have you actually come down with the plague?'

'Not plague exactly, but it was Joe's party last night,' a boy volunteered.

'Where is Joe?'

'Hanging over the toilet when I left him.'

At which point one of the girls went green and left the room.

Cassie tried to pick up the pieces. 'So have any of you prepared answers to the suggested questions, or indeed done any reading at all?'

'We meant to,' said Helen, 'but Joe only decided to have the party at the last minute.'

'So you were hoping that I would sit here and entertain you all and not notice the massive group hangover?'

There were a few embarrassed smiles.

Cassie had to fight an urge to answer the seminar questions herself. The L8s had that effect on her. She had become even more talkative than usual. Yet she knew it would be bad practice to do the work for her students. Instead she decided to use the time to improve their social relations.

'So it was a good party, then?'

'Brilliant. We started in the union then went into town. There's this new club that lets students in half-price on Sunday nights. The bouncers gave Joe a hard time – they thought he was a pusher.'

Cassie decided she didn't want to know much more. She was a little out of her depth when it came to Manchester's drug culture. Even as a student she had avoided drugs through an innate caution and sense of self-preservation. Alcohol was the only substance she regularly abused. Apart from the L8s, of course, and L8s weren't drugs: they were a herbal supplement, containing a vast number of naturally occurring ingredients . . . 'Hey, have any of you heard of a drug called L8?'

Now her students sat up. Bright, interested faces were turned towards her.

'No,' said one of the lads. 'Where do you get it from?'

'Well, when I say it's a drug, I mean in the pharmaceutical sense, like aspirin or ginseng.'

'L8,' one of the students mused. 'Sounds more like a club drug to me. Elate. What does it do to you?'

Cassie could answer that. 'Shortly after you take it, it gives you a rush of energy. You lose your appetite – or, rather, your stomach feels like it's tied in a knot. You talk ten to the dozen and you can't keep still. It makes you feel as if you could conquer the world. And then your hands start to shake.' Cassie demonstrated by holding out her hand. It trembled obligingly.

'Speed,' said Ollie. 'Dexies. Where did you get them?'

'Speed?' Cassie was confused.

'Sure. Amphetamines. Uppers.'

'No. L8s aren't a *drug*.'

Her students looked at her sympathetically. Sometimes tutors were slow to comprehend.

'These L8s sound like classic amphetamines. You know, like you get in slimming pills. They're illegal now, but not that hard to get hold of if you know where to go. You obviously do,' Ollie said.

Cassie sat absolutely still. Even her hands had stopped shaking. Was it possible that the L8s Garth had been supplying were *speed*? Did he know they were speed? What could he hope to get out of selling his clients speed? The answer came immediately; lots and lots of money, piles of it, especially as amphetamines were seriously addictive. And helped you lose weight. Her students were watching her with amusement. She had to salvage the situation.

'Did you know that the US army doled out amphetamines to their troops to give them courage to face the enemy? They were called purple hearts. In many ways the principle is not so different as giving a tot of rum to First World War soldiers going over the top. There are times when a drug that is frowned upon by the establishment is also discovered to have socially acceptable uses.'

'So, Dr Oliver,' asked Claire, 'is that how you lost all your weight?'

'No!' Cassie had to put her right immediately. 'It took blood, sweat and tears to get a figure like this. Hours in the gym, virtually no fat in my diet. You see, over six months ago I was diagnosed with gallstones and . . .' She could see she had lost her students' interest again. Good. She had more than enough to think about now. She stood up, erect and imposing. 'Since none of you were able to complete the reading, the seminar is postponed until Friday afternoon. Class dismissed.'

Gratefully the students dispersed, with some curious backward glances. Alone, Cassie perched on the table and thought rapidly. How could she have been so stupid as not to realise that the L8s were lethal? And illegal. The first thing she had to do was speak to Garth and find out whether he knew what he was doing. It was just possible he was selling the pills in good faith. He had been up-front about his activities in the gym, and she had overheard someone saying that even Jane, the manager, was taking them. Cassie became more and more certain that Garth was just as much of a dupe as she was. He wasn't that well endowed in the brains department, and with no medical training he might easily have been fooled into thinking that these profit-making pills were legal.

It took her only a short time to run back to her office, collect her things and ring Lynda to tell her she had to leave early. She drove impatiently through and out of Manchester, cursing the traffic-lights that turned red as soon as they saw her coming. Then Fit Not Fat hove into view, with a scattering of vehicles in the car park. She jumped out of her car and ran into the club, past Kendra at the desk and straight into the gym.

'Hi, Siobhan. Garth around?'

'No, he's not. He called in sick today.'

'What's wrong?'

'Something or nothing, I suspect.'

'I don't suppose you could let me have his home number?'

Siobhan looked hesitant, and Cassie realised she had put her in an awkward position. 'Never mind,' she said. 'I think I might have it.' She rooted around in her bag and found her L8s. The sticker he had put on them had his name, with an address and telephone number that she did not recognise. Could this be where he sold his pills?

She ran back to her car and got out her mobile. She rang the number immediately. Unsurprisingly, the line was dead.

Cassie had drawn a blank. She put the key in the ignition, revved up the engine, and headed back into town. Now that she was driving against the flow of traffic she made better time, at least until she got near Piccadilly. Then it was stop, start, stop, start all the way to Garth's block of flats. She drove into the courtyard and parked in front of someone's garage. She saw that the blinds were not drawn in Garth's living room and went straight to his window to try to attract his attention.

But when she got there, she could see that the flat was empty – empty of Garth, empty of furniture, even empty of his mirrors. Four white walls stared back blankly, inscrutably at her.

Damn, damn, damn, damn, damn.

Chapter Sixteen

On returning home from Fit Not Fat the day before the inspection the first thing Siobhan did was to take the letter from Trudy, which she had left on her dressing-table that morning, and burn it in the ring of the gas cooker. And if she singed her fingers, well, it was her fault for being such a fool in the first place. It had read,

Dear Siobhan, I know you've been trying to get through to me and I understand that Maria told you I was in hospital. Just in case you were worried, I can assure you I'm perfectly all right now, and that everyone was absolutely wonderful to me. You would not believe how considerate all the nurses and doctors are over here and how special they make you feel. All the swelling has gone down and I am feeling much, much better. I could have really done with you to keep me company while I was recuperating – you always used to make such a fuss of me.

In case you were wondering what had happened to the health and leisure club venture, unfortunately that's fallen through. You know how these things are – one complication lands on top of another. It was very lucky you took my advice and stayed at Fit Not Fat as I can't offer you a job now. I expect you're secretly relieved – I know that really you would have hated to leave Sunnybank and your mother, and you would have got fed up with an old bat like me! So all that remains is just a huge thank you for all the support you gave me when I started up the Sunnybank Health Club and all the best in your future career.

Love, Trudy

PS. Some very exciting things on the horizon for me! Can't say too much but wish me luck. I'll try to keep in touch. Love, T.

Now Siobhan felt numb. She had walked around in a stupor all day, trying to suppress the agonising pain of loss and shattered dreams. She had even shed a few tears in the privacy of the ladies', which had shocked her and brought her to her senses. She rarely cried. Then, on duty in the gym, she began to hate herself for being so easily sucked into Trudy's self-centred fantasies. Later she wondered if she still loved Trudy, decided she did, and felt worse than ever. Or, rather, she loved the old Trudy, not this new one. The old one was dead. She grieved for her, and grieved for herself.

As her tumultuous emotions receded, she was left with the realisation that her pride had taken a tumble. She had placed her trust in somebody worthless. At least she had kept her foolishness to herself; only Jane knew what had been afoot. That meant there was only one person she was obliged to tell about this sorry mess: Jane. And, fortunately, she would not have to tell her today, as she was busy preparing for the inspection.

Siobhan felt guilty for feeling grateful that she had Jane to look after. Putting Jane first meant that she needn't think about Trudy and chastise herself for being so easily taken in. All afternoon she had focused on Jane, who had looked pale and complained of a headache – it was unusual for her to mention her health. Siobhan felt she could give them a good shaking at Head Office – they didn't realise what they were putting Jane through. And if Head Office weren't bad enough, what about

Garth? He'd rung in sick yesterday and since then there'd been no sign of him. She only hoped he'd be in tomorrow – she couldn't imagine he'd desert them now. Which reminded her of another desertion, much closer to her heart. Like a whiplash, it stung her in the midst of her indignation and double-checking of all the equipment and records. It took every ounce of her strength not to flinch at the pain.

Now she was at home, and the letter was just charred remnants. Siobhan felt that, at last, she could begin to put the whole affair behind her. She swept the ashes swiftly into the bin as she heard her mother come down the stairs.

Garth stood by the carousel watching the luggage. One by one cases and rucksacks pushed through the rubber flaps and jerked their way along the conveyor belt. The effect was mesmerising. Garth's eyes were trained on the flaps. One arrivals lounge was very much like another, with its carousels, armed police, customs officials in peaked caps, and monitors with details of arriving flights. There was nothing to tell him where he was.

The luggage was coming through with more frequency now. And there was his new black suitcase. He moved closer to the conveyor belt to pick it up. Now he felt a rising sense of anticipation. He adjusted the handle of his case so that it formed a trolley and wheeled it towards the nothing-to-declare gate. Funny how he felt guilty as the customs officers eyed him, although he had nothing illegal with him – he would not be such a fool. If there had been anything not quite kosher about the L8s, he hadn't dealt with that side of it. That had been the stipulation all along.

And he was out into the airport proper. He stopped, looked around at the foreign news-stands and information bureaux, scanning the crowd for one familiar face. He frowned. She wasn't there. He was not a little put out. He stood still, debating what to do, hearing excited chatter in a language he did not know. He checked the crowd again.

Then, coming through the entrance, Garth noticed a sleek blonde, with immaculate shoulder-length hair, designer shades, tight top, low-slung denim shorts exposing a tanned midriff, silver stilettos finishing off brown legs. Still no sign of her. She was late or she wasn't coming. The blonde approached him. 'Garth?'

He did a double-take. The voice, slightly husky, rough round the edges, was exactly the same.

'Garth? Remember me?' She removed her shades and still he couldn't make sense of what he was seeing. The Trudy he remembered had started to wrinkle, especially around the mouth, had pouches beneath her eyes and laughter lines. This woman's skin was as smooth as a doll's, her eyes pulled apart like Betty Boop's. Her forehead was unlined, wrinkle free. 'Look at me!' She twirled round. Her figure was perfect. The love handles that would never disappear despite all the state-of-the-art resistance equipment she had bought for Sunnybank had finally gone. She was honey-coloured all over. And she had had her navel pierced. A glittering bauble hung just below it. 'What do you think?' she asked him.

'Very nice!' Garth replied automatically.

'It took months and months. I can't tell you the pain I was in, and the swelling – there was a time I thought I'd end up looking worse than before. But it's all been worth it. I feel like a million dollars. Which is almost what it cost.'

Garth could not take his eyes off her. She didn't so much look like Trudy's daughter as a conserved species, mummified.

'Everyone says I look at least fifteen years younger.'

Garth agreed. Trudy was fifty-two. She looked like a thirty-seven-year-old pretending to be twenty, and from behind she certainly did look twenty.

'Say something, Garth!'

'You look gorgeous.'

'Show me I look gorgeous.' She put her arms around him and wriggled close and her mouth met his. Obligingly Garth kissed her surgically enhanced lips. 'I did it for you,' she murmured. 'Look. I had liposuction too. Can you see how flat my stomach is? I can tell you, I've never felt better. These shorts are Armani. I bought a dress, too, which I'll wear tonight. I'm taking you out for dinner. Believe me, all eyes will turn.'

'Great!' Garth said. 'Excuse me while I –' He gestured in the direction of the toilets.

Once inside he stood in front of the mirrors over the basins, checked his reflection, put a comb through his hair, then gave a tight little grimace. He was not happy. This new plastic woman did nothing for him. If he'd wanted a young woman, he could have had his pick. What had happened to the old Trudy, the rather sad, neurotic, if scheming, woman who had wanted him so badly she'd set him up in business with the L8s so that he could earn enough for them to start a new life in Portugal? She'd gone, had been transformed into this creature who wanted *his* admiration. She'd become vain, and vanity was a quality Garth could not endure. She had made a big miscalculation: *he* was not supposed to be the lucky one, she was.

He was uncertain what to do now. However, he noticed other men glancing at him curiously, one or two with interest, so he left the gents' and made his way back to the concourse. Trudy, too, was attracting the attention of several males, who obviously thought she was a film star. When she saw him she linked her arm with his and they left the airport.

'We're getting a taxi back to my apartment,' she said. 'I used to have my own car and driver but I had to give them up to pay for the tummy tuck. We're back to basics, I'm afraid. But don't worry, there's still a job for you. The gym's only small as yet, just some weights and that, only for men at the moment, but I know how hard-working you are and I'm sure you can build it up for me. I'm afraid my L8 supply has dried up – you know how these things are. There was some investigation involving the local constabulary. Still, I've not wasted a penny of the profits – a new body and a new man! But you haven't changed a bit, Garth. You're as gorgeous as ever.'

Garth allowed himself to be led to the taxi rank and Trudy shouted something in Portuguese to the driver, while gesticulating expansively. The sun was hot and he took off his jacket. He decided he would give Trudy a week, if that. A holiday would be welcome after his long hours at Fit Not Fat. How lucky it was that he hadn't been completely honest about the L8 profits. There was a nest-egg waiting for him back in Manchester, enough for him to move on, buy a new place and set up as a personal trainer, specialising, he decided, in the over-forties.

He swung his suitcase into the boot of the taxi and grinned at his ex-partner.

On the morning of the inspection, Siobhan was the first to arrive. That surprised her, she had expected Jane to be there before her, but it didn't matter as they both had keys. As she was unlocking the premises the earlybirds came along and Siobhan greeted them. She ran in ahead of them, switching on lights, plugging in the equipment, soothed by the familiar routine. It made her feel as if nothing had changed after all.

The club was pristine. Last night they had all helped to give it a thorough clean while Jane was finalising the figures. Unfortunately Garth was still off, and they could have done with his help. Siobhan hoped fervently that he would be in today – he was aware of the importance of the inspection. They all were. For the first hour she covered the reception desk, the office, the gym, and kept things ticking over, occasionally wondering where Jane was.

Ah – there was Jane now. Brisk footsteps came down the corridor and the office door opened. But it was Jodie. 'Oh, it's you, Siobhan. Am I late? Sorry if I am. I've got such a headache. And the bus kept stopping and starting on the way here, only I had to get the bus as I wouldn't take a lift from Mum as I'm in such a foul temper today. I mean, I just can't believe that Head Office can come here and just say, 'Sorry, you're not making enough of a profit – we're closing you down.' It's just not worth it, is it? It's like everything you've worked for, gone.'

'Hold on a minute, Jodie. We don't know what the result will be.'

'Huh. Well. Shall I make some coffee? Oh, God! Damn! We're out of milk. Isn't it just bloody typical?'

One day, thought Siobhan, I'm going to force-feed that girl vitamin B6. Meanwhile she decided to tread softly around her. 'Did you see Jane on your way in?' she asked her.

'No. Kendra's in Reception, though.'

Well, that was something. Siobhan glanced at the clock and guessed that the inspection team would be with them in an hour or so. There was still plenty of time for Jane to arrive. There was no point in getting stressed. Then the phone rang. Was that Jane?

'Hi,' said a croaky, tired male voice.

'Siobhan here.'

'Hi, Siobhan. It's Darren. I'm not well. I've got a pounding headache and I've been sick. I'm supposed to be in today but I can't make it. I know it's the inspection and that, but I'm sure you'll find a replacement. Garth or someone. 'Bye.'

'That was Darren,' Siobhan told Jodie. 'He's not coming in today. He's ill.'

'Oh, really?' Jodie said, swinging her ponytail contemptuously. 'That's strange. He was well enough to attend his annual rugby-club dinner last night.'

The two women looked at each other meaningfully, and Siobhan lost no time in ringing Garth. In her haste she pressed in his number incorrectly and a silken computerised voice informed her that the number she had dialled had not been recognised. She tried again, more carefully. Still the same response. She tried a third time. Then she got Garth's mobile number from Jane's desk directory. It was switched off. Siobhan smelt a rat. But there was no time to think about that now. The inspection team was on its way, Jane wasn't in yet, and only she and Jodie were manning the club, Jodie with advanced PMT and Siobhan with a broken heart.

Still, there wasn't much to do once the team arrived. Siobhan reckoned she could escort them round the club and show them the systems and accounts if Jodie took over in the gym. But it didn't look good. Jane was right: it was vital they gave the impression of a thriving club. With half the staff off, they were at a distinct disadvantage. Nevertheless she explained her strategy to Jodie.

'I wonder where Jane is,' Siobhan mused, as she switched on the computer.

'It's not like her to be late,' Jodie said. 'Did she tell you she pulled a muscle yesterday during her lunchtime session on the treadmill?'

'Did she?'

'Yeah. She had a pain all afternoon in the middle of her back and she said it seemed to go all the way round the right side of her ribs then down to her groin.'

Siobhan frowned, concerned. 'You don't think she's ill, do you?'

'No. It was only a pulled muscle. She said she was fairly certain she felt it go.'

The phone rang again. It was an enquiry from a member. Jodie left the office and Siobhan dealt with the call. When she had finished, she checked the clock again. Half past eight. Still no Jane. It occurred to her that if it got to nine o'clock someone ought to go round to her flat and check that she was all right. But it was silly to imagine catastrophe – Siobhan's disposition was naturally sanguine – Jane would be here any minute now, frantic at having overslept. Siobhan decided to keep herself busy, tidying the already immaculate office, looking in at the studio and checking Jan was installed in the café. Among all this she spared a thought or two for Garth. Strange that he and Jane should have vanished at the same time.

Nine o'clock. Siobhan tidied herself up in the ladies' and went out to Reception to await the inspection team. 'Any word from Jane?' she asked Kendra.

'No. Funny she's not in yet.'

Siobhan stood at Reception, her gaze tricking over the pile of free newspapers, the posters advertising classes, the large Swiss cheese plant that hid a patch of peeling paint. She really ought to go and see if Jane was OK but the inspection team might arrive at any minute. And, indeed, there they were, the woman who had interviewed her, in a tailored navy suit, accompanied by two men, only one of whom looked familiar. She took a deep breath: she had not prepared herself to welcome them alone. She hated being the front person, responsible for putting people at their ease. Suppressing her self-consciousness, she advanced to meet them, putting out her hand to shake theirs in turn. 'I'm sorry,' she said, 'but Jane has been held up and has asked me to meet you.'

'And you are?' the woman asked her.

'Siobhan Murphy.'

'Of course, I remember now. Sarah Curtis, Greg Black, Colin Ricketts.'

A silence. What did you say next in these situations? Siobhan wondered. 'Did you have a nice journey here?' she asked, inspired suddenly.

'Yes, thank you,' Sarah said.

The four stood in Reception.

'Where do you want to start?' asked Siobhan.

'It's up to you.'

Siobhan decided that the best thing she could do was stall.

Jane might be here at any moment and, failing that, she would send her mother in a taxi to go and wake her up. 'Come and have a coffee in our new café. I'm sure you'll all need one after your drive. And you haven't seen the café yet anyway.'

'Great,' Sarah replied. 'I'm gasping for a drink.'

The inspection team settled at a table by the window while Siobhan took their orders. Fetching them and seeing to sugar and biscuits kept her busy. She ordered a filter coffee for herself and finally brought that over to their table. Sarah asked her a few questions about the café, which were easy to answer. Siobhan knew it was important to present a good image: she sang the praises of Jan and their coffee supplier.

It was just as Colin drained his mocha that Kendra scurried in, gesticulating urgently at Siobhan. 'Excuse me,' Siobhan said, and got herself out of the café as quickly as possible. Once out of sight of the inspection team, she asked Kendra what the problem was.

'It's Jane,' said Kendra. 'She's arrived.'

'At last! I'll go and get her.'

'No, don't.'

'Why?' Siobhan asked.

'I think you'd better go and see for yourself.'

Siobhan ran headlong to Jane's office. The door was open and Jane was sitting at her desk. When she saw Siobhan she gave her a pathetic little smile that looked ready at any moment to dissolve into tears. 'Siobhan,' she said. 'I think I've got chicken pox.'

Jane had seen similar little teardrop vesicles on her cousin's daughter when she'd had chicken pox, but she hadn't thought she could possibly have caught it. She was twenty-four, for heaven's sake. Yet Jane knew that she wasn't well: all of yesterday she had felt tired, although she'd put that down to weaning herself off the L8s. She'd had no choice: she'd run out and Garth was not around to get her some more. The tiredness stayed with her, and made her weepy and unbalanced. Part of her had argued it was only stress — anyone facing an inspection as significant as this one was bound to feel uptight, with alternating waves of lassitude and irritability, anyone would develop a persistent headache. And the fact that she had pulled a muscle in her back hadn't helped.

When she had got home the night before, she tried to look after herself. She half thought about ringing David, but pride stopped her. After the fiasco at the managers' dinner she had kept her distance. She knew he could not possibly want to take things further when she had made such an exhibition of herself. Besides, she needed to focus all her energy on the inspection. She had told him so when he'd rung her, and she had made him promise not to contact her until the end of this week. So she had made herself some tea, sat in front of the TV and even filled a hot-water bottle, which she pushed away as soon as she realised she was running a temperature and it was the last thing she needed. She took two paracetamol for the pain in her back and thought how odd it was that it travelled down to her groin in that way. Had she pulled a whole set of muscles? Or damaged nerve endings? The workings of her body were a mystery to her.

She had taken herself to bed and fallen asleep, to be haunted by dreams of Sarah, Colin, and taking an examination in a subject for which she hadn't revised. She had woken early in more pain than ever and examined her right side. She had a rash. At first she was puzzled because she couldn't think why a pulled muscle should react in that way. Then, she stood up and knew, without any doubt, that she really was ill. The pain was unbearable, she could hardly stand and had to sit back on the bed to recover.

So she was ill. This meant she couldn't go in to work. What relief! She would climb back into bed and go back to sleep — except that the inspection was today and it didn't matter whether she had tuberculosis, yellow fever and diphtheria all together because she was going in to work. Then Jane felt very brave and very sorry for herself. She allowed herself the luxury of a little weep – to get the bad feelings out of her system – and tried to stand again. If she took it slowly she found she could get to the bathroom where she switched on the light and examined her rash again. It wasn't all over her body; it was concentrated around the site of the pain. She twisted to see exactly where it started on her back. She felt dizzy with the effort. Then she looked more closely at the part of the rash she could see, and that was when she discovered it looked like chicken pox.

Naming what was wrong with her made her feel a little better. It robbed her illness of its power. But chicken pox was supposed to itch and with every moment the pain she was suffering got worse and worse. It was deep, relentless, acute. She was desperate to relieve it and couldn't think how. Gingerly she laid her finger on the spots then pulled it away hastily. It hurt like hell.

Perhaps she was only in so much pain because she was feeling sorry for herself and thinking about the pain too much. So, very slowly, she made plans. She would get washed and dressed – impossible, she was dying. No, she would get washed and dressed, and the one concession she would make to her chicken pox was that she would ring for a taxi and go to work that way.

Everything she did took an eternity. However, she had one stroke of luck. She discovered some powerful painkillers in her medicine cabinet from when she'd had a tooth extracted, and took some. They dented the impact of the pain, which helped her to get downstairs and make a cup of tea. At which point she broke into a sweat and had to sit down to try to bring her temperature back to normal. The kitchen clock told her it was already half past eight: Siobhan would wonder where she was. But the important thing, the only thing that mattered, was to get to work, to be in control in her office from where she could issue orders and cope somehow. It wasn't that she couldn't trust her staff, but what would they do without her?

It was a moment's work to ring for the taxi. Then Jane had a surge of determination that carried her out of the house and into the waiting cab. It felt odd to be going to work so late, and everything about her was lurid and unreal – the check shirt of the taxi driver, the Hindi music he was listening to, the distorted appearance of the shops and houses she knew so well. And the pain – terrible, unreal. As if one side of her body was an infected tooth, or as if she had been beaten up by a gang of hooligans, kicked viciously and left clutching several broken ribs on a deserted pavement.

There, at last, was Fit Not Fat, and she was glad to see it. Very slowly, limping a little, she had entered. Kendra had taken one look at her and her mouth formed a distinct 'Oh' of surprise. She had helped Jane to her office and run for Siobhan. And here was Siobhan and Jane knew she owed her an explanation.

'Siobhan,' she said, 'I think I've got chicken pox.'

'Chicken pox? What do you mean?'

'I've got a rash.' Automatically she untucked her blouse from her skirt and showed Siobhan, who bent over her to take a close look. 'Don't touch it!'

'It does look like chicken pox,' Siobhan said. 'Is it itchy?'

'No. It's . . . very, very painful.' And Jane couldn't help herself and began to cry.

'I don't think it's chicken pox. That's shingles. My auntie Margaret had it. You shouldn't be at work – you've got to get home. And you'd better see a doctor immediately.'

'Shingles?' Jane felt cut adrift again. The word shingles meant nothing to her except pebbles on beaches and illogically she thought the pain she was suffering was like what she would feel if she had fallen heavily on shingle, cut and bruised herself. Then she remembered that shingles was an adult variety of chicken pox. She felt better again and decided to take control.

'Well, all right, if I'm infectious nobody should come near me. Have Sarah and Colin arrived yet?'

'They're in the café.'

'Oh, Christ! Look, I'd better go and – No, they can't see me like this. I know. I'll hide in my office. You tell them – tell them I'm ill. No, say there's a family emergency. You take them round. No – they'll have to come into the office. I'll hide in the café. Explain to them about the advertising campaign I'm planning and how many of our members are active, unlike Fitness International. Siobhan, the painkillers aren't working. Take me to the staff room – no, I'm infectious.' She was crying again and the part of her that was detached from the rest of her watched her snivelling and was surprised she couldn't control herself. And the bullying pain laid into her again and again.

'Jane, stay here for now. I'm going to get you home as quickly as I can. I'll just have to tell the inspection team to come back when you're better. It's no crime to be ill.'

'Yes, it is,' Jane said.

'You're not thinking straight.'

'I am. They're looking for any excuse to shut us down. This one is perfect. If they think I'm off taking a sickie they'll have me down as work-shy. Or if we postpone the inspection, they'll think we have something to hide, or we're so incompetent we couldn't get ready for them in time.'

Siobhan gave her a steady look. 'Then we'll have to tell them the truth,' she said. 'Jodie and I can handle the inspection. You stay here. I have an idea.'

Siobhan felt herself fill with a surge of adrenaline. This was a crisis and, in some way that she couldn't understand, she was glad it was. First port of call was the gym. A few people were working out, and Jodie was there too. She could hardly raise a smile when she saw Siobhan: she was PMT personified.

'Jodie, listen. Jane's just come in and I'm sure she's got shingles. She shouldn't be here. I've got to get her home but the inspection must continue. You'll have to show everyone around. The people from Head Office are in the café right now and in a moment I'll take you in and introduce them.'

'Me? Oh, please, no, Siobhan. I feel wretched.'

'Jodie, tell your PMT to sod off. Today you've got to be your brightest, breeziest self. You're one of the main assets of the club and we all know it. Now get to the café and show them why Sunnybank Fit Not Fat is the best health club in the district.'

Siobhan saw Jodie's mind working. She saw the struggle going on inside her. Then her eyes flashed and she stood just a little more erect. 'I'll have a go,' Jodie said, and smiled.

Then Siobhan went over to the sound system in the gym and turned it off. 'Excuse me,' she shouted, 'but we have an emergency. Is there a doctor here?'

A man got off the leg press in a pair of pink shorts and a Commit to Get Fit T-shirt. It was David Richmond. Siobhan went straight over to him and, without explanation, frogmarched both him and Jodie out of the gym. Leaving him bemused outside the café she took Jodie over to the inspection team. 'Jane has just arrived but she's not at all well. One of our clients, a GP, is going to have a look at her and it's likely she won't be able to show you round. But Jodie here is happy to substitute.'

'Absolutely!' Jodie asserted. 'It'll be a pleasure. Except I know Jane will be disappointed as she was looking forward to today so much.'

Siobhan shot her a brilliant smile. 'If you don't mind,' she said, 'I'll take our doctor to Jane.' Her heart pounding, she left the café.

David was still outside, looking puzzled. 'Come with me,' she said.

*　　*　　*

Jane wiped her forehead with the back of her hand and discovered it was damp. She presumed she had a temperature. Her vision was blurred too, or else the words on her Quote-a-day desk calendar were melting. She tried to read the quote for the day and found that concentrating on something else helped her cope with the pain.

'Give a man a fish,' she read. A fish? Why a fish? 'And you feed him for a day. Give a man a fishing rod—'

The door to her office opened and Siobhan came in with a client in bright pink shorts. David. Now he was the person she most wanted to see in the world.

'David's here,' Siobhan said. 'He's going to have a look at you. I'll have to leave because I need to make a few phone calls.'

Jane did not want her to go. In her mind Siobhan had become a substitute mother and she felt deserted.

'What's wrong?' asked David.

Jane tried to explain. She lifted up her blouse and showed him her rash. He looked serious. He explained that he would need to examine her properly and suggested they close the blinds. Obediently Jane took off her jacket and blouse and was conscious of how bizarre it was to be semi-dressed in her office with David when they hadn't even kissed properly yet.

'Yes,' he said. 'I've no doubt that it's shingles. Have you had chicken pox?'

'As a baby,' Jane said.

'Yes, not surprising. Who is your GP? Ah, I remember. You haven't registered. Right, Jane. I'm going to see if I can get hold of some acyclovir. If you take it immediately it will shorten the course of the illness. Now, how long have you had the rash?'

'Since this morning.'

'Good. It isn't too late. You shouldn't be at work. Can someone take you home?'

Jane reminded herself that it was impossible for her to go

home, and realised she had to remind David. 'No. It's the inspection today and everyone's needed, especially me.'

She watched him shake his head thoughtfully. 'I think I'll drive you home and we'll see about the acyclovir on the way,' he said. She turned to the door and put her hand on the knob to open it. 'I think you'd better get dressed first,' he told her, smiling.

As she struggled back into her blouse and jacket she watched David write a note for Siobhan and leave his mobile number. 'We'd better go out the back way,' she said. 'I don't want anyone to see me like this.'

She leant on his arm as they went past the Portakabin and into the car park. It was almost as if they were running away together. Jane noticed that he was still in his shorts, and for the first time that day she smiled. He installed her in his car and in a few moments they were on the road. 'I'm in a lot of pain,' she told him.

'I know,' he said. 'Shingles is one of the most painful illnesses there is. I've heard some women say that it's almost as bad as labour pains.'

Jane was impressed by how well he understood what she was going through. She felt justified by his acknowledgement of her suffering. Most of all, she felt safe with him. He was a doctor. Whatever happened to her now, she would be looked after. The relief created the illusion that the pain was lessening. And if it was, what on earth was she doing driving away from the club when today was the day of the inspection? 'David, I think I *am* well enough to go back to work.'

'Forget about work,' he said.

Impossible, Jane thought. Life was work and work was life. What else was there? Only now, in her weakened state, she found it impossible to argue with David or even argue with herself. Yet she felt compelled to explain to him. 'I have to be there. It's my responsibility. How will they cope without me?'

'I'm sure they'll cope. It's a bad manager whose staff can't do without her. Why don't you let them show you what *they* can do?'

Jane thought about that as David parked outside the pharmacy. It conflicted with her own ingrained philosophy that she should be indispensable, yet there was something comforting in the idea that others could help you when you were in need. There was something tempting and wonderful in the idea of relinquishing control. She had never tried it before. David reappeared with a package, leapt back into the car and drove off.

Now Jane gave into the helplessness that was engulfing her. She allowed David to unlock her door, install her on her settee, and fetch her some water from the kitchen with which to take some pills. Thoughts of the inspection receded, although she vowed to return to them as soon as she had the pain under control.

David perched on the edge of the armchair and observed her. I wonder whether your immune system is somewhat depleted. I've noticed you looking rather pale lately, and you've lost weight.'

For the first time she welcomed his interest in her health. She hardly realised why. All she knew was that she was drowning and he was her rescuer. He had the power to make her feel better. Through the film of her pain she saw him with new eyes.

'I've been under a lot of pressure.'

'You'll need someone to help you for the next couple of days. Do your parents live nearby?'

'No – please!'

She saw him take that in. 'Is there anyone who can keep an eye on you?'

'I'm sure Siobhan will call round after the inspection. I'll be all right. And you must go and get dressed.'

David looked down at himself and laughed. He had forgotten that he was still in his sports gear. Jane found it touching.

He was so selfless and so keen to help her that he hadn't even noticed how he was dressed. He was a hero, she thought. If only he could stay with her.

'I'll have to go,' he said, 'I have a clinic shortly. But I'll be round again as soon as I can.'

She looked up at him. There was something new, strange and enticing about letting go like this, giving up, allowing another person to take control. That is, if it was David. She said goodbye and listened to his parting instructions about painkillers, calamine lotion and the necessity to rest. She tried to get herself into a comfortable position. Then, just as she had hoped, he came over and kissed her cheek briefly.

Then Jane was alone. Who would have thought it would all turn out like this? Illness, she thought, was like a huge hammer, a sixteen-ton weight, that descended at random and shattered everything. The inspection, her indiscretions at dinner, the failure of her plans for a pool, none of it mattered any more. Life consisted of her, her pain, the course of the illness. The only person who had any meaningful connection with her was David. Perhaps the shingles was demonstrating to her that very little actually mattered: it was the emphasis we placed on things that made them *seem* important. Or maybe she was struggling to express to herself that we make rods for our own backs — and hers was the lacerating pain that would not go away.

There was nothing for it but to crawl over to the television, switch it on, and hope that the morning programmes would distract and soothe her. Clutching the remote control panel, she sank back on to the settee.

'So that really is the history of the club to date,' Jodie concluded. 'And when we reach the office I can give you the folders Jane's prepared explaining just why we're so optimistic about future growth.' She could hardly believe she had kept talking for — how long? She glanced at the café clock. A whole twenty minutes! Sometimes being a natural-born chatterbox was a distinct advantage.

Sarah smiled at her encouragingly. 'The staff seem rather thin on the ground today. I was hoping to catch up with Garth. Is he around?'

Jodie thought quickly. It wouldn't do for Head Office to know that Garth was currently untraceable. She had better lie. 'He's been given leave,' she said.

'Leave?'

'Yes – to get married.'

'I didn't know he was engaged,' Sarah said, puzzled.

'Oh, yes. To a childhood sweetheart. But the wedding was all of a sudden – they just couldn't wait any longer.'

'A shotgun wedding!' exclaimed Sarah. 'Does Jane know about this?'

'Yes. Garth wanted her to be a witness but of course she put the inspection first.' Jodie found it was remarkably easy to make things up as she went along.

'And do you know what's wrong with Jane? Is it serious?'

'Oh, no! She'll be back at work tomorrow. That is, it's bad enough for her to be away today, but not bad enough to stop her working tomorrow. She never stops working.' Jodie could feel herself breaking out in a sweat. She wasn't sure that she ought to say what was wrong with Jane. She begged that the questions would stop or she would be bound to trip up. She attempted to divert Sarah. 'If you like, I'll show you round now.'

Jodie ushered the inspection team out of the café and pointed out the squash courts, sauna, steam room and jacuzzi. Next they passed the studios where a yoga class was just finishing. Jodie was about to take them in when she noticed just in the nick of time that only three members were in the class – Anita and two others. But it turned out not to be in the nick of time: Colin was already watching the class from the window, frowning. 'A small class,' he remarked. 'I'm surprised you can afford to run it.'

'It's normally chocker,' Jodie said. 'In fact, it's been so successful that most of the class has graduated to advanced yoga on Wednesday evenings.'

If only that were true. Jodie hoped the team would not check up on her. The three members of the class got up, yawning. Colin, Greg and Sarah paused outside a window that gave on to the wasteground where a large sign read, 'Acquired by Excelsior Holdings'.

'A pity,' the accountant said. 'I always thought the Sunny-bank branch's one hope was to expand. Do you know what's being built there?'

Jodie wondered about another white lie, but this time her mind was blank. 'Sorry, I haven't the faintest,' she said.

They approached the gym and Jodie felt nervous. If it was as empty as the yoga class it would be the last straw. Presumably Anita would be in there now that yoga was over (when was she not?) but the weather was good, and the morning was not their busiest time. She walked on ahead of them to the gym and opened the door to let them in first. She couldn't believe her eyes.

The gym was full. Men and women were walking on the treadmills, cycling, stepping, chest-expanding, leg-stretching, lifting weights, doing press-ups, and Siobhan was presiding over all of them as if butter wouldn't melt in her mouth. Then Jodie looked again. Every single one of these new members – she didn't recognise any, not one – would not see sixty again. They were the same age as her grandparents. She snatched a look at the inspection team. They looked as taken aback as she was.

Siobhan approached them. 'It's our over-sixties morning,' she explained. 'Since Jane has been advertising Fit Not Fat by going to give talks at local clubs, we can't keep them away. Everyone here today is joining – at a reduced rate, naturally, but they all have younger families and spread the word very effectively.'

An elderly lady came up to them. 'This is a grand club,' she said. 'They do a service to this community, they do. And the manager here is such a friendly lass. I'm quite partial to her second-in-command too.' Then she hurried away to wait by an occupied treadmill. Jodie was certain she saw her wink at Siobhan.

'Astonishing,' Sarah said.

'I'll tell my father about this,' the accountant mused.

'Have you seen the rest of the premises?' Siobhan asked the team. They said that they had. 'If you like, Jodie, I'll take them to the office to have a look at the paperwork. You can keep an eye on everyone in here.'

'Sure,' Jodie said. She watched Siobhan escort the team out of the gym and relaxed inside. She turned, and there was the same lady who had spoken earlier.

'I'm Siobhan's mother,' she said. 'Just you remember, you can always depend on a mother to get you out of a fix. Tell that woman over there on the treadmill that she's been hogging it. Some others of us would like to have a go.'

'Would you like to have some time alone?' Siobhan asked them.

Colin nodded. 'Yes. We have a lot to digest.'

Siobhan arranged for some coffee to be brought through and left the office. She didn't know what to do with herself. She thought of ringing Jane but imagined she would be in bed. In any case it would be infinitely better to wait until she had something concrete to tell her. She decided to join Jodie in the gym.

When she got there, it was virtually empty. Jodie explained that Siobhan's mother and her friends were all changing prior to sampling the cakes in the café. The only person still working out was Anita, jogging relentlessly on the treadmill, her expression a stony blank. Siobhan watched her. She had never quite known what to do about exercise addicts. Like any other sort of addict, she guessed, you had to leave them to acknowledge that they had a problem.

Then the door to the gym opened and a woman of Siobhan's age entered. She wasn't dressed for a workout: she had on a checked shirt and jeans and her eyes sought out and rested on Anita. She watched her for a while. Siobhan was intrigued. In a moment she would go and ask her what she wanted. Yet there was something about this woman that held her attention – it was difficult to say what it was but Siobhan felt almost as if she knew her from somewhere, although she was certain she didn't.

The woman marched up to Anita. 'Mum,' she said, in a warning voice.

Anita swivelled round. She pushed the pause button on the machine and came to a halt. 'What are you doing here?' she asked.

'I've come to take you home,' the woman said. She turned to Siobhan and smiled. 'I don't know what to do with her. She'd live in this place if I let her. Come on, Mum.'

Anita looked daggers at her. Scowling, she helped herself to some water and left the gym.

Her daughter explained to Siobhan, 'She's been like this ever since my dad left. At first I thought it was good for her to have an interest but now I'm not so sure. I've been away for the past month rock-climbing in Wales, but now I've got time to take her properly in hand.'

'Rock-climbing?' said Siobhan. 'I've always wanted to try that.'

'Have you?' said Anita's daughter, looking pleased.

Siobhan felt the stirring of something new and dangerously exciting – rather like rock-climbing.

'I'd better go and check on Mum – make sure she's not

slipped into the aerobics class. I think I'd better escort her here next time. My name's Carol, by the way.'

'I'm Siobhan.'

And Carol was gone. Siobhan hardly had time to store away this meeting in her mind before Sarah appeared.

'Ah, Siobhan, Jodie. Would you come along to the office? We'd like to have a few words.'

The moment of truth was fast approaching. Together the three left the empty gym.

Chapter Seventeen

Cassie couldn't settle to anything. A pile of paperwork in her briefcase demanded attention, but it would have to wait: she had far too much to think about. In fact, she had hardly slept all night, despite having stopped taking the L8s. She had finally crashed out at about five a.m., and had consequently woken up late. Now she was sitting at the table with a strong coffee and a copy of last night's local paper, which she wasn't reading – until she caught sight of an exposé of a double-glazing company that preyed on the lonely and vulnerable. She studied it with attention. She could identify with the journalists. She, too, had uncovered a scam, albeit accidentally. And the question now was, what should she do about it?

There was no doubt now in her mind that Garth had known he was peddling speed to unsuspecting women under the guise of a new wonder drug. It all made perfect sense. Amphetamines were illegal, although it was well known that unscrupulous slimming clinics occasionally acquired supplies and sold them as weight-loss pills. Eventually these schemes folded as either the press cottoned on or dissatisfied customers realised that their weight piled back on after they stopped taking the drug. How much more ingenious to flog speed under the general heading of an all-round tonic! It meant he could pull in custom two ways:

from those people who realised what he was selling, and those, like Cassie, who didn't. Now Garth had either cottoned on that Cassie was hot on his trail after her questions to him in the gym the other day, or he had simply run out of supplies. Either way, he had done a runner.

This discovery preoccupied her. What also preoccupied her was that Dr Cassie Oliver, senior lecturer in Medieval History, had been dallying with a common criminal. In some bizarre way she was pleased with herself, because everyone wants to do something wicked at least once in their lives. Yet she was also alarmed, because she was essentially conventional and had an innate moral instinct. She wanted everyone to know that she had almost been in the position of a gangster's moll, and she wanted no one to know. On balance, she decided she wanted no one to know. Because as soon as they did, the next question would be, what was she going to do about it?

If Garth was a drug-dealer, shouldn't she alert the authorities? It was her clear ethical duty as an upstanding citizen. But was she an upstanding citizen? No, because of the shameless way she had pursued him for his body. If the police were to interrogate her about how she had found out about his nefarious activities, what would they find out about *her*?

She had racked her brain trying to think of historical analogies to guide her through the darkness. She decided that Garth was a kind of latter-day pardoner, selling spurious relics, saints' bones, and worthless paper pardons to gullible peasants, although this comparison was not very flattering to her. However, the analogy fell down when one considered that speed was dangerous. She had to let someone know. But, on the other hand, Garth had gone and the danger with him. But did she have a moral duty to grass on him? Cassie reached for the paracetamol that were lying conveniently close on the table.

And whom should she tell? She could ring an enterprising journo on the local paper, disguising her voice and insisting she remain anonymous. Or go straight round to the police. She stared at the paper again, seeking inspiration. There was the usual collection of local stories, someone trekking across Nepal for charity, police called to a neighbour dispute, more jobs for the area in one of those new call centres, an appeal for help to find a hit-and-run driver, an advertisement extolling a closing-down sale at a furniture warehouse. And tomorrow, perhaps, the headline, 'Speed Scandal at Fit Not Fat'.

Then the penny dropped. The person she should tell was Jane at Fit Not Fat. If Garth was operating from their premises, he could get them all into hot water, and Jane most of all. Didn't they have an inspection coming up? The club would be in serious trouble if the scandal was uncovered. It was only fair to Jane, Jodie and all the staff that she blow the whistle. Then Jane could decide whether to speak to the police.

Cassie thought through the logistics of her new resolution. She wouldn't ring Jane at Fit Not Fat and create panic. No, she would speak to her in person. Unfortunately Cassie had only worked out yesterday and normally would not go to the gym today. But she had to speak to Jane about Garth. It was a moral imperative. She would drive up there and ask to see Jane, taking with her for chemical analysis the L8s she had left. It was important to be calm and measured about everything. The reports she had to write would wait. There was more important work to be done.

When Cassie arrived at Fit Not Fat, she asked Kendra if she could have a word with Jane.

'Sorry, Cassie. She's not in. She did come in this morning but she wasn't at all well. Shaking, she was, and running a terrible temperature. Siobhan had to fetch a doctor to take her home. And today of all days! We're having an inspection – they're at it now. And I have to say I'm not feeling at my best. I think it's a bladder infection. I'm prone to them, you know.'

Cassie made the appropriate sympathetic noises and debated what to do next. She realised she could not have picked a worse time. To expose Garth's activities now was impossible. She would have to come back tomorrow. She prepared to leave and then, predictably, found herself reluctant to do so. Just crossing the threshold did something to her. She wanted to get back on the treadmill and burn up some energy. Although she knew three times a week was enough, she had been putting in four sessions recently, especially as all she had been doing at home, effectively, was waiting for Terry. Since she was here, she might as well do something. As it happened, she had on a decent pair of trainers and that was the only essential equipment for a workout. She handed her card to Kendra in exchange for a locker key.

When she reached the gym it was empty, which surprised her. Normally at least two or three other people were running or lifting weights. However, she wasn't surprised to see the instructors absent: they were obviously assisting with the inspection. Cassie decided to warm up on the rower, glancing up occasionally at the TV monitor playing Sky News. It felt good to get her body moving again. She finished her five minutes and put on her Walkman in anticipation of her session on the treadmill. The tape was an old one of Terry's – Lou Reed. She began running to 'I'm Waiting For My Man'.

Of course, she thought, as she got into a steady rhythm, it was only the social and cultural trends of the past hundred years that had caused her dilemma about Garth in the first place. Before then, most drugs had been legal anyway. It was only the nanny state that had proscribed them. Why was it more wrong to take speed than caffeine? Put like that, one almost had a duty to defy the state by breaking its laws. In which case, splitting on Garth was a singularly unimaginative and cowardly thing to do. And right wing, which was worse. Or was she being a coward in coming up with excuses at the eleventh hour?

In answer, she turned up the gradient on the treadmill. The

harder, the better. Did you have to be a secret masochist to enjoy the gym? Perhaps. There might be be an element of punishment in it – a post-modern variety of self-flagellation. An excess of the sins of the flesh leads you inexorably to the gym where you beat yourself with knotted ropes and wear hair shirts, or Nike T-shirts. Just feel that pain.

Cassie knew that her reasons for coming to the gym now had to be far less healthy than they had been in the beginning. Then, she had been scared, and genuinely in need of the health benefits an exercise regime would confer. Now, having lost enough weight to pass unnoticed as an average person, she persisted out of a vague belief that some illusory but possibly attainable goal would heave into sight – the perfect figure, love, happiness, the martyr's crown, the Holy Grail. Or at least she would lose just an inch or two more from around her middle.

Maybe the last was the most true, and the most ridiculous – just as Cassie was now, jogging on the treadmill to Lou Reed's 'Heroin', her hair awry, her cheeks red, her breasts bouncing up and down. She turned up the gradient again. Now she had to slow down to a walk. She didn't know whether it was better to walk at a high gradient or run at a low one. She resolved to ask one of the instructors. Just recently such matters had been occupying her. Obviously one wanted to work out efficiently and thus one needed to know exactly how to increase intensity for the best results. She was due for a reassessment shortly and had many questions to ask. Still, there was no reason why she couldn't experiment. She increased it still further, remembering Anita. If Anita could march up a mountain, so could she.

Strange that there was still no one in the gym. Cassie discovered she didn't much like exercising alone. Part of the fun of going to the gym was working alongside other people. Your personal programme was something you worked on while others were working on theirs. It was like life, really: each of us is essentially alone, but we can't carry on unless we have proximity to others. Working alone in an empty gym was like being sent to Coventry.

Cassie had no more energy left for thinking. She pushed the display button to see how many calories she had burned up. One hundred and twenty-three. Less than a Mars bar. Feeling a bit of a failure, she decreased the gradient and speed and began to cool down. Recently she had been told that for an even better weight loss you needed to increase your muscle-to-fat ratio, and this was best done by resistance work. She was now using some of the leg equipment to trim her thighs, but wondered if she should be doing more. That was something else to ask them at her assessment. She glanced over at the weights. A few of the women — Anita in particular — lifted weights. She admired their strong backs and erect posture, their confidence that they could do what men did. Since no one was in the gym Cassie was tempted to have a go herself. A childish curiosity prompted her to wonder how heavy they were. Anyway, she was exhausted from the treadmill and wanted a rest.

She ambled over to the weights. Above them, on a TV screen, two women were confronting each other on a chat-show, observed by a delighted host. The weights sat in a row arranged in niches. Cassie selected the two lightest and raised them so that they were on a level with her shoulders. Easy. What was all the fuss about? She replaced them and lifted the next two. Slightly tougher, but still possible. She was pleased with herself. Ought she to try the next? She did, and found these were hard.

She gave up, put them back, and eyed the biggest weight of all. Did anyone ever lift that, or was it put out just to make them feel inadequate? Could she lift it? With both hands? Since nobody was about she bent over at the waist, put both hands on the bar in the middle and, with a burst of energy, raised it a foot from the ground.

A big mistake.

Suddenly a shaft of pain shot across her back like gunfire. She had done something — pulled a muscle, torn a muscle, snapped a ligament, slipped a disc, severed her vertebrae. Whatever, it hurt like hell. She was doubled over and could not reach vertical again. And there was no one to help her.

Terrified and humiliated, Cassie shuffled over to the instructors' station. There was a telephone there. Should she ring for help? Or would her back slowly return to normal? Again she tried to ease herself upright but the pain warned her to stop, like a sadistic schoolmistress. She was hunched over like an old witch. Perhaps she ought to get herself out into the corridor and find someone. Yes. That was the most sensible thing.

She edged out of the door, and attempted to make her way to Reception, praying she would meet someone sympathetic on the way. The club was unnaturally quiet. There were no classes in the studio. She heard the thwack of balls bouncing off walls in the squash courts but she could hardly barge in in her present state to request assistance so she carried on towards the front of the club.

On her way she passed Jane's office. The door was ajar, and she stopped. Voices. Life at last! Cassie considered crying, 'Help!' but that was far too dramatic and unBritish. Instead she decided to wait for a break in the conversation when she would knock on the door. She tried to tune in to the ebb and flow of the talking, waiting for a suitable gap. Since the door was open, she found she could hear all of what was being said. She felt a little guilty for eavesdropping, but she had no choice . . .

'To be honest, we have been impressed. The club is looking good – we liked the posters and literature available for the clients, didn't we, Colin? There have been some imaginative and unusual approaches to getting new members, and it is true that the new membership figures were good last month. But we have other concerns. A club can only be as good as its manager. Is Jane often absent?'

'First time,' Siobhan said. 'She's usually in first and out last.'

'Quite. Enthusiasm is Jane's strong suit. I wondered – we wondered whether at times she can be a little difficult to work for. Does she not tell you how to do your job, and give you little scope for pursuing your own ideas?'

'Oh, no!' Jodie exclaimed. 'That is so not true! She's got me to go back to college next September to get more qualifications – part-time.'

'Jane is the most generous, supportive manager I've worked for,' said Siobhan.

Now there was a pause, but Cassie said nothing. She realised she had stumbled into the inspection report. She was fascinated and, anyway, as long as she didn't move she wasn't in pain. It was just a matter of keeping doubled up like this.

'She certainly has your loyalty. That's good. But Greg has a few words to say. Over to you, Greg.'

'I have to say I've also been impressed by the standards in the club and the keenness of the workforce, and the clients. But there's a hard reality to face. Sunnybank Fit Not Fat is a small club. Small is not always beautiful. Filled to capacity, the club would have a future but, with Fitness International so close, that will be a problem. Expanding and building a pool might have provided a solution, but I gather that's now out of the question as the land on Philips Road has been sold.'

Now there was a coincidence. Cassie had been reading about Philips Road just this morning. Was that where the neighbour dispute was, or the discount warehouse? No. She remembered now. 'Excuse me!' she called from her hunched position.

The conversation in Jane's office stopped.

'Hello? Can I come in?'

Cassie did not wait for an answer. Slowly and crab-like she edged into the office.

'Cassie! Are you all right?' Jodie exclaimed.

'I know what's happening to the land on Philips Road. That's where they're building the call centre for the telephone bank. It's going to be vast. Hundreds of new jobs apparently. And I think I've put my back out.'

Siobhan was at her side instantly. 'Here. Can you stand upright? No – I thought not.' She lifted up Cassie's T-shirt. 'Uh, Cassie, I think you've slipped a disc.'

There were murmurs of commiseration from the inspection team.

Jodie came over. 'Ooh – you can actually see it sticking out! How gross!'

'Sorry, everyone,' Cassie mumbled.

'I'd better get you to a doctor,' Siobhan said. 'Is that OK?' she asked the others in the room.

'I can wait till you've finished,' Cassie said.

'A call centre, you say,' repeated the accountant. 'Next door. And all those people sitting in one place all day long, who'll be desperate to get out of the office at lunchtime.'

'We could accommodate them all,' Jodie said. 'We only need one extra studio and a few more pieces of equipment, which would pay for themselves.'

'I need to think about this,' the accountant said. 'Can you give us some more time?'

'Certainly,' Siobhan said. 'Come on, Cassie. We'll get you to the doctors.'

Cassie was glad she had decided not to tell them about Garth. This was hardly the best time to bring his scam to light. She was still determined to have a word with Jane, but later. Now she had more pressing matters to think about, and an instance of dramatic irony to explore. For the wheel had come full circle. Six months ago she had been doubled up with pain, and had been diagnosed with gallstones; she had cured herself with diet and exercise; through the exercise she was doubled up with pain again. What did it all prove? And what did she care what it all proved when she dreaded every jolt, every movement because it half killed her?

✳   ·   ✳   ✳

Cassie lay on her back in the middle of her living room. She stared at the light fitting above her. By now she knew its every curve, every colour variation, and had wondered what would happen if it came hurtling down towards her. To her left was a bowl that had contained chicken soup, made by Lynda's mother, who claimed it had miraculous curative properties. Cassie was doubtful, but it had tasted good. To her right was a box of chocolates, sent by her female colleagues at work with the message that she could afford to eat them now. Cassie had taken them at their word and scoffed the lot. Because, if you were ill, you had to. What was the point of being ill if it didn't give you permission to indulge in all the pleasures that well people sedulously avoided? Cassie had asked Lynda to bring her round all this month's women's magazines, *Hello!*, a selection of popular novels, videos of weepy romantic movies and word-puzzle books. But, best of all, Lynda had lent her Josh's Gameboy, and Cassie had discovered she possessed an impressive talent for Tetris. It turned out that in all these years when she had been teaching medieval history she could have been astonishing the world with her talent for arranging little squares in tidy lines.

The doctor had told her to stay off work until she was able to travel comfortably and was free of severe pain. He had referred her to a physiotherapist, who had shown her certain rather difficult exercises, which Cassie had been carrying out. What was out of the question was any more visits to the gym. It was wonderful not to go to the gym and not feel guilty about it. In fact, the gym had been coming to her. Jodie had been to visit her with a get-well-soon card signed by everyone at Fit Not Fat, and had kept her up to date with all the gossip.

The best news was that the club had passed the inspection. The deciding factor had been the news of the arrival of the call centre. This source of new members was irresistible to the company accountant. When Jodie also told her that Garth had vanished, Cassie felt uncomfortable and asked to see Jane. She learned that that was impossible: Jane had shingles although she was recovering well. It was then that Cassie had decided to bury the past. Fate had clearly tried to gag her, and who was she to dispute with Fate?

She was lying on her back because it was the only position at present in which she was pain-free. The doctor had told her to do whatever was most comfortable as long as she kept up with the exercises. Most painkillers had little effect, and the ones that worked made her excessively drowsy. Cassie took few; she had had enough of pills.

Lying on the floor did not burn up many calories. In fact, it was probably the activity least designed to do so. That was why Cassie could feel a thickening round her middle, which in many ways was rather comforting. It enfolded her like a soft, woolly blanket. Another advantage of being ill was that you were obliged to look terrible. She dressed now in comfortable old leggings and a sweatshirt and wore no makeup. She was elemental Cassie, raw, basic, as nature intended. Except, of course, for the pain, which was ready to ambush her if she moved in the wrong way at the wrong time. One cheering thought, however, was that the doctor had told her that her chances of a complete recovery were good. Her previous sedentary life meant that there had been little wear and tear on her joints and her back. It was sportsmen and women whose injuries never got properly better. Lucky, Cassie thought, that she had stopped in time. Of course, when she was better she would return to Fit Not Fat. She had grown fond of the people there, if nothing else. But it would be recreation now, rather than self-improvement.

The aroma of chicken soup spiced the faint breeze from the kitchen; a chat-show rumbled on in the corner on the television screen, Cassie sighed idly. This was the life. She picked up the Gameboy again. Then she heard a sound at the front door. Would she have to heave herself up to open it? No: the person at the door had a key. Cassie stiffened — not difficult, as she was pretty stiff already. She stayed stock-still. Footsteps. The thump of a heavy object hitting the floor.

'Cassie?'

It was Terry's voice. The most natural, welcome sound in the world, and her first impulse was to scramble to her feet to welcome him. Impossible. She would have to have the conversation she had been planning for days from her supine position.

'Cassie?'

He was coming closer. He pushed open the door to the living room. Cassie gazed up at him. He towered above her. 'What are you doing down there?' he asked.

'Slipped disc. Did it at the gym.'

'I know. Lynda told me.'

Terry crouched down so that he was at her level. Cassie thought how appropriate it was that she should be prostrate, but it made rational conversation somewhat impossible, let alone romance.

'It can't have been easy for you, dealing with this alone. Is there anything I can do? Can I cook you something? I presume the doctor's told you to lie down and rest, although there's another school of thought that says you should keep mobile.'

'Yes, but I prefer the first school of thought.'

Terry gave a half-smile. Cassie wished she knew what he was thinking. She was well aware, however, of what she was thinking. That she had never realised how colossal a fool she had been until this moment. That she loved him more than ever. That, felled like this, she was literally not in a position to tell him either of those things. 'How was Rome?' she asked instead.

'Great. I had some excellent meals and did some sightseeing too. St Peter's, the Colosseum, the Pantheon, the Forum — it made me think of you.'

'Why? Because I'm an ancient ruin?'

Terry smiled again. 'It was the historical connection. But now you come to mention it, you don't look in that good nick.'

'Thanks for nothing.'

It was easier to banter like this. It was an effective way of side-stepping the big issue. For Cassie found that all the speeches she had prepared suddenly seemed inadequate, inappropriate or just plain silly. And that was not all: she also discovered that she had a fear of rejection. She'd thought that working out at Fit Not Fat was hard; now she saw that the reason the gym was so popular was, paradoxically, because it was so easy. Anyone could make a physical effort. Far, far harder was managing the business of human relations — and, in the end, human relations were what mattered most of all.

'Can I fetch you anything, Cassie? A drink? Do you want me to clean round before I go?'

'I know it's a tip but leave it — there's only me here.' That was meant to make him feel sorry for her, but it didn't seem to have any effect.

'What about the shopping? I can pop down to the super-market for you. Is there anything you want?'

'Well, yes.'

'OK. Hold on a moment and I'll get a pen and paper. I'll never remember unless I make a list.'

He fumbled in his jacket pocket for a pen, and picked up an opened envelope from under the table. 'Fire away,' he said.

'One. A pint of semi-skimmed milk. Two. A small granary loaf. Three. Some apples. Oh, and another proposal of marriage from you.'

'Hold on — I didn't quite get the last one. Would you repeat it?'

'I said, another proposal of marriage from you. And this time I promise an instant response.'

Cassie was about to learn that one moment in real time in which no one said anything could, in fact, last an eternity. 'OK,' she said. 'What if I give you a response even before the marriage proposal!'

'What would it be?' Terry asked.

'Yes,' she said.

Terry lay down on the floor too, turned on his side and looked at her.

'OK, then. Will you marry me?'

It hurt like hell to turn on her side and kiss him, but Cassie decided it was worth it. No pain, no gain.

Chapter Eighteen

———✦———

Jane opened the bottle of wine in the kitchen and brought it into the living room, where David was lounging on her sofa. 'I'm afraid I need this,' she said. 'Just one glass. First day back at work. It was more tiring than I thought.'

David smiled at her. 'It's OK. You don't have to stop at one. I quite like you when you've had a few.'

'You're a bad influence,' she said, snuggling up to him.

'Did you ease yourself in gently, as I told you?'

She loved the way he fussed over her. 'I would have done, but to be honest, something happened today.'

'Did the inspection report arrive?'

'As a matter of fact, it did. Our future is secure for at least two years. But that wasn't it.' She wriggled free, put her wineglass on the table, and looked at him. 'I was contacted today by Fitness International. They're hoping to open up a new branch in the city centre and they want someone dynamic and innovative to run it. They asked me.'

David gave a long, low whistle. 'So you've been headhunted.'

Jane nodded. ''S right. The club will be twice the size of Sunnybank Fit Not Fat, with a pool and a beauty parlour.'

'Have you given them an answer?'

Jane gave a Mona Lisa smile. That phone call had been the

best moment of her life. Yet as she listened to what she was being offered, she realised she had changed. She had learnt a lot. She knew, now, that it was possible to work too hard, that nothing was worth making yourself ill over, that Siobhan was gay and going out with Carol, Anita's daughter, that there was really no need to be wary of doctors and that it was time for her to let go and relax. So she had known precisely what to say to the regional manager of Fitness International.

Later when she called Siobhan and Jodie into her office and explained what had happened, they were delighted.

'I made absolutely sure that there were limits on my hours and responsibilities,' she told them. 'And that, if you agree, I'd take my team with me. But it's up to you both. If you stay, I think there's little doubt you'd take over as manager, Siobhan – Head Office is very impressed with you. Whether you stay or go, Jodie, there'll be promotion for you.'

She told them both to sleep on it, but Jane's guess was that Siobhan would stay at Fit Not Fat, and that Jodie would be seduced by the bright lights of the city.

'I'm going to Fitness International,' she told David.

'Good for you,' he said, kissing her cheek. 'But take it easy.'

'I will,' she said. 'Just you watch me. I guarantee you'll be impressed!'